A PEERLESS FAMIL **LINEAGE . . . A PRO** **A MAGNIFICENT DE**

Late in the eighteen the revolution were heard in France, Lucien Bouchard, second son of a nobleman, fled his native country to seek the unspoiled lands of the New World. Laying claim to a matchless piece of Alabama soil, this stalwart visionary built Windhaven Plantation, which stood for decades as a symbole of one family's lofty heritage.

When the fires of the Civil War spread across the South and Windhaven Plantation lay in ashes, Luke Bouchard, Lucien's idealistic grandson, led his family to the rich and beautiful prairies of south Texas, and there built a sprawling cattle ranch. But Luke's heart yearned for his beloved South: Leaving Windhaven Range in the hands of his son and daughter, Lucien Edmond and Mara, Luke returned to rebuild his beloved red-brick chateau beside the Alabama River, and to marry his new ladylove, Laure.

Now Luke is gone, a martyr to an assassin's bullet. Laure has remarried, and her husband—the dashing, Irish-born Leland Kenniston—has brought her to New York City. From there, she must face the manifold crises that challenge her far-flung family.

It is a new age, but the legacy of Windhaven lives on in the hearts of the Bouchards, who still bring the hope, courage, and ideals of old Lucien Bouchard to their varied enterprises and cherished aspirations.

* * *

"The Bouchards are a memorable clan, larger than life."
—Donald Clayton Porter, author of
the *White Indian* Series

The Windhaven Saga:

WINDHAVEN PLANTATION
STORM OVER WINDHAVEN
LEGACY OF WINDHAVEN
RETURN TO WINDHAVEN
WINDHAVEN'S PERIL
TRIALS OF WINDHAVEN
DEFENDERS OF WINDHAVEN
WINDHAVEN'S CRISIS
WINDHAVEN'S BOUNTY
WINDHAVEN'S TRIUMPH
WINDHAVEN'S FURY

WINDHAVEN'S DESTINY

Marie de Jourlet

 Created by the producers of
Wagons West, White Indian, The
Australians, Rakehell Dynasty, and
The Kent Family Chronicles Series.

Executive Producer: Lyle Kenyon Engel

PINNACLE BOOKS NEW YORK

WINDHAVEN'S DESTINY

Copyright © 1983 by Book Creations, Inc.

An original Pinnacle Books edition, published for the first time anywhere.

Produced by Book Creations, Inc.; Lyle Kenyon Engel, Executive Producer

First printing, August 1983

ISBN: 0-523-41888-4
CANADIAN ISBN: 0-523-43023-X

Cover illustration by Bruce Minney

Printed in the United States of America

PINNACLE BOOKS, INC.
1430 Broadway
New York, New York 10018

Once again, to Lyle and Marla Engel.

The Windhaven Families

Dora Trask = Henry Bouchard = Sybella
1798-1816   1796-1836   1802-1870

Mark Bouchard   Arabella Bouchard   Fleurette Bouchard = Leland Kenniston
1819-1864   1824-   1832-1869   1837-

Lucy Williamson = Luke Bouchard = Laure Prindeville Brunton = Leland Kenniston
1817-1866   1816-1877   1841-

Lucien   Paul   Celestine   Clarissa   John
1866-   1868-   1871-   1873-   1877-

Lucien Edmond Bouchard = Maxine Kendall
1838-   1840-

Geraldine = Lopasuta Bouchard = Lu Choy
Murcur   (adoptive son of Luke)   d. 1878

                                    Luke 1878-
Dennis 1877-
Marta 1879-

Ramón Hernandez = Mara Bouchard
1840-   1837-

Luke   1868-
Jaime   1869-   Carla   1860-
Dolores 1871-   Hugo   1861-   = Cecily Franklin
Edward   1872-   Edwina   1868-
Mara "Gatita" 1877-   Diane   1870-
                      Gloria   1872-
                      Ruth   1878-

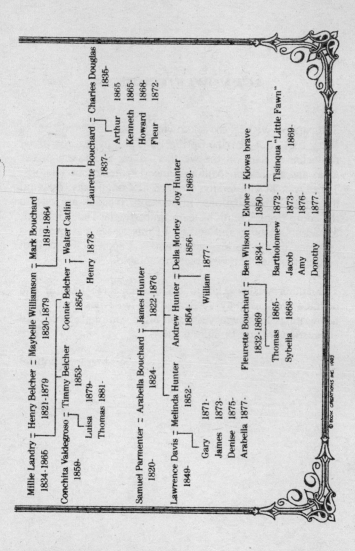

Millie Landry 1834-1865 = Henry Belcher 1821-1879 = Maybelle Williamson 1820-1879 ⚭ Mark Bouchard 1819-1864

Conchita Valdegroso 1859- = Timmy Belcher 1853-
— Luisa 1879-
— Thomas 1881-

Connie Belcher 1856- = Walter Catlin
— Henry 1878-

Laurette Bouchard 1837- ⚭ Charles Douglas 1835-
— Arthur 1865
— Kenneth 1865-
— Howard 1868-
— Fleur 1872-

Samuel Parmenter 1820- = Arabella Bouchard 1824-   James Hunter 1822-1876

Andrew Hunter 1854- ⚭ Della Morley 1856-
— William 1877-

Joy Hunter 1869-

Lawrence Davis 1849- ⚭ Melinda Hunter 1852-
— Gary 1871-
— James 1873-
— Denise 1875-
— Arabella 1877-

Fleurette Bouchard 1832-1869 = Ben Wilson 1834- ⚭ Elone 1850- = Kiowa brave
— Thomas 1865-
— Sybella 1868-
— Bartholomew 1872-
— Jacob 1873-
— Amy 1876-
— Dorothy 1877-

Tisinqua "Little Fawn" 1869-

© BOOK CREATIONS INC. 1983

ACKNOWLEDGMENTS

The author wishes to acknowledge her indebtedness to Mary Barton of Carrizo Springs, Texas, for her continued provision of data on the weather, flora, and fauna of the area; and to Joseph Milton Nance, Professor of History, Texas A & M University, College Station, Texas, for vital historical authentications. In addition, plaudits are due to the entire Book Creations team, in particular Dale Gelfand, for adroit shaping and editing of this as well as previous volumes in the series, and Pamela Lappies, for skillful editing that has likewise been invaluable.

The author wishes also to acknowledge the faithful and devoted work of Fay J. Bergstrom, who has transcribed her writings for seven years and often contributed editorial suggestions of inestimable value.

Marie de Jourlet

Prologue

It was December 18, 1880, the one hundred eighteenth anniversary of the birth of Lucien Bouchard, founder of the Bouchard dynasty. In Alabama, at the top of a towering bluff, overlooking Windhaven Plantation and the Alabama River, faithful mourners paid tribute to the great-hearted Frenchman buried here—a man who had come to live with the Creeks and had left an immortal legacy to those who had come after him. Overhead, the darkening skies predicted the coming of rain, though the air was warm.

On that same day, far to the west in Dodge City, Kansas, on the central plains, dour winter had visited and was now settled in. Drifting snow covered every surface of the flamboyant cow town, piling high on the flat roofs of the one-story frame buildings that lined the main street. Wispy, high clouds streaked the sky, and the bleak sun, which gave no warmth to the crisp, freezing air, illuminated the ghostliness of the rows of dance halls, saloons, and general stores. Snow covered the hardened ruts from wagon wheels that had brought settlers here and marked the inevitable doom of cattle trading. It covered the hoofmarks left by the wild pintos and mustangs of many a remuda, horses that had brought Texas cowboys to Dodge, where Bat Masterson and Wyatt Earp had laid down what little law and order there was. But a year ago, Wyatt Earp had decided that he had no future in a town as tame as Dodge City had come to be, so he had gone to Tombstone, Arizona, as a federal marshal, and Bat Masterson had accompanied him. Now the Kansas legislature had imposed restrictions on Texas cattle suspected to be diseased, a move that destined to end for all time the glory that had been Dodge, and marked the demise of the great cattle drive. Within a few

1

years, these drives would be over forever and would remain only in legend.

During their tenure as peace officers in Dodge, neither Wyatt Earp nor Bat Masterson ever had occasion to come to a showdown with the man who undoubtedly masterminded many bushwhackings and rustlings but, thus far, remained undetected by the law. That was Jeb Cornish, who back in 1872 bribed a corrupt Kansas legislator to sponsor his name as a federal buyer of cattle and then to the post of territorial Indian agent. Shortly after the Civil War, Cornish—who now, fifteen years later, was in his fifties—had come to Dodge from his birthplace in Baltimore, where he had tended his father's general store and inherited a considerable sum of money upon the latter's death. His father had been on the point of disinheriting him, for he was appalled both by his son's fondness for women of easy virtue and by Jeb's numbering among his favorite acquaintances confidence men and land speculators—from whom he acquired the burning ambition to make a quick fortune as easily as possible. Cornish's choice of Dodge City was entirely logical: It represented the edge of the frontier, it was a center for cattle drives, and it was virtually lawless.

Cornish had used part of his legacy to buy into a partnership in the Comique—a combination dance hall, saloon, and theater—with his crony, Frank Thompson. Here he had gathered around himself a group of desperados and with Machiavellian strategy set about rustling cattle and bushwhacking men who drove them the long way from Texas on through Kansas. As a federal buyer, he knew in advance what outfits would be expected along the trail, how many men would be driving the cattle, and how many head would be in the herd.

Cornish was of medium height, with a huge paunch and a double-chinned flaccid face, pale, watery blue eyes, and a bulbous nose. He usually wore a dirty gray Stetson pulled down to one side, but by a contrast born out of vanity, he had on a pair of gleaming new boots to which had been added authentic silver spurs. He was inordinately proud of consulting his gold-plated watch with a garishly ornamental fob, especially when he was planning an involved coup with the members of his gang. Gabe Penrock had once said, "I swear, Mr. Cornish seems to look at that damned watch and see

2

exactly how much cash he's going to come up with from whatever shindig he's worked out for us.''

With the dwindling numbers of herds coming up from Texas these days, Jeb Cornish had judiciously broken up his band of outlaws, retaining only a few of his most trusted and dependable associates. Cattle rustling and train robberies were far too dangerous, and the opportunities for them too few these days. After having lost Reuben Huntley and Jack Hayes in the aborted effort to hold up a train to Leadville and the vengeful bushwhacking of a herd that Ramón Hernandez had driven to Colorado for Maxwell Grantham, Cornish had lost Gabe Penrock in the thwarted attempt to blow up the Bouchard mine in Leadville. Since then, the corrupt Indian agent had decided to concentrate his efforts in the speculative purchase of land around Dodge City and had opened two more dance halls like the Comique. These last were profitable ventures because he dispensed not only liquor at high prices but also the carnal favors of young women who, down on their luck, had become barroom hostesses and entertainers in order to survive in the drab frontier town.

Cornish had retained a dozen of his outlaw band, and at least half were engaged in the Indian trade his post necessitated. The friendly Tonkawas, most of whom dwelt on a reservation near Fort Griffin—through which the early cattle drivers had come when they sought protection from raiding bands of Comanches—presented no problem to the fat entrepreneur. He could keep them happy with an occasional side of beef and, when they grew more demanding, see that his men sneaked them a few bottles of whiskey, though this was legally prohibited. However, since they had almost no weapons and had long ago given up raiding and hunting, Cornish saw no danger in providing this illicit treat—especially since it lulled them into not observing how he managed to cheat them by pocketing most of the government stipend granted for their maintenance, substituting weevily flour and threadbare blankets.

It was nearly sunset, and in the Comique, Cornish was playing poker with Abel Pendergast, Jerry Fox, and Tom Havison. These three men, once part of his bushwhacking band, were now involved in his current land speculations.

To Cornish's right, in an attitude of patient humility, stood a long-legged, chestnut-haired girl not quite nineteen, wear-

3

ing a spangled blue dress, black silk stockings, and lace-on high-heeled boots that rose to midcalf. Flossie stood with a look of boredom washing over her face, for in the six months or so that she had worked for Cornish, she had come to expect excitement and diversion. She was unaccustomed to the long, dull hours that characterized the Comique in winter, when very few cowboys came through town looking for entertainment. Shifting impatiently from foot to foot, not wishing to antagonize Cornish—for by now she knew her employer's penchants only too well, as well as the viciousness that could be readily aroused in him at the least irritant— she shyly and hesitatingly spoke up at last.

"Mr. Cornish, would it be all right if I were to go up to my room now? I'm kinda tired, and besides, there aren't any customers to take care of."

Cornish looked up sharply, his flaccid jowls shaking from the suddenness of movement. An irritated look crossed his face, and he retorted sharply, "Good idea, Flossie. You're ruinin' my concentration anyhow, what with all your fidgetin'. But don't get *too* comfortable. I expect to find you refreshed and ready to please me, soon as I've finished takin' money from my boys here." He laughed harshly and looked around the table at his cronies.

Abel Pendergast, a fortyish, heavyset man whose dark hair was beginning to gray at the temples, retorted. "Hell, Jeb, the last thing in the world I'm gonna give you is more of my money. I still think you fleeced us out of our fair shake from the last job we pulled off."

Cornish scowled, but glibly replied, "Now Abel, you don't think I'd mess with my men, do you? Hell, I thought we all had more trust in each other than that."

"Trust is trust, Jeb—but money is money. And I ain't gonna let you have no more than necessary. Now let's get back to poker, all right? I intend to leave here with a damn sight more than I walked in with." Cornish was doing considerably better at poker than he had done earlier at faro with his cronies. A large pile of chips was at his right, and now, after having picked up the hand that Pendergast had dealt him, he squinted at the cards and pursed his lips in a semblance of disgust. Actually, the hand was a full house—three queens and two nines.

"Your bid, Jeb," Pendergast drawled, as he leaned back in

his chair to study his own hand of four spades and a diamond. There was the possibility of a flush, and perhaps it would break his run of bad luck thus far.

"I'll open with a ten spot, Abel boy," Cornish jauntily declared, as he shoved the requisite chips into the center of the table. The other four men followed suit, but when Pendergast asked how many cards his employer wanted and learned that Cornish intended to stand pat, Tom Havison immediately folded his hand, shrugged philosophically, and leaned back to watch the play.

Jerry Fox, a gangling red-haired man in his early thirties, raised ten dollars, but his two pairs were wiped out by Cornish's full house. Pendergast, in drawing one card, had missed his flush and now swore under his breath as the fat Indian agent raked in the chips.

"Well, now," Cornish declared, "that was a right satisfyin' hand. Yep, guess I'm satisfied all around. Maybe we don't have the excitement we used to have, but there's steady money. And this landgrabbin' deal I'm workin' on, when the railroad starts expandin', it's goin' to make us profits enough so we don't have to do any more bushwhackin' jobs. They're too damn dangerous, anyhow. I've lost too many good men over the past few years, as you well know."

"Yeah," Fox glowered, "and you still never settled the score with that goddamn greaser you was telling us about, boss—Ramón Hernandez."

Cornish frowned. He didn't care to be reminded of his one great continuing failure. How he hated that goddamned greaser! He could feel the bile rising in his stomach when he thought about all the times that Mex bastard had outwitted him.

First there was that time back in 1877. Cornish had set Hernandez up to be fleeced of the money the greaser got from Cornish for his herd here in Dodge. But the badger game that Cornish had attempted had backfired, and poor old Frank Thompson had gotten killed. Determining to even the score, Cornish had sent his gang out to bushwhack Hernandez and his men during a cattle drive to Colorado—but again that dirty greaser outsmarted the lot of them, killing many of his best men in the bargain.

And who would ever have believed the incredible coincidence of Hernandez, his Texas partner—Bouchard was the guy's name—and his men being on the very payroll train that

Cornish had sent his men out to hijack? Again the greaser and his men were victorious—and again Cornish lost some of his best gang members. When Gabe Penrock came up with the scheme to destroy the greaser's silver mine in Colorado by inciting striking miners during the riots of 1880, Cornish was sure he'd finally get even with Hernandez. Hell, it was a sure-fire plan: Stir up hundreds of men into an angry mob, and while the greaser and his pals were busy fending off the miners, Gabe would blow up the mine—and the greaser with it. But, son of a bitch, what happens? Gabe went and got himself killed—and that goddamn greaser got richer'n Croesus.

Cornish shook his head to clear away the anger. Looking up at Jerry Fox, he growled, "Never you mind about him. He'll get his, when the time comes. Jeez, that reminds me—'member some months back when Gabe's wife, Rhea, walked in here proud as a peacock and told me she was goin' to fix the Mex good for killin' her man up in Leadville?"

"Yeah," Abel Pendergast recalled, as he cut the cards for Fox to deal. "Wonder what's become of that nifty-lookin' piece."

"Maybe she got herself another man," Tom Havison, a brown-bearded, stout man in his early forties spoke up.

"I'm not so sure of that," Cornish volunteered. "As I remember her, she was pretty sour on men, except for Gabe. And all she thought about when he got his was gettin' even with that Hernandez fellow. Well, since we haven't heard a word from her all this while, I guess maybe she gave up and took off for other parts. Good riddance—she's a born troublemaker."

"Don't give us that, Jeb," Pendergast scoffed. "We weren't born yesterday. You had the hots for her, and I'll bet you still have."

"You just shut your big mouth, Abel boy," the Indian agent growled, with a murderous look at his crony. "It's none of your business what I thought about her."

Then suddenly he rudely shoved the table back with such force that Pendergast, sitting opposite, let out a yowl of pain.

"What the hell was that for?" Jerry Fox wonderingly asked.

But Cornish didn't answer him. He was staring open-mouthed at the swinging doors of the Comique. Through them had come a tall, black-haired young woman with deep

6

gray eyes, bundled in a greatcoat, with sturdy black boots. She stood a moment, detailing the interior of the Comique and then, seeing Cornish, advanced slowly toward the table.

"Speak of the devil, for Chrissake!" Cornish muttered under his breath. Noticing his fixed gaze, his three cronies shifted their chairs and turned to look, then uttered gasps of surprise as each man's eyes found the same figure, almost like an apparition.

"My Gawd, it's Rhea!"

"Sure is, and she looks damn near frostbitten!"

"Hey, Rhea, where you been keepin' yourself all this while, honey?"

Jeb Cornish reached for his glass of whiskey and took a sizable gulp before setting the glass down on the table. "Rhea! I didn't expect to see you back here. Hadn't heard from you all this time. We all figgered you'd taken off. What's the matter, didn't your little scheme for settlin' Ramón Hernandez's hash work out for you?" And then, with a guffaw as he eyed Jerry Fox, "I told her she couldn't do it on her own when some of my best men failed."

"That just shows what a stupid bastard you are, Jeb Cornish," Rhea Penrock cut in as she stood facing the Indian agent. "I got me a job as cook for their outfit, and they took me on down to Texas. Then I ran away with the greaser's youngest kid. . . ."

"Well I'll be boiled in oil and tarred and feathered!" Cornish ejaculated. "Rhea, I take it all back. Gotta hand it to you, honey—that was a right smart bit of thinkin'. Jerry, be a gentleman and give Rhea your seat. Go get her a fresh glass and pour her out a slug of that whiskey. She looks like she can stand a stiff drink."

"Yes, I can, but not because of the cold," Rhea curtly interposed. She unbuttoned the greatcoat, drew it off, and then, draping it over the back of the chair, seated herself. Over her chambray work shirt she wore a leather vest, and heavy corduroy breeches completed the outfit. As she took off her Stetson, her jet-black hair, brushed to a coal sheen, cascaded wildly over her shoulders.

Jerry Fox ambled over from the bar, set down a clean glass before her, then reached for the half-empty bottle of liquor and poured out a generous portion. "Drink up, honey . . . takes the chill off," he proposed with a smile.

Rhea did not answer, but took the glass and tossed down at least two fingers of the harsh whiskey, then shuddered and set the glass on the liquor-stained table. "That hits the spot," she laconically announced.

"Well now, tell us all about it, honey," Cornish prompted. "So you snatched the greaser's brat, eh? Hmm. That gives me a great idea."

"And what could that be? I know all about your great ideas, Jeb Cornish, and they haven't panned out any too well. I told you I'd make Hernandez pay for Gabe's death, and I've done it—all on my own. Without any help from you or your friends here."

"Now, now, no need to be hostile, honey. Didn't I always treat Gabe as my best man, and wasn't I glad when he married up with you? I'm your friend, Rhea, and that's why I'm goin' to tell you about this idea that just came to mind. It'll make you a pile of cash and let you live in real style," the Indian agent declared with a smirk.

She stood up, put her hands on her hips, and glared at him. "Just what idea is that?"

"Calm down, Rhea, calm down, honey. No need to get huffy with me. Why, you know I always thought you were a hell of a woman . . . even before you shacked up with Gabe," he ingratiatingly added.

"Just keep your fat mouth shut—and I wasn't shacking up. I was his wife. You understand that, you fat creep? He was the only man I ever loved, the only man who treated me decent. You wouldn't know what that was, Jeb Cornish."

"All right, you've had your say, and I don't mind takin' a few wisecracks from you. You've had a tough life. I know all about it. And you had a tough deal when Gabe got killed. But don't blame me for that—"

"Now listen. I've got the girl, and I did it all by myself. I didn't ask you for any help, and you didn't give me any, so I'm not in hock to you. The only reason I came by was so you'd know I kept my promise."

"Look . . . you're smart, Rhea," Cornish told her, "so hear me out. Now don't you think that greaser will be out of his mind, wonderin' what happened to his brat? Listen. If you let me handle this, we'll be on easy street for the rest of our lives."

"How?" she tersely demanded.

8

"Where's the kid now?" he asked, a cagey expression on his florid face.

"Think you're smart, don't you, Cornish? I'm boarding with a widow woman—and you don't know where she is, you don't know her name, and you're not going to find out from me. I've got the kid safe and sound, and I'm not cutting you in on this deal. Get that through your thick skull!" Rhea flared.

"Jeez, I don't know why you hate me the way you do, Rhea. I've always treated all my help right. I paid Gabe a stiff price for what he did, and it was just his bad luck he got killed. Don't blame me for it . . . don't take it out on me," Cornish whined. Then, with a wheedling smile, he added, "Now here's what I'm thinkin' about. You've already proved you've got more brains than anybody else in this outfit—'ceptin' me, of course. And that's all the more reason why you and I can team up and get some real cash out of what you've just pulled off."

"I'll hear you out. But let me tell you this: I'm not going to stay in Dodge very long, and there's no way you're going to cut yourself in after I did all the hard work," Rhea defiantly told him.

The three men at the table exchanged glances. They admired Rhea Penrock, and there was not a man there who did not lust for her, but her dominant, fierce, and inimical attitude made them decide not to become involved. This, as they saw it, was a confrontation purely between their boss and Gabe Penrock's widow.

"I'll give it to you straight and fast." Jeb Cornish leaned back in his chair and made a gesture of impatience. "That greaser will give a lot to get his kid back. Suppose I have one of the boys here ride down to Windhaven Range with a note, sayin' that we've got his kid, and we'll talk turkey, if he comes up with some real cash—do you get my drift?"

"Yeah, and I want no part of it. My plan is to pay him back by keeping his daughter from him so he'll never get her. And I'm going to raise her the same way I was raised when I was a kid." Rhea moved back a little, still glaring at the Indian agent. "As you yourself said before, Jeb Cornish, I had a miserable, tough life. Gabe was the only joy I had in it, and that's why I planned all this by myself—because he was taken from me by what that greaser did. You don't figure in it at all.''

"Take it easy, take it easy. We're just talkin', see?'' Cornish gave her a smile as a look of intense concentration came over his face. He was silent for a few minutes, then a slow, mean grin transformed his expression from that of conciliation into one of evil. "I just had me an idea,'' he told Rhea. "Suppose we do somethin' that'll make 'm sit up and take notice—like cut off one of the kid's fingers and send it along with the courier just to show that damned greaser we mean business.''

Rhea Penrock recoiled, a look of horror on her face. "You disgusting bastard! How can you even think of a filthy thing like that?'' she exclaimed with vehemence, unaware that the feelings she automatically displayed were completely contrary to her intention of rearing Gatita in unhappy circumstances. Long suppressed materna' ~~cts had begun to blossom in Rhea during her time v ⌐ ine daughter of her husband's killer. Gabe's death had denied her the chance of bearing his child, a child born of love—the first love she had ever known. Now these weeks with Ramón's daughter unconsciously rekindled the feelings of affection that had lain dorment since that ill-fated, brief marriage.

"Boys, why don't you go to the bar and have yourselves a couple of rounds on me?'' Cornish grinned and winked at his cronies. "Stay outta this. I've gotta teach this little lady some manners. She's plumb forgettin' I'm the head of the gang, and what I say goes.''

"Sure, boss,'' Abel Pendergast chuckled, as he gestured to his two friends and rose from the table, heading for the bar. The others followed him, glancing back over their shoulders, grudgingly admiring the svelte black-haired young woman who had dared defy their powerful employer.

Rhea stood there, her hands still propped on her hips, glaring at Cornish, while he poured himself another drink and took a leisurely sip. "Sit down!'' he commanded her. "You're gonna listen to reason, or I might just have to push you around a little, get me?''

"I don't think you'd try it, Cornish,'' Rhea mockingly responded.

"No?'' He reached down under the table and from his belt drew out a hunting knife that he had won in a poker game

10

with an impoverished buffalo hunter. "See this, bitch? You give me any trouble, Rhea, I'll carve my initials on your pretty back—and then you'll belong to me."

"You're really a disgusting son of a bitch, Jeb Cornish!" she hissed, as she pulled out a chair and seated herself astride it, backwards, her palms on the table, staring angrily at him.

"Keep it up, honey—I like a woman with spirit. You know I always had a yen for you. Yep, Gabe sure showed good taste when he picked you out."

Seeing that her glare was still as unswerving and harsh as before, he changed his tactics and gave her another wheedling smile. "Now listen, Rhea honey, there's no reason at all for us to be enemies. Don't you see? There's dough enough for the two of us here. And I'll even go so far as to give you a fifty-fifty split, with no one the wiser. Why, I'll just guess that the greaser will go as high as five thousand for the little brat. What's wrong with that?"

Rhea reached for her glass and downed more of the whiskey, then set it down with such force that it almost smashed. She ground her teeth and finally answered, "Everything! I told you you've got nothing to do with it. I'm the one who's paying back the greaser. That's something you and all your men could never do—not with your bushwhacking, or your robbing the train, or trying to stir up trouble at the mine. All down the line, your schemes failed, Jeb Cornish. But *I* was the one who had the brains, just like you said, and *I* was the one who pulled it off. And that's exactly why you won't interfere with my plan. I'm leaving now. All I came in for was to let you know you don't have to worry about the greaser. He'll be so sick over losing Gatita that he won't be able to do his work, won't be able to do anything. And that's the worst punishment of all—worse than death or torture."

With this, she began to rise from her chair, but Cornish showed her the knife again and snarled, "I didn't give you leave to go yet, bitch! Now this is what you're gonna to do, and you hear me out. I'm gonna send Abel down to where the greaser hangs out in Texas, with a note. We can knock the kid out with booze so's she won't feel nothin', if that'll make you feel better. . . ."

Savagely, Rhea interrupted him. "You'll do no such thing! I don't want any ransom, and he doesn't get his kid back, and that's the end of it."

11

"Look, Rhea, you're gettin' me real mad at you. I think I'm gonna have to give you that lesson after all," Cornish growled as he rose from the table and squinted at her, his lips drawn back in an ugly smile.

Rhea suddenly snatched the bottle of whiskey, smashed it against the table, and used the shard to defend herself against Cornish's knife. Her eyes blazed with fury as she backed away, crouching a little and extending the broken bottle in her right hand.

"Look, boys, you're gonna have a treat tonight, for sure!" he called to his friends at the bar. "Watch me carve this bitch up and make her beg for mercy!"

Silent with fury and hatred, Rhea watched as Cornish ambled toward her, his sensual, wet lips curving in a lecherous smile. Suddenly, he lunged at her with the knife, but she twisted away and then drove the shard into the side of his jaw, drawing blood.

Not expecting her to take such swift action, he stumbled backward with a yowl of pain and staggered. Rhea was on him like a tigress, slashing at his throat with the shard, while he tried to defend himself by lunging at her with the knife. She grabbed his right wrist with her left hand, twisting it till the knife dropped with a clatter to the floor. Crouching, she picked it up and drove it into his heart.

Cornish uttered a hideous cry, his goggling eyes staring at her as if he could not believe what had happened to him. Then he slumped to the floor, rolled over onto his belly, and lay still.

There was a concerted gasp from the three men at the bar, and Abel Pendergast swore aloud. "Jesus Christ! Son of a bitch! I can't believe it. Jeb's dead!"

Rhea swiftly stooped down, noticing that Cornish had a pearl-handled derringer tucked inside his vest pocket and a six-shooter in his holster. She drew out both weapons, straightened, and whirled to face the astounded men. "Don't move, any of you! I'd just as soon shoot you as look at you, understand?" she exclaimed.

"All right, Rhea honey, don't get itchy with the triggers, especially on that derringer," Jerry Fox said, as he put up a propitiatory hand. "I didn't go along with what he wanted to do to the kid anyhow—I don't think any of us did, right, Abel?"

"Yeah, sure, only she had no right to kill him," Pendergast grumbled. Then a cunning look came over his face; he had just realized that the death of Jeb Cornish meant his enterprises were there for the taking. "Listen, you fellows, how'd it be if the three of us took over from Jeb? I mean, he's got all this land tied up in deals and a few other schemes on the side. And now that he's dead, nobody owns this here place. Do you get my drift?"

"Sure do, Abel," Tom Havison spoke up. "No reason why we can't take things over and split them between us. Hey now, what about him bein' an Indian agent and such? Who's gonna take that over?"

"Hell, it's a stinkin' job, anyhow," Pendergast disgustedly retorted. "Everybody knows Jeb cheats the Tonkawas by passing off the worst flour west of the Mississippi and blankets that wouldn't keep a polar bear warm in Florida on a hot night. No money in that. But, if one of you guys wants to write Washington and apply for the job, go do it with my blessing—"

"Fat chance," Havison sneered. "If the Feds found out where we are, they'd send out a hangin' posse for sure—and you know it damn well, Abel."

"All right, then, so we pass up the Indian trade. No big loss." Pendergast turned to the tall black-haired woman. "Well, Rhea, I guess it's high time you scrammed outa here. We got private business to talk about that don't concern you."

Rhea, still standing over Jeb Cornish's dead body, the derringer in her left hand, the pistol in her right, responded with an amused and cynical smile on her lovely face. "Talk about rats deserting the sinking ship," she jeered. "But then, maybe it's best all around. Well, seeing that none of you has any objection to my leaving, I'm going to do just that. And seeing as how you'll be getting fat off his deals, I'm going to help myself to his poker winnings. You boys don't want me to be broke now, do you? Besides, he owes me that much because I was the one that did it to the greaser."

"Sure, sure, we won't stop you, Rhea honey," Pendergast eagerly offered. He looked at his cronies, who nodded assent. "You've done us a good turn, puttin' Jeb out of the way. Take whatever's in his wallet."

Rhea laughed mockingly. "Well, looks as if everybody's happy. I'll help myself to what he's got in his wallet, and you're welcome to everything else. Just don't try to follow me. I'll go on my way with the kid, and no one's the wiser, savvy?"

As she saw them all nod in unison, she placed the derringer into the pocket of her vest and shifted the pistol to her left hand. Then she thrust her right hand into the dead Indian agent's coat pocket and drew out his wallet. Smiling to see that it was thick with greenbacks, she jammed it into the pocket of her breeches. Then, quickly putting on her greatcoat, she strode through the swinging doors of the Comique, disappearing into the gloom of twilight.

There were many who called 1881 the year of destiny. It marked the beginning of innumerable strikes and lockouts, as workers sought to improve their hours, wages, and treatment. It was a year that marked the beginning of a huge migration of Russian Jews to the United States, following the persecutions by Czar Alexander III, who had just succeeded his assassinated father. By fate's irony, the assassination robbed the Russian people of a ruler who had, by imperial ukase, liberated Russia's serfs.

Eighteen eighty-one saw Booker T. Washington founding Tuskegee Institute in Alabama; also, George Pullman inaugurating his famous made-to-order industrial town, named after him, in the state of Illinois. It was also the year in which the first pure-food laws in the United States were passed by the states of New York, New Jersey, Michigan, and Illinois.

The world-famous Anaconda copper mine was opened near Helena, Montana, and the governor of Missouri set a high price upon the heads of Frank and Jesse James, the notorious train robbers. Jesse James would be shot and killed in the following year.

It was in 1881 that Grover Cleveland was elected the "Veto" mayor of Buffalo. On January 19, the Western Union Telegraph Company was formed by Jay Gould and William H. Vanderbilt. A month from that date, Kansas adopted statewide prohibition, and three days later, President Rutherford B. Hayes, in his executive orders to the Secretary of

War, Alexander Ramsey, prohibited the sale of liquor at military posts.

On March 4, James Garfield and Chester A. Arthur were inaugurated as President and Vice President, with James G. Blaine the Secretary of State, and Abraham Lincoln's son, Robert T. Lincoln, as Secretary of War. Six days later, the Santa Fe Railroad joined the Southern Pacific at Deming, New Mexico.

In May 1881, Clara Barton became the president of a newly organized American Red Cross. The *Atlantic Monthly* published Henry Demarest Lloyd's "The Story of a Great Monopoly," aimed at the Standard Oil Company. At about the same time, an Act of Congress authorized the registration and protection of trademarks, a notable step forward in accelerating new business ventures and protecting the products and integrity of the owners.

Tragedy blighted America on July 2, 1881, when the recently elected President Garfield was shot while in the Pennsylvania Railroad Station in Washington, D.C. Garfield's assassin, Charles Guiteau, was a disappointed office seeker; on September 19, President Garfield died of his wounds, and a day later, Vice President Arthur took the oath of office as President at his home in New York City. Two months later, Guiteau's trial began, and convicted, he would be hanged in the nation's capitol on June 30, 1882.

In November 1881, the Federation of Organized Trades and Labor Unions of the United States and Canada was formed at Pittsburgh by Samuel Gompers, as the forerunner of the American Federation of Labor.

During the last month of this fateful year, Secretary of State James G. Blaine declared the Hawaiian Islands to be part of the American system and within the bounds of the Monroe Doctrine. In the same month, the Southern Pacific Railroad was completed between New Orleans and the Pacific, when the last spike was driven near El Paso, Texas. A few days later, Secretary of State Blaine resigned. A long-time friend of the assassinated President Garfield, and himself looked upon as a logical candidate for the Presidency, he retired to private life to write his memoirs. The political faction of Senator Roscoe Conkling, which had attempted to nominate U.S. Grant in 1880, had successfully blocked Blaine's own nomination for the nation's highest office. His place as Secretary of State was taken by Frederick T. Frelinghuisen, whom President Arthur appointed on December 12, 1881.

In all, it was a year fraught with uncertainty, a year whose unforeseen machinations and tortuous convolutions were to affect the destiny of Windhaven itself. . . .

Chapter One

The beginning of the second week of January 1882 was cold and raw, with the sky a dull, sullen, even gray. Yet as Laure Kenniston stared out her bedroom window to Gramercy Park across the street from the brownstone she shared with her husband, Leland, watching her five children romp in the snow under trees shivering in the wind, she felt a warmth surge within her.

She laughed aloud at the children's antics, especially the expressions on her daughters' faces as their oldest brother, Lucien—nearly sixteen and home from his private school in Ireland for the holidays—pulled them around and around on a gaily decorated sled with especially sharp runners for speed. A Christmas present from their new stepfather, the sled was in danger of being worn out in just one season, the children played with it so frequently.

Laure suddenly discounted the cold and threw open the window so the sound of the children's laughter could reach her. Celestine—now ten and a half—was squealing with joy, while clinging tightly behind her on the sled was nine-year-old Clarissa. Toward the other end of the park, Paul, who had just turned thirteen, was building a fortress out of snow with the baby of the family, John. *Dear little John,* Laure thought to herself. *How delighted with him Luke would have been.* It was so hard to believe that so much had happened to her in the four and half short years since John's birth and Luke's death barely a month later.

Laure looked down at the barely perceptible swelling of her belly and smiled. Closing the window, she walked around to the side of the bed and sat down with a poignant sigh. It had been a magnificent Christmas, the best she could recall in many a year. How much fun it had been to train down to Montgomery three weeks ago! Seeing all the wonderful people back on Windhaven Plantation had done a world of good—dear Marius . . . Burt . . . and Ben. They were doing such a fine job of maintaining the estate. And Laure thought she would faint dead away when Lopasuta and Geraldine came from New Orleans to share Christmas with her, bringing the most wonderful present of all—Lucien. What a wonderful and thoughtful surprise of Leland's this had been. She hadn't seen her son in over two years, and suddenly there he was on the most wondrous holiday of all!

A sudden sharp twinge forced Laure to lie down on the bed, reveling in the softness of the down-filled quilt. As she lay quietly for a few moments, the pain began to recede and she let her mind wander back, thinking of the twists and turns of her life. Now forty, Laure Kenniston had led the kind of life she thought existed only in books. Not that she thought of herself as a heroine—far from it. She had been the pampered, spoiled daughter of a prosperous New Orleans banker, caring for very little except her own happiness before the outbreak of the Civil War. My, how things changed after that!

It had really been John Brunton, Laure's first husband, who completely altered her way of thinking, turning her from a selfish, headstrong girl into a thoughtful, considerate woman. After knowing degradation and despair at the hands of Union soldiers, Laure had been taken in by the kindly banker, who had protected her, had loved her, and had helped her regain her self-respect.

She sighed again. Truly, she was the most fortunate of women. Who would have dreamed that after knowing such kindness and warmth from John, she would come to know, after John died, such passion and contentment with Luke? She whispered his name aloud: *Luke Bouchard. Truly you were the most considerate, devoted, and honorable man.* Luke had embodied all the hopes and dreams of his grandfather, old Lucien, when the founder of the dynasty had first come to these shores from France almost a century earlier. And Windhaven Plantation had grown into a living memorial to that man, a place where people of all races and creeds worked side by side, sharing the labors and the fruits of those labors.

What a wonderful reunion the past Christmas had been. Lopasuta—adopted by Luke and taken from his Comanche stronghold to study law—was so successful; and Geraldine, his devoted wife, looked more beautiful and radiant than ever. It had been a communicative holiday, filled with spiritual warmth, and when they had all climbed the gradually ascending trail up to the top of the red bluff to the gravesites of old Lucien, his beloved woman Dimarte, and Luke, who had so revered his courageous, heroic grandfather, they had all felt the spirit of these people.

Yes, the memories of Christmas had made Laure especially grateful for the renaissance of her life, one that she thought had been forever shattered by the bullet that had killed her precious Luke. It had been so typical of that courageous man to have died the way he did—preventing a malcontent from killing Alabama's governor, ending up a martyr himself.

"Well," Laure mused aloud to herself, "enough of this! I have two trunks of clothes to unpack and here I am lounging the afternoon away like an invalid." Rising from the four-poster bed, Laure walked over to one of the trunks and threw open the lid. She hummed softly to herself as she unpacked, glancing every now and again through the window to watch her children playing.

Again she gave herself up to the surge of nostalgia and went to stand at the window, hearing the laughter of her wonderful children by Luke, laughter that to her ears sounded like distant music. But practicality winning out, she soon returned to the opened trunk to sort away the children's clothes. Now that they were back in New York, school would resume in a few days—and Lucien would have to go back to Ireland.

There was a knock at the door, and Laure turned to the sound. "Come in," she called, and Clarabelle Hendry entered.

"Do you need any help unpacking, Laure?" she asked. While officially the children's governess, Clarabelle had become over the years a dear and devoted friend.

"That's very thoughtful of you, Clarabelle, but I'm enjoying doing it myself. By the way, Leland and I are both indebted to you for looking after the house while we were away. I hope you weren't too lonely and didn't miss going back to the plantation."

Clarabelle shook her head and replied with a broad smile, "Good gracious no, Laure! I guess I've fallen in love with New York and everything there is to see and do here. Frankly,

19

I felt I was getting a bit too dowdy and sedate back in Alabama.''

Laure came across the room to where Clarabelle was standing and impulsively hugged her. "It *is* good to be back, Clarabelle. I know exactly how you feel—and I'm so glad that you *do* feel that way, because I would be lost without you.''

Giving Laure a warm smile, Clarabelle took leave of her friend's room, closing the door, and Laure went over to the second trunk and began to unpack her clothes. There was the beautiful hand-knit shawl that Leland had given her for Christmas, one made by a woman from his native village in the County Mayo. She lifted it out carefully and buried her face in its soft folds. "My dearest Leland,'' she sighed. "I am the luckiest woman in the world. Never did I dream that life could be so totally fulfilling and satisfying as it is with my love.'' Still hugging the treasured gift, she walked ..er to the bureau and laid the shawl in the bottom drawer, ''rapping it carefully in tissue paper.

As she stood up, she felt a burning pain in her abdomen. she uttered a stifled groan, drawing a deep breath against the sudden violence. She waited anxiously. Then it seemed to pass and, after a moment or two, she went back to the trunk.

When she bent again to her task, her senses seemed to swirl. The pain was repeated, but this time it was gnawing and prolonged. "Oh, my God! What is happening?'' she gasped, as she put both hands down on the edge of the trunk to steady herself. She closed her eyes, praying that the pain would recede. It seemed to diminish somewhat, but then it returned with redoubled agony.

"Clarabelle—help me!'' she cried out frantically when the pain became too great to bear. Darkness clouded her vision, and she swayed as she fought to hold herself erect, bearing down on the lid of the trunk with all her might.

The governess opened the door just as Laure crumpled to the floor. "Laure!'' she screamed, and ran to her stricken friend. Taking but a moment to place a pillow under Laure's head, Clarabelle then raced down the stairs and picked up their newly installed telephone. When the operator responded, the governess fairly shouted Leland Kenniston's office number at the young male voice on the other end. "And hurry!'' Clarabelle demanded. "It's an emergency.''

Leland Kenniston, his handsome face wreathed in anxiety, paced up and down the hospital waiting room. Now in his middle forties, the Irish-born entrepreneur's thick black hair was just starting to be tinged with gray, and the impeccably tailored suit he wore showed off his trim, athletic figure. Nervously plucking at the fur collar on the coat he carried draped over his left arm, Leland feared for the safety of his wife, the woman who had given his life new meaning for the past year and a half.

He had fallen in love with her almost from the first moment he had met her, when she had come to New Orleans to visit Geraldine and Lopasuta. It had been one of the wonderful ironies of fate that Lopasuta had by chance saved Leland's life aboard ship some years back, thereby becoming first a business associate, then a friend, and—finally—the instrument through which Leland would know such happiness by introducing him to Laure Bouchard.

His life with Laure had been all that he had hoped for—full of tenderness, passion, sharing, and happiness. "Please, God, let her be all right," Leland whispered.

He looked up suddenly as a figure entered the room. Dr. Henry Cummins, a specialist in gynecology, had been telephoned by Leland as soon as Clarabelle had told him of Laure's condition. The physician had immediately summoned an ambulance to have Laure taken to nearby St. Vincent's Hospital. Now, having just operated on his patient, he had determined that there would be no dangerous complications to hamper her complete recovery—news that he now imparted to her anxious husband.

"But," the doctor said as he wiped his sweating brow, "I'm afraid I've bad news for you, Mr. Kenniston."

"Is Laure in danger? Be honest with me, Dr. Cummins!" Leland demanded.

"No, Mr. Kenniston, she's in no danger. She's a strong woman, and she's kept herself in superb condition. There will be no ill effects from this miscarriage. But—" Dr. Cummins hesitated, then took Leland's arm and led him to a chair. "The bad news is that she can never have another child. Of this I'm certain, and I feel it best to tell you the truth."

"Does she know it yet?"

"No, Mr. Kenniston. I think this news should come from

you. You'll have to be patient with her and more than usually considerate—but I needn't have to tell you that, because throughout her consultations with me, Mrs. Kenniston has done nothing but praise you to the skies." Dr. Cummins permitted himself a wry smile. "You're a paragon among husbands, it appears." Then, his face sobering, he added, "and that's why it's all the more unfortunate that I have to be the bearer of such bad tidings. I know how much she counted on giving you a son, Mr. Kenniston. Love is a wonderful thing, and when a husband and wife have a child that they truly want, it cements that love. She must be made to feel that in no way is she less in your eyes as a wife and lover because of her inability to procreate—that's saying it brutally, but I believe in complete frankness with my patients."

"I'm grateful to you for that, Dr. Cummins, and I'll do my very best to ease her mind. Do you agree that I shouldn't tell her right away, but wait until after she's had time to recuperate at home?"

"Unquestionably. I leave it to your discretion, Mr. Kenniston. I'm very sorry. I assure you that it just wasn't possible to have it come out any other way."

"I know of your reputation and your skill, Dr. Cummins. That thought never entered my mind. And I'm grateful to you for having saved her life and promising me that she'll have no bad aftereffects."

"I wish you both many long years of happiness. Incidentally, your wife told me how you've established a loving closeness with the children she's had by her late husband, Mr. Bouchard. That's important for both of you, and it may be a kind of compensation as the years go on."

"Yes. I'm sure that's true. Again, my sincerest thanks, Dr. Cummins."

Five days later, as the family sat around the breakfast table, the children were unusually quiet, all of them surreptitiously eyeing their mother. Leland had simply told them that she had lost the baby, but he had not explained the implications for the future.

Laure, noticing the pervasive air of stealth that surrounded them, suddenly laughed and exclaimed, "For heaven's sake, my dears, you're making me nervous by being so quiet! I'm quite all right, really I am, so please be yourselves."

22

An almost audible sigh of relief went up, and soon seven voices were babbling at once. "That's more like it," Laure said with a grin. Turning to her oldest son, she said, "Lucien, we've not had much chance to talk about your schooling, what with all the excitement of late. I want to know everything, my dear."

Leland interrupted. "You know, Laure, since Lucien is doing so well in school, it probably wouldn't matter if he were a week or two late getting back to Dublin."

"That's true, Father." Lucien had delighted Leland Kenniston by giving him that title of affection, and it was sincere. When Leland had escorted Laure's oldest son on the crossing to Ireland, he and the boy had exchanged many confidences, and Lucien had been fascinated by the anecdotes Leland had told him of his own Irish childhood and how the enterprising youth became the successful businessman he now was.

"Besides," Lucien continued with a smile, "if I do fall a little behind, my instructor will catch me up in a hurry."

"Tell me more about Ireland, Lucien," Paul eagerly demanded.

"It's so incredibly beautiful: lush green landscapes, mountains criss-crossed by babbling streams and brooks—such wonderful countryside. And Dublin is a very quaint city—all cobblestones and old-fashioned wagons. And such brogues! I have to be careful I don't get one myself," Lucien laughed. He went on to tell his entranced brothers and sisters how he had become skillful at playing rugby, a sport that the games master, Henry Brennert, coached at the academy. Then he concluded, "When our form wins its match, Mr. Brennert always takes us to his cottage, where his daughter makes us the most wonderful high tea. She's a real pippin, she is."

"Oh?" Laure eyed Leland and gave him a knowing wink. "Do I begin to detect the hint of a romance, Lucien? I suppose since you're nearly sixteen, it's to be expected that you've discovered the charms of the opposite sex."

Lucien blushed furiously. "Oh no, Mother! It's nothing like that at all! Mary Eileen is just housekeeper for her father—you see, his wife died when she was very young. And she's a capital cook. Her gooseberry tarts—well, there's nothing like them!"

"I wish I could go to school with Lucien," Paul forlornly declared.

"Maybe you will one day, youngster," Leland indulgently replied. "But right now it's wonderful to have you all here for the holidays—you especially, Lucien."

"Thank you, Father." The tall, blond boy flushed self-consciously and lowered his eyes. Laure sent her husband a grateful look for making Lucien feel so warmly welcomed after his long stay across the Atlantic.

Then, perhaps aware of the silence that had fallen partly because of his own self-consciousness, Lucien changed the subject by declaring, "You know, a lot of my school chums have commented that the situation in Ireland is very much like this country was just before the Civil War. And I suppose when you think about it, there are tremendous similarities. Economics is involved to a large degree and both sides feel that their cause is the right, just one. Wouldn't you say that is true, Father?"

"I would have agree with you, Lucien," Leland concurred. "Well, you've certainly matured since you entered St. Timothy's. Do you have any inclinations to try an American school next term?"

"Oh, no, Father!" Lucien quickly answered, almost frowning in his eagerness to put across his point. "I've made lots of friends there, and I'm learning a lot. And, besides, I think it's really important for me to understand what's going on in Europe and how people think and feel over there."

"There's no doubt that you're getting a cosmopolitan education, and it will be invaluable to you in your later years, particularly when you decide on your career," Leland said in agreement. "But remember—grateful as I am to have you call me 'Father,' your mother is the one who will have the final say as to whether you stay in Europe till you've finished your schooling, or whether you should be here with us. I'll never go against her wishes, believe me."

"You're very sweet, Leland." Laure took her husband's hand and patted it affectionately. Then, giving each of her children a gentle smile as they sat ringing the dinner table, she cleverly changed the subject. "Well now, my dears, Dr. Cummins thinks that in a few weeks I'll be able to go skating in Central Park. But just because I'm invalided at the moment is no reason why the rest of you can't go out with your father

24

and spend a pleasant day together." Laure's children—except of course John, who was still too young for such active sports—were greatly enjoying the contrasting activities that a New York winter offered, as against one in Alabama.

"We'll go uptown tomorrow morning after breakfast," Leland proposed. "Incidentally, I'll take the sled for John. I can pull him on the ice, so he won't feel left out."

"That's sweet of you, Leland," Laure beamed with another look of gratitude.

"I brought my own skates back from Dublin," Lucien proudly announced. "Last winter we watered down a place near the field hockey area, and everyone skates there. I must say, I think I'm rather good. Skating's great fun."

"I'll bet I can skate just as well as you can." Paul was not to be outshone by his older brother. "I skate with David Cohen a lot, don't I, Mother?"

"You do, indeed. And, by the way, Leland dear, I'd like to invite the Cohens for dinner—perhaps Thursday—to meet Lucien. Paul, maybe after you've finished skating, you can run over to the Cohens' and invite them."

Leland turned to Paul and said, "You know, son, David's father has really been of great value to me as the jewelry expert in my business. Since it was through your friendship with David that this came about, I want you to know that, even though it was by chance, you have helped me—and therefore *all* of us—tremendously."

"Oh, thank you, Father!" Paul gleefully declared, then flushed as Lucien looked at him with almost a patronizing smile.

Quick to notice this rivalry, Leland finished his coffee and quietly interposed, "Well then, if we're going skating tomorrow, there's no reason we can't have a little practice this afternoon. Of course," he said, turning to the handsome teenager to his right, "if you're tired or you have something else to do, Lucien, you can wait until tomorrow if you like."

"I'm not the least bit tired, Father," Lucien indignantly protested.

"Well then, let's get ready. Just for an hour or so. Laure, my dear, we'll be back long before dinner." Leland rose and kissed Laure on her cheek, then shepherded the four older children out of the dining room.

Laure sighed happily. What Dr. Cummins sometimes de-

25

fined as the "megrims" had beset her for the past few weeks, and, of course, her regrettable miscarriage had made her gloomier still. But this reunion and the obvious fondness of all her children for her husband greatly warmed her. Without their total approval of Leland—and indeed, without his sincere affection for each of them—her happiness in the new marriage wouldn't have been complete.

As the Bouchard children glided over the frozen Central Park lake the next afternoon, Leland Kenniston beckoned to young Lucien. Paul Bouchard, seeing that his stepfather had taken Lucien off for a private conference, now was able to play big brother to his sisters, Celestine and Clarissa. Taking both of them by the hand, he began to skate slowly and carefully while they squealed joyously at such attention. John, thoroughly wrapped against the cold with muffler and scarf, was being pulled on his sled by Clarabelle Hendry. She had insisted on going along, for although she was Southern-born, she was finding life in the exciting Eastern metropolis of New York fascinating and had taken to skating and other amusements like a duck to water.

"I was waiting until the proper time to tell you about your mother, Lucien," Leland quietly explained, "because I didn't want the younger children to hear. But you're old enough— why, you're practically a man—to understand what I'm about to say." He paused for a moment, then continued, "Of course, you and the others understand that the reason for your mother's stay in the hospital was that she lost the child she was carrying."

"Yes, father. I was sorry to hear that. . . ." Lucien paused. "She—she's all right, isn't she?"

"Well—yes. That is, she's made a fine recovery, and it hasn't affected her health at all. But—I have to tell you—she can never have another child."

"Oh, my God! That—that's terrible! Poor Mother! And you, too. I know how you must feel. . . ."

"Well, yes of course it saddens me, but the main thing now is to show all the more love to your mother, more attention and more kindness. The miscarriage has been a hard blow for her, and I haven't yet informed her of its consequences. I'm glad you are with us right now. You can give your mother the diversion she needs. Otherwise, I'm afraid

26

she would be much too melancholy and unhappy, thinking it was her fault that she couldn't give me a child." Leland stopped again and gave his stepson a candid look. "Lucien, I'd rather like to think that, in a way, you're my son, too—and I want to help you with your life, do everything I can to give you the opportunity of being your own man—wise and honorable and courageous, just as your father was."

"Thank you, Father. I—I do love you a lot. And I'm very grateful to you for sending me off to St. Timothy's, because I'm really happy there."

"Good!" Leland uttered a sigh. "Well now, that's enough serious talk, wouldn't you say? We're here to have a whopping good time, so let's go out and do it!" With a broad smile, Leland pushed himself off onto the ice and raced to catch up with his younger stepchildren.

Chapter Two

Leland Kenniston decided to accompany his stepson Paul over to the Cohens' attractive apartment on East Sixteenth Street, a few blocks south of the Kenniston town house.

The two families had met by chance nearly a year and a half earlier when Paul Bouchard, in the course of a long walk one lovely September afternoon, found himself hopelessly lost in the teeming streets of the Lower East Side. A boy his own age, David Cohen, rescued Paul by taking him home to a six-story tenement on Rivington Street.

When Leland and Laure went to thank the boy's parents, Jacob and Miriam Cohen, for the kindness they showed to Paul, the Kennistons learned that Jacob Cohen had been a diamond merchant in Kiev before he and his family were forced to flee the pogroms just starting to be initiated by the Czar's Cossacks. Practically penniless upon their arrival in America, the immigrant family slaved cruelly long hours under intolerable conditions just to earn a subsistance living. Leland, recognizing Jacob's intelligence and conscientiousness, hired the Russian Jew to be his jewelry expert in his expanding import-export business, and through this association, the members of both families developed deep friendships with each other.

In the year and a half since the families had met, Miriam Cohen, a tiny woman in her early thirties, had changed the most, Leland reflected. Not only had her speech become Americanized, but also her appearance. Miriam's thick raven hair, worn in a bun at the back of her neck and with curls along the top of her forehead, already showed traces of gray. She had relaxed her custom of keeping her head covered at all times. Laure had even suggested that Miriam go to her own hairdresser, and had done it so tactfully that her new friend looked upon it as an adventure. And, even though Jacob Cohen was somewhat shocked at this swift transition into the American way of life, when his wife emerged from the beauty salon, he sheepishly grinned and muttered, "What will they think of next? Now I have a new wife, it seems, thanks to you, Laure!"

Now Leland strode up to the Cohens' door and knocked firmly. His summons was answered almost immediately by the flushed wife of the jewelry expert, a food-spotted apron tied around her waist. "Leland, my friend! What a pleasant surprise. Hello, Paul, it's good to see you, too. Dear me, I apologize for my untidy appearance. . . ."

"It is I who should apologize, Miriam," the genial Irishman interposed, as Paul went in to find his friend, David. "Do forgive me for dropping in on you without notice, but we were on our way home and I wanted to invite all of you for dinner day after tomorrow."

"Oh, that would be very nice." Miriam lowered her voice so her children couldn't hear her next words. "How is Laure? I have been so worried about her. She was quite distraught—although she tried to hide it—when I visited her in the hospital."

Leland's face sobered, but he instantly responded, smiling again so that this gracious woman would in no way guess his own disappointment over the tragic circumstances. "She's doing fine. She's so looking forward, as all of us are, to having you over for dinner. I know she has lots to talk about with you."

"I am so pleased that we will finally have the chance to meet Lucien—Laure must be so thrilled to have him home from Europe. And speaking of the old country, I shall never be able to thank you enough, Leland, for the wonderful chance you have given Jacob. My goodness," she exclaimed, her eyes earnest and warm, "I still cannot get over the change in my husband—the sparkle is back in his eyes, the stoop is gone from his back, there is excitement in his voice whenever he talks about his work. I tell you, Leland, you have given me back my old Jacob."

Leland laughed, an embarrassed look on his face, and he tried to disavow responsibility for the alteration in Jacob Cohen's personality. "Really, my dear Miriam," he began awkwardly, "Jacob has repaid me a thousandfold for anything I may have done for him. Why, without his help—his very expert help, I might add—I would have paid far too much for a good deal of the jewelry that Kenniston Company has imported. Jacob certainly knows precious stones, and he has been invaluable to me as an appraiser."

"That may well be true, Leland," Miriam interrupted, "but you, too, must have noticed how much Jacob has changed in the year and a half since we had the good fortune to meet you. As I have often said, the luckiest thing that has ever happened to us was when David ran into Paul. That truly was the beginning of a new life for all of us."

Leland took Miriam's hand, pressing it in both of his. "We were equally lucky, Miriam. Paul and Celestine are so very fond of David and Rachel—your children have been a very good influence on our sometimes-too-spoiled children, and I must confess that I have done a lot of the spoiling," he laughed. "And even more important," Leland continued, "your friendship has meant a great deal to Laure. I don't know that I have ever seen her quite so excited and caught up in anything as she has been over your settlement house project. The work you two are doing has brought a new richness to Laure's life, one that she finds immensely rewarding."

"Yes, helping others *is* very rewarding," Miriam declared, "and I, too, am so pleased that I can help others who are in the same dire circumstances that my family and I were in such a short time ago. You know, Leland, I feel it must have been the hand of God that guided Paul to David. To think that something that might have been so insignificant could have led us together, and in so doing has helped so many people . . ." Her voice trailed off as she wiped a tear glistening down her cheek.

Just at that moment Paul burst back into the room, David Cohen trailing a few steps behind. "Father," Paul asked, "do you think that we should be getting home for dinner soon?"

Leland and Miriam both laughed, then the handsome Irishman observed, "My son has learned to be a diplomat, wouldn't you say, Miriam? The delicious aroma coming out of your kitchen has all too strongly reminded him that he is very hungry after an afternoon of ice skating, but, clever lad that he is, he has left the decision of getting home to our *own* dinner up to me." He turned back to his stepson and declared,

"You're absolutely right, Paul. We certainly don't want to keep the others waiting." Leland kissed Miriam lightly on her cheek and said in parting, "It was good to see you again, Miriam. And please tell Jacob how much I have appreciated his handling so many of my usual chores at the office during my vacation with my family. Well, then, we'll see you all on Thursday."

When Leland and Paul arrived back at their house on Gramercy Park, Lucien was just rounding the corner, returning from a short stroll. As Paul climbed the steps ahead of them, Lucien turned to his stepfather and addressed him thoughtfully. "Paul told me the story of how you met the Cohens. They sound like fine people, and it's good that you helped him. I'm very proud of you for that, Father. My instructor, Sean Flannery, says that the real purpose of life is to experience and express love. And by doing what we can for those less fortunate than ourselves, we receive the joy that comes from expressing love."

"Your instructor sounds like a very perceptive man, and from the many times you've quoted him, I've become quite eager to meet him. Perhaps on my next trip to Dublin I'll have that pleasure—that will be this fall, according to my present plans. Incidentally, I'm glad we're alone for the moment. Remember what I said about your mother, Lucien. After dinner, I'd like her and me to spend the evening together—you understand."

"Of course. Poor Mother! I wish—" Laure's oldest son paused, then impulsively blurted out, "I wish to God it were different, because I know how much she loves you, and it would have made you both so happy!"

"I know," Leland softly agreed, "but we mustn't think about that. I'm going to try to console her as best I can, and that's why I want to be alone with her this evening. I'd appreciate it if you and Paul will keep the girls and John occupied."

"Of course, Father," Lucien concurred, and a warm look of understanding passed between the youth and his greatly admired and respected stepfather.

It was a cold evening, and Anna Emmons, the Kennistons' cook, had prepared a simple but nourishing dinner. She had further endeared herself to the children by making them hot cocoa. Leland Kenniston had hired her about six months after Laure and the children had moved to the new house fronting Gramercy Park. She was in her late forties, plump, and wonderfully efficient. The greengrocers, the butchers, and the other tradespeople with whom she dealt saw the most practical side of her nature when she shopped for the Kenniston household. Anna questioned prices, and she deflated from the very first any tradesman's attempt to profit unjustly at the family's expense by her refusal to accept meats and vegetables whose quality she found suspect. Mrs. Emmons came by her skills through years of professional experience.

A childless widow whose husband had died twelve years earlier, she had first managed a boardinghouse catering to some twenty residents, then spent five years in a private hospital as a cook and dietician before going to work for a blue-blooded family whose scandalous divorce early the previous year had left her without a post. Leland had learned about her from one of his friends who knew the estranged couple, and he had promptly gone to see her and offered her not only a salary far above what her previous employer had paid her, but also her own private room and bath. The residence on Gramercy Park was unusually well equipped in that regard, Leland had assured the grateful widow.

Their house was spacious indeed, Leland reflected as he bade the children good night. Ironically, he had purchased the house with its several extra guest rooms with the intention of adding to their already large family . . . children that would be born to them, engendered by their love for each other, their respect and devotion. But now it would never be. And now he would have the most difficult task of his life—of reconciling Laure to the news that he had withheld from her and the same time not only consoling her, but also making her feel certain that in no way would his adoration of her and the happiness that she brought to him diminish.

From the other end of the table, she looked up at him now with a bewitching smile, then murmured, "Alone at last— isn't that from one of E.D.E.N. Southworth's novels?"

He chuckled and nodded. "I do believe it is, my darling, and so we are. It's been a most exhilarating day with the children, and I've loved every minute of it."

"One of the things I like most about you, dear Leland, is

your willingness to take off time from your business—and I know how complex and extensive it is—to spend time with the children."

"Your children—our children—are most important to me. And, after all, now that I have a family, my primary business is being devoted to making it possible for you and the children to have the happiest of lives. For them, I want the finest education that money can buy . . . and exposure to culture, comforts, of course, but in a way that will let them develop their own minds and choose for themselves what course they wish to follow when they mature. What other incentive can there be for the accumulation of wealth but this? To match your quotation with another, 'The man who hath a wife and children hath given hostages to fortune.' Well, that's my feeling exactly."

"Dear Leland! With each new day, I realize what a smart woman I was to have said yes to you! I'm so in love with you, and I always shall be."

He winced inwardly, for he knew that he must no longer withhold the terrible news Dr. Cummins had imparted to him. Brutal though it might have been, perhaps he should have told her from the very outset. No, it could not be, for it might have plunged her into such a morass of despair that, coupled with the understandable physical weakening of her system the miscarriage had caused, it might well have endangered her very outlook on life.

But before he could speak, Laure broke in, her face now very grave, and he could detect tears glinting in those marvelous green eyes: "You know, Leland, we're so terribly lucky. I thank God every day for the happiness He's given us. Just this morning, I had a letter from my stepdaughter, Mara Bouchard—you remember, she's married to Ramón Hernandez and living on Windhaven Range?"

"Yes, I remember very well. I take it from the expression on your face that they still have no news of their daughter."

Laure's lovely face wore a pained look as she shook her head and responded, "No, they haven't—and I can't begin to imagine what they're going through. Apparently no one has yet been able to figure out why this young woman—Rita Galloway, I believe her name was—kidnapped Gatita. When Lucien Edmond and Ramón hired her as their cook back in Leadville, Colorado, she told them that she was down on her

33

luck, but oddly there's been no ransom demand. I gather that she was very fond of the child—indeed, of all the children on Windhaven Range, so Maxine Bouchard told me last year shortly after Gatita was taken away—so perhaps that was her motivation."

Laure paused, a perplexed expression on her face, then continued, "Still, it doesn't make any sense. From what Maxine has said, the young woman was industrious, considerate, and very sweet. Truly, it seems absolutely senseless."

Neither of them spoke for a few moments, then Leland asked, "You said you received a letter from Mara?"

"Yes, I did. Wait, I'll get it and read it to you—"

Dear Laure,

It has been a terribly trying year for all of us here on Windhaven Range—and of course, our little girl's disappearance is the chief cause of it. There is still no word of her, and none of that infamous woman who betrayed our trust and kidnapped our daughter. Her note said that she was going to take Gatita (that is her nickname—Little Kitten, an appropriate name for our adorable child) to Mexico, where we would never find her again.

Ramón has ridden out again and again, and he and the vaqueros, as well as Lucien Edmond, have covered every possible way that woman could have gone across the border. There have been many false leads, but still no sign of her, or my daughter.

Ramón is absolutely shattered. He is not able to overcome his guilt and anger at having been deceived by that cruel woman, and he cannot understand why she would do what she did, after all the kindness all of us showed her. More than this, he blames the discovery of the Colorado silver mine for all of his troubles. He curses his greed and everyone else's, and he says—and, of course, I agree with him—"All the silver in the world can't make up for the loss of Gatita."

It is strange that I have now become the stronger one. I remember when I first met Ramón, how haughty and spoiled I was. I can hardly bear to recall how I treated him then—calling him names simply because he was Mexican. What a silly, prejudiced girl I was then! When he became my lover, my husband, the father of my children, *he* was the one who could always console me when I was in a bad mood. But this past year, Laure, it has been I who have done everything I can to pull him out of these terrible black moods in which he no longer seems to care to live. He keeps saying that he will go on searching for Gatita until he has found her—and if he doesn't find her, then he has failed as a man.

Pray for us, dear Laure, that we may find our child so that Ramón can take joy in life again. It breaks my heart to see him this way, and I feel so helpless, for there is nothing I can do.

In a happier vein, I wish you, the children, and Leland every happiness. Sometimes I think that a visit to New York to see you all would help take me out of my *own* black mood.

> Yours fondly,
> Mara

Laura looked up at her husband. "Of course, I'm going to answer her, and naturally I'll pray—and yet, words are so utterly futile in such a tragedy as this. I remember how strong and self-reliant Ramón was, and how Mara depended upon him. Indeed, he was the bulwark of Windhaven Range, along with Lucien Edmond." She sighed and shook her head.

Leland remained silent, for he was tortured by the knowledge that he must shortly reveal to his lovely wife their own tragedy, one that might profoundly affect their lives. Finally he said in a husky voice, "When you write her, my darling, why don't you tell her that if there is anything I can do to help, she shouldn't hesitate to ask."

"How sweet of you, dear Leland! I will write tomorrow morning, and I'll mention that. You're always so thoughtful and considerate of others!"

Leland's eyes turned to gaze down, and he breathed deeply. "I wish that were possible all the time, my darling. Alas, some things are impossible to do without causing others grief." At this Leland paused, then forced himself to continue. "Laure dear, I have something to tell you, something I perhaps should have told you sooner, but I couldn't bring myself to do it. . . ."

35

Laure put down Mara Hernandez's letter and stared wonderingly at her handsome Irish husband. "That sounds ominous, my darling," she said in an uneasy voice. "Please tell me. We must never have any secrets from each other."

"I know that—I promised you that from the very first, when I met you and fell in love with you, Laure. I want your forgiveness for my not having told you this before, but it was done, I swear, only to spare your feelings so that the delight we've had with our children wouldn't be shadowed." He paused momentarily. "All right, then—I'll come right to the point. While you were in the hospital, I conferred with Dr. Cummins. He told me that, although there won't be other aftereffects from the miscarriage, I'm afraid that—that you and I can never have a child."

"Oh, God!" She uttered a strangled cry, then sat back in her chair and stared at him in silence for a long moment. Finally, she murmured, "This must break your heart, as it breaks mine, Leland—"

"No, no, my darling! You mustn't say that. I was only afraid for you. Believe me, it changes nothing between us. Yes, I'm selfish enough to say that it would be most flattering and wonderful to have a child by you, for you are the only woman I shall ever love. It just can't be, however. The most important thing is that I'll have you, for from what Dr. Cummins says, you'll have a long and healthy life. And because we can't have children of our own, your children are all the more dear to me."

She rose from the table and walked toward him. Tears streamed down her cheeks as she held out her arms to him. "Hold me. Take me in your arms and hold me, my dearest one."

He took her on his lap and held her close until the sobs that shook her died away. Then, stroking the back of her neck, he cupped her chin with the other hand as he put his lips to hers very tenderly. "I love you more than ever, Laure. And I have come to think of your children as mine."

"Oh, Leland!" she broke in, sobbing once more. She put her head on his shoulders and murmured, "I'll try to make you happy, so that you won't regret having married me."

"That's something I never want you to say again, my dearest!" He was almost angry as he cupped her chin and stared into her eyes. "You have nothing to apologize for or

36

feel ashamed of. It's God's will, and I don't rail against it, or question it. It's His test for our love, to make us stronger, to make our love deeper and richer, so that we may cling to each other and protect each other against all the evils and the adversities. When I think of poor Ramón Hernandez, when I think of you now so brave and so sorrowful that you can't give me a child, I want to go down on my knees and thank God for all my blessings.''

"Oh, dearest, oh, my Leland!'' she whispered.

"I swear to you there will never be any chance for you to have the tiniest feeling that in any way am I displeased with you, or find you inadequate or lacking. Promise me you believe me.''

"Oh, I do, I do, Leland dearest!'' Laure began to sob in earnest and, as the tears ran down her cheeks, she cupped his cheeks with her soft, trembling hands and kissed him ardently on the mouth.

Chapter Three

Mrs. Emmons had surpassed even herself in preparing a superb dinner to welcome the Cohen family once again to Leland Kenniston's elegant brownstone house. She would have done so out of her own desire for perfection, for she prided herself on her cuisine; but she admired Leland and Laure, and very likely because she had been bereaved herself, she felt all the more sympathy toward the reunited family, whose warmth and respect for one another was readily observed.

A magnificent fish filet, subtly flavored with lemon and capers and just a hint of garlic, was served with delicately seasoned wild rice, snap beans cooked with almonds, and tiny mushrooms to add even more flavor. There was an excellent mixed green salad, tossed with her own special vinaigrette dressing. Since she had been given ample notice of this dinner and knew that David and Rachel Cohen would join the Kenniston brood, she had decided to give everyone special treats for dessert: baked apples with brown sugar, which were marvelously palatable.

Leland Kenniston had thought it best to remind Mrs. Emmons that the Cohens were of the Orthodox Jewish faith, and that they had certain dietary laws. To be sure, the menu that she discussed with him—apart from the dessert, which was her own improvisational idea for the evening—offended in no way these strict laws. At the conclusion of the meal, there was the finest coffee served with rich clotted cream, as was Mrs. Emmons's custom. To the men she served a fine old French cognac in large snifters, which Leland Kenniston had imported from Italy. The hand-blown glasses had giant bowls in which the burnished golden liquid seemed to swirl and change colors, and its aroma spread upwards to delight the nostrils and finally the palate.

For the women, Leland had suggested a delicate anisette, and the younger children enjoyed cocoa, rich and piping hot. Lucien Bouchard, because of his seniority among the offspring, was allowed a modest pony of brandy. So that the next youngest would not be jealous, Leland suggested to Laure, "Why don't we let Paul have a small sip of brandy—in honor of the occasion." And to his younger stepson, he pleasantly added, "Next year, you'll be of an age when I think you can handle a pony of that potent cognac."

At this, Celestine and Clarissa began to giggle until Paul silenced his younger sisters with an angry look. The youngest child, John, appeared mystified by these proceedings.

These small exchanges among the children eluded their mother, for Laure and Miriam were deeply involved in a discussion about the settlement house they had started up for immigrant families. Several months after Leland had hired Jacob Cohen to handle the jewelry division of his import-export business, the two women—who had by then become fast friends—began to talk about the importance of helping newcomers to America acclimate themselves to this new land and this new way of life.

Leland had generously contributed ten thousand dollars for the purchase of a serviceable building for the settlement house on the lower East Side. The building had a spacious assembly hall, where the men and women could listen to discussion by compatriots who had already come to New York and learned how to cope with this dramatic change in their lives. In addition, there were furnished rooms, some of them large enough for couples with children, providing temporary housing for those who had come from the old country at the behest of relatives who had then failed to meet their obligations or decided, at the last moment, that they did not want their impoverished relatives from Europe to intrude upon their lives. There was also a communal kitchen, where the women took part in preparing meals and exchanging recipes, creating a kind of social leavening that made them feel more at home in the strange new city of New York, so far from their homelands across the seas.

Leland had also engaged two highly respected social workers, who had the additional talents of being fluent in German,

Polish, Russian, and Yiddish, and who had access to larger industrial firms seeking qualified help. These workers interviewed the men and women who came to the settlement house and, after determining their skills, aided them in finding gainful employment.

"As you know, Miriam," Laure said, momentarily setting down her fork, "our house is such a success that we really need new, larger quarters. Leland has been so very generous already that I'm not going to ask him for more financial support, but I do believe that you and I should be able to raise the money ourselves. There are many people who are influential and compassionate and who realize that contributing to a settlement house such as we have is a good investment in America's future."

"That's a wonderful idea, Laure," Miriam exclaimed. Her warm brown eyes lit with excitement, and her smile was radiant.

"Well, I can spare a good deal of time, now that I'm well again," Laure proposed. "I've met the Vanderpools—they're good friends of the Gorths, if you recall. I told you all about them—"

"Oh, yes, I remember!" Miriam Cohen nodded. "Alexander Gorth manages the Douglas Department Store on Broadway, and Charles Douglas is married to your late husband's niece in Chicago."

"My goodness!" Laure laughed. "You do have an excellent memory, Miriam. Well now, the Vanderpools know practically the entire Four Hundred of New York City, and a word from them would certainly bring us plenty of contributions."

"You know, back in Kiev, we called that *schnorring*," Miriam said with a wry smile, glancing over at her husband, who was in animated conversation with Leland Kenniston. "It's a very good Yiddish word for asking for money. I don't know if there's an English word that's more expressive, not for that."

"*Schnorring*," Laure repeated with a smile. "I must remember that. But, of course, when we approach these wealthy socialites, we'll talk about the humanitarianism of our project and the help we're going to give to people who can become good, upstanding citizens. We'll let the socialites infer that we would be very grateful for a substantial check."

"Well, I must say, the American way is much more subtle than the way we used to do things in the old country," Miriam giggled.

"There are times, I'll admit, when directness produces results. But I think, with these important people we're going to ask to help us, it would be best to let them think it's their own very charitable idea, so that they can be proud of themselves when they do contribute," Laure explained.

"You're absolutely right. By the way, didn't you say earlier that a realtor has contacted you, and he mentioned a property that he felt would be suitable for us?"

"Yes, indeed. There's a warehouse building about two blocks east of our present establishment. I think it could be converted at not too great a cost to house at least another hundred immigrants, and allow some recreational facilities as well. There could be, for example, a gymnasium for the children—and even for the adults. In a crowded city like New York, it's so vital to have a place to exercise."

"Yes, even in Kiev we had many wonderful parks and gymnasiums—till the Czar decided that Jews shouldn't be allowed in them." For a moment, Miriam Cohen lowered her eyes and tightened her lips.

At the other end of the table, Lucien and Paul listened attentively while their stepfather chatted with Jacob Cohen. The subject was diamonds, and this was a fascinating topic for these two boys, who were already eager for manhood. Lucien, to be sure, had had far more experience, because of his trip across the seas to Ireland and his schooling there, and there was no doubt that his younger brother, Paul, was secretly envious. Paul determined, even as he listened, that one day he would be as well traveled and as conversant with as many subjects as Lucien was.

"Did I mention to you, Leland," Jacob Cohen was saying, "that we should soon be receiving a shipment of diamonds from the Transvaal? When I was in Kiev, I had a contact—an Afrikaner, whom I suppose you would call a Boer—who was an assistant superintendent in the great new Kimberley diamond mine. Since I dealt in the finest stones, I was able to secure superb gems from this man, which I sold at a considerable profit. Alas, as you know, when the Cossacks came and began to persecute our people, I was forced to practically give away all my remaining valuables to enable my family and me

41

to flee that tyranny. Be that as it may, the man is still dealing in gems, for I had a letter recently from Heer Pieter Tolvard in Amsterdam, another of my old contacts. He wrote me just two weeks ago that the Afrikaner has now been promoted to become one of the directors of sales.''

"But that's capital, Jacob! I have some orders in San Francisco, Hong Kong, and New Orleans for the very finest large-carat stones. Write your friend, then, and see if you can negotiate some sales with this contact of yours in the Transvaal.''

"I shall do that indeed, Leland. I wanted your approval before I negotiated such a major transaction.''

The genial Irishman interrupted with a mock scowl, "Heavens, my good man, to hear you talk, you would think that after all this time I don't trust your judgment. Why, you have far more expertise in such matters than I. Henceforth, Jacob, I want it clearly understood that when it comes to stones, *you* are the boss. Is that acceptable to you?''

Jacob shrugged, then chuckled, and both men broke out laughing; the two boys, who had followed the conversation closely, heartily joined.

When the adult conversation turned to more mundane matters, David Cohen and Paul Bouchard, who had become fast friends, began twitting each other. Last fall, at Leland's suggestion, the youngsters had joined a nearby boys' club, where they went each weekday after school. It boasted gymnastic equipment like padded horses, trapeze bars and rings, and also a boxing ring. The instructor, whom both boys took to at once, was a stout, nearly bald, retired middleweight prizefighter. He had wisely decided to end his career before he was battered like a human punching bag into senselessness, and had invested his earnings in a Bowery saloon. After four years, the profits from his business had enabled him to take life relatively easy, and to accept the modest-paying post as an instructor for a group of boys whose parents were of middle or high income.

Both boys were quite proud of their pugilistic prowess. The instructor, Herman Gingery—who had fought under the name of Battling Herman—was particularly fond of them because both were so serious and determined to show their skill. "Boys, I'll level with you. You probably won't ever be good enough to enter the real ring, but you'll sure be able to defend yourselves if some low-life bully comes around tryin' to make trouble. You gotta remember to be light on your feet and to figger out what the fellow fightin' you is going to throw your way, so you can duck out of it without losin' balance, see?''

Then he had confided, ''The real reason I got out of professional bare knuckles was that I've always had me a glass jaw. So throw your best Sunday punch and see if you can hit me right on the button. Go ahead, now. I won't get mad if you land one.'' And each boy had tried unsuccessfully during the first month to hit Herman Gingery's ''glass jaw'' until, just three days ago, David—studying the stout, middle-aged man—had successfully landed a right hook that had staggered his instructor.

''You see, Paul,'' David was now boasting, ''it's a scientific thing, just like everything else in life. I just figured out, after watching Mr. Gingery, where he was going to move to next, and I was ready for him. You can do just as well. But, right now,'' he grinned, ''I'm one up on you.''

''Oh, go on, David. I bet you that tomorrow afternoon I'll floor him,'' Paul boasted.

Leland had listened to some of this patter and chuckled as he addressed both boys. ''I can see the club is doing you two a world of good. That's great! It's good to know how to defend yourself. Sometimes you're the only person you can rely on, when it comes to self-protection.'' Then he eyed Laure and thought to himself—though he did not express it, for he knew that the Irish movement was not entirely to her liking—*Yes, and that's the plight of my fellow countrymen these days. But the danger is that they may all try to take matters into their own hands, and then we'll have nothing but bloodshed and violence. That's not the way for Irish freedom. And yet, when all the English are against them, how can they ever hope to become free men and hold their heads up high, as free men should?*

Rachel and Celestine were deep in animated conversation at their places at the table. They had started the seventh grade in September, and shared many of the same classes. ''I'm sort of scared of algebra, Rachel,'' Celestine admitted to her new friend.

''Don't worry—it's really easy if you put your mind to it. I'll help you, if you'd like. We can go over the homework together. You can come to my house whenever you like, after school,'' Rachel generously offered.

"That's real nice of you to offer. Thank you so much, Rachel."

The two girls smiled at each other; with them, too, a bond of deep and lasting friendship had grown. Celestine had learned through the eyes of her new friend how lucky she had always been in not having to be concerned over money, or clothes, or food. Not that Rachel was tactless enough ever to mention her previous circumstances and those of her parents, but Paul had often described in amazement what a dreadful apartment the Cohens used to live in, yet how impressed he had been by the fact that, despite their poverty, they had been unusually warm and loving toward each other—and to strangers such as he had been.

He had remarked to his sister after meeting the Cohens, "You know, you and I never had to think about going without anything we ever needed or wanted."

Celestine had always been relatively self-centered and aloof, perhaps subconsciously believing that she was of the privileged class and, therefore, what came to her was her due. But thanks to Rachel's pluck and serious integrity, Laure's fair-haired daughter had begun to take more interest in others.

Although she had achieved reasonably good grades at the private Alabama school when the family had lived on Windhaven Plantation, her education had been summary, with an emphasis on some of the domestic arts and the liberal arts, but without any real grounding in history or mathematics. True enough, she had been too young to receive such training, but the outlook of the rural schoolteacher had been that these were the children of the well-to-do; they should be brought up to realize only that they were superior to others—even without a good education—because of their parents' position in life.

Now, happily—thanks mainly to Rachel Cohen—Celestine Bouchard was becoming more serious, learning how to think for herself and to work things out. Laure, already perceiving this, heartily approved of it and had mentioned as much to her husband before the Cohens arrived: "I think the most wonderful thing that's happened to this family since we came to New York is that the Cohens have become an integral part of our lives, making us all better people for it because of their own family loyalty and innate honesty." Leland had been in total agreement.

Now their highly regarded guests were leaving. Jacob Cohen turned to his host. "It's been a wonderful evening, Leland. And I've so enjoyed meeting you, young man," he said to Lucien.

"Thank you, sir," Lucien warmly replied. "After hearing so much about all of you, I couldn't wait to meet you—and I'm awfully glad I did."

They shook hands, and Jacob patted Lucien affectionately on the back. "Have a safe journey to Ireland, and I guess we'll see you again during your summer vacation." Then, looking over at his wife, he murmured, "I have a full day tomorrow at the office, my dear Miriam, so let us get home and to bed."

"I'll show you tomorrow afternoon that I can knock Mr. Gingery out," Paul called after David, as the Cohens opened the front door of the brownstone, letting in a rush of frigid air.

"We'll see about that," David chuckled. "Good night, everybody. Thank you, Mr. and Mrs. Kenniston. It was a delicious meal."

"You're quite welcome, David. Good night to you all," Laure called back.

On the landing, Lucien turned to his younger brother. "Well, sprout, I'll say this for you—you've grown up a lot. 'Course you still have a ways to go before catching up with me."

"Wait till you come back the next time; I'll be even with you," Paul defiantly retorted, and Lucien goodnaturedly poked him in the ribs. The two boys then raced each other up the stairs.

Laure and Leland Kenniston stood at the front door after seeing their guests out. They gazed at each other, holding hands, and Laure whispered, "What a delightful evening this was, my dear Leland. I think it has made me truly realize how very full our lives are and how content I am. I guess I'll always feel a twinge of regret or remorse that we cannot have a child of our own, but the fullness of our life together is more than ample compensation." She kissed him tenderly, then whispered even more softly, "What I have is enough to make any woman happy."

Chapter Four

Before Rachel Cohen left with her parents, she had arranged with Celestine to play in Gramercy Park, across from the Kenniston house, the following afternoon. The sky was a dazzling blue, and the sun reflecting off the snow was almost painful to the eyes. At least a foot had fallen during the earlier part of the week, and the warm sun had helped melt the snow somewhat so that it was ideal for packing. Rachel had told Celestine, "We'll make a snowman—I know that my father has an old pipe and scarf he's about to throw away, so I'm sure he won't mind if we use them."

As she was about to run out the front door of her house, Celestine caught sight of Lucien, sitting at the desk in the study, intently reading *The New York Times*. "Want to help us build a snowman, Lucien?" the young girl inquired.

Lucien Bouchard was scheduled to leave on the steamship the SS *Megowen* the next noon, to take him back to St. Timothy's Academy in Dublin. He looked up at his sister and gave her a rueful grin. "Can't, sis. I've got to get upstairs and finish my packing."

Leland Kenniston had written a letter to Father O'Mara to let the headmaster know that, if by any chance the crossing was bad because of winter weather on the Atlantic, young Lucien might be delayed in returning for the new semester. He had added:

> He's so enthusiastic about his instructors at your fine school, that I'm sure even if he should be a few days late, he can quickly make up any work. The earlier reports you sent me confirm his keen intelligence and his eagerness to assimilate all these new experiences

and curricula, through which you and your able staff have guided him.

I remember from my own school days that I judged a school and its teachers by how enthusiastic I was about getting up each morning and going off to my classes. Well, it already seems to me that Lucien burns with eagerness to learn all he can as quickly as possible. Needless to say, my wife—his devoted mother—is as happy as I am to see what you have done with our son. You are modeling him to be a cosmopolitan man of the world, one who can understand that what happens in Europe affects our own country. God bless you and your wonderful work!

This morning he had given Laure's oldest son a five hundred dollar bank draft as spending money for the rest of the semester for such things as extra books the youth would want to read, sporting events, and perhaps even the theater. Nor had he forgotten that Lucien had mentioned—albeit rather coyly—an interest in the games master's daughter. Well, the boy was rapidly coming to an age when he would certainly be conscious of the opposite sex, and he might like to entertain her at music halls, or perhaps buy her some tea and buttered scones, and the like. He remembered his own boyhood and the arduous struggle his parents had had to survive—yet they had dedicated themselves to giving him the very best possible education so that he would advance beyond their own limited scope of endeavor. Leland vowed to do no less for Laure's —his—children.

Paul Bouchard had come home from the boys' club this Friday afternoon to discover a letter from his cousin, Joy Hunter, whom he had met for the first time a year and a half ago, and with whom he had formed an immediate friendship. Now entering her thirteenth year, Joy had sent along clippings from the Galveston newspaper. One of them, to his great delight, was a feature story she herself had contributed to the newspaper.

Paul sighed as he folded the letter. How he wished that Joy were right here in New York City. The brown-haired youth had listened avidly to Lucien talk about Mary Eileen Brennert and had been just a little envious. And he thought to himself that if Joy were here, in a year or so when they were old enough, they might do some sparking—the serious kind, of course. Both of them were so interested in much the same things—like history and stamps and writing. He read the clippings assiduously and then went to his desk and began to write a letter. Looking out his window through frosted panes to the park, he recognized Celestine and Rachel, bundled up, wearing their mittens and their winter boots, busy near a bare oak tree building a snowman.

Paul liked Rachel. In some ways she reminded him of Joy. Perhaps Joy had a bit more of a sense of humor and was more mischievous than Rachel, but he understood why: After hearing talk of the Cohens' hardships before finding freedom here in New York City, he had learned that when people had more worries, they naturally had to become more serious in order to handle the problems. David was just beginning to laugh and joke a little; well, the same thing was beginning to happen to Rachel, too. And the way Celestine had begun to grow up pleased him a great deal.

He was about to turn away from the window, when he noticed a stocky towheaded boy—whom he guessed to be as old as Lucien—chasing a black animal that at first Paul couldn't identify. The boy made a lunge and caught the creature, lifting it up by its tail. Paul gasped as he saw that it was a kitten. It was probably a stray, or else the poor thing had wandered away from home and got lost and was now starving in the cold winter air.

"That's a terrible thing to do to a poor little kitten!" Paul exclaimed aloud, pressing his nose against the glass and following the scene with an indignation that was almost instinctive. Back on Windhaven Plantation, all of Laure's children had grown up loving animals: horses, cows, chickens, even pigs, and of course such pets as raccoons. His father, Luke, had always told him and the others that the world wasn't complete without animals, that they had feelings and perhaps even souls, just as all of us did, and that was why no one should ever be unnecessarily cruel to any of them. Poisonous snakes and rats and other vermin—well, it was understandable that you would want to kill them, before they hurt you or others. But a kitten—

The boy had begun to swing the kitten by the tail, around and over his head, and suddenly he let it fly. The kitten managed to land on its four paws, but it staggered as it tried to recover itself. Instantly, the boy ran up to it, grabbed it by the tail again, and began to whirl it around his head once more.

Paul flung open his window and shouted, "Stop that!" and was about to turn away and hurry downstairs when to his amazement he saw Celestine run up to the boy. He couldn't believe what he saw now: His sister clenched her mittened right fist and struck the boy in the stomach so vigorously that he stumbled and fell back into the snow. Snatching up the mewing kitten, she began to talk to it. Paul could clearly hear her raised voice through the window.

"You big bully, you!" Celestine was angrily exclaiming to the startled boy who stared up at her—incredulous that a girl had hit him in the first place, and even more bemused by the fact that she had hit him with such force as to fell him to the ground. "That was a wicked thing to do, do you hear me? I warn you, if I ever see you hurting anything else, I'll tell the S.P.C.A. on you! I mean it! Now you just get up and take yourself away from here, and don't ever come back!"

The boy scrambled to his feet, shook his head in bewilderment, rubbed his stomach—which still pained him—then turned tail and ran out of Paul Bouchard's view. No more than the bully could he believe what had happened: His pampered sister actually had come to the defense of a kitten and, what was more, bested a toughie like that boy, who would be hard for even him to fight.

With the danger to the kitten past, Paul's thoughts turned to his boast that he would knock out Herman Gingery. Monday, he promised himself, he would prove to David Cohen that he could sock that "glass jaw" and maybe even knock Mr. Gingery onto his back—just as Celestine had done with the bully.

Rachel Cohen ran up to Celestine and hugged her. "That was the bravest thing I ever saw, Celestine!" she exclaimed. "I'm so proud of you. Wasn't he a terrible boy? What are you going to do with the kitten?"

"I'm going to take it home. Maybe Mama will let me keep it. Or give it a home until we can find out if it belongs to somebody," Celestine stoutly declared.

"I'd love to take it myself, Celestine," Rachel hesitated a moment, "but I don't think our landlord allows pets in the apartments. Besides, you've a much bigger house and room for it—and it can go out in your yard when the weather's nice."

"That's true. Well, let's go back to my house and see what we can do for this little thing. I'll ask Mrs. Emmons to give it a saucer of milk. Maybe we can make a bed for it out of a box and some towels, or something like that," Celestine proposed. "Hmm . . . do you suppose it's a boy or a girl?"

Celestine and Rachel triumphantly bore the kitten across the street and, in great animation, described the rescue to Laure and also to Leland, who, as it happened, had come home early from work.

"Celestine, I'm very proud of you." Laure hugged her lovely daughter. Then, turning to Leland, she added with a sly smile, "I think we could find a place for this little kitten somewhere, don't you, Leland?"

"I'm sure we can," the Irish businessman genially agreed. "But we're going to have to try to find out if it belongs to anyone. We wouldn't want to deprive another girl of her favorite pet, would we, Celestine dear?"

"Oh, no, Papa," Celestine nodded. "But in the meantime we can keep it from starving and being out in that awful cold."

"Do you know, I suspect there must be a little Irish in you somewhere—fighting a boy older than you and as big and strong as he was," Leland joshed his stepdaughter, who couldn't help giggling. Their eyes met, and both he and Celestine burst into gales of laughter.

Later that night—much later, when all the children were asleep—Laure turned to her husband and murmured, "Do you know, my darling, that all the love I see reflected in our children—well, I'm very comfortable and happy."

"That's exactly the way I want it to be always, my adorable Laure," he murmured as he took her in his arms.

Chapter Five

As dusk brought to an end another cool February day at Windhaven Range, Ramón Hernandez silently entered the kitchen of his house and slumped down at his place at the table.

In the span of nearly a year and a half since the abduction of his youngest child, Mara—or Gatita, as she had been lovingly called by all who knew her—he had completely altered. Just entering his forty-third year, the agony and despair caused by his daughter's kidnapping had etched deep lines in his forehead and brought a tightness to his mouth and a taciturn, melancholic air to his demeanor. His hair, formerly jet black, was now liberally flecked with gray. Always courageous and handsome, brave and loyal, outgoing and gracious to a fault, Ramón had turned into a self-recriminating, guilt-ridden recluse during the past sixteen months.

Since his daughter's abduction, he and a number of chosen vaqueros had gone searching for Rhea and Gatita on four separate occasions, spending from four to five weeks at a time, riding disconsolately from one little Mexican village to another. Silent and tortured, Ramón learned only that there had been no sight of either the woman or the child. This fortune was, indeed, exactly the kind of revenge Rhea Penrock had planned when she had learned that Ramón and Lucien Edmond had been responsible for her husband's death.

During the last cattle drive to Sante Fe, the past October, the men who had gone with Ramón had found him no longer the jovial companion who shared their campfire and their meals, laughed at their jokes, told them anecdotes of the first Windhaven drives and the dangers of bushwhacking and Indians. Instead, he had made his own solitary campfire, cooked a few beans, a small piece of beef, and a cup of black coffee, and sat there hunched over, his hands gripping his knees as he stared into the dusk. The vaqueros had accosted him, trying to cheer him up, but he had been brutally terse with them. Pedro Dominguez—who had been with him for a dozen years—realized how morose and tormented his beloved *patrón* was, and he had awkwardly approached Ramón, hesitantly saying, "*Señor patrón*, have we offended you in some way? All of us suffer with you and wish you well and—"

Ramón had turned on him, his face twisted in anger. "*¡Silencio, hombre!*" he had barked. "When I want your opinion or those of the others, I'll ask for it, *comprendes?*"

He had worked with a dogged, almost self-despising efficiency, and since he was one of the finest horsemen in Texas and a master at handling balky cattle, no one could find fault with his supervision of the herd and his ability to sell it at the best price. But, by now, some of the vaqueros had openly told their *compañeros* that they hoped they would not be chosen for the next drive Señor Hernandez commanded.

His wife, Mara, three years older than her husband, stood at the stove and glanced at the silent figure before her. Soon after the initial anguish had passed, she had attempted to restore some semblance of normality to their lives, working hard to overcome her misery. "Ramón," she now exclaimed lightly, "Pedro stopped by earlier and asked me to remind you that the fencing in the south quadrant needs refurbishing, and he—"

"Woman, I will not be nagged by you or anyone!" he burst out. Then, glaring at her, he lifted the coffee cup she had set before him and was about to fill, then hurled it against the stove, smashing it into shards.

"Stop it!" Mara angrily shouted back. "I am sick to death of your moodiness, Ramón!" A low moan escaped from her throat. "In Heaven's name, my darling, you're going to drive yourself to an early grave, if you keep this up," she declared almost sobbing, as she came toward her husband and seated herself opposite him at the table. She put out a propitiatory hand toward him, but he ignored the gesture. Turning partly away from her, crossing one leg over the other, he put his hand into the pocket of his coarse denim shirt, took out cigarette papers and a pouch of tobacco, and began to roll a cigarette. Silently and patiently, Mara struck a match and lit it for him. Ramón hardly acknowledged this courtesy, his eyes continuing to stare at the opposite wall.

Finally, he said, in a low, harsh voice, "Perhaps death would be better, after all. That damnable woman, that monster—how could I have been such a fool as to be taken in by her, posing as an abandoned woman, so helpless and naive. I—who fought on behalf of Juarez and who took a bullet in the back from the man I thought was dedicated to his cause—I should have learned those many years ago what a foolish idiot I am to swallow any story given me—"

"You mustn't torture yourself any longer! Please, Ramón, you mustn't! Don't forget, Lucien Edmond accepted her story, just as you did. All of us thought she was such a fine person—I was wrong—everyone was wrong—"

"That doesn't console me in the least!" Ramón mumbled through clenched teeth as he smashed his fist on the table, making the dishes clatter. His untouched dinner of stew was before him. He stared at it and then, with a sardonic laugh, added, "Yes, I should have been content to be a cattleman. Here's good beef for my meal, and if I'd stuck to beef, none of this would have happened. It's that accursed silver mine Frank Scolby found. If all of us—yes, Lucien Edmond, too—hadn't wanted to be rich overnight, if we'd stayed on the range and tended our cattle and opened new markets and paid more attention to our families . . . I tell you, *El Señor Dios* is punishing me! I'd give every ounce of that silver, every penny it has brought in, just to have Gatita back."

"Of course you would, my darling. Please—try not to think of this again. Eat a little—you've been looking so thin lately that I'm worried about you, Ramón." Again, Mara gently tried to propitiate her agonized husband. Gray had touched her glossy black hair as well, and there were fine lines under her eyes, indicating her own distress over the loss of her youngest child. Yet curiously it was she, who had relied so much on Ramón at the very outset of their relationship, who had become the stronger, the one who had tried to mend broken fences and to restore Ramón's faith in himself. "Be sensible, my darling. How can you expect to go on, if you lose your health and strength? Doesn't it stand to reason that you must keep well, that you must try not to let this loss of ours destroy you—"

"Do you take me for a sentimental fool, Mara?" Ramón

turned to glare at her. He took a long drag at his cigarette and then crushed it out in the untouched food. "All women are alike—they always have sweet, soft words they think can take away guilt and suffering. Well, it's not that easy, believe me! *Dios*, when I think of the wild-goose chase that treacherous *puta* led me and the vaqueros on all this last year—I swear before God that if she were here before me I would strangle her slowly, I would make her go down on her knees and beg forgiveness. I would laugh at her and tell her to beg forgiveness from Satan himself, and then I'd send her to hell by choking the monstrous life out of her throat!"

"My God, Ramón, you mustn't talk this way! Don't you see that you've become a total stranger to me? Ramón, you've even turned upon me, as if I were your enemy. Don't you know that I still love you? Do you need proof of it? I was a fool, too, when I first met you, and you were the one who guided me and channeled my life and gave me purpose and meaning. And now you want to throw it all away!"

"Words! What words can you think of now, woman, that will bring Gatita back?" he stormed, as he abruptly rose from the table and walked to the window, peering out into the darkness.

"If you don't care about having become a stranger to me, will you at least care about not becoming a stranger to your children, too, Ramón?" she sobbed.

"Stop it!" he growled, glaring at her again, then suddenly went back to the table, slumped into the chair and buried his face in his hands.

"The boys, especially Luke and Jaime—well, at fourteen and twelve, they need guidance and support; after all, it won't be long before they're men. But all they've seen of their father this last year and a half is the sour, unfriendly side. And since Edward is only nine, he doesn't understand what is going on. The poor child asked me just last week, 'Mama, is Daddy angry with us? Have we done anything wrong?' Nor does Dolores understand much better. She's quite grown up for her ten years, but she still weeps sometimes in my arms—I never tell you—saying she hopes Gatita will be back soon, so that you'll play with her again. Because you haven't, not once all this last year," Mara went on, her voice trembling with anger.

"In the name of *nuestro Dios*, stop it! I can't stand listening to you, woman!'' He dropped his hands, clenched them into fists, pounded on the table, and glared ferociously at her.

Mara turned away, trying to hide her tears. His words had hurt her deeply, more than he could realize. In addressing her as he had done, he seemed to renounce completely their idyllic union as fervent lovers. Indeed, since that fateful day when Mara and Maxine had returned from their trip to San Antonio to find Rhea Penrock's mocking and vindictive note saying she was taking Gatita to Mexico and they'd never get her back, she and Ramón had rarely shared the conjugal joys they had known from their very first awareness of each other as destined partners. When he had occasionally turned to her for a kind of tortured, if momentary, release, there had been little emotion to it other than a spiteful hatred—not so much for her as for himself, because he was so burdened with guilt for Gatita's disappearance.

At last, Mara drew a deep breath. Steeling herself to counter his inevitable contemptuous rejection, in a low, trembling voice, she averred, ''Can't you understand, *querido,* that I feel the same guilt that you do? Don't you know that when I came back with Maxine from San Antonio, my first thought was, 'Oh, dear God, if only I'd stayed home, this never would have happened!' Don't you think I've had the same nightmares you've had—often, so often, lying alone at night, when you've not come back till dawn, riding through the night to ease your conscience? I've had those nightmares, and they're worse than yours, for it was my responsibility, as her mother, to watch over her and—''

''Mara, in the name of sweet Jesus, stop! I want to hear no more!'' Ramón rose again and struck his thighs as hard as he could with his clenched fists as his face twisted in a ferocious grimace. Tears welled into his eyes, and then he said hoarsely, ''It's no use, Mara. I know I've hurt you, but I can't forget this. I've looked so hard, so long, everywhere I could think of—and there's nothing. And each day it becomes harder, not easier. I still love you and the children, no matter what you may think—but I can't go on like this. I'll go mad. I'll strike out. I've already alienated my loyal *compadres* on the range.'' He paced the floor like a caged puma. ''I've decided to go out searching again in some other part of Mexico. And I swear before *El Señor Dios* that I won't return to you and the children until I've found Gatita. I will leave in the morning.''

Without another word, he turned on his heels and strode out of the house.

Mara Hernandez burst into tears, moved over to the table, and stared at the untouched plate of stew with its crushed-out cigarette. Her tears fell the faster and her shoulders shook with strangled sobs. She moved over to the window, drawing the curtains, and even though it was dark outside, she could see the shadowy figure of her tall, wiry husband walking in endless circles. Tomorrow he would saddle his horse and ride away—and God alone knew when she would see him again.

The children had already eaten, and Luke, Dolores, Edward, and Jaime were busy doing their lessons in their rooms. In the morning, they would go to the school where valiant Catayuna, widow of the heroic Comanche *jefe* Sangrodo, served as teacher with Catholic sisters who had come from Mexico several years earlier and founded a school for the children in the area.

Mara could not bear the thought of another long month or perhaps two when Ramón would be absent from this house, when she alone would be left to answer the children's constant questions. "Where is Gatita? Why was she taken away? Will we ever see her again?" Thus far, she had been the one who had placated them, telling them that soon—very soon—Gatita would be brought home. But even they had come to doubt her words after all this long time.

With a cry, she turned and ran to the door, opened it, and went out into the chilly night. "Ramón, please listen to me! If you must go, at least talk to Lucien Edmond first. You're brothers-in-law; you're partners on this ranch. You've an obligation to him that you surely can't evade, no matter what your feelings are about what's happened to us. I beg of you, do this for me, if you love me, Ramón!"

Wearily, he turned to her, his shoulders slumped in despondency. He stared at her a long moment, and then muttered, "Well, what difference will it make after all? Oh, all right, I'll go see Lucien Edmond." He began to turn toward the hacienda, then paused. "No, I'll tell you—I need to try to shake this helpless feeling I've had so long. I'm going to take a ride. I'll talk to Lucien Edmond tomorrow if you insist—but it won't do any good. I'll leave after breakfast, and I won't come back, just as I swore I wouldn't, till I bring Gatita back to us. You can go talk to Lucien Edmond if you've a mind to, but I haven't the stomach for it now. Right now all I want to do is ride Magdalena.''

She nodded, for this she could understand, just as she understood why Ramón had called this newest mare out of the remuda by the name Magdalena. It was the name of the woman who had tended his wounds—after the bandit, Diego Macaras, had shot him in the back and left him for dead—and brought him back to health, enabling Ramón to come to Windhaven Range to warn the Bouchards of Macaras's intended attack upon the ranch. From this had grown their first stormy meetings, and then their love. Yes, it was only fitting that the young, beloved mare, so docile and gentle, and yet so strong and responsive to his reins, should be named to remind him of that blessed woman. Without her, Mara Hernandez knew, she herself might have remained a thwarted, unhappy spinster, mourning for her home in Alabama and feeling herself abandoned in Texas, where cattle thrived, but where there were few settlers for scores of miles around among whom to find a husband who would know how to fulfill her—just as Ramón had. That had been seventeen long years ago, seventeen years of utter trust, love, and passion, and the sharing of all the plans for the future. She would not, she could not, abandon him now; if she did, her life would be over. But it seemed even more hurtful to her that Ramón realized this and yet would not do anything other than persist in this stubborn, obsessed determination to find their stolen child at any cost—perhaps even that of his own life.

He brought out the black mare a few moments later, mounted her, and rode off toward the south. Mara caught her breath and then put her hand to her mouth to stifle a cry, for she feared that he was actually heading for the border to continue this endless, fruitless search.

Then she straightened, took another deep breath, and told herself that he had given her his word, and thus far, he had never lied to her. No, he would be back—perhaps by dawn, the mare bathed in lather, her withers trembling convulsively from the merciless ride that her master would have given her. But he would be back.

She knew what she must do. She walked directly to the hacienda and knocked at the door. Lucien Edmond opened the door and drew back, startled to see the tears rolling down his sister's cheeks. "My God, Mara dear, what's the matter?" he gasped.

"I—I'm sorry to disturb you and Maxine—you're not still at dinner, I hope—"

"No, no, we've finished. Come in, please, and have a cup of coffee with us."

Maxine rose and hurried to her sister-in-law. Seeing Mara's tears, she put her arms around the handsome, black-haired matron and murmured, "Come sit down. It's Ramón, isn't it?"

"Yes. I need your help because Ramón wants to go off and search for Gatita again." Wearily, Mara disengaged herself, gave Maxine and Lucien Edmond a wan smile, then seated herself at the table. Maxine lifted the coffee pot and filled an empty cup for Mara. "It's still hot, and it's strong. Drink it now; it'll do you a world of good," she urged.

Obediently, her tears still flowing, Mara took a few sips of the coffee, then set the cup down again. She looked at Lucien Edmond and, in a choked voice, said, "I beg of you, Lucien Edmond. You must help me convince Ramón that going on another long trip into Mexico won't do any good at all. All it *will* do, if the truth be known, is make all of us suffer more than we already have."

"I understand. It's been hell for you, Mara." Lucien Edmond shook his head and frowned. "Of course, we'll do what we can, Maxine and I. But you know that Ramón's always been a free spirit."

"Mara dear," Maxine gently interposed, "you and I both understand that a man's reactions may be very different from a woman's. Although, I confess I felt a bit guilty, too. I thought to myself that if I hadn't gone off on that trip to San Antonio with you—if we'd both been here to watch over all the children—that awful woman could never have stolen Gatita."

Lucien Edmond bitterly broke in, "And wasn't I the one who offered to take her to Windhaven Range to begin with— when she said she didn't like Leadville because it was so cold? That lying—forgive me, I was about to use a word I'd rather not term any woman, but, by the Eternal, that woman deserves it!"

"All the same," Maxine pointed out, "what I'm saying is that Ramón blames the mine and his being away from here

for what happened
I can understand hi

"But you will try,
our children and me?"

Maxine and Lucien
compassion, and then both
we'll talk to him. Where is

"He rode off on his new
terrible feeling when he rode
Mexico, but he promised me th
tomorrow, and he's never lied to
he ever will."

"That's because he loves you, no ___ ___ ___ ay do,
or how he may act, or what he ma___ ___ ___ a have to
remember that," Maxine urged. "Now ___ ___ don't you go
home and try to get some sleep. I'm sure he'll be back. You
must keep up your strength, my dear—for all of our sakes."

"Th-thank you, Maxine. God bless you both."

Chapter Six

Ramón Hernandez slid down from the saddle and bowed his head against the mare's heaving side, his hands gripping the pommel. It was nearly dawn, and he had ridden Magdalena pitilessly through the long, black night. Her flanks and her muzzle were wet with foam, and she turned her head to look at her exhausted master, uttering a plaintive whinny.

He did not move for a long time. Slumping against the mare, his lean, strong fingers whitening at the knuckles, Ramón clung to the pommel, as if he were afraid that to release it would mean his total collapse. There had been only a quarter moon, and its ghostly light had illuminated the landscape he knew as well as he knew his own thoughts. He had passed a small ravine into which his beloved first mare, Corita, had nearly stumbled many years ago, when a rattlesnake concealed in a clump of mesquite had sounded its ominous warning. And farther to the southeast was a gnarled live oak tree twisted grotesquely by the force of a lightning bolt, where he had once stopped to take a swig from his canteen and to share the rest of it with valiant little Corita. All these things had passed through his mind during his endless night of self-recrimination, and with those remembered scenes had come the memories of love and tenderness, of valor and the companionship of the vaqueros on each of their forays to sell Lucien Edmond Bouchard's cattle, so that Windhaven Range might prosper.

In his circling return to the ranch, he came upon that very place to which Mara Bouchard had ridden on her mare, Tamisin, despite his warning that there were hostile Comanches in the area. She had lashed him then with her quirt—telling him that he, a "greaser," was to mind his own business—and had arrogantly and heedlessly ridden off. But he had followed nonetheless, concerned for her safety, and had come upon her as the captive of three Comanche braves, whom he had killed. It was then their love had been cemented, and he had become Lucien Edmond Bouchard's brother-in-law and partner.

He paused there a long moment, reflectively touching his hand to his cheek where the quirt had marked him so many years ago, and smiled grimly. And he thought that he would take a thousand blows of the whip, even from that traitorous bitch, Rita Galloway, if only Gatita would be returned to his beloved Mara.

Riding back, he was heedless of Magdalena's snuffling and shuddering, knowing full well how he had overtaxed the courageous little horse. But he was not yet purged, even though dawn had begun to break on the eastern sky. There was no reprieve from the nagging, burning torture of his loss. He would keep his word to Mara, he would talk to Lucien Edmond today, and then he would go back to Mexico, and not return until he had found their little girl.

Wearily, slowly raising his head, he took the reins and led Magdalena round and round the corral, cooling her off before putting her back into the stable. There, he drew only a quarter of a bucket filled with water for her, for she should not drink too much. As he brought oats and some hay and stroked her muzzle, he murmured. "Forgive me, *querida*. I punished you who have done nothing but bring me trust and obedience and service. Forgive me if you can."

He flung himself down on the floor of the stable, and the sleep of exhaustion claimed him.

It was well past noon when he wakened and staggered to his feet, blinking his eyes, the pit of his stomach as hollow as if he had not eaten for weeks. He put his palm to his cheeks and grimaced at the feel of the prickly day's growth of stubble. It was time to have it out with Lucien Edmond and to tell him why he would no longer be a burden to Windhaven Range, not so long as all his mind and energy were fixed on this insoluble dilemma.

Dusting off the bits of straw that clung to his clothing, he walked slowly toward the front door of the hacienda. He knocked at it, and then, so distraught and exhausted that he did not wait for the amenities of being admitted, he turned the knob and entered.

Hearing the knock, Lucien Edmond and Maxine had quickly risen from the dining room table, where they were having lunch. Coming out to the hallway, they stopped short as Ramón approached. "My God, *amigo*, what's happened to you? You look terrible," Lucien Edmond exclaimed.

"I suppose I do, *mi compadre*. I've been riding all night long, thinking things over. I'm sorry if I've disturbed you—I suppose you're just finishing lunch—"

"We are. The children have had theirs and are off to school again." Lucien Edmond chuckled. "When one gets along in years and has growing children, sometimes it's a relief to have quiet moments—" He suddenly realized that he was touching on a subject that must be excrutiatingly painful to his brother-in-law, and stopped, abashed. Then, quickly, he extemporized, "I didn't mean that the way it sounds—"

"There's no need to keep up pretenses, Lucien Edmond. Do you mind if I sit down? I'm wearier than I was that time when I first met you—*Dios*, it seems an eternity ago."

"Please, join us. Let me pour you some coffee. Have you eaten anything?"

Ramón shook his head. "After I brought Magdalena back to the stable, I fell asleep on the floor there. I just woke now."

"You'll kill yourself if you go on like this, man," Lucien Edmond angrily remonstrated, as he took Ramón by the arm and led him into the dining room.

Maxine was startled by the comparison between the two men. Though forty-four, Luke's tall blond son was sturdy and fit, showing hardly any signs of aging. Ramón, on the other hand, was a few years younger, yet he looked like a worn-out old man as Lucien Edmond literally helped him into a chair. Maxine shook her head, her luxuriant chestnut hair flowing in soft waves about her serene face, and sighed.

The Mexican leaned back, closing his eyes, uttering a soft groan. Not only the night's exertion but also the long months of mental stress had wearied him more than he realized.

"Ramón, you can't go on like this. You have to take better care of yourself," Maxine expostulated, rising from the table. "We were having some stewed chicken for lunch and there's more than enough for you."

"Please don't go to any trouble for me—"

"For heaven's sake, stop acting like a guest! You're family, Ramón. Just sit there and relax, and I'll bring you some lunch," Maxine said almost fiercely.

A few minutes later, returning from the kitchen with a plate piled with chicken and a huge sweet yam, she set it down before the exhausted man. "Eat it while it's still hot—please, Ramón," Maxine urged. She reached out to touch Lucien Edmond's hand, and the two of them exchanged a warmly sympathetic look.

Ramón sighed again, opened his eyes, and then seized his fork. "*Gracias,* Maxine. It's good of you. And please excuse the way I look."

"Don't concern yourself about such things, Ramón. Eat first, and we can talk later," Maxine urged.

She and her husband watched Ramón attack his food, as if he hadn't eaten for weeks. To be sure, throughout the long quest for his missing daughter, he had paid short shrift to the necessity of eating meals three times a day, much to Mara's mingled exasperation and growing concern. He was leaner, his face almost gaunt now, and he looked like a derelict with the black stubble of his unshaved beard.

At last, he finished and then exhaled a great sigh. "*Por Dios,* I didn't know I was so hungry. *Gracias* again, Maxine. And now, I don't want to take any more of your time; I want to get right to the point. I've really been worthless to you, Lucien Edmond, since my daughter was taken. I am not making excuses—that's not the way I act or think, you understand. But I'll never be of any use to anybody, especially to myself, until I find Gatita."

Lucien Edmond decided to take the bull by the horns and answered in a stern voice, "Look, Ramón, if you'll just stop to think, and not go off on a tangent the way you've been doing all this time, you'll see that the ranch needs you as much as your wife and children do."

"No, that's not true. I'm a useless burden to you here. I don't do my share. And I know—" here, Ramón uttered a hollow laugh "—that even the vaqueros who used to like me have said among themselves that they'd rather not go with Señor Hernandez the next time there's a drive. Oh, no, Lucien Edmond, don't try to tell me otherwise—I know it to be true."

63

"Well, what the devil do you expect, if you keep estranging people by brooding and keeping to yourself? Don't you think your *compadres* are worried about you and don't want to lose your friendship? You don't talk to them—you sit by yourself at the campfires at night, and they think they've offended you, in some way. And then, when they do try to console you a little—"

"*Por los cojones del diablo*," Ramón burst out, his eyes flashing with anger, "I don't want pity! It's the last thing in the world I want. All I want is my Gatita. I tell you now, just as I told Mara last night, I'm going to leave again and go back to Mexico and exhaust every single village there is in the area I think they may have gone to—that detestable *puta* and my child! My poor helpless child, a little girl who's always been surrounded by love and affection and doesn't know hardship. God alone knows what that woman's done to her—perhaps she's not fed her properly, perhaps she's come down with some terrible sickness, perhaps she was left to suffer by herself—"

"You're torturing yourself, Ramón," Lucien Edmond intervened. "It doesn't do any good, *hombre*. I tell you, work is a distraction. Look, wouldn't it be better if we hired a private detective to look for her—that would make a lot more sense than your going off in every which way in Mexico, where you'll probably never find them in any case."

"Maybe what you say would make sense; just the same, I want to look for her myself."

"I think you're foolish and wrong! And as your partner you owe me a certain obligation, Ramón." Lucien Edmond half rose from the table, his face flushed with anger.

"That was unworthy of you, Lucien Edmond," Ramón shouted back. "Until this horrible thing happened, I worked hard and I asked for very little. But don't you understand that a man must right a wrong? I nearly lost my life because I misjudged Diego Macaras. Well, I misjudged that Rita Galloway—may her soul burn in the lowest fires of hell itself!—and because I hired her, I must be the one who remedies the hurt that woman has caused Mara and me."

"You're so blind with hate and desire for vengeance that you're almost as bad as she is," Lucien Edmond brutally replied.

"Take care, *hombre*! You go too far. I respect you and you

are my brother-in-law, and I do not wish to argue with you in front of your lovely wife—but I tell you that you do not say things like that to me!'' Ramón stood up now, his eyes narrowed, and he trembled convulsively as the aftereffect of the exhausting ride he had taken on Magdalena began to take hold.

"It's time somebody spoke out straight to you, Ramón," was Lucien Edmond's irascible answer. "Your obsession is going to cause you nothing but grief. You'll go to Mexico, you'll abandon everything here—especially your wife and children—and then what will happen? You won't find either that woman or Gatita, and you'll come back worse than ever. I tell you, man, you're going to destroy yourself, if you keep up this stubborn course!"

Before Ramón could answer, Maxine clenched her fist and brought it down with a crash on the table. "Stop it, you two!" she cried out in a shrill voice, and there were tears in her eyes. "Lucien Edmond, you've really no cause to tell your good friend what he should do. This is the time to be kind and gentle, to be compassionate, not angry with him. You're both behaving like schoolboys! Look, Lucien Edmond, if you were in Ramón's shoes, you'd behave exactly the same way."

"Come now, Maxine, it's different—" Lucien Edmond turned back to argue.

But Maxine was determined to be heard. "Wait a minute and let me finish!" she hissed. "You and I know that all of our children are safe and sound. Edwina, Diane, Gloria, and Ruth are happy and healthy here with us in this lovely ranch house. And from their letters, we know that Hugo and Carla are maturing every day, entering new phases of their exciting lives. We have everything—and Ramón feels that he has nothing. How can you possibly berate him for merely wanting the same for Gatita?"

Lucien Edmond Bouchard bowed his head and slowly nodded. "You're right, Maxine. You always are." He turned to her and held out his hand in an conciliatory gesture. She took it and smiled at him, and the tears began to run down her cheeks. Then he looked at Ramón and said softly, "Forgive me. I didn't mean to rant and rave at you like that. Of course I am distressed, but I understand how you feel. Yes, what Maxine says is true—we'd feel the same way if someone had

65

taken any of our children from us. Go, then, to Mexico on your quest. But please take some of the best vaqueros with you. You shouldn't do this alone.''

"No, *mi amigo*. The ranch must continue to run, and I won't further burden Windhaven Range by leaving it short-handed.''

"But the men will be back from the Leadville mine within a few months, and then we'll have all the help we need. Besides, it's only February now, so there won't be any cattle drives until spring. Even then, they'll be only short distances because the railroad has almost completed its spur down here a few miles from Carrizo Springs. So you needn't worry about taking some of our men, Ramón.''

"That may be true, but until those men come back, you'll need all the manpower we have. And remember this, Lucien Edmond, it's my place and mine alone to find Gatita.''

"Well, I can't stop you, and I won't. All I can do is pray that you'll find her quickly, so that you can resume your life here, the way it was, when we were all close together.'' Lucien Edmond put his arm around Ramón's shoulders. "I know we will be again.''

"If God so wills, Lucien Edmond.'' Reverently, Ramón crossed himself. "Well, I'm glad we had this talk and know that we're still friends—''

"You mustn't ever think otherwise, Ramón,'' Maxine said. Coming to him, she took his hands in hers and kissed him on the cheek. "We'll watch out after Mara and the children, you have our word on it.''

"*Gracias*. I ask your forgiveness for the grief I've caused both of you by the way I've acted all this time. That's another reason I want to leave, so I don't inflict any more upon you. I've done enough harm to Mara and the children. Now all I can do is try to find Gatita. And, if *El Señor Dios* so grants it, I will!''

He turned to shake hands with Lucien Edmond and then, his head bowed, Ramón Hernandez turned and walked out of the hacienda.

Chapter Seven

The year of 1882 was destined to be one of strikes for higher wages throughout the country, after a year of poor crops and the increase in prices. This made the cost of living for the average American worker far higher than it had been in some little time; however, the Scolby-Bouchard miners had a far easier time of it, owing to the very fair wages they received. In the same month that John D. Rockefeller organized the Standard Oil Trust—one of the mightiest conglomerates in American business—the last vein of silver ore in the Leadville silver mine was discovered.

By now, the first week of April, that vein had been tapped out, and the men from Windhaven who had accompanied Lucien Edmond and Ramón to this mining town two years earlier were preparing to begin the journey home.

Walter Catlin and Timmy Belcher had returned to Texas more than a year before, along with Lucien Edmond and another of his partners, Joe Duvray. Both of them had realized that this drab, almost lawless town that had begun as a mining camp could not possibly offer a permanent home for their wives. Walter, married to Timmy's lovely sister, Connie, had been anxious to return to her and their young son, Henry—named for Connie and Timmy's late father. The same reason had brought Timmy Belcher back, and the previous December, his lovely young Mexican wife, Conchita, had given birth to their second child—their first son—Thomas. The move turned out to be even more fortuitous than any of them had expected; already the past year saw many of the famous mines beginning to run out, and the town had gradually become deserted. It was now more desolate than ever, dreary and ramshackle.

After Ramón had hurried back to Windhaven Range upon learning of his daughter's kidnapping, Robert Markey was put in charge of the operation of the mine. To be sure, he was ably guided by the capable mining engineer, John Darwent, whose scientific background and mining experience had enormously contributed to the rich profits taken from the lode since its inception. The Bouchard's Denver bank account, which was co-owned by Ramón Hernandez, Lucien Edmond Bouchard, Joe Duvray, and Frank Scolby, had now, in the first week of April, reached the imposing figure of $758,900. John Darwent had told Robert only the day before that the final yield should amount to something like $65,000—meaning that old Frank Scolby's discovery would earn almost a million dollars.

Manuel Olivera and Santiago Dornado—whose wife had come to Leadville to be cook for the men—had stayed behind to work the mine and to supervise the local personnel, along with Pablo Bensares and Diego Martinez. Although these men were far from home, they were bound in loyalty to the Bouchards. All of them had evidence of how hard work and initiative were rewarded: Lucas Forsden, for example, a long-time worker of black descent, had been made a partner at Windhaven Range, as had the young Texan, Eddie Gentry, who had first come to the ranch as an itinerent driver. The vaqueros had been well rewarded with bonuses, and Lucien Edmond had told the Mexican workers that ten percent of his share of the mine's profits would be divided among them as a bonus for helping work the mine and for voluntarily giving up the chance to return to Texas, where they could have pursued their own personal lives.

To be sure, the unmarried vaqueros who had stayed up in Colorado had had occasional sweethearts among the Leadville women. These were, however, for the most part, companions with whom to pass a few delightful hours—eating, drinking, and making love, with no long-term commitments. Manuel and Diego, being older than twenty-six-year-old Pablo Bensares, frequently teased the youngest vaquero because of his fickleness and inconstancy. *"Amigo,"* Manuel had told him only the prevous week, after finding him in a saloon with a comely black-haired dance-hall girl, "this week it is Mercedes, last week it was Amy, and last month it was Joella. Would it not be better and wiser, as well as more practical, to be faithful to one girl and spend all your money on her, rather than to spread yourself so thin with so many?''

"*Sí, mi compañeros,*" the dreamy-eyed, handsome young Mexican had replied with a smile as he reached over to stroke the rouged cheek of the slim young woman who sat at the table beside him, "but then I would deny myself the joys of variety. Each woman is different. I marvel that you, señores, have not already learned this fact in all your long years.''

"Watch your tongue!" Manuel Olivera had retorted, a sly grin on his face, "I'm only about ten years older, and till now, no *mujer* has ever complained of my ability to please her." Then, with a wink at the smiling dance-hall girl, he took off his sombrero, bowed low, and declared, "If you tire of this stripling, *querida,* just let me know, and I shall show you that a mature man can provide far more entertainment for such a *linda* as you than this almost beardless boy!"

Pablo Bensares had leaped out of his chair, but when Manuel and Diego burst into laughter, he sheepishly grinned and slumped back in his seat and shrugged. "Now I see it—you are trying to steal my Mercedes from me. But it will not work, will it, *mi corazón*?''

The dance-hall girl giggled, then leaned over to whisper in his ear, making Pablo blush. "You must excuse me, señores," he stammered, clearing his throat and rising to his feet as he offered the young woman his arm. "I will pay for your drinks at the bar, but I urge you to forget that I am here for the rest of the evening. Incidentally," he concluded, almost offhandedly, "Mercedes is a *compañera;* she comes from San Luis Potosí. So you see, we have much in common.''

With this, the young vaquero escorted his pretty companion up the stairs and disappeared down a hallway to one of the private rooms provided by the saloon owner.

Diego sighed and shook his head. "San Luis Potosí—well now, perhaps if I'd known that, I might have taken the girl from him. I once had a *novia* there, before I came to work for Señor Hernandez. I wonder how this *mujer linda* came so far north, where there is no warmth at all, even in the summer, and where there is so much snow. Brrr!" he hugged himself and pretended to shiver.

"That's true enough, *amigo,*" Manuel gloomily nodded. "Back on the ranch it would be warm now, and we should not need greatcoats when we go out. Come to think of it, we

69

would not see any snow at all. Oh, well, let us have that drink Pablo is treating us to. By next week, we shall surely start back for home where it is warm. And then, Diego, I for one intend to find a real *novia*, for it is high time I thought of taking a wife and having children by her and settling down. I have saved my wages, which the good Señor Bouchard has made so high because, of course, I am *un gran vaquero*—"

"As am I," Diego interrupted, then he sighed. "I have the same feeling, Manuel. I'll tell you what—I will buy you the second drink, and we shall make a toast to your finding a *novia* and having many fine children."

Arm in arm, they walked off toward the bar. The bartender of this, one of Leadville's largest halls, had learned that the Scolby-Bouchard mine vaqueros preferred tequila; moreover, many other Mexican workers had come to Leadville during the silver boom, and so tequila was almost as popular as whiskey at his establishment. He had even managed to procure limes, a rarity in Leadville, though, of course, he charged extra for each lime that accompanied a glass of tequila. Diego and Manuel watched happily as the bartender expertly went to work cutting the lime and spilling salt from a shaker onto a little saucer. "You see, we could almost pretend we were back in San Luis Potosí," Diego sighed.

"Then you must have a more vivid imagination than I, *amigo*," Manuel snorted. "Just step outside and you will find out at once the difference. Brrr! I, for one, will be very happy to go back home!"

Robert Markey had plunged himself into his work with a dedication born out of his deeply rooted feeling of obligation to Ramón Hernandez, as well as to Lucien Edmond Bouchard. He would never forget how Ramón had saved him from lynching at the hands of the vaqueros almost five years before when he had tried to cut a steer out of the Bouchard herd on its way to the Kansas market. The mare that Ramón had given him before sending him on his way unharmed had been Robert's salvation, for after a terrible blizzard, in which his wife and infant child had perished, the mare had enabled him to reach Windhaven Range and effect a reunion with his benefactor. Lucien Edmond Bouchard had given him a chance to become a wrangler, even though he had at first shown little aptitude for it. By dogged persistence, Robert, who had been a failure as a farmer, had proved himself capable. Then he volunteered to work the Leadville mine, vowing to pay back the debt, and to demonstrate that he was worthy of acceptance as a man of ability and fealty.

When Gabe Penrock—Rhea's husband—had staged a rebellion of miners (ostensibly to strike for higher wages, but in reality to be used as a blind against his true purpose of blowing up the mine), it had been Robert who had saved the day. Although he was troubled by having to kill Penrock, it had gratified Robert enormously to have rescued the mine before Penrock blew it up and perhaps killed Lucien Edmond and Ramón, the two men who stood out so prominently in his new life. Now that he was virtually in charge of the profitable mining operation, even though he was a stranger in a dismal town, Robert Markey attacked his work each new day with the same assiduity with which he had first tried to become a wrangler on Windhaven Range.

Black-bearded and moustached—his tall frame much sturdier now, yet still wiry—Robert had clear blue eyes that showed the peace of soul he had achieved through dedication to his work and to the debt he had purposely imposed upon himself almost as a spiritual discipline. He had become a new man with growing optimism for the future, and although he had not forgotten the circumstance of the deaths of his wife, Marcy, and their infant daughter, Lucille, those memories came back infrequently now. When they did, they did not torture him as they had during the terrible aftermath of the blizzard that had taken their lives, compelling him to ride southward through snow and sleet and freezing air with but a single clue to guide him toward the only man who had really ever befriended him, Ramón Hernandez.

The journey had purged Robert, making him reflect on the elemental need for survival. It was a catharsis, easing the incredible guilt he had borne, and the feeling that his loved ones' deaths meant that he had been a failure as a provider and a husband, as a father and a lover.

He had not thought, all during these long months of work at Leadville, of having a family again. Nor had he sought the transient easing of his physical needs with some pretty dance-hall girl as the vaqueros had. Not that he was a Puritan, or righteously prim, but he had been brought up to believe that physical love was the concomitant of a lasting, steadfast union—of marriage. To have found consolation in the arms of a woman who tendered a facile welcome to any man with the price would, in his code, have been flagrant promiscuity, and he would have despised himself for it.

It was true that he was lonely, and particularly after Ramón had been summoned back to Windhaven Range by that terrible wire announcing the kidnapping of Gatita. Robert liked the vaqueros, and they knew and liked him in return. Old Frank Scolby, who had become quite fond of this personable, twenty-nine-year-old man, made a point of sharing his meals with Robert and regaling the wrangler with colorful anecdotes about his prospecting days, when he was as young as his listener. But still it was not quite enough.

Often, when his work was finished, he would take long solitary walks far beyond the town, taking with him simple provisions. Reaching a plateau, he would build a campfire, cook some beans and bacon and coffee, roll a cigarette, and smoke it while looking reflectively at the skyline and the mountain peaks as dusk fell.

For him, the drabness of the town itself slipped away from his memory when he looked beyond and saw the mountain ranges in the distance. Moreover, with so many mines cutting down or actually ceasing their operations—and without the smoke of their smelters, which had been a constant irritation and, indeed, had created the clouds of smoke that hung like a pall above the mining town—he could now see through the clear air to the distance and marvel at the majesty of the Colorado mountain ranges.

Three days before the departure of all the Windhaven men for Texas, Robert Markey decided to take a last long walk through these mountainous hills that he had come to enjoy, as a farewell to his present life and a symbol of the forthcoming resumption of his life on Windhaven Range. He packed a knapsack with an extra jacket and sufficient food, in the event that he would have to seek shelter in one of caves in the area through which he intended to hike. He had long since learned that springtime in the Rockies could be treacherous, that a clear, warm afternoon could turn, without warning, into a blinding snow squall.

He had the afternoon off, for there was no further work left to do: The last deposit had already been made in the Denver bank, and only three men remained on duty at the mine, just to close it down and board it up. So, shortly after lunch, Robert decided to set off on his energetic hike. Bidding his companions goodbye, he walked out toward the northeast.

Two hours after he had started, clouds began to gather rapidly. At first, a few gentle flakes flitted down, which contrasted strangely with the patches of bright blue sky and the clear air. But fifteen minutes later, the sky was completely blotted out by snow, falling furiously, painting the entire landscape a ghostly white. The firs and spruces, the pines and even the gnarled scrub trees took on a look of wintry decor, and the earth, scarred in so many places by all those hopeful prospectors who had dreamed of becoming rich overnight, was completely hidden. Robert began to walk with extreme care, lest he stumble into a gulley hidden by the drifting snow and sprain an ankle, or worse.

Robert paused a moment to reflect that the squall was all too painfully reminiscent of that dreadful blizzard that had snuffed out the lives of those two whom he had loved most of all in the world. He sighed, shook his head, then plodded on. About a ten minute walk from where he stood, he knew there to be a broad, deep cave. He had discovered it and had spent a night there last September, when he had gone on another one of these solitary excursions. It would be a good place to stay until the sudden blizzard ceased.

As he moved unerringly in the direction of that refuge, he suddenly heard a muffled cry for help. He could hardly see now and directed himself more by instinct. But he quickened his footsteps toward the sound and suddenly uttered a gasp as he practically stumbled into a young woman who was trying to make her way along the path.

"Oh, my goodness," he exclaimed. "Here—take hold of my hand—there's a cave not far from here. We can stay there until this subsides."

The young woman was about twenty-two. Her dark-blue eyes were huge in her heart-shaped face, and her teeth were chattering from terror as much as from the cold, but she managed to tell Robert, "I—I've lost my way. Oh, thank God you found me—I hate to think what would have happened to me if you hadn't—"

"No time for talk, miss. Here!" Robert took off his knapsack, quickly opened it, and drew out the extra jacket. "Put this on. That's it. Okay then, grab my hand and walk

73

steadily. It's clear ground, from here to the cave. You'll be fine once we get there."

"Gracious, h-how awfully stupid of me, g-getting lost in a snowstorm like this. I'm so grateful to you, Mr.—Mr.—" she gasped. She bowed her head, as the wind swirled the snow viciously against them.

"My name's Robert Markey, but save your breath, miss. It's lucky I came this way. Here's the cave, just ahead. Duck your head—that's it." He led her inside the cave, then gently eased her down and seated himself beside her, putting the knapsack between them. "Now then, we're safe and sound."

She put a hand to her hair to brush the snow away, and her teeth kept up their relentless chattering. "I—I'm Eleanor B-Beale, Mr. Markey. My husband's a miner here, but I only a-arrived in Leadville about f-five months ago."

He nodded and smiled encouragingly. Seeing how frightened she was, he knew that talking about herself would ease her anxiety.

"My husband and I . . . well, I suspect you've heard about 'mail order brides.' We corresponded with each other for almost a year. Anyway, Michael keeps reminding me that the weather here in Colorado is unpredictable. But this morning, after I prepared his breakfast and then sent him off to work, I looked out and saw it was such a beautiful sunny day—I didn't think anything like this could possibly happen. But I certainly was wrong, wasn't I?" she confessed with a rueful grin.

"That's understandable; if you've never been out to Colorado before, you couldn't be expected to know what the weather is like."

"It's very kind of you to reassure me like that. Just the same, I certainly learned a lesson—and I'm very indebted to you, Mr. Markey."

"I'm only happy that I was there when you needed someone to guide you, Mrs. Beale. Look—" He rustled around in his knapsack. "I've got some food here, and I think a bit might do you good. I'll just build a small fire with some of those twigs over there, then we can have some beans and bacon and coffee."

"That sounds like a feast!" She leaned back against the wall of the cave and smiled at him. The color was coming back to her face, and her teeth had stopped chattering. "It's awfully nice of you to take such good care of me."

"My pleasure," he said gruffly, for the warm, grateful expression on her face reminded him very painfully of Marcy. His wife had looked at him almost that same way when they had sat in the kitchen of their Kansas farm almost five years earlier in the autumn of 1877, just after little Lucille had been born.

He turned away from Eleanor and gathered up a bunch of twigs that were scattered just inside the mouth of the cave. Reaching inside the knapsack, he withdrew his tinderbox and expertly started a fire. In short order, he had the food cooked. There was only a single tin plate, but he piled it high with beans and strips of bacon, then handed it to his unexpected guest, along with the tin fork he always carried. Then he washed out the small pot with snow, scouring it carefully until it was clean. Adding fresh snow, he set the pot back on the fire to boil the snowmelt for coffee. He sat again next to Eleanor and said, "Here you go, Mrs. Beale."

"That's most kind. Umm, it tastes so good! You cook very well, for a man," she complimented him, as she began to eat.

"Well, when you work on a Texas ranch, you frequently have to make your own meals—unless of course you're on a cattle drive, when we have a chuck wagon cook."

"Oh, yes, I suppose you would have to fend for yourself, in that case." She suddenly looked up from her plate of food and said, "But you aren't eating at all."

"I will, as soon as you've finished. I just brought one plate along," he told her with a grin. "Don't worry about it—and take your time. I'm not all that hungry anyway." He rose and declared, "I think I'll take a look outside and see what is happening. Say now, the snow seems to be letting up. Maybe by the time we've finished lunch, we can go back to Leadville."

"That would be wonderful! It would be just awful if Michael got home from work and didn't know where I was— fortunately, he doesn't get home until very late, not till seven or eight o'clock at night." She stopped and sighed. "I—well, I was a schoolteacher back in Missouri, and I don't know anything at all about mines, mining, or miners, for that matter. I'm trying very hard to learn because I've come to love my husband, and I want him to feel that we've something in common besides the loneliness that brought us together.

75

I—I think I told you that we got together by writing letters to each other. Michael had been here about three years when he wrote to a newspaper that forwarded letters on to female correspondents.'' Eleanor looked down at her plate and paused a moment. "I really have to say that it's a strange place to live in—it seems to be so lonely."

"That's partly because most of the big mines are played out, and the rush of prospectors who came here hoping to get rich quickly is over, Mrs. Beale. A lot of them have given up and have gone elsewhere looking for work—like Nevada or California."

"I suppose that's true. Well, luckily Michael still has a good job, and he's happy with it. As I said, I do love him, and I want to be a good wife to him. I guess what I'm saying is that I don't want him to think that I'm more of a fool than I am—he certainly would think that, if he knew what a stupid thing I did today by strolling out here so unprepared!''

She laughed softly, as if at herself, and Robert felt a warm surge of sympathy. He could understand her loneliness, and he could understand how it was to try to start a new life in a strange place—he and Marcy had done that when they had gone out to Kansas, where they had known no one at all. They'd had only each other until the baby came. Then, when he lost them both, he had had to start all over again. Yes, he could feel exactly what she was feeling—and she wasn't stupid at all. He only hoped that her husband was a decent man and appreciated her, because she was attractive and intelligent and womanly and gentle. While she ate, he told her a bit about his own life and how he had come to be in Leadville.

She finished eating at last and handed the partially full plate back to him. He nodded and gave her a warm smile, then quickly ate the remaining beans and bacon, washing down the meal with half a cup of coffee. He carefully extinguished the fire and put the cooking things back in his knapsack. Then he crawled outside, straightened, and exclaimed, "Look! The sun's out again! Your husband was certainly right when he said it was unpredictable out here. I think it's safe to take you home now, Mrs. Beale."

"I—I can find my way—" she began to protest.

"It's no trouble, I assure you. It's just a short walk back to the mine, where there's a buckboard, and from there I'll drive you to your place in town."

"I've certainly put you to a lot of trouble, Mr. Markey."

"No, you haven't. Not at all. Come along now."

As they walked slowly through the fast-melting snow, Eleanor and Robert continued to talk. She said to him now, "You said you left Indiana to go to Kansas and be a farmer. Then you were a wrangler, and now you're a miner. Do you plan to stay here in Leadville, then?"

"Well, Mrs. Beale," the handsome, bearded young widower explained, "the fact is the mine's played out, and we're all going back in a few days." He grinned, and declared, "Although I think the scenery out here is wonderful—once you get away from the town—it'll be a pleasure to get back to the green grasses and the rich land of Texas near the border, where my bosses' ranch is."

"I—I see. You're a very interesting man, Mr. Markey. You're also very gentle and kind—at least, so far as I can judge from my own experience." Eleanor Beale gave him another warm look.

"I have a lot of respect for people, Mrs. Beale—I guess I was brought up that way by my parents. I know how my father and my mother loved each other and worked hard all their lives, even though they didn't have much to show for it in the end. Here we are. Let me help you up." He lifted her into the buckboard, then went to the stable and led out a spirited brown gelding. After harnessing the horse to the rig, he got into the driver's seat and took hold of the reins. "Now I just need to know where to drive you," he said, flashing her another grin.

She told him, then leaned back and stared straight ahead, her face almost wistful. He had touched a sympathetic chord within her, for he was certainly different from anyone she had thus far met since leaving the small Missouri town where she was born. As for Robert Markey, he was silent during most of the journey back to the town, for he was thinking of the past again. But this time there was a kind of warm glow inside of him, and he knew that his chance meeting with the lonely, yet courageously eager, young woman had been the reason.

"Well now, we made pretty good time, Mrs. Beale," he

chuckled as he alighted from the buckboard and helped her down. "Would you like me to stay until your husband returns, so I can tell him that you're quite all right?"

"Oh, no! I mean—you mustn't misunderstand what I said before. What I mean is, Mr. Markey, I said that I didn't want Michael to think I was stupid, and I'm afraid he'll think just that if he learns what happened to me. Really, I'm fine now, thank you."

"I'll see you to the door, at any rate," he told her. When they reached the door, he was about to open it for her when she turned to him and kissed him softly on the cheek. "You saved my life, Mr. Markey, and I'll never forget you. And if—" here, she paused and blushed furiously, "—and if I ever have a son, I'll name him after you. I'll name him Robert." Then she giggled and added, "If Michael asks who Robert is, I'll tell him that Robert was a dashing young man who once saved my life, and that's all he'll ever need to know."

"Thank you, Mrs. Beale. It's been a wonderful afternoon for me—you'll never know quite how much—and I'm the one who's really grateful. Goodbye now. Lots of good luck, and I hope that you and Michael will have many happy years together and all the children you both want."

"That's very sweet. Thank you again—and bless you." She looked at him for a long moment, then blushed again and hurriedly went inside, closing the door behind her.

As Robert walked slowly back to the buckboard, he whispered aloud to himself, "And bless you, too, Eleanor Beale. You've freed me from an old debt. My Marcy died in a blizzard, and now I've saved your life in just such a storm. Yes, God *does* work in mysterious ways. I believe it now, more than I ever did."

Chapter Eight

All was packed and in readiness for the departure of the men who had come to dreary, cold Leadville to glean a silver treasure that would be invested in the future of the Bouchards—their families and partners and workers. Here, in the frigid northwestern region of the young United States, Lucien Edmond and his brother-in-law, Ramón, had continued the legacy that old Lucien Bouchard, who had founded the dynasty nearly a century before, had bequeathed to his descendants. They had carried out their ancestor's ideals of hard and honorable labor, repeating the simple, yet timeless pattern of a life of work and fulfillment, of loyalty and love.

Like Lucien Edmond and Ramón, the workers who had accompanied them from Windhaven Range had greeted each new day—filled with adversities and joys—with a steadfast equanimity born of their own courageous endeavors. Perhaps that was why, on the frosty yet sunny April day that was set for the departure from Leadville, these people, too—who in no way belonged to the Bouchard family—had brought the Bouchard credo to their work in this far-flung enterprise. For each of them, each with his own beliefs and hopes and dreams and sorrows, each with his own driving force and touch of fearful insecurity, had found a pathway to a far more hopeful life by having come originally to Windhaven Range in search of work—work that was the salvation for the soul as assuredly as it was the means of earning a livelihood. Each of them had been touched by that special aura with which old Lucien Bouchard had been imbued, who—valiantly alone, yet hopeful—had carried it from the Old World into the new frontier with its ever-expanding horizon. . . .

These five men and one woman, along with John Darwent

79

and old Frank Scolby, sat at the kitchen table for their last breakfast in the house they had built near the mine. Maria Dornado had prepared a farewell feast consisting of flapjacks, bacon omelets, baked apples rich with carmelized brown sugar, and biscuits with honey. They sat around the table joking and laughing in easy camaraderie, eager to return to the warmer clime of Texas and its rich, fertile soil.

The night before, Robert Markey had called at Phyllis Boyd's boardinghouse to see Sister Martha and the three nuns who had come up from Texas with the men to help the poor and the needy of the mining town. The stately mother superior warmly welcomed him and invited him into the kitchen, where she and her three assistants were sitting with their genial landlady. They were having coffee and cookies, which Mrs. Boyd had just baked, and Robert was asked to join them.

"Thank you, Sister," Robert replied, respectfully doffing his Stetson. "I wanted to remind you that in the morning we're going to leave Leadville for Texas, and I came to ask one last time if you want to join us. We can always delay our departure a day or so, to give you time to pack up."

The elderly, yet still vigorous nun shook her head with a gentle smile. "No, my son. We've talked it over among ourselves, and we are unanimous in wishing to stay here. We've done much good work, but there's much more to be done. You can see yourself, Mr. Markey, that the town is dying, and most of the miners who work here aren't sure how much longer they'll be able to find employment. Their wives and children have come to rely on us for what help we can bring them, both spiritual and material. Besides, we wouldn't want to leave Mrs. Boyd, who has been a bulwark of strength and compassion and love for the impoverished people of Leadville, to have to carry on our work alone."

Robert seated himself and turned to Mrs. Boyd, smiling at her. Then, earnestly addressing Sister Martha, he went on, "I just hate to think of you sisters being left alone here in this dreary place. There's no future to this town."

"Every place on earth has a future, since it was God who was instrumental in its creation," Sister Martha gently rebuked him. "And indeed, our test of faith comes when things seem the darkest and the most miserable—for then we are bound by our faith and our love for our brethren to do all we can to lighten their burdens and brighten their horizons. We've received many contributions from important men so that our two settlement houses, our school, and our commissary can continue. Those who have been out of work or whose savings have been exhausted or who have been ill or unable to work depend on the food we offer. You do understand, don't you, Mr. Markey?"

Ruefully, he nodded his head. "I suppose I do, Sister Martha. But the men and I—well, we'll sure miss you back in Texas. I do hope you'll keep in touch with us. I promise you that the minute you want to come back, we'll come and get you and bring you safely back to the other nuns."

"You're very kind, Mr. Markey." Sister Martha suddenly grinned at him and declared, "I hope you can also promise that the trip back won't be nearly as eventful as the original train ride!"

Robert laughed in appreciation of her wit, remembering the harrowing gun battle that had taken place when the Denver & Rio Grande train they were riding had been attacked by Jeb Cornish's bandits.

Sister Martha composed herself once again and stared at the black-bearded young man. "You know, my son," she at last said, "I have seen many changes in you, and now I see peace. I think that you have found yourself closer to God, and this has eased your own burden."

He looked down at his plate self-consciously, then nodded. "It's true, Sister Martha. I *have* found peace."

"You are a good man, Mr. Markey. You know very well what wickedness, slothfulness, and greed abound in a place like this, but you did not let the temptations besmirch your soul. You maintained your own ethics, and"—she smiled wryly—"even if you are not of my faith, you are a man on whom the Creator smiles. I know that you have been burdened with guilt, but I hope by now you realize that it was not you who caused the deaths of your wife and daughter. God decides why this or that shall happen. One day you will learn the reason, when you stand before Him for judgment as all of us must. Mr. Markey, go back to Texas and look toward the future with those clear eyes and that constancy of purpose and that inborn kindness and respect that I have found in you. These qualities will serve you well in finding

81

happiness and the joys of a family once again. I'm sure of it.''

He had listened to her spellbound, tears running unbidden and unchecked down his cheeks. He took out a bandanna and mopped his eyes, and then he said in a hoarse, unsteady voice, "God bless you, Sister Martha. I will pray that all of you will be safe, and that your work will continue. But I pledge to you that if ever you need me here, I will come back swiftly to be of aid."

"I could ask no more of any man, and it is good of you to say this to us. It will comfort us, for we shall miss all of you, you and your strong vaqueros."

"Thank you."

"And so, the mine is closed now?"

"Yes, Sister Martha. We have taken from the earth all that it will give. But the money will be shared, for I know that Mr. Bouchard will give a good deal to charity. And the lives of the people who work on the ranch back in Texas where your other sisters are will be eased by part of it.''

"This is a great kindness." She paused, a gentle smile on her craggy face. "Well then, this is farewell for a time, is it not, Mr. Markey?" Rising from the table, she came to him and made the sign of the cross. "As your Señor Hernandez would say, *vaya con Dios,* my son."

"So the sisters are definitely set against returning to Texas, Roberto?" Manuel Olivera asked, as he helped himself to more flapjacks.

"Yes, Manuel. They're quite firm about wanting to stay on here and help the miners and their families for as long as they're needed. But I told them that all they have to do is send a wire to the ranch, and we'll be back for them when they've a mind to come back," Robert Markey declared.

"I shall pray that no harm will come to them here." Manuel made the sign of the cross. Then, to lighten this sober mood, he turned to the grizzled old prospector. "What about you, Señor Scolby—will you be sorry to leave here and go back with us?"

"Boys, I don't know how to break this to you, but I've been doin' a heap o' thinkin'," Frank Scolby said, as he set down his coffee cup. "My, that's what I call great vittles. I tell you, if when I'd started out prospectin' I'd had vittles like

82

this, I'd probably be a damn sight heavier on the hoof—just like one of those fattened steers you fellas drove to Kansas. Hee hee, I surely would, I reckon!'' The others joined in laughing for a few moments, then they looked at the grizzled old prospector, waiting for Frank's reply. He looked around at his companions, then said, "You see, boys, I guess prospectin's jist in my blood. I've been doin' it so long— why, hell, fact is, I wouldn't rightly know what to do with any other way of life.''

He cackled gleefully, a twinkle in his watery blue eyes, then added, "I got to confess, though, it's gonna be quite a treat havin' a brace o' mules to haul my gear and to know that I kin buy anythin' I need to do my own grubstakin'. Yessirree, quite a treat!''

"Oh, no, Señor Scolby! Don't say you're going to leave us now,'' Santiago Dornado moaned with a woebegone look on his face. "Why, when the work was the hardest, it was you who made us laugh by telling us some of those tall stories of yours. Señor Scolby, you *must* come back with us. Who will we talk to on the train and on the stage all that long ride back to the ranch?''

"Well, boys, I reckon you'll have plenty of things to swap yarns about, after all that's happened here. Gosh sakes alive, it sure was excitin', now that we kin look back. That train robbery, when we first got here; that miners' strike, and that fella who had it in his mind to blow up the mine and kill Mr. Bouchard and Mr. Hernandez. Land sakes, I never had that much excitement on any of my other prospectin' trips, I kin tell you that fer certain!'' Then he cackled again, his eyes sparkling. "All the same, this sure was fun. And now that I'm rich, I kin look on all the excitement with a lot more 'preciation than if I was still poor as a churchmouse, like I always have been.''

"You won't change your mind, Señor Scolby?'' Diego Martinez hopefully asked, as he passed the plate of biscuits to the old prospector.

"Land sakes, you fellas are tryin' to fatten me up so's I'll fall asleep and then mebbe you'll hogtie me and take me back. Don't do that to an old man, boys.'' He slapped his knee in appreciation of his own wit, then continued, "No, serious-like, I really mean it. I've always been a loner, though that's not to say that I haven't had a helluva good time

83

with all you fellas. You're the nicest bunch I ever met, and that ain't no lie. I ain't jist sayin' it 'cause I'm figgerin' on splittin' up with you. It's the truth. But it's hard for an old feller like me to shake his ways. No, I've thought it over and I've finally decided: I'm gonna head out all by myself and see what my luck will be. But I'll be damned—the fact is it won't matter whether I'm lucky or not, 'cause I've already been luckier'n I ever dreamed I would be when I started this whole game.''

"Where do you think you'll head, Mr. Scolby?'' Robert Markey poured himself some more coffee and helped himself to another biscuit.

"Don't rightly know, exactly,'' the prospector said as he shook his head. "Been thinkin' o' headin' down to Nevady. Ain't much in the way o' mountains compared to here in Colorado, but it's sure a damn sight warmer in winter! Hell, boy, don't look so glum!'' he suddenly exclaimed, as he saw the sadness in Robert's eyes, for the young man had come to love the eccentric old miner. "Now don't you think you've seen the last o' me. Sure as I'm born, I promise you one o' these days, I'll jist pop me down to Texas, and then will I ever bend your ear, tellin' you all about what I've been up to. And listen here, boy, when I *do* come, I expect to find you got yourself a beautiful wife to do the cookin' for me and pamper the hell out o' these old bones o' mine!''

Robert gave the old prospector an affectionate hug. "I'll do my best to make that prediction of yours come true. Tell you the truth, I'll admit I wouldn't mind a bit of pampering myself. Not one bit would I mind it.''

And so, Frank Scolby clambered into the buckboard the vaqueros had harnessed and rode with them into Leadville, leaving Stray Horse Gulch for the last time. The mine was boarded up, completely empty of activity and life. It had served its purpose. When they reached the recently completed train station, where they would begin the first stage of their journey back home, the prospector warmly shook hands with all of them, saying one final time how much he had enjoyed being with them.

John Darwent, the young mining engineer, planned to go back East for a time and enjoy a well-earned vacation. His part of the profits, as he jovially explained, "will give me time to do some hard thinking about whether I want to go on with mining here, or maybe even try my hand along the Eastern Seaboard. Then there's a certain girl I'm thinking of courting, who lives in Harrisburg, Pennsylvania. She was a student in a women's college when I was going to school, and we started corresponding again lately, and I think it's going to be serious. I surely hope it will be."

"We all wish you good luck, John." Robert held out his hand, which the affable mining engineer enthusiastically shook. "And you, Mr. Scolby," he turned again to the old man with almost a wistful look on his face, "I suppose you're going to take your brace of mules and start out for Nevada?"

"That's right, son. Tomorrow morning bright and early, I'll come down here to the stable, pack up my mules, all my gear, and I'll be off hell for leather. Why, who knows—I might even find gold in them Nevady hills! And if I do, I'll save up out of it for a special wedding present for you, when you pick the right girl."

"I'll hold you to that!" Robert said with a broad grin on his face. "God bless you, Mr. Scolby. May you have many long years—but don't let too many of them pass before you come back and see me down in Texas."

"I may see you sooner than you think, Bob, boy."

Chapter Nine

On the same day that the men of Windhaven Range prepared to leave for the sunnier clime of Carrizo Springs, the sun was bright over the high plains of southeast Wyoming. A few miles outside the small town of Rawlins, in the kitchen of a small, sturdily built house made of hewn timber and solid red bricks, Hugo Bouchard sat breakfasting with his wife, Cecily.

She had been Cecily Franklin until the previous October. Hugo had proposed to her the day both of them had received their diplomas from Rush Medical College in Chicago. They had met there, after Hugo had decided that cattle ranching was not for him and had gone off to study medicine.

Throughout the last year of their studies, Hugo and Cecily had been almost inseparable, and throughout most of their courtship, the main topic of discussion had been their medical future. Cecily, a strong-willed young woman, had already determined to go to Rawlins, where her widowed aunt—her only living relative—was working hard to maintain her sheep ranch. Cecily's uncle had been killed in a range war with cattlemen, and she was fiercely devoted to her Aunt Margaret.

She had been the only female student at Rush, and her determination to become a physician against what had then seemed insurmountable odds had been motivated by her love for her late father, who had been a general practitioner in New Hampshire. It was her belief that once she received her medical degree, she could serve the desolate area west of Cheyenne, and Cecily had declared to Hugo that she felt she could be of use to all of the people scattered throughout the region.

It had been easy for Hugo to fall in love with her. Not only was Cecily intelligent, candid, and honest, but she was also unusually attractive. Now twenty-one, five feet four inches in height, she had expressive dark brown eyes that called attention to her lovely heart-shaped face. During her time at Rush, she had worn her light-brown hair in a severe bun to create the illusion that she was older than she was—mainly as her defense mechanism against the preponderance of males in her classes who mocked her, thinking that she had come to Rush Medical College only to find a man. Now, however, she felt secure enough, not only in her chosen profession but also in her personal life, to wear her hair flowing in loose waves around her shoulders.

The contrasts of femininity and severity, of aloofness and candor, had fascinated him and made him fall deeply in love. And that was why, after they had their graduation ceremony and each had been awarded honors, Hugo had taken the bull by the horns and proposed marriage: "Cecily, I love you very much. I want to marry you—more than that, I want to share your life in every possible way."

Cecily had been hesitant at first, feeling that Hugo would try and sway her from the decision to practice out west, but to her surprise, he suggested quite the opposite. Recognizing the source of her uncertainty, he had told her, "I'd like nothing better than to go with you and work as a doctor out in Rawlins and be of service near your Aunt Margaret. From what you've told me of the country, the settlers are far flung, and there certainly aren't many doctors. So they could surely use two, instead of one."

She had looked at him for a long moment and then murmured, "I love you, too, Hugo. I was afraid you'd want to go back to Texas and perhaps practice in Dallas or San Antonio. Or maybe even stay here in Chicago—you could go anywhere. I've become familiar with your work, and I know how you think. The fact that you're willing to bury yourself in a remote area so far away from all the wonderful things that Chicago has to offer convinces me that you're very sincere. Yes, dearest Hugo, I'd be proud to marry you. We'll make a wonderful team."

Cecily had willingly agreed to go back with Hugo to Carrizo Springs to meet his mother and father, Lucien Edmond and Maxine. They were married there in the church, and Cecily quickly endeared herself to all of the Windhaven workers by her spontaneous and generous giving of this, her honeymoon time, to treat their ailments and occasional injuries. Although the lovely young woman liked all the men and their families, still she had found it hard to reconcile her admiration for these ranchers with her innate sense of distrust for cattlemen in general, owing to the brutal murder of her uncle. Nonetheless, she believed in the firm tenets of honor and decency, goodness and compassion. She believed—as did her doting young husband—that the Hippocratic Oath bound her to give help whenever and wherever it was sought.

After three weeks at Windhaven Range, they had gone by train to Rawlins. Cecily and Hugo had gone at once to meet her aunt, Margaret, and Hugo had, at the very first meeting, warmed to the outspoken, defiantly courageous, fifty-six-year-old widow. Helped by eight workers—some of whom were itinerant and ready to leap to another employer at the first sign of a higher wage—Margaret Denton tended a flock of some two thousand sheep. The gray-haired woman sat Cecily and Hugo down in the kitchen of her sprawling ranch house, served them hot apple pie and fresh coffee, and then leaned back to study Hugo Bouchard's earnest face. Finally, she declared, "Sonny, I have to say, I like the look of you."

"You—you've made a decision about me in just a few minutes, Mrs. Denton?" Hugo replied in astonishment.

"Land sakes, son, don't you think my niece has been writing me all about you ever since you stood up against those other young rascals in that medical school you both were going to?" the elderly woman blustered. "Gracious me, half her letters went on telling me what a fine upstanding doctor you were going to make, and how she was sweet on you—"

"Aunt Margaret, that was a secret!" Cecily gasped, turning a vivid crimson and looking, at least in Hugo's prejudiced eye, more delectable than ever. Indeed, he suited overt action to mental impulse, and then and there leaned over to kiss her resoundingly near the mouth. "Good heavens, Hugo Bouchard, don't be so demonstrative in public!" Cecily giggled. And then she hugged him, and Aunt Margaret tilted back her head and laughed uproariously.

"I can see you two sprouts are going to have a great life together. Yes, Cecily girl, I like your choice of a husband. He's got spunk, and he isn't afraid to sass an old woman and get sassed back. He'll do fine. And if he's half the doctor you tell me he is, why, this area out here can sure use the two of you together.''

"That's why I married your niece, Mrs. Denton,'' Hugo soberly declared. "It would be easy to stay in a big city and make a lot of money, but that's not why I became a doctor. I want to do something worthwhile—contribute to the community and earn my salt.''

"Well, you'll have some problems out here in Rawlins. Everybody knows that Cecily is my niece—and that means she's on the right side of the blanket of a sheep-raising family. All the rest of the town and the surroundings are going to be down on you and her because they're raising cattle. They can't see sheep for dirt—and they'd rather see dirt, if truth be told.''

"Is it really as bad as that?'' Hugo naively asked.

Margaret Denton snorted. "It's worse than that. I guess that wherever you have sheep and cattle close by, you're going to have fights. Well now, I know for a fact there are plenty of sheep in Texas—and even in Colorado in some parts—where the grazing was good for both species of critters. But out here, the way the cattlemen act, it's a matter of life and death. Their claim is that the sheep eat the grass down to the roots and don't leave anything for their poor steers and cows and whatnot. But I say that's not true; I say there's enough grass for everybody, and if it's fenced off and we all treat each other the way the Lord Jehovah intended us to do—which is getting along with our neighbors—there wouldn't be any need for all this nonsense. Trouble is, it gets worse than nonsense—it gets into gunfighting and work for the undertaker. Only last week, just before you kids got here, old Hosea Perkins was shot down deader than a mackerel by Ed Solters, who has a spread he calls the Lazy J up about fifteen miles northwest of here. All poor old Hosea did was to put up some barbed-wire fencing, so his sheep could graze without bothering old man Solters's cattle. But one of Solters's prize bulls got in a rampage with some of his heifers, and the next thing you knew, he had skedaddled into that barbed-wire fence and torn his ornery hide.''

"And that was the reason Mr. Solters killed the old man?'' Hugo asked, aghast.

"That's the long and short of it, sonny. Don't mind me calling you sonny. Harold and I never did have any kids, though the Lord knows we both went to church when we weren't too busy working. So that's why, after Cece was orphaned and after my Harold was killed in the same stupid war that's been going on longer than I care to remember, I sort of adopted this lovely young thing." She turned to smile fondly at Cecily. "So she's more like my daughter than my niece."

"You're a wonderful woman, Mrs. Denton," Hugo averred. "You're also a wonderful cook. This is even better than the apple pie my mother bakes."

"I like this feller of yours, Cece honey," Margaret chortled. To Hugo's amusement and delight, she got up from the table, walked over to him, and clapped him resoundingly on the back. Then, going back to her seat, her mood changed to one of grave concern. "I know you wrote me, Cece sweetheart, that Hugo's daddy was going to supply you with the money for brick and good timber for your house. You'll find enough of the boys around here who are just plain farmhands and settlers who'll be right smart happy to go to work for decent wages building that house. Are you going to have your office there as well, you two?"

"Might as well," Hugo responded. "What Cecily and I plan to do, Mrs. Denton, is to go around in a buckboard—well, let's make that two buckboards and two horses, because each of us will have different patients, I should guess—"

"Whoa, now, back up a mite, sonny." Margaret Denton held up a lean, bony hand to halt him. "Like I said, your first problem is that everybody's going to know that you and your wife are on the sheepherding side, whether it's true or not, simply because my niece is related to me. All right, we've covered that ground. But the next step is, you're very young and very new. People around here think that doctors oughta have gray beards down to their knees, and when you two kids come out there and start prodding around a fat man's belly to find out why he's got a pain, when he oughta have had better sense than to eat what he ate, he's going to resent it and tell you to go right back where you came from, which is Chicago. So you see, it's not gonna be easy out here."

"I don't want anything easy, Mrs. Denton," Hugo avowed.

"That's the spirit, sonny! Here, have another piece of pie—I know you've been ogling the tin. That's all right, you can stand to put some fat on your bones. You're nice and lean and it won't hurt. Won't hurt me, either; that's why I make a pig of myself. You see, I'm Cece's father's sister, and he, being a doctor, told me long ago that I was blessed by nature because I could eat all I wanted without showing it. I have all this energy, and then, when I married Harold Denton and he came out here to start ranching, I got into lending a hand just like another man, and it worked out great. Since we couldn't have kids, I figured the least I could do was to team up with him—yes, just the way you and Cece are doing now. It makes for a good marriage because you have a lot in common and the same interests. And you're devoted to each other because you're fending for the two of you, and not just for yourself."

That had been Hugo Bouchard's welcome to Rawlins. Now, after half a year of marriage, both he and Cecily had discovered that Margaret Denton's predictions about their having a hard row to hoe were more than accurate. There were, it was true, a few farmers in the area who had nothing to do with either the sheepmen or the cattlemen. But even they were reluctant at first to accept the services of either a female or a male doctor as youthful as Cecily or Hugo Bouchard. During the first month of their practice, one local farmer had ridden to the Bouchard house, wanting to ask Hugo to come look at his wife, whose leg was badly swollen. When he learned from Cecily that her husband had already gone out in the opposite direction to call on a man who was suffering from rheumatism, he had responded, "You mean the doctor ain't home now, Mrs. Bouchard?" Controlling her temper, Cecily had explained that she, too, was a qualified physician, and that she would be glad to minister to the man's wife. She had started to pack up her medicine bag, but the farmer held up an obdurate hand. "I don't like that one little bit, nosirree. Can't have a woman doctorin'. Tain't decent, no how. No, ma'am, you just let me know when your husband will be back home; then you send him out to my place. It's three miles southeast of here, and you can't miss it because there's a big blasted oak tree with the bark all stripped by lightning. You send him over just as fast as you can, you hear, Mrs. Bouchard?"

Cecily had indeed heard, and after gritting her teeth and politely agreeing, she closed the door. Then picking up the object nearest to hand—a needlepoint pillow—she threw it furiously across the small room. She didn't dare express her anger to the backward farmer because she couldn't afford to offend or antagonize any of their patients.

Cecily was concerned about their paltry income, but what Hugo did not tell his lovely, intrepid young wife was that his father had given him a generous bank draft and told him, "Hugo, if you want to look upon this as a loan, that's fine with me. I want to start you off right in your practice. I know of that territory, and I know a little about what's going on between the sheepmen and the cattlemen. So it might be tough sledding for you for a year or two, maybe even more. This way, you and Cecily won't have to scrimp and worry where the next meal is coming from. This is your choice, but I want to stand by you. Your mother and I will pray for you and write you often, and you'll always have our blessing. I admire what you've done, and all the vaqueros remember what a courageous man you were on that drive to Colorado."

Thus, the desperate anxiety of earning a livelihood in so hostile and isolated a community was lessened for them, but Hugo did not tell Cecily this, for he wanted to test his own skills in cooperation with hers, believing that they could and would survive on their own earnings. In time, they might be able to found a clinic. Perhaps they could even get contributions to build a hospital for their isolated area of Wyoming, for more and more settlers were coming in almost every month.

Cecily and Hugo had talked over their future even before they had left Chicago to get married, and with the wonderful candor he so admired, she had said to him, "Darling, although marriage to me means motherhood as well as companionship, we mustn't think of this at the outset. We have to establish ourselves as doctors. That's what brought us together; that's what will keep us together."

"I agree with you, Cece—but, of course, I want us to have a child someday. Several, in fact," he told her with a smile.

Cecily had turned to stare lovingly at him with her sweet smile, which always bewitched him. "I want them just as much, Hugo. But let's agree to wait at least three years. By then, we'll either make it as doctors out here or we won't. And if we do make it, there's time enough to plan a family, a family we'll want and love and have time to devote to. I'm not interested in the monetary aspects of a practice any more than you are, but I think we'll feel richly rewarded if we can help these people out here.''

They had begun with high hopes and dreams and love. And their profession, to which they were dedicated and which they respected, would help them solve many an arduous problem. But many more still remained as yet unseen . . . problems that would test not only their courage but also their own beliefs in each other.

Chapter Ten

Cecily Bouchard set down her coffee cup and leaned back in her chair as she looked intently at her handsome young husband. "Hugo, do you realize that it's almost the six-month anniversary of our mutual practice as doctors in this community?" she asked.

"Yes, I do, darling. As a matter of fact, I've been reflecting on what we've done and what we still hope to do."

"Well, we've made some small inroads, even with all the prejudices Aunt Margaret told us we were bound to face—and heaven knows we've certainly faced them." She giggled and shook her head. "I still can't forget the time you were out tending to a patient's rheumatism and that farmer came to me and, when he found out you weren't here, left in a huff at the idea of my being a doctor."

Hugo chuckled. "And as I recall, he came back the next day and sheepishly told you his wife much preferred a woman examining her."

"I certainly hope you weren't jealous about that, darling," Cecily twitted him.

"Of course not," Hugo indignantly retorted. "We're a team of doctors who are happily married. What benefits you benefits me, and vice versa."

"That's a very sensible way of looking at it. All in all, I'm quite pleased with this anniversary of ours—both anniversaries, darling," she said, and gave Hugo a sweetly endearing look. Hugo flushed, for though he had learned candor on the range, this vivacious, superbly intelligent girl often confronted him with unexpected sallies and intimacies that drew conditioned reflexes from him. She had, if truth be known, proved to be a magnificently enthusiastic lover, and no man could have asked for more ardor and total devotion to her husband. So far as Hugo Bouchard was concerned, the happiest day of his life was when Cecily Franklin had agreed to marry him. Looking back now, he assured himself that not for all the profits of the silver mine and Windhaven Range combined would he have traded his present life to go back to the ranch if Lucien Edmond decided to retire and wanted his son to take over.

"Let's see now," Cecily continued, "I have three sheep ranching families I look after and four farmers and their families. You've got just one sheep rancher's family, but four cattlemen's families and two farmers and their families." She paused, frowned, then went on. "You know, Hugo, just looking at the facts, I'd say that you have a marked partiality for cattlemen."

"That's just the way it happened; it wasn't of my own doing," he replied, somewhat irritated. "I can't help it that I was born to a father who owned a big cattle ranch. I personally have nothing at all against sheep."

"Well, that's very noble of you," she said sarcastically.

Hugo scowled. Such an argument reminded him at times of the way his sister, Carla, used to flout him for his lack of appreciation of modern art. Indeed, since he was still young enough to be sensitive and to have his feelings ruffled, Hugo's only domestic conflicts with his gifted young wife sprang from what he privately termed her one-sidedness concerning the problems between cattlemen and sheep ranchers. Several times over the past year, they had wrangled over this issue. One evening just two weeks before, she had remained silent and ignored his awkward overtures of reconciliation till at last, when they retired to their bedchamber, she had relented and told him, "Hugo darling, it's ridiculous to have arguments like this. You have to be flexible enough to see the other side. I know you can't help your birth and origin any more than I can mine. But just look at it impersonally, as if you were standing off to one side and weren't involved. These people are decent, law-abiding citizens; all they want to do is to make a fair living. They work hard, they have families, just as you and I hope to have; and they're expanding the frontier of this growing country. Why should they be considered outcasts and pariahs simply because they happen to raise sheep?"

He had taken her in his arms and kissed her tear-wet cheek,

murmuring, "Cecily darling, for God's sake, I understand all that. But my feeling is that if anyone goes to extremes, he's breaking the law. I abhor violence just as much as you do, God knows. However, these sheep ranchers came out here long after the cattlemen had already marked off their land, fought off hostile Indians, built their homes, and reared their families. Simply as a matter of priority, they were here first; naturally they would resent intruders."

"I know a little something about history, too, Hugo Bouchard," she had said that evening, while nestling in his arms, though she had turned her face away so that he couldn't kiss her again. "So I remember that right after the Civil War, when Texas cattlemen wanted to drive their herds up to Sedalia, the citizens were afraid that Texas cattle had fever ticks and would contaminate their cattle. There was bloodshed and resistance, and the cattlemen felt that was unjust."

"And it was, it was," he had protested.

"Hugo, in spite of the fact that I think you're one of the most brilliant young men I've ever known, sometimes I think you're a dolt!" she had sniffed.

But then he had turned her toward him, kissed her lovingly on the mouth, and whispered, "Cecily, my God, I'm so much in love with you it almost hurts me—and here we are having a fruitless argument over cattle and sheep. I love you; doesn't that count for anything?"

Then she had giggled, ruffled his hair with one hand, and pulled him to her. "A little. Suppose you make me forget all about cattle and sheep for the time being."

Although that reconciliation had been passionate and thrilling, Hugo was inwardly concerned about this difference of opinion between them. He looked over at this lovely young wife as she sat sipping her morning coffee, and inwardly sighed. He was afraid that it would flare up into something magnified beyond its true proportions. . . .

Cecily looked up from the piece of paper on which she was writing a marketing list, for this was Saturday, the day they usually drove into Rawlins for their weekly supplies. "We're running low on flour, bacon, and coffee, Hugo. And we can use some additional canned fruits and vegetables and some seeds. This summer, I'd like to start a small produce garden at the back of the house."

"That sounds like a good idea, honey," Hugo volunteered.

"Sure—if the farmers can raise produce, no reason why we can't, and Aunt Margaret says we've got good, rich soil. Well," she said as she rose from the table, "that's something to think about for the future. Why don't you go be a darling and hitch up the buggy, while I tidy up a spell?"

Hugo nodded in agreement, rose, and leaned over to kiss her on the forehead. Cecily laughed and put her arms around his neck, drawing him back down to her for a far more satisfying kiss on the mouth. "The way you kissed me just then, Mr. Bouchard," she dryly informed him, "suggests that the honeymoon is over. I certainly hope you don't feel that way, even if I do nag you at times."

"You don't nag me, and the honeymoon isn't ever going to be over, darling" was Hugo's answer. He left the kitchen and walked over to the small stable that adjoined the house, and Cecily looked up and smiled warmly after him. Then she sighed, shook her head, and then briskly rose and went to the bedroom. Humming to herself, Cecily made up the bed and put away their nightclothes. Opening up the wardrobe, she pulled out a heavy sweater and drew it on. Since it was Saturday, it wasn't necessary to dress up, so Levis, a plaid woolen blouse, sturdy boots, and warm woolen socks comprised the rest of her attire. Even though it was April, there was still snow in the Wyoming mountain ranges and on the high plains, and the air was not much more than ten degrees above freezing. She decided to put on her greatcoat, for to come down with a spring cold now would be absolutely silly—and then, of course, there was the danger she might infect Hugo.

As she drew on her coat and buttoned it, Hugo came in to announce that he was ready. Offering his arm, he escorted his lovely wife out to the buggy and helped her into it. He clambered onto the driver's seat, took up the reins, and the couple started off for Rawlins.

There was only one general store, but it was a large one that carried everything from cough drops to maple syrup, ready-to-wear clothing for both sexes, as well as dress materials, farming and ranching equipment, boots, pistols and rifles and shotguns, and a relatively complete line of foodstuffs and sundries. One shelf was devoted entirely to patent medicines, none of which Cecily and Hugo prescribed for their patients, much to the annoyance of the burly, gray-bearded shop owner,

Martin Overman. His affable wife, Bertha, was considerably younger than he, and she was already a good friend of Cecily Bouchard's. Knowing this, her husband seldom expressed to her his resentment that the Bouchards did not recommend the line of elixirs and general medicines (such as Lydia Pinkham's tonic, which he believed would cure every female disorder from megrims to lack of appetite). But he usually pointedly expounded on this subject to the young doctors whenever his wife was not in the store. This Saturday afternoon was one of those occasions.

Cecily greeted him with a vivacious "Good morning, Mr. Overman!" and then added, "Can we go over this list, please? I need quite a few supplies, and, of course, my husband will help carry them out into our buggy."

"Glad to, Mrs. Bouchard." He paused and tugged at his beard. "I suppose I ought to call you Dr. Bouchard, but I can't seem to get used to the idea."

"Well, you don't have to stand on ceremony with me, Mr. Overman," she responded with a smile.

He squinted at her and then pulled on the thick, gray hairs of his moustache. "I do wish, *Doctor*," he said, emphasizing the title with a kind of sarcastic politeness, "you wouldn't go around on your high horse over these medicines I carry here. Don't forget, I'm the only one in Rawlins who has the stuff, and it's done a lot of folks a world of good."

"I don't mean to insult your wares, Mr. Overman," Cecily was icily polite. "I just don't recommend these medicines, that's all. They certainly don't cure everything, as most of them claim—there isn't any medicine that does or, so far as I can tell, that ever will. Every person has a different metabolism."

"And what's that supposed to mean, pray tell?" His sarcastic tone was one of patient exasperation this time.

"Simply, Mr. Overman, that everyone's body is different; their insides are different. A medicine that works on one person might be fatal to someone else—that's what that means."

"Oh, I see. Thank you so much for telling me, *Doctor*." After a brief, awkward pause, he said, "Well, I guess that's about it. Do you need any dress material?"

"Not this week, thank you, Mr. Overman. When I do, I'll come see Bertha."

He glared at Cecily, bristling at this statement. Putting his palms down on the counter and leaning forward, he declared,

"I'm the one who owns the store. I just let her work here and help out—you understand, Doctor? If you want to know something about what I've got in stock, just ask me."

Cecily tried to smooth his ruffled feathers. "But it stands to reason, Mr. Overman, that a woman would know more about dress materials than a man, not to mention you're always so busy. Besides, I want to be more of a friend of your wife."

"Yes, I guess that's all right." He seemed dubious about it. "All the same, when you go seeing your patients, don't go telling them not to buy what Martin Overman has stocked here for a good many years—long before *you* ever came out here, Doctor. And that's a fact."

His offensive sarcasm nettled Cecily. "I always appreciate facts, Mr. Overman, and I'm sure that you've been of great help to the community. But speaking of facts, my husband and I got our training at Rush Medical College, where they specialize in prescribing treatment, the proper medicines, and diet for sick people. As you may be aware, many of these stock medicines have laudanum or even spirits in them."

"And that's a blessing for a lot of people, I can tell you," Martin Overman angrily defended himself.

"That may very well be true, but laudanum and spirits are rarely used these days for medicinal purposes. One can become addicted if one keeps taking laudanum all the time. However, I see no reason for prolonging this argument, so what do I owe you?"

He glowered at her, picked up the stub of a pencil, then began laboriously to write down the prices of the supplies she had brought. When he had finished, he looked up and tersely told her, "Twenty-three dollars and twelve cents, if you please, Doctor."

Cecily nodded and extracted her purse, taking out three ten-dollar bills and laying them on the counter. Overman made change, turned his back, and walked to the end of the counter. Ostensibly, he was going to put her supplies in one convenient place, but the effect of his movement and the look on his face, as well as his tone, annoyed the young woman. However, not wishing to deepen the enmity between Overman and Hugo and her, Cecily ignored this contemptuous gesture. Hugo, who had gone across the street to the tiny post office to see if there had been any letters from his father and mother, now returned. "Have you finished, honey? I'd better start loading the supplies into the buggy," he asked.

"Thank you, dear." Then, raising her voice to get the store owner's attention, she called, "My husband is here now, Mr. Overman, and we're ready to leave. Could you help him with some of the supplies?"

"I suppose I could. I'll take the heaviest stuff out, since your husband's sure a mighty slim young fellow. Incidentally, I'd have thought Rawlins was too small a place to have room for two doctors."

"We've managed quite nicely, thank you. We like it out here, Mr. Overman," Cecily pointedly told him.

"Here, I'll carry your sack of potatoes out," he volunteered. Then, eyeing Hugo, he added, "You can start taking that coffee and that sack of flour up there on the counter, and then I'll come back and get all the rest."

When Hugo and Cecily finally made their way down the dusty main street, the young man glanced over at his wife and remarked, "I presume Mr. Overman took up his pet subject again?"

"Yes, he did, and I do wish he'd stop it!" Cecily fiercely declared. "He's trying to make us feel we're taking the bread out of his mouth." She suddenly laughed. "As a matter of fact, doing that literally would be a very good idea for him. Not only is he overweight, but his coloring suggests that he has high blood pressure as well. If he keeps on like this, he could work himself into a major coronary. Unfortunately, poor Bertha tells me that he's so set in his ways he doesn't really believe in doctors, and so he's held off going to any. Of course, there haven't been any near Rawlins for a good long while, but now he has a valid reason—so he thinks—for not consulting either of us. I really am sorry for her. She's such a nice person, and she tries so hard to please. He's always browbeating her whenever she's there working with him. You know, Hugo, what I like most about you is that you look upon a woman as an equal."

"That's the way I was brought up—and besides, Cecily, the simple fact is that you're smarter than I am in a great many ways."

"What a lovely thing to say, darling! For all your faults—not that there're that many—you always manage at the right

100

time to reassure me, so I have no doubts as to the wisdom in having said yes to you," she teased him.

Hugo merrily glanced at her, then flicked the reins and quickened the mare's pace toward their house. He was quiet for a time, enjoying the passing scenery. Then he remarked in a reminiscent tone, "You know, Cecily honey, I was just thinking that at this time of year in Chicago, everything is turning so green, and there's even some decidedly warm weather."

"Not always," she countered. "I can remember some cold driving rains, even hail, and raw winds from the northeast. This is a healthier climate, and personally, apart for the lack of entertainment and restaurants, I like living in a small town. It's better for one's peace of mind. Are you sorry you've come out here to settle with me?"

"That's a leading question, and the answer is, of course, no. Wherever you were, I'd be happy—whether it was Calcutta or London or Paris or Milan or Chicago. But because you're here, I'm happy here."

"That, my darling, happens to be the exactly right answer." Cecily gave him an arch smile and leaned back and closed her eyes.

Hugo had driven toward the southwest, taking a more circuitous route because it was sunny and the sky was a marvelous, almost cloudless blue. As he breathed in the pure air, exhaling deeply, he thought how happy he was, all things considered, and he was particularly glad they had that little nest egg tucked away for those dreary days when no patients cared to knock at their door.

They were skirting the lower edge of a large cattle ranch belonging to Brand Calkins, a middle-aged ranch owner who had settled in the Rawlins area some twenty years ago. He was a widower with two ungainly, trouble-making sons, both of whom liked to come into town of a Saturday night and get drunk and paw the nearest unattached girl. Since both of them were married, their antics hardly set well with either the deacons of the Lutheran Church—the only viable sect in the community—or with the girls themselves. Only last month, Calkins had had to come to town to pay for damages caused when his younger son, Mack, had been ogling a girl and got into a fight with her boyfriend—during the course of which the bar mirror, two tables, and a dozen chairs were smashed. Mack himself had spent an unhappy night in jail.

Suddenly Hugo reined in the mare. Crossing the road just ahead were some two hundred sheep. A gray-haired man in a tattered greatcoat and dusty boots, together with two young Mexicans, was feverishly directing the flock. Their bleating filled the air, and the man, whom Hugo recognized as Elmer Cranshaw, whose wife had died from pneumonia not quite a year earlier, was urging them to hurry, glancing over his shoulder as he did so.

As they watched, they saw three horsemen approaching at a gallop. Cecily leaned forward, her eyes wide with concern. "Why, that's Mr. Cranshaw! What's he doing this far north? Does his land come up this far?"

"Well, I'm not sure where his spread ends. Maybe his sheep strayed a bit. Look at those riders; they don't look particularly happy about it!"

"Then this must be Mr. Calkins's land, isn't it?"

"Let's see—yes, look over there. See that old upright marker? The initials B.C. in that circle mark the end of the Calkins's boundary," Hugo replied.

The two young Mexicans, seeing the oncoming horsemen, urged the sheep on with explosive Spanish oaths, even belaboring the frightened animals with their staffs in their apprehension.

The horsemen reined in and the foremost rider leaped down and strode over to Elmer Cranshaw. This was Ashley Calkins, Brand Calkins's older son, a stocky, brown-bearded man in his early thirties, with small, beady eyes set closely together and a broad Roman nose. He was scowling. "Look, Cranshaw," he growled, as he advanced toward the gray-haired sheep rancher, "Pa 'n me told you to keep your goddamned sheep off our land a couple times. This is just once too much, you get me? All right, boys, let's teach this son of a bitch a lesson he won't forget in a hurry." He gestured toward the two frightened Mexicans. "You better stay out of this, if you know what's good for you!"

"*Sí*, Señor Calkins. We w-want no trouble," the older of the two sheepherders, who was not more than twenty, nervously stammered.

The other two horsemen dismounted and came toward the sheep rancher, who began to back away. Holding up a hand in propitiation, he hoarsely exclaimed, "As God is my witness, Mr. Calkins, I didn't mean for my sheep to get on your land, honest I didn't! My men didn't see the marker—"

"That's a goddamned lie, if ever I heard one! You got this coming, and it's long overdue," Ashley Calkins snarled, as he drove his fist into Elmer Cranshaw's belly. The sheep rancher doubled up and uttered a screech of agony. He clutched at himself, then stumbled onto all fours, shaking his head groggily.

"Get up and take your medicine, you bastard!" one of the two riders, a lean, beetle-browed man in his late twenties, mocked him. Not satisfied with the older man's reluctance to regain his footing, he leaned down, seized Cranshaw by the scruff of his greatcoat, and dragged him to his feet, then sent a right hook to his jaw, sprawling him flat on his back. The other rider, a few years younger and towheaded, with a vicious smile and cold blue eyes, ran forward now and seized the sobbing old man by the wrists. He pulled him to his feet, only to send him sprawling again by pummeling him with both fists against his ribs and chest. In an unconscious gesture, the rider touched the butts of his pearl-handled Colts holstered around his waist.

"For God's sake! Please s-stop it—I told you I didn't mean to. Lemme go—it won't ever happen again!" Elmer Cranshaw sobbed.

"Hugo!" Cecily's eyes were blazing as she stood up in the buggy. "That's the cruelest thing I've ever seen! Three men using all that force on the poor old man!"

"We can't interfere, Cecily. They're all armed, and they wouldn't take kindly to any interference. I—I can try to talk to them—" Hugo hesitantly began.

But already Calkins had reached down and pulled up the old sheep rancher by his armpits. His face a mask of sadistic gloating, he stared into Cranshaw's tear-filled, blinking eyes and hissed, "Maybe you'll get the idea now. If I ever see another one of those goddamned sheep of yours cross even one inch onto our land, my men and I will come out to your place and burn it down—and we'll shoot your sheep, too, you hear me?"

"Why—why—yes—s-sir—I promise it won't ever happen

again. Please—I can't take any more now! Oh, sweet Jesus!'' His frantic protestations ended in a scream of pain, as the cattleman's older son smashed his fist into the sheep rancher's face, and blood spurted from the old man's mouth. The punch left him crumpled on the ground, breathing stertorously.

The three men stood over him, exchanging quips and mocking taunts: "I got no use for a whiner." "Me neither—gimme a guy who can take his lickin' without a peep out of him." "What do you expect? He's only a goddamned sheep raiser—probably buggers the sheep in the barn at night, now that his wife's dead!''

Cecily Bouchard uttered a cry of indignation and then called out at the top of her voice, "Leave that poor man alone! I'm warning you, if he dies, I'll have you charged, all of you, with murder—do you hear me?''

Ashley Calkins, who heretofore had been unaware of the Bouchards' presence, so intent had he been on his vendetta, whirled to determine from what point this unexpected interruption had come. "Oh, it's you, Doc Bouchard. Well, now, guess you might say we're drumming up some business for you. You better take care of this son of a bitch, Doc. I think we worked him over pretty good.''

"You ought to be ashamed of yourself!'' Cecily yelled, her color high and her eyes sparkling with contemptuous anger. "Three against one, and he at least twice the age of you and your two bullies!''

"Whatcha gonna do, Doc, slap my wrist and call me a bad boy?'' he sneered.

Hugo clenched his fists but knew very well that interference would be futile. Not only were the three cattlemen armed but he had no weapon at all.

"I'm going to tell the sheriff what you've done. My husband and I witnessed this brutality from the beginning,'' Cecily declared. "Now, if you've quite finished with your victim, we will try to save his life. I shouldn't be surprised if you hurt him very seriously! And if he dies, I hope they'll hang you high!''

"Well, fancy that!'' Calkins jeered. "You're a real spitfire, Doc!'' Then, leering at Hugo, he sniggered, "Think you can handle a filly like that?''

Cecily turned crimson and looked imploringly and angrily at her husband, who merely shrugged. There was no possible way in which he could come out of the situation looking like a hero, unless he wanted to have a quick death.

By now, Ashley and his two cronies had tired of their sport. "Come along, boys," he said. "Let's go back to the ranch." Then, as a last venomous reminder, he spat out, "And you, Cranshaw, you buggerin' bastard, remember what I told you: The next time we find you on our land, we'll give you six free feet of it—all below the ground!"

Mounting his horse, he and his two cowmen rode back in the direction they had come from, glancing back and making obscene gestures.

Hugo and Cecily hurried to the fallen man and began to tend to him. Very carefully, Cecily palpated his ribs and stomach. "He's badly hurt. I'm sure he's sustained some fractured ribs, and his jaw might be broken. Those vicious bullies! I *would* like to see them hang. I mean it!"

"Cecily, you have to understand what made those men beat Mr. Cranshaw up," Hugo began, as he felt the old man's pulse.

The young Mexicans, who had been terrified by the three cattlemen, came scurrying back like frightened rabbits. The younger one asked, "Did they kill him? Tell us, *señor médico!*"

"No, they didn't kill him—but almost," Hugo retorted. Then, meeting his wife's angry glare, he went on, "As I started to say, honey, this is probably an old feud that goes back for many years. Cattlemen just don't like having sheep on their property. I know they reacted badly, but they *were* here first, as I told you before."

"So you think might makes right, do you, Hugo Bouchard? You're a fine doctor!" Cecily angrily exclaimed. "Help me lift Mr. Cranshaw. We're going to take him back to the house and look after him."

"Of course. We'll have to take him home since we don't have a hospital in Rawlins yet," was Hugo's reply.

"Now that's very observant of you, isn't it, Dr. Bouchard?" Her tone dripped with sarcasm.

"Cecily, please, for God's sake! I don't say that I condone what they did, but I understand why they did it," he protested.

"Of course you do. You were born on a cattle ranch, and you think that cattle rule the roost—if you don't mind my mixing metaphors." She stared at him, color high on her cheeks, her eyes sparkling with anger.

"Cece, honey, for God's sake, don't take it out on me," he pleaded, trying to mollify her.

"Don't talk. Just help Mr. Cranshaw into the buggy. That's all I want from you at the moment, Dr. Bouchard." Her tone was icy, and her lips were tightened. Hugo rolled his eyes to heaven, as if wondering why women were so predictably unpredictable. He knew that they would argue at length, late into the night, after they tended Elmer Cranshaw. He felt the same sort of perplexity he had had when his sister, Carla, had attacked him and called him insensitive about her feelings. It wasn't that way at all, but she didn't want to understand—and neither did Cecily.

"All right, here we go—easy now—that's fine." He announced to the young Mexicans, "We will take your *patrón* to our house where we can look after him. As soon as he is well again, we will bring him back to his ranch."

"*Muchas gracias, señor médico.*" The younger one bobbed his head and grinned. Then, turning to his companion, he whispered animatedly, and the two men hurried off with their flock of sheep.

Cecily sat in the back of the buggy, solicitously looking after Elmer Cranshaw, while Hugo drove the mare back to their house. The drive was made in stony silence. He felt somewhat resentful and almost had a surge of self-pitying despair because of the way she had reacted. If only she weren't the niece of sheep ranchers. . . . He only hoped that he would not be put in Coventry for too long, for the fact was—and he did not know how he could conceal it—Hugo was almost desperately in love with his beautiful young wife.

Chapter Eleven

It was April of 1882, and France was entering upon a golden age of arts and letters. That such a climate of creativity and optimism could exist was remarkable, considering that the French people had, a mere eleven years earlier, suffered a crushing defeat at the hands of Germany's Iron Chancellor, Otto von Bismarck, during the Franco-Prussian War. That war toppled the Second Empire, the regime of the vain and often misguided emperor, Louis Napoleon III.

As Bismarck had cunningly anticipated, Napoleon III declared war on Germany on July 9, 1870. Napoleon III himself took the field and was caught in the debacle of Sedan on September 1, 1870. Captured by the Prussians, the emperor was then deposed by the French Chamber of the Corps Legislatif, and the Third Republic was born.

The new Provisional Government was almost immediately faced with the greatest crisis threatening any nation: occupation by a foreign power. Toward the end of September 1870, German troops were advancing on Paris, and the citizens of France rallied and rose up in arms to defend their homeland against the invader. The new Foreign Minister, Jules Favre, declared, "We shall yield neither an inch of our territory nor a stone of our fortresses," and this defiance set the stage for the next scene in France's bitter drama—the siege of Paris.

The citizens of Paris resisted the German army for one hundred and thirty-one days, but despite heroic efforts—and only because of the imminent threat of starvation—Paris capitulated on January 28, 1871. The defiant populace had been subsisting on only a few grams of bread daily, and by the time they surrendered, the storehouses held only enough flour to have lasted ten more days.

However, new storm clouds appeared on the French horizon. An armistice was signed and the Germans withdrew, leaving Paris once again in the hands of newly elected officials of the Provisional Government. One of the first acts of the new government was to disband the National Guards—a decision much resented by the populace, many of whom depended on that organization for their sole source of income. The National Guards mounted their own army of one hundred thousand men and fought the government forces, a fight in which they were supported by radical extremists in Paris who now saw an opportunity to foment a proletarian revolution.

The Commune, as the revolutionary movement in Paris was called, waged a civil war with the Provisional Government that lasted two months and led in the end to an orgy of death and destruction. Fifty-six hostages, including the Archbishop of Paris and several priests, were killed, and some of the most historic and beautiful buildings in Paris—including the Tuileries, the Palais of Justice, and the Hotel de Ville—were burned.

The government exacted a severe toll, and thousands of people—including a great number of innocents—were summarily executed, imprisoned, or deported to New Caledonia. Thus ended a spontaneous, patriotically inspired uprising that signaled the climax of a half century of dispute between workers and bourgeoisie.

Humiliated by Germany, toppled from its pedestal as a world power, France very nearly turned to a monarchy again by electing Marshal McMahon, a royalist sympathizer, as President in 1873. It was McMahon's hope to turn over the power and then the throne to Henri, Count of Chambourd, who was a legitimist pretender. But the pretender's stubborn inflexibility and refusal to negotiate quashed this plan, and in 1875 a republican constitution was finally adopted.

Yet despite the collapse of the Napoleonic regime, which left the nation dwarfed by the emergence of its militaristic conqueror, Germany—a national shame that would not be erased until World War I—Napoleon III achieved one permanent glory: the planning of modern Paris.

This City of Light had come about when the Emperor had named Baron Haussmann as Prefect of the Seine. Haussmann had devised a master plan, creating magnificent tree-lined boulevards and eliminating narrow, confining streets and slums.

He created parks and gardens, built bridges across the Seine, and installed electric light and sewer systems, as well as erected monumental buildings. His corps of architects were motivated by a credo that, if truth be told, was hardly calculated to create good will among American city builders: The baron's aim was to avoid the monotony of American cities, whose straight streets crossed at right angles with nothing to attract the pedestrian at the end of the corridor.

Thus, Paris was planned as a kind of gigantic park, with monument-decorated avenues radiating from *ronds-points*— traffic circles—and it was divided into twenty *arrondissements*, of which fourteen were on the north (right) bank, and six on the south (left). As newly laid out, the city became a place of surpassing beauty, an inspiration to artists of all kinds, as well as a haven for *bon vivants* and pleasure-seekers from the world over.

It was to this renovated City of Light that Carla Bouchard, Hugo's beautiful sister, had gone in September, 1881. After Carla had completed her studies at the Chicago Academy of Fine Arts the previous June, her mentor and chaperone, Cordelia Thornberg, had urged Carla to continue her artistic education in the birthplace of the Impressionist movement, to which the young woman had been so greatly attracted. Now that Hugo, who had never really appreciated her artistic talents—or so at least Carla had firmly believed—was no longer in Chicago, Carla felt no pressure on her against making such a bold decision. Immediately after her last term, Carla had written a letter to Maxine and Lucien Edmond announcing her graduation with honors and her intention of spending the summer with Cordelia on a trip to New Orleans, then New York, and thence to San Francisco and Los Angeles. Cordelia had friends in all of these cities, some of them painters, others art dealers; and during her last few months at the Academy, Carla had finished two exquisite landscapes and a full-length oil portrait of Cordelia herself.

The talented young woman was introduced to art notables in the cities she and Cordelia visited, and to her great delight, all three paintings were sold for a total of one thousand dollars. This money, Cordelia ingenuously intimated, would be a sizable investment in a trip to Paris early that fall—and Carla's commercial success was the final augury to convince her that she could make no wiser decision at this stage of her young creative life.

Cordelia's gifted brother, Dr. Max Thornberg, who was on staff at Rush Medical College and who had spent some of his sabbatical leaves in Paris, enthusiastically recommended several delightful *pensions de famille* not far from Montmartre. Since Montmartre was the very center of artistic life in Paris, Carla boarded the steamship at the New York dock bound for Cherbourg, accompanied by her enlightened and uninhibited chaperone, with a sense of almost feverish anticipation.

She and Cordelia spent the first two weeks in Paris as any tourists might, visiting Fontainebleau, the Tuileries, and the great Louvre. That magnificent museum of the arts had been opened on Friday, August 14, 1857, by Napoleon III, completing a plan created for France's glory three centuries before. On the façade of this imposing edifice was the following inscription: "François I commenced the Louvre in 1544. Catherine de Medici commenced the Tuileries in 1564. Napoleon III united the Louvre with the Tuileries in 1852–7."

Cordelia Thornberg had, of course, seen Paris several times. But for her protégée, it was fascinatingly new and at complete variance with what Carla had seen in any of the American cities she had visited. The breadth and scope of Paris intoxicated her, and as she told Cordelia at the end of their first week, "I think I could spend my life here and never go a whole day without seeing something new! It's just marvelous! I feel so free and eager; it's as if I were reborn!"

"*Chérie*, that's what I've been trying to tell you," Cordelia assured her with a smile. "And, after we've settled in a bit, I'll take you to some of the soirées where you'll meet *la crème de la crème*—the writers, painters, and poets, the musicians, sculptors, and intellectuals. To someone as intellectual as you, my darling, as sensitive and perceptive, these soirées will be a veritable Lucullan banquet for the mind and soul and heart!"

Their *pension* was owned by a delightfully rotund, gregarious, white-haired woman named Catherine de Laurmier. Twice widowed, she had five happily married grandchildren and two great-grandchildren. Her sister, some ten years younger but equally white haired, was in exact contrast: slim, with the traces of a mustache on her upper lip, extremely prim, and punctilious to a fault in keeping track of their tenants' comings and goings in her role as concierge. Both sisters—the plump, easygoing proprietress and the wiry, taciturn concierge—took an immediate liking to Carla Bouchard, doubtless both savoring her absolutely unadulterated pleasure in experiencing Paris for the very first time. Indeed, on their third evening, Raymonde, the concierge, looked up from her desk, methodically entered a check mark opposite the listing of Carla Bouchard in her ledger book, then favored Carla with a prim little smile and almost wistfully declared, "I can see that you enjoy Paris, *n'est-ce pas, mademoiselle?*"

"It's absolutely heavenly! I shall never tire of it—if I lived here all the rest of my life, I think I'd still love it anew each day," was Carla's answer.

The concierge was sufficiently warmed by this burst of enthusiasm for her natal city and continued in the same wistful vein. "Ah, it's lovely now, but it is lucky for you that you were not here ten years ago. We Parisians endured terrible hardships during the horrible war against the Prussians—*les sales boches.* Why, there was almost no food. In the market of Les Halles, they were selling rats, horsemeat, dog and cat flesh, even rare animals from the zoological garden—at unheard-of prices!" Then, straightening her shoulders and with a satisfied smile, she added, "But we survived, and this is the result. Ah, Mam'selle Bouchard, wait until you see Paris when it is late spring in the Bois de Boulogne, and everything is green and beautiful and the sky is blue! Then you will really paint—I am told by your companion, Mam'selle Thornberg, that you are a very capable painter."

"*Oui, c'est vrai,*" Carla smilingly replied. "Thank you for taking such an interest in me—you and your sister are so kind to us."

"That is because you are kind to us in turn, Mam'selle Bouchard. I wish you a very pleasant evening."

At the beginning of the third week of their stay in Paris, Cordelia took Carla to meet an art dealer whose elegant gallery was on the edge of Montmartre. Though most of her time during these first two weeks had been taken up in following Cordelia around through a delightful tour of Paris, Carla had nevertheless begun a watercolor of the River Seine with one of its many bridges in the rain. It was half finished, but Cordelia insisted that she take it with her to show Monsieur Giles Vertrier. "He's an old darling," Cordelia explained, "and he was a dear friend of Emile's."

Carla Bouchard's eyes widened. "You mean the man you told me about, the Parisian you were engaged to and who died before you could marry?"

"Yes, Carla dearest. Emile and Giles were great friends, and when Emile died, I had the most beautiful letter from Giles. Naturally, I continued the correspondence, and on the occasions when I've come to Paris alone, I've always had dinner with him and talked over old times. Ah," the auburn-haired spinster reminiscently sighed, "it was twenty-five years ago that Emile and I were engaged. I was so in love—but then you know the rest. But the point is, as I've always told you, you mustn't let your life be upset by a cross in love, and the way to rebound is to plunge yourself into some useful endeavor which brings out your creative essence. For many women, of course, it's marriage and motherhood, their creativity being procreation. Understand me, I don't disparage that because otherwise the human race wouldn't survive. But, for me, it's been my interest in the arts, my making new friends who remain loyal and true through the years, and my helping people with genuine talent whenever I can.

"I think, Carla, young as you are but with the talent you've already displayed, your only limitation will be yourself. Here in Paris, you can find yourself. You'll find the way of life here more bohemian, shall we say, which simply means that no one expects you to conform, so long as you don't harm anyone, and this leaves you totally free to develop whatever you innately feel you must express. Oh, this age is so remarkable! We have painters like Cézanne and Monet and the other great Impressionists, and among writers, there's Zola. That reminds me, next week I plan to take you to a soirée at which they'll discuss Zola's very risqué novel, *Nana*, which was published two years ago. It's all about a woman of easy virtue and her tragic end. Zola is a great realist. And, when you combine impressionism and realism, you've plumbed the very heights and the very depths of man's creativity."

Carla found all of this fascinating and readily absorbed it. When she accompanied Cordelia to the gallery, she first saw Giles Vertrier, a nearly bald man of about fifty-two, with a neat Vandyke beard and a pince-nez, as he was examining a new painting. Seeing Cordelia enter his gallery, he hurried up to her and, with typical Gallic effusiveness, hugged her and kissed her while exclaiming in the most flamboyant phrases how enchanted he was to see her and how beautiful she continued to look.

Carla drew back, a bit shy at feeling herself something of an intruder. But Cordelia quickly turned and, still clasping one of the art dealer's hands in hers, beckoned to her. "Carla dear, do come meet Giles. Giles, *mon ami très cher,* let me introduce you to Mademoiselle Carla Bouchard. She has been staying with me the past few years in Chicago while attending the Chicago Academy of Fine Arts. She has a real talent, as may be evidenced by that half-completed canvas she is clutching in her hands. Knowing you to be the best judge of works by new artists, I insisted that she bring it along. Do show it to him, *ma chérie.*"

Carla blushed and uncovered the canvas for the dealer's scrutiny. Giles Vertrier bent over it, adjusting his pince-nez, pensively frowning as he studied it for a long moment. Then he turned to Carla. "Mam'selle Bouchard, my dear friend Cordelia is right, as she always is. You wish to convey the mood of the rain. It is a theme which that poor genius of a poet, Baudelaire, immortalized in that wonderful poem from his collection, *Les Fleurs du Mal.* I wonder if you know how it goes, Mam'selle Bouchard. . . . *'Il pleure . . .'* "

Carla brightened, then hesitated. She was familiar with the quotation that Monsieur Vertrier had in mind; however, she recognized the words as those of a different poet. "I believe, monsieur," she said, "the lines you have in mind are: *'Il pleure dans mon coeur comme il pleut sur la ville.'* . . . But if I may be so bold as to say so, I believe the poet is Verlaine—"

"Of course! You are absolutely right, mam'selle."

"—However, I have also read the works of Baudelaire, and I've found them most intriguing," Carla added politely.

The Frenchman smiled. "Ah, yes, what a genius that man was! He lived only forty-six short years of a life burdened with debts, misunderstandings, and excesses. Throughout his work, there is inner despair. And yet, if one searches, one finds an occasional ray of exquisite light, of hopeful fantasy. The same might be said of Verlaine, of course."

"You speak very movingly about poetry and poets, monsieur," Carla complimented the art dealer. Cordelia smiled approvingly at her protégée, for Carla's fluency in French was rapidly improving and she made herself readily understood. This, to be sure, creditably reflected on the spinster.

"You are very gracious to say so, Mam'selle Bouchard. I will say this about your work—it shows great promise. Finish it, think it over a few days, and if you still like it, bring it back to me. Perhaps we may find a place here for some of your works. I take it that you plan to stay in Paris for a time?"

Before Carla could answer, Cordelia broke in, "She will stay here until she has found herself, Giles. I wish I could have had her opportunity twenty-five years ago. Perhaps, *mon ami*, it would have been you who would have consoled me when poor Emile was taken from me."

"Alas, it was not meant to be—but I should have been a very happy man if it had happened, *ma chère* Cordelia." Giles Vertrier gallantly inclined his head and kissed Cordelia's hand.

One evening the following week, Cordelia Thornberg and Carla Bouchard dined in a small, intimate bistro just off the Rue de Corbier, where the proprietor, a fat, jovial man with an enormous paunch, hurried out from the kitchen in his apron to hug the spinster and insist that she and her lovely companion be his guests. "This is François Monvoisin," Cordelia informed Carla, "and, since you now know French so well, I'm sure you've already translated his name to mean 'my neighbor.' He was literally that three years ago, when I visited Paris by myself while Max went to the Swiss Alps for mountain climbing. Monsieur Monvoisin makes a magnificent quiche lorraine, and he has some beautiful Beaujolais, don't you, *mon vieux*?"

For you, the finest quiche I have ever created with these fat, ungainly hands, *ma belle*." The bistro owner dramatically exhibited his hands and flexed his fingers, then burst into jovial laughter. "But tonight, there is a specialty, *lapin en crème*—a rabbit stew cooked with cream and delightful liqueur that is very subtle but which makes all the difference. Allow me to prepare a meal worthy of this young beauty and you, who will never age or lose her beauty."

The stew was quite as good as François Monvoisin had promised, and Carla—savoring the delicate subtleties of French cuisine—was impressed and also ravenously hungry. Cordelia urged her to drink a good half bottle of a fresh, young Beaujolais, mellow and fruity, with no bite to plague the stomach the next morning.

Thus it was in an effervescent mood that they took a carriage to the soirée held in the apartment of Madame Madelaine Roucalier. "We are invited, *ma chérie*," Cordelia told her young protégée as the fiacre drew up before the apartment in the fashionable Rue des Moulins, "because I've known Madelaine for many years. Since the end of the Franco-Prussian War, she has become one of the leading sponsors and patronesses of the arts, and it is here that we shall enjoy a reading from *Nana*. Did I tell you about Zola?"

"A little. And I did read most of *L'Assommoir*."

"That's right—I gave you my copy last year. It was published in 1877, and it's part of an enormous project that this great genius began just after the dreadful war. Personally, I believe art and culture were reborn after they deposed that stuffy, tyrannical Napoleon III. Anyway, Zola calls it *Les Rougons-Macquart*, and *Nana* is in this series. He depicts the realism of lower and lower-middle class family life and their difficulties, through disease, debauchery, drink, and all the other vices to which mankind so often falls prey. At heart—and I think you've read enough of *L'Assommoir* to agree with me—he is really a social reformer. He is aiming at showing those in power in France that there are still misery, slums, wretched people who subsist on a *sou* or two a day. He has yet to be truly appreciated in the United States, but I predict that, one day, all the world will hear of him, for he battles valiantly against injustice."

When they entered the town house, received by a footman in livery who took their wraps and escorted them into the foyer, their hostess, a sharp-faced but extremely warm woman in her mid-fifties, bejeweled and beautifully gowned, received Cordelia with cries of joy. She then turned to contemplate Carla, pronouncing, "This *petite* of yours has an air, *très raffinée*. She will go far. I see in her eyes a keen eagerness for knowledge, and she is not at all a convent type of girl."

"Decidedly not. I brought her away from a ranch in Texas, and she has already learned to try her wings. Not incidentally, she has great talent as a painter, and one day, Madelaine, I

115

predict that one of her portraits will hang in your salon and be admired by all your distinguished guests. But please, let us go into the salon because I'm eager to hear the reading."

Their hostess led the way, pausing now and again to introduce Cordelia and Carla to several of her guests, who were about to take their seats. Gilt-covered chairs had been drawn up around a podium. The man who would read, Cordelia whispered to Carla, was a professor at the Sorbonne, himself distinguished as a writer, and hoping one day to be elected to the Académie Française.

Carla's first impression was one of almost disbelief: The audience was more than half comprised of women—single women by themselves, all elegantly dressed, chatting, and to her total shock, smoking cigarettes. They held white porcelain ashtrays in their hands and nonchalantly flicked the ashes into them as they continued their whispered conversations. On the far side of the room an elegantly dressed young man, an aesthete, sat next to an exquisite older woman who could have been an artist's model. The woman suddenly slipped her arm around his waist and whispered something into his ear that made him tilt his head back and laugh uproariously—and then he repeated her sally to the man next to him, who joined in the laughter.

There was enthusiastic applause as a tall, gaunt-faced man in his forties walked across the floor, cleared his throat, set a book on the podium before him, and then began to discuss the work of Émile Zola that he was about to read. Carla listened attentively.

Cordelia had told her shortly after their arrival in Paris that the ideal way to use the language was to think in French, not laboriously search for the translation of the English word into the French equivalent. "We have good schools in the United States, *ma chérie*," she had told her protégée, "but unfortunately they treat any foreign language as if it were a classical museum piece. When you wake up in the morning, the first thing you should do is to start talking to yourself in French about how well you slept; and when you breakfast, confirm your impressions. The more you think in the language, the more easily it will come to you. It's true that you have yet to learn the beauties of Parisian *argot*, slang, but that too will come. Besides, you've made wonderful progress—I know that Giles was delighted with you when you could recall that great line of Verlaine's. It shows that you respect his country, his language, and also its great artists. *Brava, ma chérie!*"

The reading lasted a little over an hour, then all of the guests retired into a enormous dining room that had been set up as a buffet, where hors d'oeuvres, various kinds of wine, liqueurs, pastries, and several hot entrees in chafing dishes awaited them on sideboards. Caterers, impeccably groomed in evening dress with black ties and long waistcoats, stood waiting to serve the guests. Carla saw some of the single women she had noticed in the audience approach some of the unattached men and begin to talk quite familiarly, without the least inhibition. She turned to Cordelia. "I can't believe my own eyes! These women are being accepted as complete equals!"

"Precisely. This is the great secret of Paris, which makes it the most intellectual and sophisticated city in all the world, for my money. That's why I brought you here. When you decide to return to the United States, I hope that you will already be an artist of some acclaim. But, even if you aren't, you'll have gained an invaluable and priceless experience that will enrich your life for all the years ahead of you. Contrary to what your father and mother might think, the role of a chaperone, as I see it, is to educate you in the broadest sense, not to keep you hidden away from life. And so, if you find a lover or a husband, depending on your preference, the intellectual freedom you will have here in Paris will make you more of a woman, and thus more of an equal. That's my view, and I shall be eager to see how things turn out for you."

"I can't believe this is happening! It's like a dream, Cordelia. I'm so happy I came!" Carla turned, her eyes shining. "I'd forgotten tonight that I ever was the dutiful daughter of a Texas rancher. Understand me, I love my mother and father very dearly, and I love my brother and sisters, too. But I feel as if I'm a different person tonight."

117

Chapter Twelve

After Ramón Hernandez had left the hacienda of Lucien Edmond and Maxine—on tenuously good terms, following their argument over Ramón's proposed trip—he returned to his own home. There, he had dinner with his family and forced himself to be as genial and tender as he could, though it was an all-too-obvious effort—at least, so far as Mara was concerned. He told the children that he was going off to find their younger sister, Gatita, and that he would come back with her. "And then you will see how happy all of us will be, niños."

That night, for the first time in many weeks, he made love to his wife; yet she felt him to be a stranger in her bed, for he kept his eyes closed while his lips were silently working, and she knew exactly what he was thinking all the while he caressed and embraced her. She tried valiantly to reassure him, to ply him with the sweetest kisses and exhortations, so that he would know she still loved him. Her only assuagement came from telling herself, *This shows that he needs me; it must show that, for otherwise he would not have turned to me when he was in such agony, such black despair. Oh, dear God, I pray to You to bring him back to me safe and sound—in his mind, as well as in his body.*

When she awoke at dawn, the bed was empty beside her, and when she went through the house, she realized that he had already taken his leave. In a way, she rationalized, it showed that he was concerned about her feelings, to spare her this last parting scene. They had had their farewells last night, and so now it was over, and Ramón had gone on with the business at hand. Their lovemaking had renewed her hope for their marriage. It was something she would continue to comfort herself with in the coming months, when she would receive no word from him. And it was her faith in him and her love for him that would sustain her, even when the long, dreary hours and days and nights went on, without any sign of hope, or news of his return. . . .

Ramón had packed his saddlebags with enough provisions for a week and had taken his rifle and a brace of pistols, with sufficient ammunition and gunpowder for all the weapons. In addition, he had strapped around his middle a hand-worked leather belt, decorated with colored beads in the Comanche picture-characters that signified a great hunter, and thrust a Bowie knife into the special holster that Catayuna had made for him.

The belt and its markings had been her Christmas present to him last year. He had thanked her, telling her that if these symbols brought him good luck, then he would believe in her Great Spirit. This remark had distressed the beautiful Mexican woman. Brought up in the Catholic faith, she had succeeded in Christianizing her late Comanche husband, and she now worked with the nuns teaching school at Windhaven Range, piously attending church with unusual regularity. Knowing that Ramón too was of Mexican birth and had always been an unswervingly faithful Catholic, Catayuna interpreted his remark to mean that he was beginning to lose his faith, which disturbed her greatly, though she could sympathize with him. The loss of a child was a horrible tragedy, and she had seen, all during these long, bitter months, the deterioration of his marriage with Mara and his estrangement from the vaqueros.

Ramón headed off toward the south. He had thought of stopping at the small village of Miero, to see his namesake, now almost sixteen, and to visit Magdalena, the woman with whom he had had the son. Never would he forget his debt of gratitude to that kindly woman. She had taken him in all those years ago when he had lain in the dust, bleeding from a near-fatal wound that the bandit chief, Diego Marcaras, had inflicted. However, it would be all too easy to seek solace with her; moreover, she was married now and would be faithful to her vows. No, his appearance in that village would doubtless cause unhappiness—certainly to the husband whom Magdalena had chosen and who deserved much better than to be confronted by a living ghost out of his wife's past. He remembered that Magdalena had said to him, when he had returned the silver crucifix that Macaras had stolen, that she had told the priest about their liaison, and that he had absolved both Magdalena and Ramón of any wrongdoing. No, it was wise to let the past remain buried.

All of the past, that is, except the hellcat who had stolen his child from him and destroyed him in this way. She had done more than kidnap Gatita; she had nearly broken up the marriage between himself and Mara and had made him a pariah among his men, who had once idolized him and would have followed him into the jaws of hell itself had he ordered it. It gnawed on his mind like a cancer, constantly spreading, ever more painful. All through the last year and a half he had heard rumors that someone in a stagecoach, or a lonely rider on horseback, had seen a woman and a little girl fitting the descriptions of Rita Galloway and Gatita—and each time it had turned out to be a false lead.

Perhaps she had taken Gatita closer to Mexico City. Yes, that must be it. Thus far, he had been through the Mexican provinces of Coahuila, Nuevo León, even Chihuahua, and nowhere was there any word or even a hint that a white woman had been seen in that region with a five-year-old girl accompanying her. That *puta* must have gone right to Mexico City; and since she was a *puta*, perhaps she was even now plying her trade in some elegant bordello in the capital. Hot rage flowed through him at the mere thought that his innocent daughter should be exposed to the kind of life that took place in one of those damnable *casas des putas*.

Briefly, he had thought of going in the opposite direction, to the northwest province of Sonora. But to reach sizable towns like Hermosillo or Guaymas, the woman and his daughter would have had to cross the brutal Sierra Madre mountains, only to be then confronted by an endless desert before reaching the Gulf of California. He quickly discarded that locale for the accursed woman and his little girl. The *puta* had enjoyed comparative luxury at the ranch, and back in Leadville, they had treated her to good food and drink, and even bought her clothes. No, she would not have taken the little one to Sonora and starved to death there; the only inhabitants were *peones*, who could probably not manage even a few *centavos* to have a *mujer* when they lusted for one.

So patting Magdalena's neck, he turned the reins first toward Nuevo Laredo, a thriving town to which he had been at least three times. Once there, he would go south through Sabinas Hidalgo, and then on down to the province of San Luis Potosí. This was an area he had not yet visited. Then, he would continue south and west. It would take weeks, months. But he would find her.

As he rode through the brightening day, his face grim with resolution, he glanced up at the cloudless sky and said aloud, *"Dios,* all my life I've lived by Your teachings and those of Your beloved son. Help me believe in You. Why have You visited this upon me? What evil have I done in Your eyes, that You should take Gatita from me and let Mara and me and the children suffer so? If I have sinned, I will atone for it. I beg of you, just and merciful *Dios,* to take pity on a lonely and unhappy father and give him back his child. Surely You, in Your mercy and wisdom, will not let a horrible, accursed woman make away with our innocent little one, unless there is some reason. Give me some sign, I pray to You. I demand it of You, after all these terrible months! Help me restore my faith in You—or I shall lose it, as surely as I am riding south!"

The mare was remarkably sturdy and seemed to have recovered from the exhausting ride that Ramón had demanded of her two nights ago. Remembering that and being contrite, this time he did not drive her quite so hard. When dusk fell, he chose a grassy knoll fortified by a kind of semicircular hedge of mesquite, and just beyond it were a half dozen gnarled scrub trees. He had tethered Magdalena to one of the trees, then made certain that she had enough water and oats to satisfy her. Then making a lonely campfire, he squatted before it, took out some beans and a couple of strips of jerky, and washed this meager dinner down with a swig of coffee. Finally, exhausted, he spread out his sleeping blanket.

At dawn he wakened, paused only long enough to drink more coffee and to gnaw at a strip of jerky without bothering to stew or boil it, then bolted into the saddle and was off again.

When he reached Nuevo Laredo, he went at once to the *posada* of Ernesto Romero, a jovial, enormously fat man in his early fifties who amazingly possessed an exquisitely lyric voice and almost a genius for playing the guitar. He and

Ramón had been friends for at least a decade, and Ernesto had sent several young vaqueros who wished steady employment with opportunity on to Ramón at Windhaven Range. Ernesto was twice a widower, and as Ramón entered his *posada* on the second evening after his departure from the ranch house, the older man was having a party to announce his forthcoming third marriage, to—as he described her—"an absolutely enchanting señorita, *mis amigos,* with glowing black eyes, long legs, and such skin! Ah, I tell you, I feel like. a young *caballero* whenever I am in the presence of *mi dulce* Alicia!"

Catching sight of Ramón, who was edging his way through the enthusiastic customers who filled the *posada,* Ernesto flung up his arms and bellowed, *"Mi compañero, Señor Hernandez! Ven aquí, pronto!"* Then, turning to his customers, he declared, "Here is one of the greatest vaqueros who ever came out of *Nueva España! ¡Es verdad, mis amigos!* Ramón, you are just in time to drink to my health. I am to be married tomorrow."

"Again? What about your second *esposa*?" Ramón called as he made his way toward the bar.

"Alas, she also died, but it was not my fault. My first wife, you may recall, fell from her horse, though I warned her not to ride the animal. The second, may heaven take her sweet soul," here he crossed himself and bowed his head, "ran off with a muleteer, and only last month I learned that he strangled her because she was unfaithful to him. Let us hope that Alicia, who will be my third, will be the charm with whom I can end the long days *nuestro Señor Dios* may see fit to allow me!"

"Amen to that. *Gracias.*" Ramón nodded as Ernesto shoved a glass of tequila toward him. After licking some salt, he lifted the glass and gulped down a large portion, then quickly bit into a lime. He shuddered, for the tequila was raw and fiery, but in the mood he was in, it suited him precisely. "Ten thousand devils must themselves have individually brewed this elixir!" he said in ribald Spanish, at which the crowd roared approval of his good humor—gallows humor, though they could not know it.

"It is true that it is raw and young, but that is precisely what I hope to be on the morrow." Ernesto Romero smirked with a broad grin to overplay the joke, and again his customers burst into laughter and applause.

"What brings you down this way again? Do you need more vaqueros for your fine *estancia*?" Ernesto asked.

"No, *mi amigo*. I am here for the same reason I was last time I saw you. I am still trying to track down that infamous woman who stole my daughter, and I still have no clue as to where they have gone."

"Forgive me." The fat man was humbly contrite and held up a hand to silence the chattering and laughter of the nearest customers who crowded toward him. "I did not stop to think. Here I am in the midst of my merriment, making ready for a wedding, and you have lost that which is almost the dearest thing in the world to you."

"Yes. And why it happened, I still do not know, and I never shall until I track down the accursed *puta*!" Ramón growled, as he turned to his glass, again repeated the ritual of the salt, tequila, and lime, then set the glass down loudly on the table.

"I wish I could console you, *mi amigo*. I am truly desolate. You still have no clue as to where she has gone with the child?"

"I just told you I haven't, you fat pig!" Ramón almost hysterically burst out, glaring at Ernesto. Silenced by this unexpected and vindictive outburst, the men closest to him drew away, whispering among themselves. Ramón put his hand to the handle of his Bowie knife and glared back at them. "Do not look me down, *mis amigos*! I do not seek a quarrel with any of you, not tonight surely. But do not provoke me into one, for I am in a murderous mood. It is not your fault—perhaps it is that of *El Señor Dios*—but, at the moment, I care only that I must go on until I find my child. Ernesto, it was a mistake for me to have come here on such a night. Forgive me. I ask you only, since I was last here, have you heard anyone speak of the woman and the child? I gave you their description when last I was here, and you have a good memory—"

"No, my friend," the fat *posada* owner said, sadly shaking his head. "I have heard not a word."

"Well, this time I shall seek her until I find her, and I shall bring that woman to justice, if it be only by my bare hands around her filthy neck! And if God will not help me, may Satan himself come to my rescue to teach me how to cope with such an evil creature!" Ramón finished his tequila, then

123

hurled his glass against the wall, shattering it. Then he turned on his heel and strode out of the *posada*.

There was a long silence behind him, and some of the men uneasily turned to Ernesto Romero and began to whisper. But the bartender shook his head and put a finger to his lips. "The devil rides with him now. I will pray for him when I go to the church tomorrow to wed with my Alicia. I almost did not recognize him when he came in this evening, *mis amigos*, and I swear to you this is the truth. What has come upon him has changed him terribly." He sighed and shook his head, and the silence in the *posada* was almost palpable. Then Ernesto looked up again and forced a smile to his lips. "*Amigos*, let us regain our happy mood! I shall buy drinks for all of you. Only," he wagged a reproving forefinger at the nearest customer, "you, Humberto, must watch over me as if you were my old *tío* and tell me when I have had too much to drink. Alicia will not marry me if she sees a fat, drunken husband-to-be stagger down the aisle of the Church of the Heavenly Angels."

The powerful tequila Ramón had drunk that evening, far more potent than he had realized, had made him fall fast asleep in the stable to which he had taken his horse. He had slumped down beside his mare, Magdalena, in her stall, and the old stable owner, eyeing him and understanding his condition, had shrugged in commiseration and gone off to leave him in his dreamless sleep. By noon of the next day, he was in the saddle again, having breakfasted only on black coffee and a tortilla. Food meant little to him now. He rode directly southward, exactly as he had planned. Two weeks later, having stopped at almost every little village and hamlet along the way to inquire after Gatita and Rita Galloway and receiving the usual news that no such pair had come that way in the last six months, he rode into the town of Montemorelos in the province of Nuevo León.

On the outskirts of this town there lived a retired *hidalgo* of Madrid, Don Santiago de Colomar. Eighteen years earlier, when young Ramón Hernandez had joined the forces of Major Alfredo Gonzalez on the side of Benito Juarez and had been wounded in the thigh by a French lancer, he had been hidden by friendly villagers who nursed his wound. Six months after that, he joined the band of Diego Macaras, mistakenly believing the man's pompous declaration that he would fight for the justice of Benito Juarez to free the common people against the French usurpers and to unite all of Mexico in a holy war.

Just a month before Ramón had joined this ostensible patriot—who had become the vilest of brigands and assassins—he had been riding alone out of Montemorelos when he had seen an ornate carriage pulled by three superb white horses. Suddenly out of a clump of woods, three bandits flourishing muskets and pistols had come riding, killing the coachman with a single shot and halting the carriage. The occupants were undoubtedly aristocrats, the very class that Ramón had reason to hate because of his father's cruel death at the hands of the corrupt *federalista*, and the young Mexican drew up his horse in the shade of a huge saguaro and waited to see what would take place.

The bandits forced out the occupants of the carriage—the elderly *hidalgo*, his frail, white-haired wife, and their daughter, who was with child. They helplessly stood while the three bandits rode around them, making obscene comments and vicious threats as to what they proposed to do with the trio. Ramón could not stomach this, and so he had spurred his mustang and ridden upon them without warning, leveling his musket and bringing down the leader with the first shot. His pistol accounted for the second, and then, leaping from his horse, he had flung himself at the third bandit, who was reaching for a pistol just as Ramón stabbed him to the heart.

The elderly man he had saved turned out to be Don Santiago de Colomar; his wife died three months later in her sleep. Their daughter was on her way to Matamoros, whence she would embark on a ship bound for Cadiz to rejoin her husband, who had been called back to the Spanish court. Don Santiago had tearfully praised the courage of the young Mexican patriot and had told him that if ever he needed a friend, he should come to Montemorelos.

Ramón did not even know whether the old man was still alive—he would surely be at least eighty by now, he estimated. But in his desolate mood, a friend out of the past would be a welcome anodyne to his maddening grief.

Sure enough, the villa was still there. There was also a majordomo, resplendent in a livery such as used to be worn in the court of Spain. Yes, the majordomo assured him, Don

Santiago was very much alive. He was ushered into the *hidalgo*'s presence, and Don Santiago, after a few moments, slapped his thigh and cried out, "But of course I remember you! You saved my life and, what was more important, that of my daughter and her unborn first child. I have often wondered what has happened to you, *mi amigo*. Come, you are travel weary, I suspect, and you look like you have not bathed or eaten. My majordomo, Luis, will take charge of you and show you to a room. You shall be my guest here."

Ramón remained there for a week, passively enjoying luxuries that he had not known for weeks: warm baths, excellent food, good wine, and conversation that went eternally back to the olden days, when Benito Juarez, a humble peasant, rose to become *el Presidente*. And yet, though this was a welcome respite out of the long months of his agony, Ramón felt once more the torment of balancing what had taken place with what was now.

He told Don Santiago of his despairing and futile quest, which continued to lead nowhere. In reply, the old man was a veritable relic of piety: When he was not talking of the past, he was telling Ramón of his gratitude to God and His wonders for this long, rich life now ending so serenely in a villa where he had no troubles or concerns with what took place beyond his own physical limitations. Don Santiago urged Ramón to attend each morning mass with him in the private chapel at which a young priest presided. Ramón complied, but every time he left the chapel, he felt all the more miserable. What good were prayers, if they would not bring Gatita back, bring that damned *puta* to the justice that even an avenging and fearful God must surely recognize as her merited due? At last, he had saddled his horse, thanked the old man, and promised to return one day—he did not know when.

That week of pious observance had left Ramón even more dubious than ever of the faith to which he had so unswervingly adhered since his boyhood. He did not think he would ever visit Don Santiago again, even if the old man lived on. No, there was nothing here except ghosts of the past, and although they had been happy ghosts at one time, they only served to lead him down this terrible corridor, into a black room where skulls and eerie laughter and the gargoyles out of hell itself mocked him.

*   *   *

By May, he had come to the town of Charcas in the province of San Luis Potosí. Here, at the largest *posada*, he again made inquiries, and by now the questions tumbled into words slurred from the weariness of anguished repetition and the hopeless anticipation of what the answer would be. No and no again, as it had been for months upon endless months. No *gringa* and no little *niña* had been seen in this part of the country. And when the leering owner of the *posada* leaned over the counter, winked at Ramón, and slyly asked, "Is it perhaps your mistress you seek, who has gone off with your child to wed another man?" Ramón seized him by the throat and nearly strangled him. It took three strong men to break that stranglehold and to throw the furious, despairing man out of the *posada*. He lay there all night long, unconscious; in the morning, aching and weary, he mounted his faithful mare, who had stood all night long waiting for him to come back to consciousness. And then he moved on.

This time, aimlessly, he turned to the west. From Charcas, he rode into Zacatecas, the principal city of the province of that name. From there, he followed the road south to Aguascalientes, where, having drunk a whole bottle of tequila during a poker game with three surly Mexican *peones*, he flared into a savage rage when one of them asked him whether he had enough money to afford a *puta* for the night. "I seek only one *puta*, and I will kill her, for she has taken my child from me!" he hoarsely cried out.

The Mexican shrugged, then leaned over to say to his cronies in a stage whisper, "*Un pococito loco, no es verdad?*" Aloud, he jeered, "Señor, I think the fact is that you have no *cojones*. Let us find a *puta* for ourselves, since you will not need one."

With a mad roar, Ramón had lunged across the table, his hands gripping the man's throat. The man's two friends clubbed Ramón into insensibility, then robbed him of what money he had in his pockets, along with his pistols and knife, and flung him out into the night. And once again, faithful Magdalena, whinnying and nudging at him with her muzzle, waited till he came back to consciousness and could again stumble back into the saddle and ride on . . . hopelessly on and on.

By June, Ramón was in Guadalajara, in the province of Jalisco, from where he planned to go west. The *peones*, the

127

travelers, the soldiers on the main road that led from Guadalajara northwest to the coastal plains called him the bearded drunkard. His face was haggard, his beard untended, his eyes unseeing, and many times during the day, he halted Magdalena to lift his canteen filled with tequila to his parched lips, and swallow down a few mouthfuls. He had almost forgotten his name. He knew only that he was a Godless one, for in Zacateras, in Aguascalientes, in Guadalajara, he had shouted in *posadas* that he did not believe in a God who was unjust and cruel and who would punish a man for no reason whatsoever. He had even said this to a priest along the way as he headed westward, and the old priest had crossed himself and said that he would pray for him. "Pray for yourself, fool. It is an illusion—no one will hear you, for no one has heard me!" Ramón Hernandez cried, a glint of madness in his eyes.

When the old priest had vanished into the distance, Ramón stumbled down from his horse, sank down into the dust of the road, covering his face with his hands, and wept. He sobbed aloud, "I cannot believe! I do not believe! I want only my Gatita—and He to Whom we have prayed all these centuries turns a deaf ear to me. Why should I then hearken to His words? But I will find her without Him, in spite of Him—and this I swear, even by hell itself!"

128

Chapter Thirteen

After Rhea Penrock had helped herself to the greenbacks in Jeb Cornish's wallet, she had hurried back to the boarding-house on the outskirts of Dodge City. The best way to elude any possible pursuers, she had decided, would be not by running away constantly and seeking new places in which to hide out, but by remaining in the Kansas area. There, she felt certain, would be the last place people would think of looking for her. Even assuming that Ramón and his partner, Lucien Edmond, could connect her to Dodge City and to her alliance with the dead Indian agent, they would surely assume that this area would be the very last place she would choose in which to evade them.

She had no way of knowing what Cornish's cronies at that card table—at which she had dealt him his last and fatal hand—would tell the authorities about the circumstances of his death, but she correctly reasoned that they would seize the chance of replacing him to their own individual advantage. If anything, they would be the ones most likely held for questioning, and it would require a good deal of inventive skill on their part to extricate themselves from the danger of being jailed and hanged for murder.

These were her thoughts as she left the Comique on that wintry day in December 1880. Back at the boardinghouse, she gave the widow who ran it a ten-dollar bill and thanked her for looking after Gatita. This done, she swiftly packed, and having already purchased a buckboard and two sturdy geldings, she left the boardinghouse with Gatita and headed eastward. Once out of town, she turned the geldings to the northeast, went for about ten miles until she found an abandoned barn, and led the horses into it for the night. There was not a soul around for miles. It was an easy matter to prepare a small fire, take out her cooking skillet and coffee pot, and prepare an adequate, if simple, meal. She had told Gatita, "Now we're going to have a picnic, and then we'll go to sleep. Bright and early tomorrow, we're going to find you a nice new place to live. Maybe we can have a garden and grow flowers."

"I would like that, Auntie Rita," Gatita gleefully replied, but then a frown creased her small forehead. "Won't my mommy and daddy worry about us?"

"Never you fret, Gatita," Rhea had glibly assured the girl as she began the preparations for their supper. "Your mother and father said it was all right for you to come with me. You see, they have to go on a long trip, all the way down to Mexico."

"Oh, my! Daddy is from Mexico, Auntie Rita. Why do he and Mommy have to go there now?"

"They have to visit some friends, Gatita," Rhea quickly countered. It was Rhea Penrock's belief that, within the next few years, she could manage to obliterate all those old memories, leaving nothing but the impressions the child would know from this point onward, those of the rough, cruel way of life Rhea had intended for her little victim.

Yet all during her stay at Windhaven Range the vengeful young woman had spent most of her spare time with Gatita, who had from the very outset shown an affection for her that she had not, in any way, anticipated. That affection had troubled her just before she kidnapped Gatita as the culmination of her vengeance against Ramón Hernandez.

Now, studying the little girl as she prepared some biscuits and warmed a bit of meat, she saw adoration and trust in the child's dark eyes that wrenched at her heart. Until now, Rhea had known the most brutal of lives, and only Gabe Penrock, more considerate than any other man she had ever known, had shown her interest and respect. It was true that their marriage had been based on a violently physical attraction for each other, yet as a lover Gabe Penrock had satisfied her without demeaning her; he had almost erased the painful, awful memories of the run of men who had visited her mother's brothel, like the vicious river pirate who had killed her mother and then raped Rhea.

When Gabe Penrock had died, there had been a tremendous

void in Rhea's life, and she had not dreamed that her intended victim would so swiftly replace and supplant Gabe in her secret affections, in her capacity for love and tender communication.

Looking at Gatita's eager, expectant face, Rhea felt herself touched by the total and unswerving trust from the child whom she had considered as only a pawn in this cruel game of retaliatory chess that she had devised to avenge Gabe's death. She had not been prepared—nor was she now—for its aftermath.

The cold air and the excitement of moving about, together with the food she had consumed, had made Gatita sleepy. As Rhea sat staring into the depths of the gloomy, deserted barn, the girl lay down beside her, turned over onto her side and held out her arms. "Tell me a story, Auntie Rita, please!" she drowsily entreated.

Rhea frowned. The only stories she had known for some years were those bawdy, violently obscene ones with which her customers had regaled her in the hope of proving their virility. This was the first time Gatita had turned to her so confidingly and asked something that she might well have asked her own mother. Once again, Rhea was troubled by the conflicting feelings rising in her. As she searched her mind almost feverishly to remember some story that would satisfy the sleepy child, she glanced almost crossly at Gatita, resenting the child for having forced herself into a situation that she had never in the world anticipated. But those dark eyes, warm and wide and tender, fixed on Rhea with such unswerving attention that she felt her harshness give way to a feeling entirely new, one that she mocked with a kind of angry impatience: *What's all this nonsense about? I didn't bargain for this, and I wish the little brat—no, I can't really call her that, but just the same, why does she have to turn to me as she would to her mother? Her mother and her father will have me strung up quicker than you can spell my name, if they catch me— don't I know it!*

"Are you thinking up a real good one, Auntie Rita?" Gatita again wistfully queried.

As Rhea wracked her brain trying to come up with a story that would satisfy the child, it dawned on her that she really should get Gatita used to calling her by her real name, not Rita. After all, no one here in Kansas—except for Cornish's men—knew that she had kidnapped the little girl, and if Hernandez and Bouchard were out looking for her, surely they would be tracking a woman named Rita Galloway, not Rhea Penrock.

She put her arm around Gatita's shoulders, drawing the child to her. "Gatita," she tentatively began, trying to come up with an explanation that the girl would understand and accept, "you know how you've got a nickname? That is, that your real name is Mara but everybody calls you Gatita?"

"Sure, Auntie Rita."

"Well, I've got a nickname, too, and I prefer it to my real name. Do you think you could call me by it from now on?"

"Sure, Auntie Rita. What is it?"

"It's Rhea. I know it's not too different from my real name, but I just like the sound of it better."

"That's a nice name, Auntie Rit—Rhea. I like it."

Rhea smiled. "So do I. Now, where were we? Let's see . . ."

Then suddenly, as if by a miracle of recall, Rhea remembered one of the stories her mother had told her in the bordello, a story that had nothing to do with the rough, cruel, and brutal life both of them had had to lead. It was the story of "Jack and the Beanstalk."

Her eyes widened and her face brightened. "Sure I have a story, honey. Now you lie back there and close your eyes and listen. I want you to fall asleep. You need it; we've been on the go practically all day, and it's too much for a little girl like you. Okay?"

"Mmmm hmmm, yes, Auntie Rhea. Tell me the story . . . Auntie Rhea. Oh, I'm so tired! Tell me the story right now, please, please?" the little girl begged, her voice slurring off, as exhaustion began to claim her.

Leaning back, closing her eyes, Rhea falteringly began the fairy tale as her mother had told it to her. She had reached the point where the fearless boy had begun to clamber all the way up to the sky, when she turned, her face taut with concern because she had forgotten the next sequence. But Gatita was fast asleep, her arms still clinging around her Auntie Rhea's waist.

Very gently, she grasped the child's limp hands and placed them at Gatita's sides. She then grimaced and said to herself, *Boy, if anyone had told me a couple of years ago I'd be telling bedtime stories to a kid—it's crazy—it doesn't make sense—but what the hell. She's been as good as gold—she's gone along with everything I've said to do, and never complains. . . . Yeah, I'm sure glad that that bastard Jeb Cornish didn't get his hands on her. I hope he's rotting in hell right now.*

Rhea Penrock lay for at least an hour studying the serene, smiling face of her little charge, until at last sleep claimed her that cold, snowy December night. Almost compulsively, she gathered the child to her, under the sleeping blanket, and her face was fanned by the soft, gentle breathing of the girl she had kidnapped from Ramón and Mara Hernandez.

When she awoke at nearly ten o'clock the next day, she stared uncomprehendingly at the still-sleeping, trusting child, and shook her head. Again Rhea was amazed at her protective, almost maternal feelings for the little girl. She recalled now a conversation she and Gabe had had about someday having children. That possibility was forever gone, but Gatita was here now, and Gatita needed her.

After the child woke up, Rhea made breakfast, then harnessed up the geldings to the buckboard. She bundled Gatita up in layers of clothes, and gently lifted the child into the buckboard while she took the driver's seat. Then they went on, heading east. Rhea knew exactly where she was going: toward Preston, where she knew about an abandoned farmhouse. If it were still there, it would make the perfect hideout. There they could live, and no one would bother them. Hernandez would never think of looking for her in Kansas, not after her note. From what she'd stolen out of Jeb Cornish's wallet, they had enough to live on for almost a year, if Rhea was frugal. After that, when it was time to look around and decide what to do next, she would worry about where to go from there.

Gatita threaded her arm through Rhea's and smiled. Rhea looked down at her; she never thought that she would like this innocent little girl, who'd never had anyone to say no to her or do any harm to her. The child's life was totally different from the way Rhea had been brought up. Perhaps one day, when the girl was old enough to understand, Rhea would tell Gatita her story.

"We're going to find a place to live in, honey," she told Gatita, as they jogged along in the buckboard. "Like I promised, we'll have a garden there when spring comes, and you can plant flowers. And we'll grow vegetables, and we'll have picnics and everything.''

"That sounds real nice, Auntie Rhea!" Gatita crooned. She was looking around her, fascinated by these new surroundings.

Rhea felt it obligatory upon her to explain, "The house we're going to, if I can still find it, is going to be dry and comfortable. You'll see.''

"All right, Auntie Rhea," the little girl murmured. The excitement of the last few days, the many new experiences and sights and sounds, the rocking of the buckboard began to tire her, and she closed her eyes, falling fast asleep. Rhea eyed the child; a strange smile softened her incisive mouth, and then she shrugged. *I must be getting soft in the head*, she thought, *as well as in the heart. I am really falling for this little kid. I'll bet the greaser's missing her something fierce by now. Good! He'll know what I felt when Gabe was killed. That high and mighty greaser and the rest of the people on the ranch—they've had it easy all their lives. Now maybe they're suffering a little—maybe a lot. I sure hope so.*

Rhea Penrock remembered that northwest of Preston, about three miles from town, there had been an old but sturdy farmhouse. Gabe had pulled off a robbery in the town with three of Cornish's desperados and told her that a house was there for the taking. Nobody had lived in it for a couple of years, so far as he could figure. He and the trio had stopped there after the robbery to elude any kind of posse that might have been forming, but there hadn't been. Well, that house would make the perfect hideout.

As well as she remembered, there were mostly farms in that area, small places where couples raised pigs and chickens and had produce gardens. They weren't the sort of people who would bother you; they would let you be, so long as you didn't cause a ruckus. Nobody in the world would think of looking for her and Gatita there, she was certain.

It had taken three days to reach Preston after leaving Dodge City. The second night out, they had stopped over at an isolated farmhouse, planning to offer to pay for food and lodging. There'd been an old couple living there, and they'd been so glad to have the young woman and child for company that they refused to take a penny for putting them up. In addition, when Rhea and Gatita were about to leave the next morning, the old homesteaders insisted that they take provisions for a few days.

Shortly after two o'clock of the third day out they came upon the deserted farmhouse. It was exactly as Gabe had described it, and it was in pretty good condition, too. It would need plenty of dusting and cleaning, of course, but she was used to that. She'd tidied up Gabe's place when they'd been married, and he told her she was a darn good housekeeper, and a good cook, too.

She lifted Gatita out of the buckboard and went on into the house to inspect it. Whoever had built it had done a good job combating the bitterly cold winters in Kansas. The hewn logs were fitting, and the chinks had been so tightly sealed that the cold wouldn't blow in. There was even a fireplace, and the first thing Rhea did was to build a fire after making sure the chimney was clear and the damper was open. An hour later, she was preparing a meal in a cast-iron kettle that had been left behind by the previous owners. Gatita was wide-eyed and eager to know what they were going to have for their picnic supper.

After she had fed the child and put her to bed, using the blankets and sheets she had brought with her from the Dodge City boardinghouse, she stalked through the house, planning how it could be made into a comfortable, permanent home. Gabe had shown her how to do a good many things, like using a hammer and saw, and whenever he had been away she had always relied on herself; this would be no different, except that it would mean more chores. Still and all, it was worth it. Here they would be absolutely hidden away from everyone. There was a small general store in Preston, and the next day she would go there and purchase enough supplies— and various sundries to improve the house—to get them well through the first month or two. There was an old ramshackle barn, which would be fine for the buckboard and the geldings. She was used to riding bareback, but she could always buy a saddle in town.

Hidden in the duffle bag she had brought along from Dodge City was the money from Jeb Cornish's wallet, which had amounted to over eighteen hundred dollars. That would be quite enough to live on for a good period of time if she managed properly. The land here was not too bad, so it would be easy to raise some fruits and vegetables. As for meat, she was pretty certain that she could buy a steer and have a farmer slaughter and even cut it up for her.

The duffle bag also held a bottle of excellent rye whiskey. Rhea thought that she deserved a drink after what had been accomplished in this brief week. She was at last free of the odious influence of the fat Indian agent—indeed, if anything, she figured that she was owed a reward for having rid the world of an out-and-out bastard, thief, and murderer. Of course, Gabe had been an outlaw, but what he had done paled into insignificance beside Cornish's nefarious schemes all through the last few years. How different life would have been if Gabe hadn't been killed. . . . Her face hardened as she poured herself a stiff drink, gulped most of it down, then sat brooding and thinking.

The following morning, she hitched up the buckboard and drove into Preston to the general store. There was an affable, bespectacled, wiry old man in his late sixties—so far as she could judge—who ran it, and he greeted her with the kind of courtesy and attentiveness that only a rural shopkeeper could muster. She told him that she had just come from Philadelphia, where she had attended her brother's funeral, and her widowed sister-in-law had run away with a traveling drummer, leaving the little girl behind. Out of deep concern for the child and love for her brother, she had decided, since there were no other living relatives, to bring the child to Preston with her to settle down. Her story was readily accepted; the storekeeper clucked his tongue in sympathy and shook his head, commenting on the amorality of the world in general and of flighty wives in particular. She bought Gatita a few dresses, some shoes, and underclothes, as well as some furnishings for the house. A rickety old table and several chairs had been left there by the last owner, but the bed was nothing more than an iron cot with a sagging mattress. So she purchased a new bed and mattress and was told by the shopkeeper that he would be happy to deliver it late that afternoon. Finally, she bought food supplies and some candy for Gatita.

Having established herself as an acceptable newcomer to Preston, she went back to the house and began her task of

136

mothering the little girl, who with each new day had begun to depend more and more upon her for love and affection, for conversation, for things with which to occupy her curious young mind.

By the following April in the year of 1881, Rhea Penrock had turned the old farmhouse into an extremely comfortable home. The seeds they had planted in flower beds around the house had started to come up, and in the vegetable garden out behind the house, Rhea and Gatita had planted tomatoes and potatoes; there would even be some golden bantam corn ready by late summer. She had planted two rows of it after learning from the hired hand at the nearest farm some four miles southeast how to plant and how to lay furrows. She had bought a small plow, and attaching one of the geldings to it and steering it with her hands, she had dug the rows and planted the seed. Gatita had made a game of it with her, and that had made the task cheerful and not the least onerous. When the stalks had begun to grow, it was a good feeling. She had also repaired the roof with some shingles and bought some more secondhand furniture and additional housewares.

Now, in this second warm spring, she was teaching Gatita how to read and write. Rhea had discovered that she had a certain skill in making homemade toys, and she made Gatita a doll that the child took to bed with her every night, hugging it and kissing it. By now, also, Gatita Hernandez had stopped asking anxious questions on the subject of when she would go back to her mother and father. She followed Rhea around the house like a little puppy, laughing and telling stories, plainly happy to be with the handsome young woman.

For Rhea Penrock, whose life had been bitter and harsh and who had grown up on a diet of distrust, suspicion, and wariness, this attention had the effect of a spring sun's thawing winter ice. Rhea's brooding moods and her fits of despondency had been lifted, and she quite frankly enjoyed having Gatita around her all the time. The child's quick praise—for Rhea's making a toy or preparing especially tasty meals, which the child still referred to as "picnics"—had given the vengeful and vindictive young widow a singular new motivation. She strove to win the girl's favor by good works, and to herself she had even begun to gloss over the real reason for having stolen Gatita from her parents.

137

By using the money wisely and by supplementing their diet with vegetables from their garden, Rhea estimated that she and Gatita could easily manage through all of this year. After that, doubtless it would be time to move on. But for the moment, she was happier than she had been since the day Gabe Penrock had asked her to marry him.

As for Gatita, the intense concentration of attention—solely upon her, with no brothers and sister to be rivals for it—made her blossom. She was enthusiastic and excited about the wonderful new things that were happening to her. She particularly enjoyed the daily lessons in reading and writing—especially Rhea's warm praise when she spelled out a difficult word, or was able to read from a dusty primer the young widow had purchased at the general store.

Indeed, Rhea comprised so much of Gatita's world that already—in just a few short months—the child seldom thought of, nor even remembered, her home and family on Windhaven Range.

Chapter Fourteen

This spring of 1882 along the Eastern Seaboard was seasonably warm, and in New York City pedestrians were massing on the streets throughout the bustling, growing metropolis. The Italian organ-grinders were out in full force, sometimes as many as three or four on a single block, creating a jangling cacophony that at least delighted the children. There were also brass bands, groups of four of five street musicians, mainly of German extraction—since by now the city's population had been greatly swelled by heavy German immigration, which had begun three years earlier. Taking pains not to congregate on the same street, these bands drew the attention of adults who stopped to listen to sentimental airs that recalled to them other springtimes years ago, when they had been young and courting and carefree.

There were vendors pushing handcarts filled with hot chestnuts, plying their wares and ringing handbells to attract the passersby. Others sold pretzels and buns with Thuringer sausages, flavored with thick dollops of horseradish or strong mustard. New Yorkers with strong constitutions could walk as far as the Fulton Market on the East River, where catches from scores of fishing boats were unloaded and sold on the spot. There one found open-air stalls purveying oysters, beer, watermelons, and steamed buns with meat or cheeses. Or, if a pedestrian wished to avoid the teeming area of the East River, he might go over to the West Side, to visit the Washington Market, which extended along the Hudson River from Fulton as far as Vesey Street. At that market a panorama of low, straggling sheds was separated into irregular lanes and stalls, where vegetables, fruits, fish, and meats were sold both wholesale and retail. The Manhattan Abbattoir was located between Eleventh and Twelfth Avenues and Thirty-fourth and Thirty-fifth Streets, and here about ten thousand head of cattle each week were slaughtered and cut into meat to feed the hungry populace. The cattle were landed on the Hudson River dock through a tunnel leading from the wharf, and their carcasses were refrigerated in ice houses until they were ready for shipment and carted off. From this wharf, more than forty-one thousand live head of cattle were sent abroad each year, mainly to England.

Other harbingers of spring were the auctions, informal sales held out of booths or stalls located on many corners throughout the residential areas of New York. The housewives who lived in this crowded city arrived at the auctions early to search for bargains, especially when the weather was as fair as it was on this bright April day.

But the fine weather had also attracted gangs of toughs from the slums, youths ranging in age from fifteen to nineteen—some even younger—taking up entire sidewalks and jostling aside passersby with sullen looks and verbal threats to those who would not give way. As their fancy took them, they accosted the elderly and solitary walker, who would be easy prey. They would beat and rob the defenseless man or woman and laugh over the victim's helplessness as he or she lay in the gutter, wailing for the police, who rarely came quickly enough. By the time the authorities did arrive, the gang usually had already vanished, to spring up blocks and blocks away to continue their depredations. Many of these toughs carried cudgels, and some even used knives and brass knuckles, which let a wiry stripling of thirteen administer a blow that would shatter an adult's jaw or skull, or break his nose.

Leland Kenniston had established a suite of offices for his import-export business uptown near where the new Metropolitan Opera was being erected at Broadway and Thirty-ninth Street. It was to this area that many of the wholesale trades were moving, and the city officials were predicting that in a few years' time, many of the major department stores would also be heading northward. Always anxious to be in the forefront of new movements in enterprise, Leland had decided to move out of his old office downtown—which was by now too small to comfortably house his business—and relocate. This new location gave him the bonus of much-needed additional warehouse space.

Many of his employees—as well as Leland himself—gravitated at lunchtime to a nearby tavern, one of hundreds in New York City where one could eat what amounted to a full-course dinner for the price of a single drink, with a varied assortment of dishes from which to select. It was customary at these elaborate establishments to tip the waiter twenty-five cents. Jacob Cohen, Leland's jewelry expert, however, rarely ate at any of these restaurants and bars because he adhered to the diet prescribed by his Orthodox Jewish faith. At times, though, if he had to work late, he would go to one of these establishments that specialized in kosher food for a filling soup, a roll, and strong coffee.

On this April evening, Jacob had to work later than usual; he had to answer correspondence from Amsterdam—where he had established valuable contacts for the acquisition of quality diamonds—regarding an assortment of smaller cut stones that could be made into rings or bracelets. Leland had authorized Jacob to employ a number of expert jewelers and goldsmiths to fashion the unmounted stones into finished pieces, and these men, who were from Russia or Germany, unvaryingly shared Jacob's religious beliefs.

Leland had arranged for these employees to work in a narrow two-story building next to that in which his offices were quartered. As a precaution, the building displayed no sign that might induce robbers or thugs to visit the workshop and make away with a valuable haul of precious stones. To further guarantee the safety of these men—most of them of middle and advanced age—the doors were kept bolted, and the only access was through a code of special knocks. When the workmen left, they left individually and at staggered times, so that there would be no suspicions aroused among those who might be watching the building and find it singular that a group of five or six men would emerge at one time.

The letter from Amsterdam told Jacob Cohen that a large shipment of cut diamonds would be sent, carefully packed and camouflaged, on a steamship leaving Rotterdam at the end of the month. He was relieved to learn of the shipment, for he knew that his workmen were running low on merchandise, and that there were several large orders coming in from New Orleans, San Francisco, and Hong Kong. A rich dowager in San Francisco, for example, had ordered a diamond necklace, no stone of which should be less than three carats, all matched and flawless, set into a pure platinum filigree chain. It was an extraordinarily profitable order, and Jacob was particularly anxious about it. He would have liked to argue the setting, for the metal might be spun too thin to bear the weight of the stones; also, he privately considered such a necklace grotesquely exaggerated and, if worn in public, a sure invitation to theft. Nonetheless, the woman had already paid a deposit of a third of the estimated price, and she could not be denied, for her word carried considerable weight in the socialite circles of the City by the Bay.

Jacob suddenly looked up from his work and realized that a good three hours had passed since he had bidden a cordial good night to the middle-aged woman, Mrs. Ellen Hartung, whom Leland Kenniston had hired as a combination filing clerk and stenographer. He smiled to himself, thinking of her prim efficiency when he dictated his letters to his foreign contacts. She took them down in that strange language she called Pittman Shorthand before transcribing them on the Remington typewriter, which sat on its own special table. With a weary sigh, Jacob rose and stretched, and then he locked up the office and walked down the stairway out into the street.

He walked to the adjacent two-story loft, where his artisans were laboring, and unlocked the street door. Going up the stairs and down the hall, he reached the door and gave the signal of five short, quick knocks, a pause, and then three short knocks. After a moment, the door was opened by Max Brundig, a stoop-shouldered Jew from Berlin wearing a *yarmulke*. His only vice was the constant smoking of hand-rolled cigarettes, of which he was inordinately fond and about which his pious wife, Rebecca, indignantly sermonized him every day when she detected the odor of tobacco on his clothes and beard. *"Wie geht's, Herr Cohen?"* Max inquired.

"Ganz gut, mein Freund." Jacob Cohen inclined his head to the other workers, who greeted him by making gestures with their hands, their eyes still glued to their work. "I have some very exciting news. There will be a large shipment of the finest quality grade stones due here in about three weeks. This will help us to make Mrs. Gowdy's famous necklace. You, Max, will be responsible for the filigree work—and I confess I am still worried about it."

"Have no fear, *lieber* Herr Cohen. I shall be very careful

with it. It shall have the necessary weight for strength, and be of delicate-looking appearance, which is essential.''

"I agree. Well, I just closed up, so now I'll be going home. Thank you, gentlemen. Incidentally, very soon, my wife and I would be happy to have you all as our guests at *Shabbes*, perhaps in two or three weeks. Let me know which Friday would be best for you.''

This time, the others turned away from their work and acknowledged the warm invitation with smiles. All of them liked Jacob Cohen because, although he was the "big boss," he was, as Max Brundig put it, "a real *Mensch*." Aside from other considerations for his employees, Jacob had seen to the installation of a gas burner, so that his men could have strong, hot tea whenever they wished. Next to a rack of cups was a plate of sugar, for some of the workers of Russian descent liked the old way of drinking their tea through a lump of sugar, which they kept in their mouths as they swallowed. There was also a plate of *matzohs*, to ease any hunger that should come upon them during the late hours of their toil.

"You go home now, Herr Cohen, and have no fear. The work will be done to specifications, *wie immer*," Max Brundig assured him with a patriarchal smile.

"And so *you* do not fear, Mr. Kenniston has arranged to have a patrolman stand near the building in the evening, just to make certain that no one comes upon you with any evil intentions," Jacob retorted, and grinned. "Do not forget, also, that this new-fangled telephone is connected to the precinct police station, so that if you suspect anyone is trying to break in, or you do not like what you hear outside, you have only to pick it up, and they will send men who will protect you.''

"*Ach*, this is better than the old country, for certain," Max chuckled. "I feel safe now, and it is a good thing. When a man has freedom and safety, he can do his best work. I wish you and your family a *guten Abend*, Herr Cohen.''

Jacob nodded, shook hands again with the old German, and waved a farewell to the other workers. They responded with mumbled greetings, for already they were back to their work so as not to lose a moment of time.

Jacob Cohen closed the door behind him and heard the bolt thrust home, then nodded with a smile of satisfaction as he went down the stairs and out onto the street. For some reason, he felt the urge to walk home, although it would be many blocks from here to his home on the East Side on Sixteenth Street. It was a pleasant night, and there was a half-moon. A ring around it foretold the coming of rain the next morning, but the air was still warm and the wind had died down so that he fancied that it was almost late May or early June. The news from abroad about the diamonds had excited him, and his mind was occupied with the intricate details of putting together the ornate necklace for the San Francisco dowager. It would certainly be a striking piece, extremely unusual, and if this woman's influential and wealthy friends saw her wearing it, they might well inquire where she had obtained it. That would mean more business for Jacob's benefactor, Leland Kenniston.

He felt a surge of great affection when he thought of that man, and an equal liking and fondness for young Paul Bouchard, who had become such a good friend to his own son, David. Jacob was still, on occasion, tempted to pinch himself for reassurance that all that he had was not a dream: a spacious new apartment, so wonderfully clean and with so many devices to ensure comfort such as they had never known in the old country; good schools for the children; a fine salary that allowed him money to spend on his family, as he'd not been able to since fleeing Kiev; and such warm, good friends to brighten his mind and let his intellectual capacities come to full flowering. He was happiest for Miriam; her involvement in the settlement project was a wonderfully humanitarian thing. Assuredly, there had been nothing like that in Kiev, where the old people were expected to die as quickly and unobtrusively as possible—especially if they were Jews—so that they would not be in the way of people who really mattered.

He had reached Twenty-sixth Street near Sixth Avenue when he saw a group of five shabbily dressed youths come out from the shadows of a corner store across the street. "Wait a bit, Grandfather," one of the boys called, then burst into laughter and turned to whisper something to his friends, who nodded as they advanced toward Jacob.

Feeling uneasy, he quickened his footsteps and looked around. There was no one else on the street, and the shops were all closed. He kept walking, but their footsteps kept apace with his.

"Didn't I tell you to wait, old man?" the same harsh, jeering voice broke in upon him. Then a rough hand grabbed his shoulder and spun him around. Jacob found himself looking at five smirking, leering youths, some with the scraggly beginnings of mustaches over their mouths. Two of the boys could not have been more than fourteen, but they were sturdy and stocky: typical products of the slum, who had grown up and learned to defend themselves and to be the aggressors, so that they would not themselves be the victims.

One of them, a black-haired, surly-faced boy with a bad eruption of acne on his cheeks and lower forehead, sniggered, "Hey, Teddie, this guy's a kike!"

"Yeah," agreed the tallest boy with the harsh voice who had first hailed him. "Sure is. You can tell just by the size of that beak on his face. Hey, Grandpa, you've gotta learn to have more respect for us West Side Terriers, get me?"

"Gentlemen, I want no trouble. I am on my way home now, after a hard day. I would be appreciative if you would allow me to go on," Jacob said, forcing a pleasant smile to his face. His heart had begun to beat faster, and he could not suppress the trembling that suddenly seized him. He saw still more ominous signs. All of the five had their fists clenched, and they were forming a half circle around him, backing him up against the window of a clothing shop.

"Oh, guess he doesn't like our style, Buddy," one of the younger boys piped up. "This kike has got to be taught respect for the Terriers. Let's give him a good lesson." Then, grabbing the lapel of Jacob's coat, he thrust his leering face up against his victim's and snarled, "First off, you'd better dish out all the money you've got in your pockets, Grandfather Kike! Come on! If you don't, you'll get a worse wallopin'!"

Jacob resigned himself to being robbed; besides, his Orthodox faith prevented his defending himself in a violent manner. He had a sickening feeling in the pit of his stomach, but he hoped that if he gave them money, that would be enough to buy his release. He swore to himself that he would never tell Miriam or David or Rachel about what was happening now. It was unbelievable! Why, these young toughs acted like Cossacks back in the old country!

"Hurry up now, get a move on—we ain't got all night,"

145

one of the older boys growled, and then with his fist he struck Jacob a soft, glancing blow on the side of the neck.

"I'm doing it, I'm doing it! Please don't hurt me! I just want to get home to my family, don't you understand?" Jacob pleaded. At the same time, he fumbled for his wallet in his trousers pocket and drew it out.

Before he could open it, the eldest boy—the first to accost him—pulled it out of his hand and opened it. "Hey, this kike's rich—sixty bucks! Well, that's your contribution, you dirty Christ-killer! It ain't half enough, no how!"

"Please, I've done nothing to you—I don't know you—I want no trouble—"

"But you're gonna get it, just like every other goddamned kike should!" the gang leader growled. Then, without warning, he balled his fist and struck Jacob in the stomach, doubling the man up and making him collapse onto one knee. He was instantly hauled up by his coat, and all five boys began to pummel him with their fists. His face was so lacerated that his clothes were spattered with his blood. He fell several times to the pavement, only to be pulled up and mercilessly struck again and again by all of the toughs. After the last beating, he lay panting, nearly unconscious from the pain, his face covered with blood, his lips and eyes swollen, and his nose badly bloodied. The youngest boy, standing over him, spat at him and jeered, "Mebbe we oughta give the kike back a couple bucks so he can buy a steak for that shiner he's gonna have, haw haw! Okay, Terriers, we've done with this dirty Christ-killer—"

The gang leader pushed his younger crony out of the way and, standing over Jacob, spat into his face. He angrily growled, "Don't you ever let us see you again in our territory, Grandfather Kike! Boy, won't we have something to tell Father Delaney when we go to mass tomorrow night! Any time us Irish Terriers can't give a Christ-killer what's coming to him, we ain't fit to wear the green! Awright, guys, let's beat it before a copper comes along!"

Then the street was totally silent. Incredibly, no one had heard or seen this brutal beating. Jacob struggled to his feet, gasping for breath. He groped for a handkerchief and began to touch it to his face, grimacing at the sight of all the blood. There was no help for it; he had to go home—and now he didn't have a cent left to hire a hansom cab. He was so dazed and incredulous over the unexpected and brutal attack by such young boys that he did not stop to think that Miriam would have money at home to pay the driver.

And so Jacob unsteadily started homeward, putting a hand against windows and walls for support until he had regained some strength.

About a half-dozen blocks onward, he was stopped by a policeman, who took a look at him and in an unmistakable Irish brogue solicitously asked, "What's the matter, mister? Can I help you?"

Jacob was about to tell the man what had happened, but then hesitated. He irrationally feared that this Irish patrolman would take the side of his attackers. "No—th-thank you, Officer—I—I'm going home—I fell down and hurt myself, but I'll be all right."

"I dunno about that, mister." The policeman scratched his head and dubiously eyed Jacob. "You sure got a lot of blood smeared all over you. You just fell, you said?"

"Yes, s-sir. Please—I'm very late now, and my wife will be worried about me. I can manage. Thank you, Officer."

"Well, if you say so, mister. Good night, then. You better get yourself patched up when you get home, though. Good night."

Jacob lifted a weary hand to acknowledge the partrolman's salutation, took several deep breaths, and again steadied himself with his right palm against the wall of a corner building. Then he continued his journey.

He did not reach home until after ten o'clock, and by then Miriam Cohen was extremely worried. He had seldom stayed out so late before, certainly not without telling her in advance. David and Rachel were busy doing their homework in the kitchen, and she had made them strong, hot tea and some *challah* as a late snack. She wondered if Jacob had eaten, and she turned to the pot in which she had made a rich chicken-vegetable soup. She would keep it hot because she was sure that Jacob would enjoy a bowl when he got home, even if he had eaten dinner at the kosher restaurant near where he worked.

She heard the key turn in the lock and hurried out of the kitchen to greet her husband. When she saw his face, swollen and puffy with dried blood on it, she threw up her hands and

147

uttered a cry of horror: *"Gottenyu!* What in the world has happened to you, Jacob? Oh, what has happened to you?"

"It is nothing, my dear one. I—I fell down. I—I lost my footing because the street was dark, and I stepped down off the curb and fell. That's all. It's nothing to worry about."

"Nothing to worry about, indeed! With your clothes soiled and torn, your eyes swollen, those terrible bruises—and your nose and mouth! Oh, my poor darling, Jacob, it was more than a fall!"

Hearing the voices of his father and mother, David hurried out of the kitchen. He gasped when he saw his father. "What happened? Papa, you're all bloody—how did it happen?"

"Your father says he fell," Miriam said as she turned to her son. "I do not really believe it. A single fall on the street couldn't do all that damage. Jacob, you are hiding something from us! We have a right to know! We are your family."

"It—well, it—there were some boys. They saw me, and they—they asked for money. But even when I gave it to them, it didn't satisfy them. So—well, they—they beat me up, you might say."

"And you didn't fight back, Papa?" David indignantly countered. "We're in America now, Papa, and we have to act like Americans!"

"I know, *boychik,* but—" Jacob faltered.

"No, Papa, I have to say it. Once before, you didn't fight, but you let the Cossacks take everything you ever worked for. Papa, are we going to have to run away again? Do we always have to run away? I won't run, Papa! I'll fight! You know I'm taking boxing lessons with Paul, and if that ever happens to me, I'll fight them!"

"But it says in the Torah that a soft answer turneth away wrath, and that a good Jew does not show violence, even to his enemies."

"Then the Torah is wrong, Papa, and the Torah doesn't know anything about America, where everybody is free and equal!" David indignantly declared.

"David, David, that is no way to speak to your father." Miriam was consternated at her young son's fiery stand.

"I'm sorry, Mama, and I don't mean any disrespect. You know I don't, because I love you both very, very much. Only I can't stand to see Papa just take a bearing without defending himself. I wouldn't ever do that. That only encourages stupid people like that to try it again. You have to defend yourself, Papa. Then they'll respect you, and they'll let you alone the next time."

"Instead of lecturing your father, you who are still green behind the ears, *boychik*," his mother irritatedly countered, "you would do well to help your father lie down on the couch and then to get some towels. I will heat some water, and we will try to wash the blood off his face and make him comfortable."

"Of course I will, Mama. Here, Papa, lean on me. . . ."

Wearily, Jacob let himself be led over to the comfortable couch, sank down on it, and uttered a long sigh of relief. His head throbbed from the merciless beating, and he was feeling nauseated from the blow to his stomach.

Rachel, who had heard the raised voices, came running into the parlor, and she began to cry when she saw her father lying on the couch. But, being of a practical nature, she hurried to get a towel while her mother carried a basin of hot water into the room. Rachel dipped the towel into it and began very carefully to lave Jacob's bloodied face. She then got a pillow and put it under her father's head, so he could be more at his ease.

"Have you had anything to eat, Jacob?" Miriam asked her husband.

He shook his head, too exhausted to speak.

"Then you are going to have a large bowl of my chicken soup, Mr. Jacob Cohen," Miriam announced, "and do not give me any argument about it."

He smiled wanly, shook his head, then winced at the pain it cost him. "I—I'll eat it, Miriam. Maybe it will make me feel better."

"You would have felt better if you had fought against those brutes." David could not resist another sally.

But a warning glare from his mother told him that he was on dangerous ground, and so David shrugged and went out to the kitchen to ladle out a brimming bowl of hot, rich soup. Drawing up a chair, he sat beside the couch and spooned soup to his father's lips. Jacob docilely ate it and then closed his eyes. "I just want to rest a little, David. Thank you, my son. You are very kind."

"Papa, come with me and take boxing lessons." Again

149

David could not suppress his anger and indignation at the treatment his father had received from the hooligans.

Miriam, who was heating more water and had sent Rachel to get another towel, overheard this. Her hands on her hips, she came back into the room and berated her young son. "I told you, that is enough of that sort of talk, David! Good heavens, are you forgetting that a boy owes his father respect? You are lecturing him and scolding him as if you were grown up, and you have no right to do that. Your father works hard to provide for all of us, and you must not criticize him because of his faith."

"I don't mean to, Mama." David's exasperated yet contrite tone showed the struggle taking place within him. "It's only that I wish Papa had been able to fight back against them and make them feel some of the pain they forced on him, that's all."

"I suggest we not talk about it any more. Then maybe your father will be able to forget it," was Miriam's tart reply.

Chapter Fifteen

Jacob Cohen felt well enough the next morning to go to work, though Miriam tried to dissuade him. "You look just dreadful, my dear," she anxiously decided. "Your eye is still swollen, and that terrible bruise below it—I must say, unless you really have to go in, you should stay home and rest."

"No, Miriam, it is my duty. I feel well enough, truly I do. Besides, I need to tell Leland that the workers have been told about the shipment of diamonds. They will need to give priority to some of the other jewelry on order before the stones arrive, so that then they can concentrate on the San Francisco piece."

"He will probably already know that, my dear," his wife patiently retorted, "but I won't stop you. I know what you mean when you say that it is your duty. And a wife should never interfere with her husband's duty. That, too, Jacob, is in our Torah."

"Now are you sermonizing me, woman of my heart and life?" he mockingly countered, rolling his eyes ceilingward. "You begin to sound a bit like David."

"Well, it would do you no harm, with all respect to the Holy Book, if you were to defend yourself, so that things like this do not happen again," she admitted. "Wait, I will pack you a lunch, so you will not have to go to the restaurant this noon."

"You spoil me, Miriam." Awkwardly, he put his arm around her shoulders and kissed her on the cheek. She turned to him, her eyes suddenly sparkling with tears. "I don't spoil you; I just love and respect you—you, the husband who fulfilled all my dreams and who brought me to this wonderful country of freedom, the father of my children, two such wonderful children of whom we could not be prouder. Now you sit down and close your eyes and rest a bit, while I prepare your lunch.''

"To hear is to obey, for there is no discounting the wisdom of a woman,'' he sallied as he made a wry face.

"And from what part of the Torah is that, Jacob?'' she asked suspiciously.

"It is not. I simply made it up on the spur of the moment.''

"It is not bad. You may have missed your calling. Perhaps you should have been a rabbi.''

"And you, a *rebbitsin,* a rabbi's wife, who is herself ordained to preach the holy words.''

"Oh, get along with you, Jacob Cohen! You cannot hope to soft-soap me by making up these quotations of yours. But I tell you what I will do—I will write it down after you've gone to work, and I will look at it and say, 'This is what my wise, revered husband says, and so it must be true.' Yes, Jacob, your words of wisdom will be remembered. Now rest, as I told you to!''

He made a hopeless gesture with both hands, as if to indicate that there was no accounting for the disposition of women and of his wife in particular. But the tender look he gave her when her back was turned belied any irritation.

Then minutes later, she handed him a metal lunchbox lined with paper. "There is an egg sandwich and one of cheese, and there is an apple. That should be nourishment enough until you come home tonight, Jacob. Don't forget to eat slowly. And most of all,'' she wagged a reproving forefinger at him, "forget about the business when you eat. Your lunch hour is certainly your own time, and you should cleanse your mind of all unnecessary thoughts about work. Close your eyes and relax as much as you can. It will help make the pain go away.''

"Truly, woman, perhaps instead of being a *rebbitsin,* you should have been a doctor.''

"I know. I am certain that I missed several callings—but when I met you in Kiev, I knew that you would be my life from then on. You surely do not regret that I did not pursue the other fields you tell me I may be qualified in,'' she gently poked fun at him.

Jacob hugged and kissed her. "Woman, I know that your bark is worse than your bite, and that you do this out of love

152

for me. I did not mean to tease you, and I love you very much. Now, I will go to work.''

"May *Yahweh* guide your footsteps and bring you back safely. And try not to fall off the curb again." She could not help a last sly little joke.

Jacob laughed, then winced, for his face still hurt. He nodded a goodbye, then left the apartment.

He had gone into the office by the side door, wanting to avoid the clerk who sat in the foyer of the suite and announced visitors and clients to Leland Kenniston and the other managerial personnel of the firm. But, as luck would have it, just as he was about to slip into his office undetected, Leland turned down the hall and came up to him. "My God—what happened to you, Jacob?"

"Oh—g-good morning, Leland—" he stammered. "It—it is nothing. I—I fell down the stairs." Almost childlike, the diamond expert put his right hand behind his back and crossed his fingers, the age-old symbol of seeking exoneration for a white lie or a fib. "It was very foolish of me to be so clumsy."

"You fell down the stairs? You mean, in the building next door where your workmen are?"

"Why, yes, that's it! Down the stairs next door," Jacob repeated, seizing upon the escape gambit just offered to him.

"That could have been very dangerous, Jacob. You might have broken your neck. I'm worried about you. Maybe you're working too hard. Perhaps what you need is a vacation."

"Oh, no, Leland! I'm fine. I was just clumsy and didn't look where I was going and it was dark."

"There is a gas jet and a globe on the stairs there, which should be light enough, Jacob. Wasn't it working?"

Uncomfortably, Jacob fidgeted, inwardly pained. He regarded lying as a moral sin, and here he was compounding it by inventing details of an incident that had never taken place. Even the matter of crossing his fingers behind his back did not purge him, for he was the very soul of ethics, a characteristic that was the spiritual effect of his deep devotion to his religious faith.

"Well," he hedged, "perhaps I had my mind on that necklace for the San Francisco woman, L-Leland. Yes, that's it. I was thinking so much about it and the filigree work that

153

has to hold the diamonds together and yet be strong enough without looking cumbersome—I didn't have my mind on my footsteps, and that's how it happened."

"All right, then, maybe that's a good lesson to you to be more careful and not to worry so much about business. I don't want you going home from here, Jacob, so full of the job that you jeopardize your health or a normal life with your family. I don't think I'm that severe a taskmaster."

"Oh, you're not, Leland. You know you're not! You're a wonderfully kind and sympathetic man, and I value your friendship beyond what I can tell you."

"And I feel the same way about you, Jacob. That's why I insist that you take better care of yourself."

"I—I promise I will, L-Leland."

"Good! By the way, you told your men that the diamonds should be here within a month?"

"I did, Leland, and they're all very excited. Max Brundig promised he'll give us his very best."

"In that case, we'll make the woman happy, and we'll probably get a great many more orders as a result of her influence in San Francisco society. This is how modern business expands, Jacob—and you're the one who's responsible for it. Well now, I've got to go back to my office. Now you remember what I said: Take good care of yourself!"

For the rest of the day, Jacob did his best to avoid Leland. At five-thirty, having worked an extra half hour after he had been told that his employer had left for the day, Jacob decided to go home. He hailed a passing cab to take him to his apartment, and the friendly hack driver tried several times to engage him in conversation about the weather and politics. But receiving only a few monosyllabic words in reply, the man gave it up as a bad job and drove on in dogged silence.

All during the journey home, Jacob pondered over the sin he had committed by lying to his employer. It had weighed upon his mind all through the day. So much so, in fact, that he had forgotten to bring home his lunchbox. This he remembered as he was unlocking the door of his apartment and ruefully shook his head, knowing that he was in for a scolding from Miriam.

"Jacob dear, how did it go today?" Miriam affectionately asked, as he seated himself at the dinner table.

"Well enough."

154

"I see. Did Leland say anything about the way you look?"

"Er—why, yes he did, Miriam. But it was only for a minute, and then he was busy the rest of the day." Jacob looked down at his plate and winced. It was a topic he did not wish to pursue, and he desperately hoped that Miriam would divine from his expression that he wished to change the subject swiftly.

"Oh, by the way, Jacob, I did not see your lunchbox."

"No, Miriam—I—I was so busy, I forgot it. But it's safe in a drawer of my desk."

"It will not do much good there when I make your lunch tomorrow, dear. You will have to take it in a paper bag."

"So, I will take it in a paper bag. Now please let me eat in peace."

For the rest of the meal, Jacob was strangely laconic and answered only briefly his wife's attempts to engage him in conversation. Finally, when supper was over and Miriam had gone back into the kitchen to do the dishes, he turned to David and said, "My son, I would like you to take a walk with me. Would you mind?"

"I'd love to, Papa. I must just take a few moments to complete my schoolwork, if that is all right," David replied.

"Of course." Jacob watched his handsome young son hurry back to his room, then sighed heavily and shook his head. He was in a gloomy mood, and he only hoped that he had wisdom enough to clearly articulate the words that came crowding all too awkwardly into his mind, so that he could communicate with his son and make David understand. He admired David's spirit and his youthful zest for freedom—but then, the boy was still so young, in his early teens. How could he know the suffering and the compromises that one had to make when one had begun life in the Old World, where freedom was only an illusion and a hope that few people realized?

Jacob Cohen glanced up at the sky and smiled. "What a very nice night it is, *boychik*. The air is quite warm enough so an old man like me doesn't actually need a shawl—but of course, your mother insisted I wear it because she's afraid I'll catch my death of cold."

"That's because she worries about you, Papa, just the way I do."

They had come to the park, and Jacob turned to his son and put his hand on the boy's shoulder. "Let us sit down. I—well, David, I have been thinking about something all day at the office, and I . . . please sit down, David. And bear with me for a moment. I want to get my thoughts together so I can express myself in a way you'll understand."

"Certainly, Papa." David dutifully seated himself on the bench and quietly waited for his father to speak.

For nearly ten minutes there were no words between them, as Jacob mulled over in his mind the proper way to begin this discussion. The events of last night had convinced him that he and his son had somehow grown apart, and this disturbed him even more than the telling of that lie to Leland Kenniston. He pursed his lips, frowned, and then finally declared, "David, I have been doing a great deal of thinking over what you see as my cowardice."

"I didn't say you were a coward, Papa. I just said that you're an American now, and sometimes you have to stand up for your rights and even fight for them. I think it is a terrible thing that someone can beat a person up just for looking at him cross-eyed."

"What expressions you are learning in your school these days!" Jacob laughed briefly and shook his head. Then his face sobered as he continued, "But I understand what you meant—and I want you to know that I respect your feelings. Yes, I think I can understand how you would want to act as an American would under the circumstances I found myself in yesterday. In fact—" Jacob stopped and gathered David into his arms to give him a bear hug "—I think you already have proved yourself to be a man, even before we proceed to the ritual of the *bar mitzvah*."

Hearing these words, David's face was radiant, for this was the most glowing compliment a father could pay his son, but he remained silent while Jacob carefully pursued his thinking. Jacob did not want to offend David, yet he needed to clearly express the points he meant to emphasize. Finally he went on hesitantly, "You see, my son, my ways are the ways of my father and his father, and his father before him—this is what we call tradition. Although it saddens me that you are moving away from this tradition, all the same, I can understand your doing so."

"Yes, Papa." David had bowed his head and was listening attentively.

"What I ask of you is that you understand why I must do what I must do, and not think the less of me because I do it."

David's eyes suddenly filled with tears; then he turned to his father with an unflinching look, and he softly replied, "Yes, I *do* understand, Papa. And forgive me if I have hurt you."

"But you haven't hurt me, David. You've just made me realize that the difference between us will continue to grow, and I must expect that to happen. Although I may not always agree with these differences, mind you, all the same, I will respect them—for I respect you."

"Thank you, Papa," David murmured. Then he added, to lighten the moment, "And don't worry, Papa. If those thugs ever so much as look at you the wrong way, Paul and I will take care of them. We can outbox any other boy in our club!"

Jacob tightened his arm around his young son's shoulders and looked at him for a long, silent moment. "You would defend your old father, would you?"

"You're not old, and of course I would, Papa!" David almost indignantly replied, straightening and stiffening his shoulders. "I love you and Mama more than anybody else in the whole wide world; of course I'd fight for you. In school they tell us that here, in this country, we're supposed to fight for our freedom so we always have it and don't lose sight of what it is."

"Ah, yes," Jacob reflectively mused. "Freedom can be like a *Hanukkah* gift one gives you: At the time you think it is very wonderful and impressive, but you put it away and almost forget about it. Then soon you begin to think that there's no reason to look at it again and be reminded of it because you *know* it's there. And soon perhaps, without even realizing it, someone takes it away. You don't know it's gone until you miss it and try to find it—and then, it's too late. Yes, David, you are right. I did run away from the Cossacks. Even if all of us who were oppressed had stood up and fought together, still we had no weapons. The Cossacks had their lances and their sabers and their rifles. They would have crushed us mercilessly. We would have been martyrs—we would have died, and some people would have said that we were heroes because we fought for freedom. And then to

157

punish us even after we were dead because we had revolted against the authorites, the Czar would have sent more Cossacks—to the villages and the cities like the one in which your mother and you and Rachel lived. They would have taken you all to prison, or made you slaves, or even killed you, all because we had wanted to stand up for our freedom."

"I see what you mean, Papa. Please forgive me—I didn't mean to call you a coward. Honestly I didn't!"

Again Jacob hugged his son. "I know that. I know that very well. When you are young and the blood is hot in your veins and you think you are immortal and you can conquer the world, then you talk about Cossacks and tyrants and kings and czars. And you think that you can beat them all. Only, as you get older, you realize that the odds are against you. You can die for a cause, yes, but sometimes you wonder what it has accomplished. If it puts the rest of your family into danger, then it is really not so heroic and so brave after all. So, if one judges things by that standard, David, I for one would much rather be a live coward than a dead hero. I think I could do my family more good being a live coward."

David thought a moment about this, looking away and screwing up his face. Then he finally replied very softly, "I guess by the time I grow up, I'll know a lot of things I don't know now."

"A man always does, my son. As he grows older, he realizes that he doesn't have quite so much wisdom as he thought he did as a boy. And he begins to think that perhaps his father has got smarter while he himself has been held back—held back, perhaps, so that his father could catch up. It is the eternal law. Youth is impatient to be grown up—but all too often the grownups sigh and think of their lost youth and wish they could be young again. Yes, I suppose even I do. But certainly I would rather be your age here in America than back in Kiev!"

"I would too, Papa. I love New York!"

"Yes, so do I, my son." Jacob took a deep breath and then smiled broadly. "You have eased my mind a great deal this evening by talking to me as you have. It is good for a father and a son to talk together, to understand what there is between them that holds them back from communicating so there will never be any deceit or mistrust between them. I did not fight those bullies because in the Torah, it says that we are not to give violence for violence, but rather to turn the other cheek—like the good Samaritan, who may even have been a Jew for all I know. It says also that we shall not lie for our own advantage. I did this, I'm afraid, with Mr. Kenniston today. He asked me how I had hurt and bruised myself so much, and I told him that it was because I had stumbled down the stairs. That was a lie, David, and it has bothered me since I uttered it. So tomorrow, when I go to the office, I will ask to have a few minutes with him. And then I will tell him that I was embarrassed over what had happened, because the group of five boys who attacked me were, so far as I could tell, all Irish. Now, since he was Irish-born, my son, this news may disturb him because he is so much on the side of Ireland. Yet I have to do this, or I would not feel right within my soul.''

''I understand, Papa. And Papa—I think you're terribly brave, braver than I am. I guess it takes a special kind of bravery to sit back and let other people do cruel things to you, without wanting to put yourself on their level and pay them back.''

''That is exactly why the Torah's words say what they do, my son. To strike back out of hatred and a desire to be superior to one's enemies is human frailty. It is selfish and self-centered.''

David stared gravely up at his father's face and then smiled warmly, as he hugged his father. ''I love you so, Papa. You make everything sound natural and right.''

''Even with me, *boychik*, do not take my words as the only truth on the matter. A wise man is he who seeks many opinions and weighs and judges and makes a decision for himself of what he will accept, according to his code of ethics. For me, who have lived by the Torah all of my life, it was natural to act as I did. Under other circumstances and without my religion, very likely I would have defended myself.'' He suddenly stood up from the park bench and held out his hand to David, saying, ''And now, my son, let us go back home before your mother starts to worry. Perhaps we can persuade her, if we ask very diplomatically, to make us some cocoa.''

''Or a snack. I'm starved!'' the boy burst out.

Jacob smiled and then chuckled. ''I do not know where

you put it, my son. After what you ate for dinner, and I would have thought you'd be completely full.''

"I was, but walking out here in the night air got me hungry again, Papa."

"Well then, we shall just have to feed you. Never let it be said that the son of Jacob Cohen went hungry. Come, let us go in now."

Jacob rose a half hour earlier than usual the next morning. He tiptoed out of the bedroom so as not to disturb his wife, scribbled a quick note so that she would not worry when she woke to find him absent from the apartment, and then went out onto the street. He had determined to walk all the way to the office, to straighten out his thinking and to clear his mind. Last night's man-to-man chat with David had convinced him that he had been guilty of a kind of intolerance, which he could decry in others when it was obvious, yet which he had failed to recognize in himself. Because of tradition, he had put up an impenetrable barrier like a glass wall inside his mind, refusing to believe what he could clearly see simply because it did not jibe with what he had been taught, what he had been conditioned to expect as inevitable.

No, David was right. This *was* America, where freedom was precious and where one didn't have to worry about Cossacks suddenly riding into a village wielding their rifles and sabers, ravishing women, killing old men and children simply out of a whim, and terrorizing the occupants of that village simply because they were unfortunate enough to be Jews. Here a person could be Jew or Gentile as he chose. Yes, truly it was worth fighting for.

As he walked the rapidly awakening streets, he concentrated on exactly what he would say to Leland Kenniston. Perhaps it wasn't tactful to mention that these young bullies had all been of Irish descent, but it had to be said. And what had to be said, also, was that they had probably attacked him because he was Jewish and perhaps for no other reason. Even if they had at first chosen him quite by chance as a victim of their rowdiness and bullying, when they discovered that he was Jewish, their intolerance and bigotry had become even more vicious.

He arrived at work a quarter of an hour before anyone else and went to his office, where he sat with his head bowed and his hands pressed against his cheeks, rapt in thought. He hoped Leland would realize that he was hardly denouncing the Irish simply because those boys had been of that lineage. Certainly Jacob did not want any rift in his happy association with such a warmhearted, generous man.

At last he heard the door of the large office suite open and the woman receptionist greet the entrepreneur with a cordial and respectful, "Good morning, Mr. Kenniston."

Gathering up his courage, Jacob rose swiftly from his desk and went out into the hallway. "May I have a private word with you, Leland?" he inquired.

"Of course, Jacob, come right along. Here, would you like to read the morning paper? I want the second section, though, because I need to check a report from the Stock Exchange on certain commodities. . . . ''

They had reached Leland Kenniston's office, and he closed the door and gestured toward a comfortable chair opposite his desk. "Make yourself comfortable, Jacob. I'm going to send Mrs. Tolson out for coffee and some sweet rolls from that bakery around the corner. Would you like something?"

"Just the coffee, thank you. And no cream or sugar."

"That's the way I drink it too—unless at night I make an Irish coffee, with cream and whiskey," Leland chuckled. He went to tell the receptionist what he wanted and then returned, closing the door behind him. "Now go ahead, Jacob. What's on your mind?"

"Leland, I—I didn't tell you the truth yesterday."

"What? My goodness, Jacob, you're such a man of honor and integrity that I would never in the world think you would falsify anything—certainly nothing of any great consequence. But I see you're upset, so please tell me what it is that's troubling you."

"I told you, when you asked me yesterday what had happened, that I had stumbled down the stairs. The truth is, when I left the office the other night, a group of five boys beat me up. They called me a kike, a Christ-killer."

"That's damnable!"

"Yes, Leland. And the reason I wanted to spare you the truth is that all of them were Irish."

"You're sure, Jacob?"

Jacob Cohen nodded. "There's no doubt about it. One of them referred to the group as the Irish Terriers. They were talking of going to mass and boasting to the priest of what they had done.''

Leland abruptly rose from his desk and strode over to the window, where, clasping his hands behind his back, he stared out into the street. After a few moments, he exhaled slowly and said, ''Thank you for telling me. I appreciate your tact in not wanting to burden me with the truth. Perhaps I should have guessed—there have been accounts in the newspapers—quite a few of them, more's the pity—of attacks on decent people by gangs of young bullies and rowdies.'' Then his face tightened. ''I think you know that I've always been proud of my Irish background, Jacob.''

Jacob Cohen nodded. ''As I am of my Jewish background, Leland.''

''Just so. And I've read enough history to know that the Jews have been persecuted in many countries over many centuries. Well, I told myself, so have the Irish, mainly by the English, who seem to be their nemesis. I've lived in hopes that one day I'd see an Irish Free State, independent as our own United States are, able to manage its own affairs without any help from what the English like to call the Mother Country. I have had a blind faith in my country, in my countrymen—in everything Ireland stood for. I felt that Ireland and the Irish could do no wrong.''

Jacob nodded his understanding, his eyes grave and sorrowful, as he listened intently.

''I've seen accounts in the newspapers, reports that there are signs on factories all over the country saying 'No Jews Need Apply.' But because prejudice against the Irish was once equally overt, I guess the fact is that I've tended to ignore the plight of your people, my friend.''

''Leland, I—''

''Please, Jacob, I want to say what I am feeling without interruption. Knowing you, I realize it was a very difficult decision for you to have told me the truth. You are too gentle a man not to have wished to spare my feelings. But if we focus on my feelings, then the important issue is overlooked: the significance of the brutal actions of those hooligans against you, Jacob. That is the only thing that matters. That is what I am sickened over. Irish rebels resort to violence ostensibly to achieve independence for their nation. It is so easy to rationalize their motivations. We go to great lengths to invent high-

162

sounding reasons for all the violence we perpetrate under the sun.''

Leland strode back to the window and peered out again. Then he turned to face his gray-haired employee. "The simple fact of the matter, Jacob, is that you were victimized, cruelly victimized. The fact that those boys were Irish should perhaps increase my anger, my resentment, my shame—but I am not my brother's keeper. I can try to set an example for others, but I am not responsible for others' acts. I am greatly disgusted that this terrible deed was done to you, and would feel the same way no matter who the culprits were. I am telling you this, Jacob, because I don't want you in any way to feel guilty for being truthful—and because if anything like this should ever, God forbid, happen again, I want you to know that you should immediately call in the authorities and report it. You do not have to spare my feelings, I assure you.''

Leland smiled sadly, just as there was a knock at the door. "That's our coffee. Let's drink it in friendship and to a renewed and better understanding of each other's principles, Jacob.''

Chapter Sixteen

For Lucien Bouchard, the world was a magnificent fresh oyster in whose depths there was certain to be concealed a pearl without price. Indeed, to carry on the analogy—which he was fond of doing in his creative writing class—there were at least two pearls: One of them was Mary Eileen Brennert, the games master's daughter, whom he had described as a "pippin" to Laure; and the other, assuredly, was his instructor, Sean Flannery. Between the teacher, who though considerably older showed the youth great respect, and Mary Eileen, Lucien's days at St. Timothy's Academy were a halcyon period in which life seemed gloriously rich and wonderfully promising.

He had made many friends at school, for he was not at all standoffish. Because of this his classmates did not snub him when he happened to show greater scholastic ability and more diligent zeal in pursuing his studies than they did. Since he greatly enjoyed sports, he went rowing (several times already this early spring with Mary Eileen in the stream that meandered by the campus of St. Timothy's), and was learning to play cricket and soccer with as much aplomb as if he had been born abroad and had never lived in the United States. He was generally regarded by everyone as "a good sport, even if he is an American." From the Irish, especially the adolescents who sometimes tended to be more insular than their elders, this was about the highest praise Lucien could have expected.

Quite apart from his chums, his instructors also liked him, for he was honest and direct. And when he asked questions—though they might prove troublesome because they involved a good deal of logical thinking—their difficulty was a kind of tribute to the instructors themselves, since it was they who had inculcated the precept of searching for truth in the receptive, impressionable student.

Lucien loved the countryside beyond the campus, and since Dublin itself was about two miles from the school, there were all the fascinating temptations of a large city—but with a difference. There was an unusual quaintness to Dublin that Lucien Bouchard would not have found in any American city. New York, New Orleans, or Chicago offered very little that was analogous to Dublin, which combined antiquity with contemporary urban building, yet with that rusticism that calls for flowers and trees and shrubs, for which the Irish have always been renowned. It was no mere accident that Irishmen who met throughout the world would say that they formed a fellowship born to the wearing of the green. Nor was it strange that Ireland itself should be called the "Emerald Isle," because the city and town planners of that spirited and freedom-seeking country emphasized always the beauty of nature, even when it was confined within a city.

In March of 1882, Lucien Bouchard had attained his six-teenth year. In this very year, and in this same city of Dublin that so fascinated young Lucien, James Joyce was born, one of a family so large as to be described by his father as having "sixteen or seventeen children." In letters home to his parents, Lucien rhapsodized about the city—the sights and sounds and smells. He had, for example, discovered the delight of ginger beer in its stone crock, an effervescent and thoroughly satisfying drink in warm weather. He had also found extremely palatable a dish that many of the students ordered when they went into the town and visited what was called a "refreshment bar" or restaurant: hot grocer's peas, liberally seasoned with pepper and vinegar. And finally, Lucien Bouchard was on the threshold of young maturity and his first true love affair.

Like most sensitive and intelligent adolescents, the experi-ence of an awakening sexuality meant an awareness and a sharpening of all Lucien's senses. When he hiked with some of his school friends into Dublin to go to a restaurant or to see a vaudeville show, his eyes were filled with the sights of the city. These included the pretty Irish girls in their finery, showing off and coquettishly flirting with their eyes. It was, indeed, an age-old ritual: The female made herself known to the male and rejoiced in her own womanhood, while the male in turn delighted in his observations of her attire, the look of her face and her eyes, and thereby conjured up from all this a fantasy of wooing and courtship and happiness. It was innocuous, yet it was almost intolerably exciting. Lucien had never before experienced these emotions, and since he was at an age when one could fall in love with love, his infatuation for Mary Eileen Brennert was ever increasing by leaps and bounds. As he wrote in his secret diary on the last Friday in April, "I think she is the most beautiful girl in all the world. Sometimes I wish I were a painter, so I might reproduce her face exactly as it is and bring it home with me during summer vacation. A painted portrait would capture on canvas for all time all the perfections on which I dote."

Nonetheless, his eye could still wander. A week before, he and three of his friends, Ned Riordan, Daniel O'Toole, and Jimmy Moynihan, had gone into Dublin and walked down Merrion Street. It was a great event to dine out on a Sunday in Dublin itself and then to walk the streets, see the sights, and espy the pretty colleens. They had seen a young woman going to church, wearing a blue serge skirt tightly cinched at the waist and a white blouse over which was a short, navy jacket with mother-of-pearl buttons. A corsage of red carnations was pinned to the jacket's bodice.

She had eyed the four young men, smiled an insouciant little smile, and went on walking. Jimmy Moynihan, whose father was a butcher, had been sent to St. Timothy's to acquire some smoothing out in the hopes that perhaps he might decide to enter a seminary, rather than pursue his father's rough trade. The lad gawked at the young woman and actually turned around to stare after her. When she abruptly twirled back and flashed a mocking yet provocative, inviting look from her gray-green eyes, Jimmy blushed. Ned Riordan had hoarsely whispered, "For heaven's sake, Jimmy my boy, are you going to undress her with your eyes? That one, my friend, can be had for a ten-shilling note and for the night entire, I tell you. She's a trollop, Jimmy! She'd send that look after any man who could pay her fee. I did think you had better taste than that."

At the mention of that coarse word—one which so many men sanctimoniously use by way of condemnation, thus covering up their own secret lusts for such an unfortunate creature— Lucien Bouchard had crimsoned. It was not that he was ignorant of what a scarlet woman was, it was only that he had an intensely romantic concept of a female, and the use of the word "trollop" sullied it. It even besmirched his rhapsodic thoughts of Mary Eileen Brennert, whose sparkling eyes had been brought to his mind by the eyes of the attractive colleen now being discussed. He had put the lovely young daughter of the games master on a pedestal, worshiping her from afar, attributing to her all those virtues the ideal woman must have.

But, now that this condemning word had been spoken, the boys seemed to unleash all their hitherto pent-up feelings about the opposite sex. Each of them had at least one bawdy story to tell, bragging of his carnal prowess. Lucien could not believe his ears; what he did believe was that those who talked the most knew the least.

While his cronies boasted of their experiences with Dublin's women of easy virtue, Lucien was too self-contained and sensitive, even though he was essentially gregarious, to discuss such matters. He had even taken great pains to keep his friendship with Mary Eileen as secret as was possible on a campus of impressionable adolescent boys. Thus, to view her as one of the females of whom his friends talked with such contemptuous ease and slyly salacious innuendos would have been to destroy his belief in the beauty and purity of womanhood.

Lucien had adroitly sidestepped a direct answer to Jimmy Moynihan's query, "And what about you, Lucien boy? Have you some light o' love hidden away right here in Dublin that we know nothing about?"

"Perhaps," he had said with an elusive smile, leaving them all guessing yet sacrificing nothing of his standing with them. The young men then continued to promenade in search of fanciful adventures, adventures that might never take place except in the mind and the spirit.

It was with Sean Flannery that Laure's oldest son felt himself most fulfilled intellectually and spiritually, and the disparity in their ages was offset by the meeting of their minds as well as by Lucien's willingness and eagerness to assimilate his instructor's beliefs. Like many other zealous youthful students, Lucien tended to romanticize the capabilities of his history and sociology instructor. Lucien's devotion to Sean might not have been so readily formed had the older man not been of the stuff out of which sensitive, imaginative teenagers are capable of evolving an idealistic hero.

The wiry twenty-eight-year-old was black haired, with keen dark-blue eyes and a firm mouth. Thick sideburns framed his handsome face, from which a broken nose did not detract. He walked with a decided limp, the result of a wound inflicted by British troops during a skirmish Sean had been involved in as a postgraduate student in 1877. He spoke crisply, with a definite Irish brogue, and had the interesting habit of pausing after a long, involved sentence to gaze out the window, ignoring all his students. His students, further romanticizing the man, decided that at such moments he was ruminating over what had happened in his past. Lucien was keenly sensitive to this protagonist of freedom and had inwardly marked him as a sympathetic soul who could guide him to a better understanding of what was taking place in the Old World and set him on the path to noble, emancipated thought.

Though he was ardently in favor of an Irish Free State, Sean had never been a fanatic. Eschewing emotional and physical violence, he had always approached the question of how best to achieve liberty with a calm deliberation, carefully weighing all the options before he decided on what he thought was the best—though not necessarily the most expedient— choice. It was small wonder, then, that his students gave greater credence to Sean's opinions than to those of any other instructor at St. Timothy's.

During Lucien's very first semester at the academy, the young, idealistic instructor had delivered an impassioned lecture on Ireland's history, from the early days when the Celts, the Picts, and the Romans were engaged in the struggle for the conquest of these islands in the North Atlantic. He had traced with wit and elegant sarcasm the emergence of England as the ruling power, an England that, from the days of Queen Elizabeth onward, had spurned the concept of Irish freedom. He had not altered the facts of history, but yet he tinged them with his own special colorations of opinion. Lucien had come to accept these opinions as truths, and he found the instructor extremely sympathetic and marvelously communicative.

A few weeks after the lecture, Sean Flannery had invited Lucien and some of the other leading students from the history class to a private tea in the instructor's quarters.

Taking Lucien aside, Sean had complimented him on his quick mind. "You have a cosmopolitan outlook, Lucien, and it will serve you in good stead to balance facts and to weigh arguments and make your own decisions. This is all I ask of any student, but I consider you one of the best I've had in years, and from you I think I can expect much more."

Now, in his second year, Lucien Bouchard was more committed than ever to his instructor. It was almost inevitable that Lucien would become involved in the "Irish Ireland" movement, for which the groundwork had already been laid. Leland Kenniston had told many tales of his own Irish background during the initial voyage over to Ireland, when Lucien had first entered St. Timothy's under Leland's sponsorship. With Lucien being far away from home most of the year, it was inevitable that Sean Flannery, shaping Lucien's young, fertile mind, should become a kind of surrogate father.

There was yet another motivation for Lucien's involvement in the Irish movement: Because he had been brought up with an unswerving acceptance of Catholicism—a gentle kind of Catholicism that did not condemn as heathens those not of the faith—he was shocked at the blatant religious antipathy of the British toward Irish Catholics. Moreover, he had personally witnessed examples of religious persecutions since coming to St. Timothy's.

Edward Cordovan was a fifteen-year-old with a brilliant intellect. He had been brought up by a spinster aunt after the tragically early death of his parents by drowning in the Irish Sea. Because of his background and the pampering of his aunt, Edward was extremely timid. One day, as the boy walked down a Dublin street with Lucien, a British soldier with a blowsy woman on his arm came down the sidewalk from the opposite direction. Edward suddenly stumbled, and did not get out of the British corporal's way. With a mocking laugh, the man shouldered the boy brutally, knocking him into the gutter, and then turned to the woman to loudly declare, "That's where all the Papists ought to wind up, Jenny." The soldier and the woman sniggered as they strode away, while Lucien hurried to help Edward.

Another episode occurred just the previous February, soon after Lucien had returned from the holidays with his family. It was a Saturday, and he and Mary Eileen Brennert had watched a soccer match between first-term and second-term boys being coached by her father.

As it chanced, that day some English soldiers had been given a furlough and had decided to hire a horse-drawn carriage to make a tour of the environs of Dublin. As they passed St. Timothy's soccer field, they halted their driver and alighted to watch the match. All six of them, including a corporal and a sergeant, had taken places behind Lucien and his pretty young companion.

Halfway through the match, Edward Cordovan had won a position on the second-term team, and had just adroitly scored a goal with a "header" that took the opposing goalie by surprise. Lucien turned to Mary Eileen, his face glowing with pleasure, and exclaimed, "Well done, wasn't it?"

Hearing Lucien exclaim praise for Edward's unexpected goal, the sergeant turned to his corporal and, in a sneering voice, remarked, "Not bad for a Papist. But those kids wouldn't stand a chance against an English team—what with losing all that sleep going to mass and taking their orders from Rome."

Lucien turned to glare at the offending commentator, and the sergeant chuckled and said in an even louder voice, "They're touchy, too, when you talk about their religion. Shouldn't wonder, if they have to confess to their priest about having nasty thoughts about us because we spoke out of turn against Papism, eh what, Corporal Tordley?"

Lucien had wisely learned that discretion is usually the better part of valor, so instead of retaliating, he murmured to Mary Eileen, "Let's get away from here. We can't hear ourselves think."

She nodded, her brown curls bobbing, and she gazed at him with those wonderful gray-green eyes. Of medium height, her oval-shaped face held thick dark-brown eyebrows and a dainty Grecian nose. Her mouth was soft, ripe, and tremulous, and adorable dimples appeared whenever she smiled, which was often. Lately, Lucien had had the irresistible impulse to kiss those dimples, but thus far he had resisted any overt gesture that in any way could have been deemed an impropriety.

Mary Eileen had a soft, clear voice, made even sweeter by her lilting Irish brogue. To Lucien, it was an exquisite voice, and its overtones, particularly when it pronounced his name, made him feel all the more that she was very fond of him. He worshiped her and, indeed, even dreamed one day of marrying her.

Mary Eileen's mother had died three years after her birth, and Henry Brennert had brought up his daughter with the help of a widowed cousin. Three months younger than Lucien, Mary Eileen attended a girls' school about two miles north of St. Timothy's. Although Mr. Brennert was fiercely vigilant in making certain that his only child was not exposed to the uncouth importunities of adolescent boys, he had taken an early liking to Lucien, particularly admiring the youth's supportiveness to Edward Cordovan.

Moreover, he had learned that Lucien stood high in his class scholastically and was regarded as one of the brightest prospects to win honors. Knowing this, he had granted Mary Eileen the unheard-of privilege of accepting Lucien's invitations to tea in a local restaurant, or even to a visit to Dublin on a Sunday. Though not to his discredit, it must be said that Henry Brennert's inquiry concerning his daughter's young squire had revealed the fact that Lucien came from a wealthy family. Since Brennert was nearly as poor as the proverbial churchmouse, his acceptance of Lucien as a companion for his daughter was all the more understandable.

This third Sunday in April was a bright, warm day. Lucien Bouchard, Edward Cordovan, and Ned Riordan took advantage of the serene and almost summery day to go into Dublin for sightseeing and windowshopping, to culminate in a sumptuous high tea at Kelly's Restaurant. Ned, a London-born boy three months older than Lucien—whose Irish grandfather had almost belligerently demanded that the lad's parents send him to Ireland to continue his education—suggested they indulge in Kelly's suet pudding engorged with plump raisins. Lucien had become almost greedily fond of this treat himself and offered no objections.

They had strolled along High Street for about an hour and a half, pausing to look into windows, commenting to each other about the ideas tendered to them by their instructors during the previous week. Lucien recalled that Sean Flannery had been tutoring his pupils on the Irish kings, mentioning some of the legendary Irish heroes. He had concluded his long lecture with these words: "What we find as a cohesive force

171

throughout Irish history, as well as Irish legend, is the untrammeled, indomitable will toward freedom.

"Doubtless, when our ancestors first set foot upon the soil of Ireland, they were conscious of the flora and the fauna, of the stretches of hills and wooded dells, and the green beauty of the rich, fertile soil. They may not have expressed themselves, yet in those early days of time they must have known what it meant to be free and dependent only upon their ability to survive. But now, the extraneous forces inflicted upon Ireland, mainly by usurpers, have compelled all of us Irishmen to yearn for the freedom that has been stolen from us—and, indeed, history bears out that this was exactly the case. Remember, though, that the educational process sometimes takes hundreds of years. It cannot be accomplished by force overnight, nor should it be so conceived. A thinking man abhors violence and bloodshed, as the end does not justify the means. Yet, the end will be glorious, one to which all of us who have Irish blood in our veins should dedicate ourselves."

As the three friends ambled across from a book stall a few blocks south of Kelly's Restaurant, they decided to stop and browse and then enjoy their high tea. They were exhilarated, for the warmth, the sunshine, the smiles of the pretty young women who saw them walking with such buoyant confidence, had made them relish life. Lucien recalled Wordsworth's lines, "Bliss it was in that hour to be alive, but to be young was very heaven!" He mentioned this now to Edward and Ned as they strolled leisurely toward the bookseller's.

As they crossed the cobblestoned street, they saw four British soldiers—three privates and a corporal—stop to bar the path of a young fishmonger. Selling cod and halibut from her pushcart, she wore a gray dress made of cotton worsted, and solid shoes for walking Dublin's uneven streets. A lace-trimmed cap perched on her coppery hair, and she had a piquant, saucy face. Doubtless the soldiers had espied this, though two of them wrinkled their noses at the smell of the fish from her handcart.

"Excuse me, sirs," she said in a soft, husky brogue, "but unless I sell my wares, I'll not have even a bob for supper this night. Do let me pass, there's good laddies!"

"Come now, sweetheart, you can always sell fish, but it's not every day you meet four handsome soldiers of the queen like this." The corporal, a corpulent man in his early thirties with an enormous handlebar mustache, moved to confront her, while his three cronies leaned against the pushcart to prevent her from going on.

"Please, it's a very steep street, and I've not the strength to keep this cart suspended this way. Do let me go, sirs!" she pleaded prettily.

"Not without a forfeit, you sweet colleen," the corporal sniggered, winking at his fellows. "Just one kiss, that's all I'm asking of you, dearie!"

"Faith and I'm not your dearie, nor no man else's!" she hotly retorted. "You're four big gawking hulks of men against a poor girl who's trying to make an honest living. Do go away and let me be. I want no truck with the likes of you!"

"Oh, now, I suppose she thinks she's too good for us," one of the privates spoke up, a wiry, stoop-shouldered man with a day's growth of blond stubble on his dissipated face. "Tell you what, *dearie*. I think I can manage a quid for your favors—that should more than make up for the few bob you'd earn peddling this whole smelly lot."

"I'd rather die than do a thing like that! I'm not that sort of girl! Let go of my cart—you've no right to treat me this way!" By now, the pretty young redhead was almost in tears.

All four of them were now holding onto her cart, and she could not budge it, try as she would. The three schoolboys overheard every word, and not only were Ned and Lucien incensed but so was reticent young Edward Cordovan. Lucien called out, "Do the British have so little courage it takes four of the likes of you to bother a single Irish girl?"

"Did you fellows hear a gadfly buzzing about there?" The corporal turned and favored Lucien with a cross-grained look, then shrugged. Then he yelled, "Schoolboys trying to be heroes! Go home. Your mother wants to nurse you."

"Leave the lady alone," Lucien indignantly exclaimed. "Or we'll see that you're reported—all of you—to your commanding officer."

"Oh, you will, will you, squirt? Be careful now, sonny, or I'll take you over my knee and paddle your backside for you," another private jeered. His handsome face was crowned by an unkempt mop of black hair, and his nostrils flared as he spoke. He whispered something to his cronies, then loudly addressed Lucien. "We're going to count to four, and if you haven't gone by then, we'll paddle the lot of you—and you can be sure you'll remember it for a long while!''

Lucien, red with anger, clenched his fists, but he contained himself. Then Edward unexpectedly bent, picked up a large stone, and flung it at the head of the obstreperous private.

"Well now, if they want to fight, we'll oblige them, the dirty little Papists!'' the corporal snorted, and he and his three friends came menacingly toward Lucien and his two companions. The young fishmonger screamed, "Help, someone! Now the British soldiers are bullying little schoolboys who just tried to help me!''

The corporal doubled his fist and sent Edward sprawling with a vicious punch to the young boy's chin. Ned Riordan let out a bellow of anger. Lowering his head, he butted one of the privates in the belly, making the man double up and yell with pain. The private then stumbled backwards, losing his balance, and sprawled onto the cobblestones.

The corporal swore, giving Ned a venomous look. Then, advancing on the youth, he sent Ned stumbling back against the brick wall of a building with a blow to his stomach. With a stertorous moan, Ned slumped down to the sidewalk, his head bowed, breathing painfully.

Two of the privates now made for Lucien, who stoutly defended himself. With his back against the wall, he struck out with his fists and, unexpectedly, launched a good hard kick with his hobnailed boot. The kick took one of the privates in the shin, putting him out of action as he rolled on the sidewalk and clutched his leg in pain.

The young fishmonger, who had pushed her cart up to the top of the street, turned back to cheer the boys on. "Give it to them! They've got it coming! Strike a blow for every decent Irish man and woman here in Dublin!''

A shrill whistle suddenly interrupted her words, and a burly, red-faced policeman came running down the street, brandishing a polished nightstick. "That'll be enough of that! We'll have no scuffling on a Sunday in Dublin!'' he called out in majestic tones.

The corporal turned with a wheedling smile and addressed the helmeted policeman. "Constable, these boys attacked us. We was minding our own business, just talking to that pretty colleen up there, when all of a sudden these louts began to insult us because we're wearing the uniform of the queen—God save her! One of them actually threw a rock! I swear to you, my good man, one of us could have been killed, the way they carried on!''

"I think," the policeman said, puffing out the chest of his blue uniform and staring long and hard at Lucien and his two friends, "you'd best come along with me, gentlemen! We'll go see His Honor, Mr. Dougherty, who's sitting magistrate of a Sunday afternoon in Hanraty Lane. Come along now; don't give me any trouble. I wouldn't want to have to clout you on the head with me nightstick! Shame on the three of you, giving those helpless soldiers such a difficult time!"

"Helpless indeed!" Lucien hotly defended himself and his friends. "You should have been here a long time ago! Then you would have seen how they insulted the fishmonger, trying to have their pleasure with her! It was an abomination, I tell you, Constable!"

The young woman had watched the proceedings from the top of the street, and now yelled, "Faith and these boys were only trying to help me, sir! Don't you be taken in by those English bastids!"

The policeman turned, hands on hips, and scowled at her. Then he called out, "For shame, lass! A word like that doesn't belong on a decent girl's lips, and that's no lie! Now, sure as me name is Francis Murphy, you'll be taking yourself off if you don't want me making certain you've a license to sell fish on a Sunday. Then *you'll* spend the night waiting to see the magistrate. Get along with you now, lass!" Turning to the by now apprehensive boys, he commanded, "You come along with me, foolish lads, and I'll have you brought up before Magistrate Dougherty. Like as not you've not been before him—or have you, now?"

"No, sir," Lucien answered for all of them, as he eyed his two friends.

"Well, His Honor'll no doubt let you off with just a scolding, I'm thinking. Mind you now"—he gave them a broad, indulgent wink—"I didn't see any violence, or any other shenanigans. Maybe this will teach you not to pick on the whole British Army by yourselves. Come along now, that's good lads!"

Lucien murmured to Edward and Ned, "I sure hope Father

O'Mara doesn't hear about this—I shouldn't like to be expelled."

"It would be worth it," Edward declared with a beaming smile.

Ned patted him on the back and whispered, "That's the spirit, Edward! Up the Irish, down the British—forever!"

Chapter Seventeen

The magistrate at the High Street District Police Station was an angular-faced man who wore a wig that did not quite fit him. He frowned through thick spectacles at the three boys brought before him, and at the indulgent Irish policeman who had charged him. Clearing his throat, Magistrate Dougherty spoke to the youths in stinging tones. "Young gentlemen, your conduct has been most unseemly, and we shall not tolerate it. Sunday is the Lord's day, a day of peace and harmony. I personally know your headmaster, and Father O'Mara will be as displeased with you as I am. Undoubtedly you are boys of exceptional scholastic merit, from good, decent families—for it goes without saying that any enrollee at St. Timothy's must necessarily be passed upon by Father O'Mara, who has exemplary judgment when it comes to weeding out the wheat from the chaff, so to speak."

Lucien Bouchard glanced uneasily at his two companions; they squirmed from foot to foot, adjusting their collars, feeling thoroughly sheepish and miserable. The court was empty except for a bailiff and a clerk, who—sitting with his eyes closed—had hardly bothered to write down the testimony given by the arraigning policeman.

"I shall let you off this time with a warning. I shall not tolerate this in my district, and any repetition will carry with it far more punishment than I have indulgently decided to grant you young gentlemen. You are dismissed back to your academy, in the company of this policeman. You are fortunate that Constable Murphy gave a good report of you and did not indicate any harm or malice or damage." He turned to address the policeman. "I hold you responsible for their return."

"Faith, Your Honor, it's a charge I'll carry out as if I were taking me own boys back to school," the garrulous, grinning policeman responded.

"Thank you, Constable Murphy." The magistrate adjusted his spectacles and glared down at the three boys. "Your names have been registered, and although you will not have a criminal record, if you repeat this nonsense the next time you come to Dublin for your outings, you will find yourself in a far more critical predicament. I dismiss this case, and, Clerk Ponsby—" The clerk awoke with a gasp, hastily eyeing the judge with a fawning respect. "Pay attention, sir! Enter that I have dismissed the charges, but that I have put these boys on their honor not to repeat this flagrant offense."

"Yes, Your Honor!" The clerk wrote industriously.

"That will be all. I hope you have learned a lesson. I do not want to see you before me again, is that plainly understood?"

"Oh, yes, Your Honor," Lucien Bouchard spoke up with a certain bravado. He heaved a sigh of relief at hearing the magistrate's final words, and as the boys left the courtroom, he gave his two companions a knowledgeable wink.

Father Patrick O'Mara, a tall man in his early sixties garbed in the black robe of an ordained priest, sat without uttering a word. There were slight wattles on his neck, made more pronounced by his ecclesiastical collar, which was uncomfortably tight. Invariably, since he preferred this kind of self-penitence, it forced him to maintain a more severe expression on his ascetic face than might have been expected from a man who, in his early twenties, had won two firsts in English poetry at the University of Dublin. His hooded eyes were gray, and his bushy eyebrows were a stark contrast to his sparse white hair. His broad Roman nose dominated his face, and altogether he gave the appearance of a stern, elderly hawk.

Lucien, Ned, and Edward had been summoned to his study directly after breakfast at seven-thirty in the morning. Sean Flannery had been noncommittal, but he had hinted to Lucien as the youth left the dining hall, "You're in some trouble, my lad. You're going to get a tongue-lashing, a very severe one. Luckily for you, Father O'Mara decided to give up the cane for refectory students about two years ago, or you might be expecting at least a dozen of the best over your knickers. Good luck—keep your mouth shut, and remember that there is always a price for freedom. It is now time for you to pay yours."

This Monday, in direct contrast to the day before, was gray and rainy and chilly, and winds from the North Atlantic battered the Irish coastline. The sullen, gray mood also prevailed in the headmaster's study, where the priest sat contemplating his three headstrong pupils. For five interminably long minutes, he had stared at them with a baleful glare. Then at last marching to the huge bay window and turning his back on them, he declared, "Magistrate Dougherty happens to be a distant cousin of mine. But he shows absolutely no partiality or favoritism, which is exactly the way a member of the bench should act at all times. However, knowing that you were from St. Timothy's—and perhaps for that reason out of a kindness to both of us—he deferred the matter of your punishment to my judgment. Still, the three of you are extremely lucky. If you had been adjudged guilty of a criminal misdemeanor, I feel that I should have had no recourse but to send you packing from St. Timothy's forever. Are you aware of this?"

A mumbled "yes" came from all three simultaneously, and Lucien, Ned, and Edward looked uncomfortably sheepish as they stared down at their high-gloss polished shoes that were obligatory during class periods at St. Timothy's.

At last he turned and looked at them, his lips tightening, his eyes narrowing, and then he went on in a tone of harsh and almost contemptuous irritation. "I closeted myself with Constable Murphy, gentlemen, and he told me of your reprehensible conduct in the city of Dublin yesterday afternoon. I warn you, I do not tolerate this sort of brawling, no matter how right the cause. Yes, I know there are members of my faculty who would take a stronger and more daring stand on a Free Irish Republic—but this school does not condone, nor do I in my official post as headmaster of St. Timothy's, the substitution of the use of force in place of clear logic and patient education to gain an immediate end or advantage. You will be wise to remember that, all three of you."

His gaze seemed to fix on Lucien Bouchard, who held it incumbent upon him to mutter a "Yes, Father O'Mara."

"I am happy to see that some clarity is left to you, Mr. Bouchard. But you disappoint me. Your marks at the present moment rank at about the third highest in my entire school, regardless of form. You would have been due special notice of praise from this office; however, you have forfeited such praise by endangering the reputation of this academy. And I repeat—regardless of your standing—had you been found guilty of a criminal misdemeanor against those English soldiers, I should have had no alternative but to expel you in disgrace. You are fortunate that the arresting officer was indulgent and, admittedly, of Irish descent. If it had been an English policeman, had you been in London, you may be certain that all three of you would have spent at least a week in jail, without the possibility of bail, even on *habeas corpus*. Think on that awhile, gentlemen."

Once again, he turned to the bay window, deliberately staring at the scenery beyond, frowning as he saw the sky darken with the advent of a storm.

Finally, after another lengthy pause, he turned back to his recalcitrant charges and said, "I daresay that Magistrate Dougherty considered your tender ages. He knows also that boys from St. Timothy's are wont to set high scholastic records, to be recluses and novitiates in the pastures of learning, and not to take a brawling and contumacious attitude when they visit the city. The policemen, the magistrates, and the civic authorities know very well that I trust you enough to grant you leave from campus on Sundays. *Trust*, gentlemen. This does not give you free license to act as you please, to defy all precepts of ethical behavior, and, in short, to make asses of yourselves."

He glared at each in turn, and Lucien squirmed uncomfortably, lowering his eyes again to his shoes.

Then, in an almost didactic tone, as if he were lecturing a class, he half turned from them and went on. "Although I am hardly obliged to do so, I will give you something of my own antecedents. I was born in County Cork, and my family belongs to one of the greatest clans of all Ireland. But this did not prevent them from acting with humility, one that comes from a fine name and the obligation of setting a good example for one's *poursuivants*. I have more reason than any one of you—and certainly more than you, Mr. Bouchard—to seek with all my heart and soul a free Ireland. But you observe that I am not found in a Dublin street on a Sunday, taunting and challenging British soldiers. That way is madness, and it would do more harm for the Irish cause of the Free State than anything I can think of. Be advised of that, and be advised also of my official displeasure with all three of you. You, Mr. Cordovan—I have told your form master to give you a special assignment. When you reach class tomorrow morning, you will find that he will have you write an essay for him, due at the end of the week. The subject will be, 'The Discipline of Self-Restraint.' And one more thing, Mr Cordovan—''

''Father?''

''After you complete this essay, you will also write two hundred lines of the Latin equivalent of this sentence: 'I am truly and humbly contrite for my stupidity, and I promise by all that I hold dear not to repeat my blunder.' Is that clear, Mr. Cordovan?''

''Yes, F-Father.''

''You, Mr. Riordan, will say a hundred Hail Mary's, and you will work in the refectory for the next week, breakfast, lunch, and dinner, serving your fellows. When they see you thusly, they will know that you are in disgrace and earning your pardon. You are a touch too proud, and this is a trait I do not at all find admirable, either in the young or in the old. Do you have any further questions?''

''N-no, sir,'' the boy quavered.

Lastly, Father O'Mara turned to confront Lucien Bouchard. ''Mr. Bouchard, you will write the Latin phrase, '*Mea culpa*' five thousand times and turn in your pages, which must be neat and without a single blot of ink, by Friday morning. I wish you also to write a short story in which you are the villain and the British soldiers the heroes. You will avow yourself wrong from the outset; you will write the essay as if you had been one of them having to deal with an irascible young man like yourself. Do you question the assignment?''

''No, F-Father.''

The three boys eyed each other again with hangdog expressions. Father O'Mara smiled coldly. ''You, Mr. Riordan . . .''

''F-Father?''

''I am somewhat amused by the irony of your situation. You were English-born, yet your grandfather, who is paying for your education here, counts this beautiful country as his birthplace. He would be greatly disappointed if you did not graduate when you have completed your studies at St. Timothy's. I mean to see that you do not disgrace him." Ned gave the Father O'Mara a duly contrite expression before the headmaster concluded, "I shall expect the three of you in my office next Friday morning, directly after breakfast. Now then, gentlemen, you are dismissed."

The three boys hastily left Father O'Mara's study and were walking back to their dormitory. They had been exempted from the morning's study courses, told by Father O'Mara that they would better be served by going to chapel and offering prayers of pardon for their escapades. Then, after luncheon, they would resume their studies with their various instructors.

"Well, we really got off lightly. I think he saw through it all," Lucien Bouchard commented.

"I was really scared there for a minute," Edward Cordovan hesitantly confessed. "I want to make my first, and I don't dare get expelled. But nonetheless, Lucien, I don't think any of us overreacted to those stupid soldiers."

"Edward, Ned," Lucien fiercely broke in, "it's time we took a vow. You might call us the Three Musketeers. Perhaps one day we'll find a fourth—our d'Artagnan, if you recall your Dumas. What I'm getting at is, we have to pledge that we'll continue to do whatever we feel is necessary—but we'll take special pains not to get caught so that another session with Father O'Mara won't be our reward. Do we all agree?"

Ned Riordan walked to the window and looked out, heaving a long sigh. "All for one and one for all, Lucien?"

"Yes, Ned. I won't stand there and pretend not to take notice while some British soldiers are abusing a nice young woman. That's the way I feel, but both of you will have to make your own decisions. Don't follow me if you don't want to."

"But you're our good friend, and you're the best in the school. Of course we'll follow you," Edward loyally spoke up.

"All right, then. Whenever we see things like what we saw yesterday afternoon, we're going to make ourselves known. Maybe that'll be one way of getting Irish freedom faster. I'm not a great one for education solving all problems, and I think that it's possible for us to take a definite stand and do whatever we can so people can live with a little less worry.

182

Let's all shake on it. I think we should have a name; let's call ourselves the Free Irish Republicans, and we're the charter members."

"I'll go along with that," Ned vigorously nodded, as he walked over and sat down at the desk loaded with a pile of books.

"We'll make a difference, just see if we don't," Lucien boldly declared. "The important thing is to do it without getting into any more trouble—and I think we're all smart enough for that."

The three friends clasped hands and, with the impudence that only youth allows, believed wholeheartedly that they were impervious to misfortune.

Chapter Eighteen

Lucien Bouchard had tentatively agreed to play cricket with the second-form team the following Thursday, but that noon he decided he would much rather take a walk with Mary Eileen Brennert. Her classes let out about thirty minutes after Lucien's last afternoon class, and so, after hurriedly telling Ned Riordan—who was to be a wicket keeper in the match—that he was feeling somewhat out of sorts and would not play, Lucien set out across the campus toward Saint Eulalie's Institute for Girls.

Actually, Lucien was not so much out of sorts physically as he was emotionally chastened by a conversation he had had just before luncheon with Sean Flannery. The young instructor had taken Ned and Edward aside the day before and interrogated them on the previous Sunday's escapade. Since Edward was extremely pious and believed lying to be a venial sin, he had at last lamely admitted that he, Ned, and Lucien had sworn a pact that they would fight against the injustices of British soldiers toward Irish citizens.

The instructor had said nothing, letting neither of the boys know his true feelings of the matter, but this morning, after his class in history, he gestured to Lucien to stay after class. The moment the last student filed out, closing the door behind him, and Lucien and Mr. Flannery were alone, the instructor let his anger out: "I understand you have set yourself up as a would-be Brian Boru, one of the great and early Irish kings."

"I don't follow you, Mr. Flannery," Lucien replied, somewhat puzzled by his sudden and challenging attack.

"Lucien, I believe you misinterpreted my remark last week about paying a price for freedom. True, I admired your trying to stand up for a woman, but it was hardly well-advised to

184

draw the attention of the police to you and your friends. Henceforth, you and they will be marked men, so to speak. And if there should be any further dramatic episodes, you may rest assured that Magistrate Dougherty will show you considerably less indulgent treatment. You might even be sent to jail for a day or two, which would be a terrible blot on your record. I trust you are aware of that?''

"Yes, sir, but I don't propose—''

"Let me finish, Lucien. Perhaps I've been wrong in rhapso-dizing so much about Irish history, our heroes and kings. Lucien, there is a vast difference between a king of the tenth or eleventh century who, with hundreds of loyal followers, quested for Irish independence and a boy of sixteen who, with two romantically inclined companions of that same age, has determined to take this ancient political burden entirely upon his young shoulders. Such a burden will crush you, ruin you, Lucien. What would you do next? You merely threw a stone and insulted those British soldiers this time. Next time, your indignation might lead you to some impulsive, more violent act, one that would be cited as criminal. Your father's influence, the fact that you are an American enrolled here under the benign supervision of our good Father O'Mara, would not save you then from the magistrate's almost Mosaic justice. Even though he might secretly admire your stand, admire it all the more because here you are an American who wants to take up the cudgel—or perhaps I should say the shillelagh—on behalf of a free Ireland against the hated British, he must by virtue of his legal role as a mediator maintain peace at all costs. If anything, he must veer toward the side of the British, so that he could never be accused by them of being biased. Do you follow me?''

"Yes, I think so, Mr. Flannery.''

"Very well. Now listen to me carefully. You are a brilliant student, with a quick, assimilating mind. There's no limit to where you can place yourself mentally—or spiritually for that matter, because you have an excellent code of ethics and morality, innate decency and honor. All these things are to the good. But a single impulsive and rash act may destroy all this in the minds of others and create an image of your being a rowdy or a hooligan, as bad as any child of the slums who knows only to strike out against injustice because he lives in poverty and encounters violence daily. Do you not see this parallel?''

''I suppose you are right, Mr. Flannery, but—'' Lucien hedged.

''A moment, please, Lucien.'' Sean Flannery held up a hand and shook his head. ''Think what you like; write your essays about fanciful episodes in which you become the hero and put the hated English to flight. Have your triumphs in a literary way. If you become a fine writer, you can get across your point to a large audience, whereas this present course of action severely limits your audience and puts you in jeopardy. Do you follow me there?''

''Yes, sir, I do.''

''I'm relieved to hear it. Please promise me that you, Ned, and Edward will not try to be a band of young heroes who plan to right all the wrongs done our fine country over the centuries. Such utopian hopes would never be realized—and, as your exploits could grow bolder, British military opposition would put a swift and, I fear, dangerous end to these exploits. Please promise me that while you are at St. Timothy's, you will digest what I tell you, you will form your own well-advised opinions, but you will not go out on the streets of Dublin and defy British soldiers.''

''I—I'll try not to, Mr. Flannery.''

''I want you to do more than try, Lucien,'' Sean Flannery said in an exasperated tone. Then he shrugged and sighed. ''As I've said, perhaps it's my own fault. But never once, so far as I can remember, did I propose that all of you go out and turn the tables on our oppressors. From now on, I'll try to emphasize that we may *think* what we like—that is the beauty of freedom of the mind—but we may not always *do* what we choose. We must cope with the social order, an order not yet advanced enough to accept our ideas all down the line. In other words, try to temper your valor with discretion, and restrict your notions to your writing, your examinations, your discussions in class. You will find all your instructors sympathetic, for we Irish here at this academy—being good Catholics and digesting the heritage of Ireland along with our mother's milk—are at least as much concerned with the Irish Free State as you could ever possibly be. When you have concluded your education here, you will doubtless go back to America. You will take with you all your high resolves, but you will not have to defy the English on Irish soil—a defiance that must be guided by calm, unfevered thinking. We must convince the English that we deserve our freedom, but that will not be done by violence, for one act of violence leads to others in reprisal. This is how wars start, young Lucien Bouchard. Never forget it.''

Mary Eileen Brennert, who stood seventh in her class, had a quick mind and always did well in written examinations, although her natural shyness and diffidence held her back from topmost honors when it came to oral examinations. However, the headmistress, Sister Ernestine—Father O'Mara's cousin—had several times commented to the priest that in her opinion, the games master's daughter was an excellent, steadying influence on Lucien. She felt Mary Eileen had definitely helped this intrepid young American teenager to assimilate Irish culture and come to terms with the quieter, more reflective way of life that both educational institutions sought to inculcate in their charges.

Although Sean Flannery's lecture had smarted, Lucien's distress was at once dispelled when he saw Mary Eileen walking toward him. Her smile was exquisite, and he thought again that the dimples at the corners of her soft, tremulous mouth were the most enchanting sight he had ever seen.

"Good afternoon, Mary Eileen," he greeted her.

"And the same to you, Lucien. Oh, my, the girls have been buzzing for days over what you and your friends did in Dublin last Sunday. Were you severely punished?"

"Not really. But Father O'Mara and Mr. Flannery gave me the very dickens, and told me never to do anything like that again."

"Well, I think you're very brave and what you did was just wonderful! You're almost one of us, the way you think and feel about wanting Ireland to be free from the English," she declared. Then, to his almost incredulous delight, she slipped her soft hand into his and murmured, "Let's walk down by the stream—that is, if you've a mind to."

"Very much, Mary Eileen."

They walked silently, holding hands all the while until they reached the quietly flowing stream. Sitting down on a fallen log, Lucien broke the silence by asking, "Would you like to go into Dublin with me Sunday and have high tea at Kelly's?"

"I don't know if my father will let me—he said something last night about Aunt Patricia's visiting with my cousins. But I'd like to, if I am allowed. . . ."

"I do hope you can. Maybe you can let me know tomorrow, if you find out tonight?" he hazarded.

"Of course I will." She lowered her eyes and blushed exquisitely. He stole a glance at her, and his heart beat faster. The soft touch of her hand, her flattering praise of him, had gone to his head, and he thought himself deeply in love. Though he was wise enough to understand that they were both too young to be serious, he could dream about a future. He envisioned Mary Eileen as his fiancée and dreamed of bringing her back to America, for Laure and his stepfather to inspect, and announcing their engagement. Of course, he could not think of marriage for a number of years, but the thought that this girl liked him so much enchanted him.

Suddenly, he blurted, "When will you be finished at St. Eulalie's, Mary Eileen?"

She pursed her lips and frowned thoughtfully, looking even lovelier, at least in his opinion. Presently she said, "In about two-and-a-half years, Lucien. Why do you ask?"

"I—er—well, I was just curious. I've the same time to go at St. Timothy's—that is, if my parents want me to keep on here. I daresay they will. I certainly like it very much, and one of the main reasons—" He caught himself short, realizing that he was becoming too bold.

She gave him a sidelong look. "I hope we shall be friends till you have to go back to America."

"And maybe even after that!" he blurted, without meaning to. The touch of her hand in his, her dimpled smile, and the quizzical look in her gray-green eyes made him tremble with an awareness that was not so much carnal as euphoric and totally romantic. He had not yet kissed her, although many times at night when he was alone in his room he dreamed of doing so.

"But as to the present, Mary Eileen," he managed to say in a controlled tone, "I hope you'll be able to go out with me Sunday."

"I'll tell you tomorrow after classes, Lucien. But, if I can't . . ."

He shrugged, adopting a man-of-the-world attitude to impress her. "Well, then, I suppose I'll go with Edward and Ned."

"I do hope you won't get into trouble again!"

"I don't plan to. But I couldn't just stand by and let those four bullies bother that fishmonger, could I?"

"I don't suppose so. You know, I'm sure the policeman didn't understand and thought it odd because of your not being Irish."

"I have an Irish stepfather," he countered with a boyish smile.

"That's true," she laughed, although a worried look shadowed her face.

Lucien smiled at her, instinctively straightening his shoulders. Suddenly he felt himself a champion, a courageous protector, and imagined that the delicious girl who sat beside him was pledged to him. He swore to himself that like St. George he would slay any dragon that should cross her path. They sat a few more moments in silence, and then she asked, with a quizzical glance, "What are you thinking of, Lucien?"

"Oh—well, Mary Eileen, just—I guess I was thinking that I hate to see all those English soldiers swaggering around thinking they're so much better than the Irish. I don't like it at all."

"I know, Lucien. My father doesn't like it, either, but he says that we mustn't get involved. He says the political leaders have to sit down and talk things over sensibly. That's the only proper way to work things out. Otherwise, people will be hurt, lots of innocent people." Then she impulsively added, "I must say, had I been taken before a magistrate, I'd have been scared to death. And my father would have given me a good paddywhacking for it, too." Putting her hand over her mouth, she blushed and looked away. This innocent reference to her anatomy had suddenly brought to mind an intimate subject, one not to be mentioned in conversation with members of the opposite sex. Standing hastily, she declared, "I have to go now. My father will be wondering why I'm not home directly from school. I'll see you tomorrow—at the same time and the same place."

She turned away and began to run, and he stood marveling at her shapeliness, her entrancing femininity. As she ran, the wind played with the hem of her skirt, momentarily lifting it above the tops of her high-buttoned shoes and giving Lucien a hint of her shapely calves encased in black cotton stockings. He felt the blood rush to his head and then turned away quickly. With that tantalizing vision embossed on his mind, he walked slowly back to the dormitory.

Over the next few days, Lucien had pondered Sean Flannery's words, ultimately deciding he could never take a passive attitude toward what he deemed rank injustice, especially if it were demonstrated in his presence and sight. As he confided to Ned, "It seems to me that Mr. Flannery's approach is much too intellectual. I mean, if we hadn't done something last time, who knows what those four British soldiers might have done to the fishmonger. They might have manhandled her, dragged her off somewhere to have their way with her. . . ."

Ned had nodded and agreed with him. "A fellow has to do what is expedient at the moment, depending on the situation. Yes, heaven knows what might have happened to her."

"Naturally," Lucien went on, "if we take such overt actions, we'll have to be careful that there isn't a policeman about. I've no wish to have another scolding from Father O'Mara—the next time, he'd probably give us good wigging!"

Ned laughed, declaring, "Rather! He'd no doubt be so bloody furious that he'd have forgotten he no longer gives out canings and would promptly drag out the swishy cane I know he still keeps in his closet. But, nonetheless, I don't like the way British soldiers treat people here any more that you do, even if I am of English birth. But then, as you know, my grandfather stipulated that I had to come here, or else he wouldn't leave me a farthing. My mother thought it a great shame and all that, she being Church of England herself, but in the end, Grandfather prevailed—and I'm glad he did. I like it here very much."

As it turned out, Mary Eileen could not go into town with him the next Sunday. Nor could Edward Cordovan, who had come down with a bad case of the sniffles, the house physician strongly advising him against leaving his room until all symptoms had disappeared. Ned Riordan, however, was at loose ends and readily agreed to accompany Lucien on a jaunt through Dublin, planning to culminate their outing with that famous high tea at Kelly's.

Before he left his room that morning, Lucien wrote a long letter to Leland Kenniston, addressing it to his stepfather's office:

Dear Father,

This second term is even better than the first, and each week makes me feel happier that I'm in such an atmosphere. The instructors are wonderful, and I've made lots of friends, including Miss Brennert, who continues to favor me with her interest. She is very refined, and I assure you that our meetings are extremely circumspect. Perhaps one day you and Mother can meet her.

Father, by the end of next month the school term will be out, and I'd like very much to stay here. It's a long trip each way across the ocean, and since I spent the Christmas holidays home, I was hoping you'd agree. I'd like to concentrate on some projects I have, such as writing, and—I'll be honest—I'd like to see Mary Eileen as much as possible. She stands very high scholastically, and this pleases me. She's also very gentle, but she has a certain amount of skepticism so that she isn't a pushover for anyone. That's very healthy in a girl, don't you agree?

I think you would have been proud of me last Sunday. Ned, Edward, and I saw a girl selling fish being rudely accosted by four British soldiers. I told them several times to leave her alone, but they didn't pay any attention. Finally, we took them all on with fisticuffs. A policeman intervened, and we were taken to the magistrate's court and there given a strong lecture. The headmaster gave us an even worse one on Monday.

I'm sure you agree that it's important to take a stand, because I know how much Ireland means to you, Father. Mr. Flannery, whom I respect and like very much indeed, tells me that I shouldn't go so far in my reactions to this kind of tyranny. There I don't agree with him. Understand, I don't mean to get in any trouble or risk myself unnecessarily, but I do feel I must act when I see brutality and contempt and even violence trying to replace sanity. I'm sure you would, too.

Give Mother my love, and tell her I hope she won't

be too disappointed in my decision not to come back this summer. Honestly, I can get a good deal of work done and prepare for my next semester, while at the same time enjoy a vacation and have a lot of fun. Some of the other boys stay on during the summer, so I know it would be all right with Father O'Mara for me to do so. I won't exceed my allowance, you can depend on that. Do make Mother understand that my not wanting to come back home this summer has nothing to do with not wanting to see both of you—for, of course, I do. But I would prefer to wait until the Christmas holidays again, if you've no objection.

Please tell Paul, Clarissa, Celestine, and John that I miss them all, just as I miss you and Mother very much.

Your son,
Lucien

When Leland Kenniston received this letter in early May, he read it twice over and then scowled. "The young fool wants to play the role of hero, when he is not yet dry behind the ears," he said half aloud to himself. "Laure won't like this at all, and still less the fact that he wants to stay over there until next Christmas. The boy's getting some ideas that are way beyond his grasp, in my opinion."

He decided that when he went home that evening, he would share parts of the letter with his wife, but not refer to the episode of the Sunday arrest. That would only worry Laure unnecessarily. No, he would concentrate on softening the news that Lucien preferred to stay in Ireland through the summer, rather than come home to his family.

Lucien might well have added a paragraph in his letter to his stepfather, but he had decided against it. Quite apart from wanting to be with Mary Eileen Brennert through the summer and making preparations for the classwork he would have in the following semester, his main reason for wanting to stay in Ireland was to do what he could for the cause of the Irish Free State. He had even gone so far as to think that perhaps he might attract other classmates to join Ned and Edward and himself in a kind of vigilante group, patrolling the streets of Dublin and preventing episodes of British bullying. In his idealism and patriotic zeal for the country in which he was receiving his advanced schooling, he quite overlooked the dangers attendant upon such a course of action. He did not stop to think that if he had seriously injured one of the soldiers, the others might have been justified in drawing a pistol and shooting him down in retaliation, in spite of his age. For his act surely would have been one of criminal assault against an officer of the Crown. He did not understand that men are not always rational, not always even tempered. It was well for Lucien that the four soldiers had been so, or he might indeed have had a physical injury done to him.

As Lucien and Ned had set out for Dublin in high spirits, the young American was blissfully unaware of the real inspiration for his errant idealism. Had he been more introspective, he might have realized that the underlying motivation for his espousal of the Irish Free State cause was not patriotic zeal; rather, it was a way of impressing Mary Eileen Brennert with the fact that he was a mature man capable of forthright decisions.

In addition, young Lucien could not forget how gallantly and nobly his father, Luke Bouchard, had died by sacrificing himself for the life of Governor Houston. And he remembered other examples of how his father had taken a stand against oppression and bigotry and evil. With this background and admiration for his stepfather—together with the elemental desire to win Mary Eileen's esteem for him as a man of courage and judgment—it was no wonder that Lucien ignored Sean Flannery's wise advice: to be moderate in all things, to let the mind be as free and imaginative and daring as it would, but to temper the hot blood of youth with rational intellectualism.

Ned and Lucien had spent a long afternoon trudging through the poorer sections of Dublin, exchanging impassioned views on the curse of poverty. They were retracing their steps toward High Street, so as to be at Kelly's by four-thirty on this windy early spring afternoon, when they came up behind an elderly woman pushing a barrow filled with potatoes along the sidewalk. She paused from time to time, heaving mournful sighs, looking up at the sky and muttering to herself. At that moment, two British soldiers came down the sidewalk from the opposite direction, one of them a thickly moustached sergeant major. In his gloved right hand, he was carrying his drill stick, and as he walked, he beat out a cadence with it on his polished boot.

He and his companion advanced, both so engrossed in conversation that neither of them noticed the old woman approaching until the sergeant major walked smack into the barrow. He growled, "You stupid old woman, get that barrow off to the street where it belongs. Let us pass!"

Flustered and apologetic, the woman tried to turn the barrow, but the sharp incline of the street slowed her action. The sergeant major strode impatiently past the barrow and, with his shoulder, gave her a nudge that made her stumble and then fall to her knees. "That'll teach you to obey the rules of courtesy," he angrily told her. "Come along, now, Private Hearn. Look sharp."

Lucien was boiling inwardly at such a brutal lack of consideration for the aged. He whirled, caught the sergeant major by the arm, and exclaimed, "That was no way to treat that poor old woman! Don't you see you hurt her? Go help her to her feet and apologize!"

The sergeant major stood, hands on hips, staring incredulously at his young interlocutor. Then he burst into laughter. "Listen to this lad trying to tell me how I should behave toward that old crow!" Then, with a stern and harsh look, he told Lucien, "I don't need any more of your lip, my lad. Suppose you go off, you and your pale-faced friend there, to wherever your business takes you. You'd best, if you don't want some trouble."

"I'm going to report you to the military authority, Sergeant Major," Lucien Bouchard announced, a righteous expression on his face.

"Oh, are you now, my fine bucko?" He turned to the private, who guffawed and slapped his thigh. "I'm warning you, take off and get out of my sight, before I take this drill stick to your stupid skull!"

Incensed beyond control, Lucien doubled his fist and struck out, hitting the sergeant major just below his left eye. With a bellow of rage, the soldier retaliated with a savage punch that sent Lucien stumbling back against the wall of a shuttered store. With an angry cry, Ned charged the sergeant major's companion and, before the man could get in a blow, sent both fists thudding into the private's belly.

194

As Lucien stood, unsteadily reeling, the sergeant major raised his drill stick and slashed at him, livid with rage. Instinct alone saved the youth from a cut across the cheek, and the stick whistled over the top of his head as he ducked. Then, lowering his head, he butted the sergeant major in the belly and sent the man sprawling into the cobblestone gutter. "Let's get out of here fast!" he panted to Ned, who needed no second invitation, and the two boys took to their heels. The sergeant major stumbled to all fours, then righted himself and, pulling his whistle out of his tunic pocket, blew a shrill blast. He bawled, "Come back here, you little Irish bastid! I'll skelp you raw for this, see if I don't!"

Fortunately for both boys, this time no policeman was in the offing. The two of them ran as if the devil himself were after them; they went around the corner, ducked into an alley, and thence crossed over into Martry Lane and were soon lost from view.

Winded, panting, having completely forgotten their anticipated high tea at Kelly's, they slumped down on a stone bench and looked at each other as they tried to regain their breath.

"Sink me if that wasn't a narrow one, Lucien," Ned gasped, then began to laugh. It was contagious, and Lucien joined him in gales of uncontrollable laughter.

"I think," Ned concluded, when he had finally regained his composure, "we'd best not go back to Dublin for at least a fortnight, just in case that sergeant major should run into us. He might not take kindly to seeing us again."

"I don't think he would, at that," Lucien chuckled. Then, clapping Ned on the back, he declared, "Up the Irish! Down the British and damnation to all of them!"

A week later, Lucien wrote another letter to Leland Kenniston:

Dear Father,
   I want to tell you about what happened when my friend Ned and I went into Dublin last Sunday. We saw two British soldiers elbow an elderly Irish woman out of the way and send her tumbling into the gutter. I told them what I thought, then I sent my fist into the

belligerent face of one of them. It was very satisfying, believe me.

He was the most disgusting bully, Father. You would have been proud of me. I nursed a sore stomach where he punched me back, but I've never felt better. I have, to use a poetic expression, struck a blow for Irish freedom.

We shan't be going into Dublin for two more weeks at least because we want to avoid this sergeant major, lest he drag us before a magistrate again. But, you see, Father, I feel I'm doing something for the cause of Irish independence. I know it's a small thing, but it excites me, makes me feel worthwhile. I have a mission in life while I'm here.

At any rate, I presume that by now you've received my first letter, telling you about my decision to stay here for the summer. I hope you've broken the news to Mother, and that she isn't too disappointed. I'll keep writing to you because I know you'll want to know what's going on here.

Your affectionate son,
Lucien

The Irish entrepreneur opened the letter in his office, read it swiftly, and then rolled his eyes and uttered a groan. "The harebrained young fool!" Leland ejaculated. "He's just daring them to do something to him, catch up with him. He thinks what he's doing is clever, but I don't agree with him at all. I think it's senseless and that he's just feeling his oats. He's interpreted my theoretical belief in the Fenian movement as an open invitation for him to indulge in whatever heroic acts—as he terms them—may suit his ego."

Leland reread the letter slowly, then shook his head again and put the letter into the drawer of his desk. He drew out several sheets of paper and laboriously wrote a long letter to his stepson:

My Dear Lucien,

I have just read your last letter detailing your exploits with the sergeant major. My opinion is that you are now a marked man, and I use that word advisedly. You are still immature, and you cannot solve the problems of a nation until you have learned to solve your own.

Petty acts of violence, petty and small, will not help the cause of Ireland against the tyrannical English. Even I—who am many years older than you and supposedly wiser—had to revise my thinking when I discovered facts you do not yet know.

The Irish movement toward freedom and emancipation from English rule cannot be achieved—as I see now—with blood. You would allocate to yourself the role of martyr and hero and devil's advocate all in one—and you would be a fool.

No one wins a war. Study your history a little more with Sean Flannery, of whom you are so fond. Even he must necessarily tell you that the common people, the so-called masses, are the ones who suffer most. In every war, from the days of Troy to date, the victors were those who furnished the weapons, and who bided their time well behind the front lines until all the fighting was done, then claimed victory for their side. And their side was not necessarily the moral one.

No, Lucien—not you, nor any martyr who kills an English soldier and willingly gives his neck to the hangman's noose, can expect to right the wrongs done for hundreds of years. It will take an intelligent breed of statesmen on both sides to decide how to resolve this agonizing question of independence.

Remember also, no man can consider himself worthy of ruling a nation or even a town or a borough until he learns to rule himself. You are still too young to have learned this, but one day you will, I hope in the not-too-far-distant future.

As to your request, I have broken the news gently to your mother that you do not propose to return here for the summer vacation. She is unhappy over your decision, but she accepts it. She wishes you well and bids you take care of yourself. She and I are both more interested in your friendship with Miss Brennert—she seems like a sensible girl—than in your intrepid gallantry. You have read, of course, that famous poem "The Charge of the Light Brigade"—what a glorious show it was, but what a tragic waste of lives it was. There is a lesson there for all of us. Grand gestures are marvelous—they satisfy the soul—but if the individual is dead, I very much doubt that he or she can enjoy the so-called victory.

With this letter, I'm enclosing a small check. I admonish you to spend it on the simple pleasures of taking Miss Brennert to the theater, to tea, and with further injunction that, when you are with her, you are in no way to endanger her by continuing your single-handed war against the British soldiers. I know that your own wisdom will tell you that involving her would be madness, and beyond that, it would estrange the two of you. I can tell by your letters that you are smitten with this girl in a very decent way. That is all to the good. Do not spoil it, and do not spoil your hopes for your future with her by playing the hero role just once too often.

Your concerned father,
Leland

Chapter Nineteen

Nearly two years had passed since Mei Luong, the Chinese girl who had been Lopasuta and Geraldine Bouchard's nursemaid, had married Eugene DuBois, the ambitious young Creole, and since that time she had known unbounded happiness. Her husband was thoughtful, ardent, and tender, and though the New Orleans newspapers occasionally carried stories of violent attacks against Chinese—particularly in the far west and northwest of the country—she encountered no animosity in New Orleans. To be sure, part of this could be attributed to her having adopted Western ways in dress and coiffure, mostly at Geraldine Bouchard's urging.

Mei Luong had blossomed, and her delicate beauty was enhanced when, on the last Friday night in the month of May 1882, she told her husband that she was with child. He was overjoyed and kissed her hand, treating her like a princess. "You have made me the happiest man in the world, my dearest Mei Luong," he told her. "I love you more now than when we were first married. This news is more than I could have hoped for. Since I passed the Louisiana bar two months ago, making me a full-fledged lawyer, I didn't think I would be entitled to any more happiness for a while!"

Eugene held his wife in his arms and whispered, "Lopasuta will always be my dearest friend, and not just because he saw my potential and helped me realize it, not just because we now work together. I will be indebted to him mostly because it was he who invited me to his home, where I first met you, my exquisite flower of beauty."

Mei Luong felt tears come to her eyes at so poetic and ardent a declaration, and she embraced the young Creole and murmured, "All these things were in your destiny, dear Eugene."

As soon as Eugene DuBois had received his certificate from the Louisiana Bar Association, Lopasuta had written to his employer, Leland Kenniston, and proposed that he be authorized to promote the young Creole, making him a staff lawyer. Leland had at once wired a hearty agreement with this proposal, delighted with the fact that he would have two excellent legal minds working for him to solve any problems that might arise for his import-export firm. He also praised both men for their extracurricular work on behalf of the poor and proposed that a separate storefront be rented as a legal clinic, to better serve the community.

Judith Marquard had been for some years Lopasuta's invaluable legal assistant. She had proved herself endlessly resourceful in going all over the city to obtain financial reports, performing private detective work of the most discreet and intensive kind. Indeed, it was her ability to search out obscure facts that had enabled Lopasuta to win two important cases before the Louisiana Court of Appeals, where a conveyer had sought to reverse the decision of the lower court in an action against Leland's business. Thanks to what Judith had uncovered, the Appellate Court had dismissed the plaintiff's plea on the grounds that he had furnished no new point of law to warrant the changing of the lower court's ruling.

As a result, Judith had received a handsome Christmas bonus the previous December plus a substantial raise in salary. The housekeeper she had engaged took excellent care of her children, leaving her free to pursue a career that spiritually and materially satisfied her. Her marriage to the blind Bernard Marquard had proved to be a total salvation and regeneration for Judith, a woman who years before had been traduced and reviled by a scheming ne'er-do-well.

Just this morning, she had received a letter from her former employer, now living in Arizona, wishing her and Bernard well. Jason Barntry, the former New Orleans bank president, had been stricken with an inevitably fatal disease, but he had peacefully and calmly prepared himself for his end. As he wrote:

When a man knows that he is going to die and he is along in years, he begins to take stock of himself, and

200

his mind wanders toward the past. I pride myself in remembering that I served the Bouchard family faithfully to the utmost of my abilities, and during the last years of my tenure, dear Judith, your help was invaluable in that service. Be assured that if I can help you or your husband in any way that has to do with the banking industry, I stand ready to serve you both.

I am happy for you, Judith. I have great faith in you because you are a sensitive, intelligent woman. It pains me that you once suffered so needlessly and unjustly. Perhaps this is the lesson we oldsters learn as our days are ending: that somehow, however long it may take, our Creator moves inexorably to right the wrongs done us. Persevere and enjoy life. I shall be your friend until death claims me—and beyond that, if it is possible.

Yours affectionately,
Jason Barntry

Judith was terribly saddened to learn how ill her dear benefactor now was, and she quickly sent off a reply, hoping her letter would reach the good man in time. Although she had often in the past expressed her great appreciation to him, she felt that to do so now, once again, would comfort him. She would never forget his having given her the first chance to escape the past—and his treating her with a respect that she had not then felt for herself. Truly, she would miss his guidance.

As a parallel to the happy unions between the DuBoises and the Marquards, the marriage between Lopasuta and Geraldine Bouchard was more durable than ever. But even now, after so many years had gone by, Lopasuta could still occasionally be amazed at his good fortune.

As a young Comanche, he had been adopted by Luke Bouchard and given the chance to develop his keen intelligence. He had chosen the field of law, believing that this would enable him to help those who were circumscribed by poverty and unfamiliarity with the law so they might gain an equitable voice before the courts. It was after arguing just such a case that his beloved wife, Geraldine, had first approached him, extolling him for his concern. Now, after surviving several tragic events—including Lopasuta's being kidnapped to Hong

Kong, which resulted in the birth of his second child, a son born to the woman who rescued him—the Comanche and his wife were idyllically happy. Geraldine was dedicated to her husband's endeavors, and Lopasuta constantly received inspiration from her dedication.

Being a member of a tribe despised by whites as "murderous savages," he understood only too well what stigmas were attached to those who were minorities. He saw this happen to blacks, Chinese, Indians, and immigrants who fled to America as the one land where they might find freedom from oppression and bigotry and prejudice. In this young, growing country there were all those evils, and thus he had taken as his life's work the challenge of combating them, hoping that America might be the one bulwark in the world where justice could prevail, no matter what a man's bank account might be, or his antecedents. Granted, it was a romantic idealism, but it served to shape Lopasuta's character and make him a far better husband and father than he could have been without such purpose in his life. And because Geraldine was not the helpless, clinging type—whose life began and ended in her husband—but rather was amplified and expanded by her husband's very profession, their marriage was unshakably steadfast, loving and loyal.

Shortly after Eugene DuBois had passed the bar examination, Lopasuta assigned him to a curious case in which there were overtones of contraband. One of Leland Kenniston's shippers, one the firm used sporadically when their regular shippers were unavailable, had been unable to fill one of Leland's contracts for cargo delivery, owing, he said, to an unexpected storm. After Lopasuta had filed a lawsuit, claiming nonperformance of contract, the shipper, in turn, had pleaded that an "act of God" in the form of the alleged storm had prevented that performance, and thus sought the quashing of the suit against him.

Lopasuta had advised Eugene to go to the levee and talk in a friendly way with many ships' captains and first mates. What the Creole learned had led Lopasuta to be suspicious of this particular shipper: The man had a history of nonperformances because of similar acts of God. Investigating further and checking several of the maritime logs of ships that had traveled in the region, as well as the harbormaster's records,

Eugene discovered that there had been no such storm reported by any of these other vessels during the period in question.

The previous Saturday afternoon, he had gone back to the levee and, quite by chance, met an unemployed stevedore, an extremely gregarious and friendly mulatto nearing his fortieth year. The man had come up to Eugene and, nodding his forehead, had mumbled, "Cap'n, I hear you're tryin' to find out about the man who owns the *Benjamin Benrow*. Fact is, Cap'n, I was a second mate on that ship up to last year, and I didn't like the cut of the man's jib no way. He's a thief and a pirate, and he's runnin' smuggled goods, and I'll just bet my next month's pay against a good stogie he gave you his usual runaround."

Eugene had taken the man to a nearby restaurant and there bought him a huge meal. He had also made careful notes of the man's testimony. Then he had given the stevedore a five-dollar bill out of his own pocket and promised to help the man find new employment.

The stevedore, Malachi Evans, was effusive in his gratitude. "Cap'n, you're a real fine Christian man. I didn't know where my next dollar was comin' from, truth to tell. God bless you." Then Eugene had gone back to the office and written a letter to the shipper, hinting at the facts he had discovered.

On this morning, exactly one week later, Leland Kenniston's New Orleans office received an apologetic and almost feverish note from the shipper agreeing to pay the claim of damages in the suit, but asking for a compromise so that the damages themselves would be cut by two thirds. Following Eugene's careful report to him, detailing all of the circumstances of the case, Lopasuta sent off a telegram to Leland advising that, in view of the shipper's unsavory reputation, based on the evidence Eugene had uncovered, Leland should cease doing business with him henceforth. Further, the Irishman should accept the settlement, for it was unlikely that anything more could be derived from such a questionable source. A wire followed back the next day, commending both lawyers and suggesting that the stevedore who had been indirectly responsible for the information be given a substantial monetary reward.

The stevedore had given Eugene his address—a small,

cheap rooming house not far from notorious Gallatin Street. Luke's adoptive son had good reason to remember this dangerous area, for it was there that an enemy by the name of Milo Brutus Henson had arranged for a thug to waylay and try to kill him.

However, now that all those conspirators who had been involved in the abduction that had taken him to Hong Kong were dead, Lopasuta decided that there would be no harm in going to Gallatin Street in broad daylight. He was anxious to meet the man who had been so helpful in resolving the Kenniston Company's suit against the delinquent shipper. Accordingly, after having lunched at one of his favorite Creole restaurants with Eugene, the Comanche sent his associate back to the office and then set out for the stevedore's address.

In response to his tugging the bellpull, a slatternly woman with hideously bleached hair and a face disfigured by the pitting of smallpox opened the door and peered out at him suspiciously. Seeing how well he was dressed, she snapped, "Ain't got no gals here, mistuh. You go on to Rampart Street, if that's your fancy. Me, I'm a respectable woman."

Before she could close the door in his face, Lopasuta interposed with a polite smile, "I was looking for Mr. Evans."

"Oh, him!" the woman contemptuously sniffed. "He cleared out two days ago. What's more, he skipped owin' me a week's rent. If you find him—though I don't know what a fine-lookin' gentleman like you'd be doin' havin' a friend like that no-good, shiftless nigger—you can tell him he owes Amy Blodgett two dollars room and board, and he better pay up, or I'll have him jailed next time I clap eyes on him."

"I'll do that, of course. Then you've no idea where he might have gone?"

"Didn't I say no? Sneaked out in the dead o' night, he did, after tellin' me a lot of fine talk about makin' a passel o' money at a job he was gonna get any day now. Huh!" She snorted indignantly. "As if anybody with good sense'd pay that no-account nigger any big money, when all he can do is talk a poor respectable widow outa room 'n board for a week!"

"He didn't mention what kind of work it was, did he, ma'am?" Lopasuta politely inquired.

"Not so's ah kin recollect. Wait a mite—it seems to me he said somethin' 'bout goin' into the swamps—out near Lake

Pontchartrain—but that's all he said. Now, if you'll excuse me, I got work to do in the kitchen, gettin' supper ready for my payin' lodgers.'' With this, she closed the door with a finality that clearly pronounced there was no more information to be derived from this source. Lopasuta frowned, puzzled, and then slowly retraced his footsteps back to the office.

When he mentioned to Eugene DuBois what he had learned, the young Creole thought a moment and then said, "You know, Lopasuta, lots of things go on in the bayous. There used to be smuggling in the old pirate days, when Jean Lafitte and his gang ruled the roost out there. I shouldn't be surprised if there's some smuggling going on even to this very day. It's a good place to stay out of. If somebody wanted to murder somebody and never have the body found, he'd probably try to lure him out there, would be my guess. All kinds of snakes and alligators and lots of quicksand, too, to suck you down, without a trace.''

"I can see that your legal training has done nothing to dispel a very vivid imagination, Eugene,'' the Comanche lawyer chuckled.

When Lopasuta arrived at the office two mornings later, Judith Marquard told him that a shabbily dressed black in his early forties had come up to her, just as she was opening the door, and handed her a note, "For that lawyer fella who was lookin' for my friend Malachi. Tell him I'm mighty worried 'bout him. I'd be mighty pleased if the lawyer fella could find him for me. We been friends nigh on to fifteen years, we have, 'n our pappies worked on the same sugarcane plantation.''

He had respectfully bobbed his head, shoved a piece of folded paper into Judith's hand, and then hobbled down the street.

Puzzled, Lopasuta opened the note and read the following:

I hear tell my friend Malachi Evans is gone into the swamp. I was supposed to go with him but he left not saying a word. Now I scared. Can you help me, Mr. Lawyer? I got some nigger friends tell me you done real good for them and didn't charge them much. You can find me over on Bush Street, upstairs over the saloon.

205

The note was signed, "Eddie Henry."

"What is it all about, Lopasuta?" Judith asked him, after he had frowned and, folding the piece of paper, put it back into his pocket.

"It's all very strange, Judith. You know about Malachi Evans, the black man who helped us out by informing on that shady shipping company and saved us the cost of a long, protracted lawsuit? Well, Mr. Kenniston wired me to give him a reward to show our appreciation, only when I went over to his boardinghouse, he'd gone without notice—leaving a very angry landlady. And now this man says he's a friend of Mr. Evans and fears the stevedore has been lost in the bayous or something, and says I can help find him somehow. It's very mystifying, to say the least. But I suppose I should go see him."

"Where is he, Lopasuta?"

He put his hand back into his pocket, took out the note and let her read it. "Hmm. That's not a very good neighborhood—you certainly shouldn't go there at night."

"I'll be careful. And I think I'll go there right now."

When Lopasuta Bouchard arrived at the address he had been given and climbed the narrow stairway that led above the saloon to a rickety second-floor hallway with three apartments, he stood a moment irresolutely, not knowing at which door to knock. The problem was solved for him when the door far down the hall to his left suddenly opened and a heavyset black man with closely cropped graying hair stepped out. Hobbling up the hallway, he eagerly asked, "You the lawyer—Mr. Bouchard?"

"Yes, I am. You're Mr. Henry, I take it. I'd like to know more about this friend of yours." He stopped and looked around the dingy landing. "Tell you what," he suggested. "I'll take you to a restaurant I know and buy you lunch. It's close enough to lunchtime, and I'm hungry. Come along."

When they reached the eating place, Lopasuta ushered the lame black man to a table at the back of the restaurant, then spoke in a low voice to the man. "Now what's your opinion about all this, Mr. Henry?"

The black glanced around warily, as if afraid someone would overhear his conversation. Then he leaned forward across the table and, in a guarded whisper, replied, "I've heard mighty strange things 'bout these here swamps, Mr.

Bouchard. *Mighty* strange things. You know what I think? I think poor old black Malachi Evans went there for this job he was talkin' 'bout 'n got hisself made a slave again.''

"Made a slave again?" Lopasuta echoed, an incredulous look on his handsome face. "But there isn't any slavery in the United States any more, Mr. Henry, and there hasn't been since Abraham Lincoln freed them all nineteen years ago."

"I know that. You knows that. But there it is. I's scared, honest I is. I's afraid maybe they'll come for me, if Malachi tells 'em 'bout me and how I wants to work, too. 'N he ain't able to get away no how, if he's where I think he is. Can you help?"

"Let's eat lunch first, Mr. Henry, and then come back to my office with me. I want you to talk to my associate, Eugene DuBois. He grew up around here, and he knows a great deal more than I could possibly know."

An hour later, the lame black man told his story to Eugene. Lopasuta was still incredulous about the entire affair. "How can there be slavery going on in this day and age, and so close to New Orleans, Eugene?" he asked.

"It may not be so impossible a notion as you think, Lopasuta. I know the bayous. My father and I used to hunt and fish there, and civilization doesn't reach very far into them. The Cajuns who live there are a very insular people, and if anything like a slavery ring were operating there, they'd be the last people in the world to go to the authorities to tell them of its existence."

Lopasuta sat with his fingers tented to his lips. Finally he said, "This is most interesting. Just by accident, we may have stumbled onto something very criminal—and we should do what we can to get someone to investigate it."

"Yes, I agree. It could be dangerous, though. Very dangerous."

Chapter Twenty

The meeting with Eddie Henry had more than aroused Lopasuta's interest in a possible criminal misdeed. It had also awakened a part of himself that had lain dormant for years. At the moment, all of his employer's legal matters were proceeding smoothly, and he had no court cases for at least a week. The curious story that the aging black had told him, together with Eugene DuBois's comments on the mysterious insularity of the swamps, had reminded him that he had come from an Indian tribe noted for its scouting and hunting. Since he had left the Comanche stronghold in Mexico to study law and subsequently pass the bar examination in Alabama, Lopasuta had done nothing to compare to his extremely active boyhood as a member of that aggressive tribe. True, years before, he had fought off an attack by the Ku Klux Klan led by a rival attorney who had hated him for having triumphed in the courtroom against his own clients, but since then, he had sometimes had the feeling that those primitive, yet powerful abilities he had learned while living with the Comanche were of no use in this thoroughly urban life of his.

He reasoned that if he were personally to try to track down the supposed illicit ring of slavers in the murky swamps northwest of the city of New Orleans, he would call upon all of his resourcefulness, all of the survival instincts that had been sharpened by his daily life in the Comanche stronghold. For that reason, after his meeting with Eddie Henry and his subsequent discussion with Eugene, he told the Creole the next morning, "Do you know, Eugene, I feel very much like going into the swamps myself to determine whether this slave ring really exists. Besides, the idea is so bizarre, the officials probably wouldn't believe it anyway."

"I agree with you there, Lopasuta," the young Creole lawyer said. "But you may not realize the extent of the danger—and not just from the snakes and the alligators you're likely to find in the bayous. I shouldn't be surprised if a certain amount of smuggling still goes on in that area even today, and those men wouldn't take kindly to an intruder."

"Well, of course, I'll take a weapon along, Eugene. I'd be a fool if I didn't. And I'll get a pair of high, thick boots so the fangs of a poisonous snake won't end my days as a successful lawyer," Lopasuta declared with a grin.

"But more than that, you'll need a guide—and I'd like to volunteer. It's the least I can do, considering all you've done for me." He gave his friend a wry smile and added, "Anyway, my own curiosity has been piqued. I'm good with a pistol or a rifle, and besides, I can speak the *patois* of the Cajuns. They'll be more open with me than they would be to outsiders. They'd clam up in a hurry if you tried to find out any information by yourself."

"I see your point. And I'm grateful for your offer of help, Eugene. It'll be an adventure," Lopasuta chuckled, his eyes sparkling. "The fact is, I've wanted something like this for a few years, without really knowing what it was. Now here's a golden opportunity to use my physical skills and do a fine humanitarian service, if we actually do find slavers and can bring them in for prosecution."

"I practically lived in the bayous for a long while, my father and I hunted there so often. It'll be like going home for me, too. . . . Well, if you've no objection, after lunch today, I'll go make some inquiries about supplies. We'll need a pirogue first off. And I'd like to get a good rifle and also some revolvers, plus plenty of ammunition."

"That's a good idea. But why would you take a pirogue over, say, a flatboat?"

"For one thing, it's smaller and lighter, easier to handle. You're thinking of the old Mississippi and Alabama River flatboats, where you had two or three boatmen pushing with long poles down in the mud to thrust it onward. It's something I wouldn't care to do, especially against the current."

"It sounds a little bit fatiguing," the Comanche lawyer chuckled.

"It's that and more," Eugene explained. "A pirogue is actually a canoe hollowed from the trunk of a tree, and of course its keel doesn't go deep into the water. This is important because swampwater is shallow for the most part, except for places like Blind River, which we'll probably cross if we go farther to the north. Also, we won't get held up by thick plant growth, as we would using a vessel that sits deeper into the water with its keel."

"I leave that entirely to you. You evidently know a good deal about it, and I bow to your superior wisdom. Take all the time you want to get supplies this afternoon, Eugene, because I'd like to get started tomorrow and wind this thing up before the week is over."

"*If* we're lucky—and if the Cajuns don't betray us to the slavers, if slavers really are there." Eugene was guarded in his assent. "At any rate, it'll certainly be exciting, as well as dangerous. Maybe we both need that."

Lopasuta peered closely at the young Creole. "You know, I'm glad I met you and that you're my friend and associate. I have great confidence in you, Eugene, and I foresee that one day you'll be a very important attorney."

Eugene bowed his head slightly before saying, "I'm not interested in being important. I just want to be a good lawyer. I want to help people, the way you do. If I can do half of what you've already done, I'll settle for that."

"No, Eugene"—Lopasuta put out his hand and clapped the Creole on the shoulder—"you'll do even more than that because you're driven, and you can't stand evil and injustice any more than I can. Besides, you're younger, and you haven't met the rebuffs I've had, and because you've made this early start, something tells me that you'll go far beyond what you even dream. I want that for you." He philosophically smiled, then added, "We of the Comanche, the People, believe that every man has within himself the power to create beyond his father, who in turn believed that he could create beyond *his* father. That is the way of life."

"There's much truth to that, Lopasuta," Eugene solemnly agreed. "Well, I'll go into town now, and buy the boat and weapons. Tomorrow morning, at dawn, we'll start out for the bayous. I hope I can find a carriage driver willing to leave that early, but since its a good fifty miles to the area Malachi told Eddie he was heading for—past Pontchartrain and Maurepas—we'll have to leave that early if we expect to make any distance at all the first day. And I for one," he grinned, "don't intend to carry our supplies all that distance on my back. Nor, of course, could we leave a carriage and horses just tied up for days. After the driver leaves us, we'll be on our own in a different world."

"It sounds as if we're beginning a new chapter in our lives together, Eugene," Lopasuta said with a grim smile.

Lopasuta had thought at first that it might be advantageous to bring along Eddie Henry, if only to identify his missing friend, should Malachi be found. But Eugene had emphatically rejected the idea. "Please, Lopasuta, it's going to be tough enough getting into those bayous and past the Cajuns with just our two selves, you understand me? Some of the Cajuns may well be on the slavers' side because they feel that in the swamps the only law that goes is what they hold to. Bringing along this black man could very well make things even rougher for us. We'd be risking Mr. Henry's life. No, sir, it'll be just the two of us, and we're going to see if our brains and our wit and your Comanche training oughtn't to be enough to lick a band of slavers. That's the long and the short of it, as I see it."

And so, at dawn on a June morning that threatened a scorching day in New Orleans, Lopasuta Bouchard and Eugene DuBois boarded the carriage taking them northwest of the Queen City. Tilting up toward the already sunny sky was the sharp prow of the pirogue that Eugene had purchased the day before. There were two rifles, both of them the Spencer repeating kind, and a pair of Colt revolvers, plus over a hundred rounds of ammunition. In addition, Eugene had purchased two pairs of riding boots, of the thickest leather he had been able to buy, at a bootmaker's on Branch Street. Lopasuta had eyed them suspiciously, but when he had looked at Eugene, the young man said laconically, "I don't think a snake's fangs can penetrate these, Lopasuta. I don't believe in taking extra risks. We'll have trouble enough with the Cajuns and the slavers."

In an old trunk he had brought from Montgomery, Lopasuta had found the leggings and buckskin jacket he had worn as a stripling. He explained this to Eugene as the carriage bounced along the cobblestone street, adding, "They will be good camouflage."

Eugene was also sensibly dressed in a costume that would

obscure his presence in the shadowy, mysterious bayous. He wore a pair of faded Levis and a drab gray cotton shirt. These clothes and heavy boots were all he would need in the oppressive humidity and dense enclosure of the bayous. It was an almost prehistoric world, where death and danger lurked for the unwary. The strange insects, whose buzzing was more usually heard at night, the pelicans and flamingos, the owls and the dark-winged hummingbirds, as well as huge bats hanging on the ends of cypress trees in the very heart of the swamp—these were the eerie winged denizens of the dense forest, where the water and the silt and the intense, cloistered heat made vegetation flourish. It was a primeval world, and those who lived within its boundaries were a tribe unto themselves, who recognized no law save their own—the basic law since the world had begun, that of survival. Those who had survived were hardy because of it and were proud of their difference from the world society called "civilized"—because here there were no tenets of decency and morality, justice and honor, only the constant battle against quicksand and snakes and alligators and poisonous insects whose bite created miasmic fever and inevitable death by hideous, unrelenting pain. . . .

Hours later, the driver pulled into the shade of a huge live oak at the very edge of the swamp. Then Eugene and Lopasuta lifted the pirogue and set it down carefully into one of the tributary streams that ran northwestward.

"This is an inlet of the Blind River. It's sluggish and stagnant, and we'll have to paddle quite a spell," the Creole declared. The two men then carefully placed the weapons and ammunition on the bottom of the pirogue.

Eugene also brought a gunnysack of food—dried beef, a slab of bacon, a pound of coffee, cans of beans, and a sack of rice, plus a tinderbox. Also, he had brought tobacco, both for a pipe and for cigarettes. "Cajuns in these parts," he told Lopasuta, "look upon the gift of tobacco just as the Indians did—you, as a Comanche, know the value of tobacco to your people."

"That's true," Lopasuta chuckled, remembering. "I remember that my chief would often rob a Mexican caravan of mules and be very happy when the booty included boxes of hand-rolled cigars from Chihuahua. These were almost as good as the calumet, the pipe of peace."

"Well, there the analogy fails," Eugene pointed out,

"because the most we can expect is an uneasy truce with these Cajuns. I'll do all the talking, if you don't mind. They'll trust me because I speak their dialect. I'll vouch for you, and if they accept me, you'll be included. That's the best we can hope for."

"I told you I had complete faith and reliance in you, Eugene. It still goes. Now let's shove off. I must say," Lopasuta chuckled again, as he unbuttoned his buckskin jacket, "the fine restaurant meals of New Orleans have added an inch or two to my waistline. I think that our efforts here will help lose them for me—and Geraldine will quite approve."

Eugene handed one of the short broad-leafed oars to Lopasuta, then took the other and, dipping his into the algae-covered green water, shoved the pirogue off. Lopasuta followed suit, taking his cue from Eugene's vigorous movements of shoulder and arm as he wielded the oar, dipping it cleanly and neatly, propelling the boat along the course of the narrow stream.

As they threaded their way along the stream, the Comanche lawyer felt that they had left the city of New Orleans at least several hundred years behind them. Around them grew clusters of palmetto and ferns, cypress and tupelo-gum trees, and weirdly shaped bushes and stunted growths. Few of the plants that grew here were recognizable to Lopasuta in the little sunlight that filtered through the immense thickets and trees shrouding this hidden junglelike world.

Lopasuta slapped at his neck, and Eugene gave him a wan smile. "Mosquitoes. They're the least of the problems in the bayous. Let's just hope the one that bit you didn't have the yellow fever bug."

"I hadn't thought of that. That's an ever deadlier menace than the snakes and the alligators, which you can easily see," the Comanche lawyer responded, glancing back as he dipped his oar into the stagnant water.

They poled silently along for a while, with Lopasuta amazed at the spectacle. He watched dozens of dragonflies dart over the water, scooping up prey and then disappearing into the long gray tangled skeins of Spanish moss clinging to the cypress trees. Suddenly he saw a sinuous movement just below the water. He squinted at the dark form, and Eugene, who had also seen it, turned and exclaimed, "That's a water moccasin. You don't want one of those things to bite you, that's for sure. Well, let's keep paddling. We're a long way from the Cajun village. As I recall—and it was a good many years ago—it's off to the northeast somewhat."

"What could slavers do here that would bring them money, Eugene?" Lopasuta wanted to know.

"A lot of things. Apart from smuggling, they could go after alligators. Tanned alligator hides, as you know, are highly prized for leather goods."

"I wonder how the people who live here know how to avoid all the unforeseen dangers," Lopasuta mused.

"By instinct. But when they do make mistakes, they can easily end up dead. If the alligators don't get them, the quicksand will. Also, there are probably hundreds of unsolved murders in this area, I shouldn't be surprised."

"Well," Lopasuta quipped, "it would be difficult to prove any of these murders, without a *corpus delicti*."

"That's true. Nobody knows of their existence, and the ones who sent their victims to the bottom of the bayou or into the jaws of an alligator aren't about to have any pricks of conscience bother them of a night."

"It appears to me that much of our law, most of our morality, and certainly all of our conscience depends on our surroundings, then," Lopasuta philosophized.

"I've come to that conclusion myself," the Creole nodded. "When I was studying for the bar, I learned the basic laws, but when you enter a place like this, you forget all that. It's as if you were starting over again, with nothing to go on except your own body's ability to withstand what you must, if you want to keep alive. And when you figure that people have lived here for years without ever going into New Orleans, it becomes all the more amazing."

"That's true. If we could go back in time, Eugene, if we could go back to what I believe I have heard called the neolithic age, we'd probably revise our entire opinion about the law as it stands today."

"Yes, surely we would. We'd find that nothing would apply, except the art of keeping alive. I'm sure the race was to the swift and to the strong."

"Yes, life gets reduced to its lowest common denominator. Here we are, two reasonably well-educated men, living toward the end of the nineteenth century, and now we realize how

214

little we know and how poorly most of us are equipped to come into a world like this.''

"That's true. But you'd best save your breath for paddling now because the water gets weedier and shallower up ahead. See that fork up there? As I remember, we turn to the left. We'll have to be careful not to get grounded, because I wouldn't want to have to step out onto that bank. There's no telling what might be hidden in the swamp grass,'' Eugene warned.

They reached the fork in the stream and Eugene leaned to his right and pushed with the end of his oar at what looked like a thick, partially submerged tree root. There was a gurgling snort, then a bellow that reverberated off the enclosed canopy of trees, and the water thrashed as a huge bull alligator disappeared. The men looked back through the sticky, thick haze; there was no sight of what they had left behind. It seemed almost dusk in the bayou, though outside and beyond them it was bright day.

They had been inside this strange, isolated world for more than three hours, and their faces were covered with sweat, and their garments clung to them. Through the miasma they now and then heard the splash of an alligator sliding off a bank into the water, or a huge catfish breaking surface to gulp down a bluebottle fly that had ventured too close to the surface of the water.

Eugene turned his head to the left and squinted, then murmured to Lopasuta, "Up ahead a little ways is the first Cajun village. You'd best take your jacket off and put it over the weapons. We don't want them thinking that we're the law, or we'll certainly never leave here alive. I venture to say that a lot of them are wanted men—except, by now, the warrants are probably long forgotten.''

"That's a good idea, Eugene. I must say, I'm glad you're with me. I'm beginning to get back some of my feelings for this kind of tracking, but it's been so long that it would be easy to forget seemingly unimportant matters. I guess I've become too civilized.''

"I know what you mean. I guess it doesn't hurt a man once in a while to break away from what he expects and to try to confront something about which he knows very little. That is, if he's confident in himself.''

The two men exchanged a long, understanding look. Lopasuta

smiled. He felt a companionship that made him almost anticipate the Creole's feelings, moods, and warnings. The years
seemed to have slipped away, and for a moment, he could
almost forget Geraldine and their children and his practice.
Now, alone with Eugene DuBois in the very heart of this
swamp, he sensed that his life was as much dependent on the
young Creole as it was on his own ability to anticipate
danger. To find a friend so loyal and trustworthy at such a
time was heartwarming and reassuring.

There was a small cove to the left, and the men paddled
toward it. Eugene leaped nimbly onto the bank, then reached
down and held out his hand to Lopasuta, who swung himself
ashore. Then they lifted up the bow of the pirogue and
dragged it onto the bank, so that it could not drift away and
leave them stranded.

Before them stood five cottages, if they could be called
that: The Cajuns had borrowed the design from the early
Indians, using sturdy poles with thatch, fibers, vines, and
solidifying mud to construct their dwellings. In some ways,
they were not unlike the huts one would have found among
the Seminoles of Florida. The entrance was low, and a man
had to stoop to enter his shelter. There was a small ramshackle
shed built of timbers toward the rear of the encampment.

The nearest hut, or cottage, was about twenty feet directly
ahead of the men, and as they stood there waiting, a man
came out of the entrance, stooping to clear the low door. He
aimed an old Sharps buffalo gun at the two visitors, and
Eugene glanced at Lopasuta as if to say, "I told you it would
be like nothing you'd ever seen before."

"You will stay still now!" the man with the Sharps commanded in a slurred, deep voice.

Eugene raised both hands above his head to show that he
carried no weapons and came in peace. Slowly, he advanced,
conversing in a *patois* of strange-sounding combinations of
vowels and consonants in which Lopasuta recognized only a
few French derivatives. The man lowered his Sharps, his eyes
widening with surprise. Then he turned, made a peremptory
gesture with his left hand, and two other men came from out
of the entrance through which he had emerged.

Eugene greeted them as he had done the first man, and
both these men eyed each other, nodding slowly. Then all
three advanced very slowly toward Lopasuta and the Creole.

The first man spoke, and once again Lopasuta recognized only a few of the words. Eugene, however, listened intently, smiling and nodding, then answered in the same dialect. The first man pointed to the northeast, then turned to his friends and said something to them, and all three began a rapid, animated conversation. Lopasuta felt himself entirely at the mercy of Eugene's inventiveness and knowledge, but he sensed that these three men were not hostile. Indeed, the first man had lowered the Sharps buffalo gun so that the muzzle pointed toward the damp, fetid ground.

The man with the gun suddenly eyed him, turning to Eugene and directing a lengthy question, all the while continuing to glance warily at the Comanche lawyer. Eugene answered, and the man pondered a moment, then nodded. The Creole murmured a quick aside to the Comanche lawyer. "They figure we're not enemies, but they wonder what we're doing here, and how we knew about their camp. There's a trading post here, that supplies about four other encampments. The men without the guns are brothers—and sometimes they travel to the outskirts of New Orleans to buy supplies, especially tobacco. I told them we have some for them, and they're quite friendly now."

"Good! Give them whatever they want. Have you asked them yet about the slavers?" Lopasuta asked.

"Yes. But they're holding off answering till they see how much tobacco we've got to give."

The Creole walked back to the pirogue, reached down into the gunnysack, and pulled out a large leather pouch. Then he walked slowly over to the man with the Sharps and exhibited the tobacco. The other two men began to talk to Eugene in the *patois*, which Lopasuta still found impossible to comprehend, save for an isolated, bastardized French word.

Eugene finally turned to Lopasuta and said, "They told me about the slavers. They say there are two brothers who trade in alligator hides, and they are using black slaves to do the hunting for them. That way, if an alligator should get anyone, it won't be the brothers."

"A practical if somewhat callous arrangement," Lopasuta sardonically concluded. "Did you find out where the brothers are?"

"It's a good day's journey from here, and I wouldn't advise going on in the midday heat. Besides, this man—his name is Etienne Cardot—has invited us to have lunch with them. They've got gumbo and alligator steak." Eugene laughed when Lopasuta automatically grimaced, then said, "I had alligator steak some years back, and it's not all that bad."

"Are they alone here?"

"Oh, my, no. All three of them have wives. But the women are told to stay out of sight until everything is clear. I think we can trust them. I told them you were a friend, and I told them also that you were an Indian. That made them less worried about you. Still and all, this fellow Etienne wants to know why we want to find the slavers. He doesn't see anything wrong with what they're doing."

"Tell him that we met a man who helped us greatly, and we think the slavers may have carried off the man and brought him here. So we're here to find him."

"I think they'd understand that. Down here, they believe in friendship and loyalty."

"Not bad virtues in any age or climate," Lopasuta declared.

Chapter Twenty-One

Etienne Cardot was in his early forties, short and dark. It was obvious from the tremendous musculature in his wrists and forearms that he was immensely strong. His two companions, whom he introduced as cousins, were in their mid-thirties, somewhat taller than he, with dark bushy hair, thick sideburns, and heavily tanned skin. Like the vegetation, they seemed a species distinct to this swampland that had been their family's home for generations. Inside one of the cottages, two women were busy preparing the noontime meal, while the third laid out plates on the rustic table. Lopasuta and Eugene smacked their lips over the gumbo that was set before them, but when the soup was finished, Lopasuta hesitated somewhat over the alligator steak. Eugene, more accustomed to the unusual fare, tackled it at once and pronounced it extremely palatable.

The women did not speak and seemed shy, keeping their faces averted from the strangers. Etienne and his two cousins, meanwhile, carried on a guarded conversation.

Eugene made a sign to Lopasuta not to be too hasty in leaving the hospitality of his Cajun hosts. Accordingly, Lopasuta engaged in some friendly conversation with the three men, which Eugene translated. Finally, the Creole arose and ostentatiously thanked Etienne Cardot for the splendid lunch and the cordial welcome accorded to him and his good friend.

The Cajun grinned, showing stained teeth. "Food in your belly, rum to warm you. You go on now. We will not help you any further. It is our law that anyone here who seeks refuge is not to be betrayed—and that includes the men you seek."

"I understand and respect your code," Eugene placatingly murmured.

219

"That is good. I trust your word that neither of you is from the authorities, the *gendarmes de Nouvelle Orléans*," Cardot replied.

"On my honor, we do not belong to that body of men. If our friend is being held by the slavers, we want only to free him and to bring him back to New Orleans." Eugene bowed to his hosts, then to the women, who remained with their faces averted from them, and then muttered to Lopasuta, "We'd best leave now, before we wear out our welcome. It should be a bit cooler, and we've a long way to go. We'll have to camp out all night, and while that's not a very pleasant prospect, it's the only one we've got."

The Creole and the Comanche lawyer walked back to their pirogue and lifted it into the water. Paddling upstream, they entered a broader tributary. An otter floated by on its back, not even bothering to look up from the meal of turtle arrayed on its stomach. The water here was pure and clean, and mirrored in its surface were the splashes of color of the tree orchids clinging in profusion to the cypress. Here and there, a lonely palm raised its pointed leaves toward the hidden sun, as if hungry for the light that gave it life.

"I feel this is a ghostly place, where many men have died," Lopasuta murmured.

"Your feelings are probably right. Federal authorities have come into the swamps hoping to pick up criminals, and they were never heard from again. We've definitely an advantage in having made friends with Cardot and his cousins. I know he didn't lie to me when he told me where the slavers are. Dip your paddle deeper, Lopasuta—that's it!"

They went on for another two hours, moving slowly through the rapidly thickening muck. Here, at the tributary of the Blind River, along which Etienne Cardot had directed them, was a thick, oozing substance of mud, slime, and water, and Lopasuta soon understood the value of the short-keeled pirogue against a sturdier type of vessel. In the very heart of swamp, the air was even more fetid, and because beyond this isolated world the sun was beginning to lower in the heavens, it seemed darker than before. Only at rare times could Lopasuta catch a glimpse of the serene blue sky. He and Eugene were isolated within a singularly archaic place, and it seemed the familiar world they had left behind that morning was just an illusion in the frame of such overwhelming reality.

There was suddenly a loud squawking overhead, and Lopasuta reached for one of the Spencer rifles. A great blue heron flew over them, startled from its perch by their approach. As Lopasuta relaxed, his hand slipped from the butt of the rifle, which then splashed into the muck. Angry, swearing at himself for such clumsiness, the Comanche lawyer managed to make a quick retrieval of the weapon.

"I'm afraid you've fouled it," Eugene said, shaking his head. "It'll take more than just a cursory cleaning to be able to use it. You'd best put it back in the bow and forget about it. We've still got the other rifle and revolvers, plus our knives. That, I hope, should be enough. But then again, we don't know how many slavers there actually are, since Cardot didn't tell us."

"Well, we'll just have to manage. How much farther should we go today? We seem to be slowing down, no matter how hard we paddle."

"Cardot told me it'll be tougher going from now on in, as we head south by southwest. The farther away these waters get from their source in Lake Maurepas, the more sluggish and shallow they become—unless of course there's a hurricane."

"Well, I think I'd prefer to do without that kind of help," Lopasuta laughed, though he inwardly quivered at the thought of such natural fury in this wild place.

They paddled on in silence for another half hour. Often, they bent their heads as huge dangling clumps of Spanish moss brushed over them, obscuring their vision, and once a mink ran out of its nest with an uncanny scream that made Lopasuta instinctively flinch.

The Comanche lawyer turned to look at the wet ooze through which they so arduously were paddling and shuddered as he saw a deadly cottonmouth slither off a bank and disappear. Even more fearsome, a coral snake was barely discernible in the undergrowth of the levee off to the right.

"How are we going to spend the night—or rather, where, Eugene?" he at last asked.

"Cardot said that around sundown, if we've made good time, we should come to a small, fairly well-elevated island. He said we'll find initials carved in a big live oak. That's our landmark. We'll camp there. Apparently, it's reasonably safe from snakes, and there aren't many alligators in this particular area.''

"That's true, I haven't seen or noticed one for quite some time,'' Lopasuta agreed.

"Of course, we'll have to take turns standing watch. A snake can crawl up on you before you know it. Well, we'll just have to pray that luck continues to be with us.''

An hour later, Eugene leaned forward and exclaimed, ''I can see the island, Lopasuta! We'll have a bit to eat, and then rest—we'll need all our strength tomorrow.''

"You've done a remarkable job, Eugene,'' Lopasuta praised his companion.

"I'm lucky that I know something of this place—that and the fact that I speak the Cajun *patois*. I didn't want to frighten you, but just beyond all the foliage along these banks I've seen signs of other encampments. There must be at least thirty or forty Cajuns and their families between where we ate lunch and where we are now—and we haven't seen hide nor hair of them.''

"No, we haven't. I'd say that the Comanche would pay them a tribute for their cleverness in camouflaging themselves,'' Lopasuta declared.

Reaching the island, they dragged the pirogue onto the higher ground, finding it quite dry and hard. Lopasuta started a fire, and they cooked some jerky, beans, and coffee, and conversed while the oppressive darkness gathered around them. All around them came strange sounds, life and death struggles being waged between hunter and hunted. Soon, though, the intense, shrill sound of thousands of cicadas drowned out everything else.

Lopasuta offered to stand guard during the first shift, so Eugene spread out a blanket, stretched himself out on it, and was soon fast asleep.

The Comanche stood, watching. It was almost like being back at the stronghold, and yet he knew himself to be less adept and skillful than he had been as a boy. Still, those early experiences had sharpened his wits and keened his senses, and he was grateful for them. He did not regret the arduous effort and the time expended on this search for the slavers.

Chapter Twenty-Two

Eugene DuBois woke shortly after midnight, and Lopasuta gratefully took his turn on the blanket. The young Creole armed himself with the usable Spencer rifle and stood guard near his sleeping friend.

Crouching against the trunk of the live-oak tree, Eugene found the solid ground reassuring after those long hours through the water. The darkness was thick, inky, and muggy. Mosquitos landed on his face, neck, and hands, and he swatted at them furiously, their incessant buzzing seeming to echo in his eardrums. But even this annoyance did not detract from the exaltation he felt over the mission.

They had come a long way and thus far were safe—but what dangers awaited them, Eugene could only speculate. A horde of black flies suddenly swirled around him, and he swore under his breath, slapping himself, crushing some of them on his cheek, on his chest, and on his forehead. Then, as suddenly, they were gone.

He squatted down, double-checking the rifle to make certain that the chambers were filled and that it was ready to fire. The loaded weapon was reassuring; it was a tangible reality in a world of fantasy and grotesque terror. And the night magnified such distortions, the night with its attendant dreads and childlike fears that attacked even the bravest of men. What a man could not see, what he could not envision, made him the more fearful, and thus the more vulnerable.

He glanced down at the sleeping Comanche lawyer and sighed softly. Here was the man who had brought him to such happiness as he had not dreamed he could have. Now he was a lawyer, with a reputation and solidity to back his name. The taint of black blood in his veins that had once downgraded him among the aristocratic whites who did not know what it was to struggle for a living, to wrest self-esteem out of denigration, to know contempt and low wages, seemed a thing of the past, and even those who had denigrated him now recognized him, if only grudgingly. And all this was due to the man who lay sleeping before him, whom he guarded now as a kind of sacred trust. He thought tenderly of Mei Luong, and of the child she would soon bear him. He was grateful to God for having brought him into touch with a friend like Lopasuta. Leaning up against the tree, he sighed contentedly, prepared to sit in vigilance through the long hours of the black, sightless night.

The Creole took out his watch and glanced at it in the half-light. It was more than an hour after dawn, but only the face of the watch let him know that outside this sequestered, bizarre world there would be daylight. He wiped his forehead with a damp handkerchief. The heat and the stickiness, the insects and the eerie sounds went on interminably, as they had perhaps from the very dawn of time. Lopasuta slept a deep and exhausted sleep. Eugene was loath to wake him, but it was time. To cling to such discipline as they had brought with them, two men whose lives were disposed toward orderliness and law and fact, was the way to remain in control in the fantasmagoria of the brooding, pitiless bayous. Reluctantly, he leaned forward and shook Lopasuta's shoulder, first gently, and then somewhat more firmly. The Comanche lawyer came awake, abruptly sitting up, then smiled up at Eugene. "It's time, is it?"

"Yes, Lopasuta," Eugene answered in a low voice. "Everything's fine, incidentally. No sight, no sound of any trouble. Wherever those slavers are, they're nowhere near this island. Well, let's have some breakfast, and then we'll start out."

"You're a good man, Eugene. I knew that the first time I talked with you. We'll come out of this very well, I'm sure. Do you know, I dreamed about the Cajuns. I wonder how people can live here all their lives." Lopasuta pondered a moment, then reflected, "That kind of living takes a great deal of courage, the sort of courage that Indians had, living solely on their wits in hostile surroundings—the way we're doing right now. I'm rather proud of myself, and even more of you, Eugene.''

"Well, that's—" A long yawn interrupted the rest of his response. "I guess I'm more tired than I thought. Breakfast should help wake me up.''

"Why don't you sleep for a while, Eugene? A few more hours won't matter.''

"Well, we want to catch those men before the end of the day, and who knows? They could be even farther away by now than the Cajuns realized.''

"That's true. But I'm sure even an hour's rest will make you feel better. We'll catch them. They're not expecting us, and chances are they haven't moved their camp.'' Lopasuta took the Spencer automatic rifle from the Creole and nodded toward the sleeping blanket. Eugene needed no second invitation. He stretched himself out, closed his eyes, and fell asleep almost at once.

After a quick breakfast, Lopasuta and Eugene resumed the slow, laborious journey in the pirogue. They had to contend with vines, weeds, cypress trees, rotting pieces of driftwood, and sometimes even more sinister shapes in the dark, brownish water of the narrow tributary. Still the sounds of the junglelike forest seemed less fraught with danger to Lopasuta now—perhaps, he thought to himself, he was actually getting used to this primitive world so different from the one they knew of lights and laughter and noises and brightness.

"How much farther do you think it is, Eugene?" Lopasuta asked as he thrust his oar down hard to propel the pirogue a little faster. It was exasperating to move so slowly.

"Etienne Cardot said that we'd find the slavers somewhere at the end of the stream if we kept following it all the way to the Blind River—although I wouldn't exactly call it a stream. It's barely flowing at all. My God! Look out!" The Creole raised his voice in a hoarse shout of fear. An enormous bull alligator had just crawled off the bank only a few feet away and splashed into the water, making straight for the pirogue. Lopasuta felt the snout of the creature hit hard against the canoe, which swayed so violently that he almost lost his balance. Groping for the revolvers at his feet, he took one of them and aimed it just as the hideous jaws of the alligator yawned only a few feet away from his face. He fired point-blank, and the sound was deafening. There was a terrifyingly harsh roar, unlike any other sound he had ever heard, as the alligator rolled over and thrashed about in the water. Yet, horribly, it continued to follow the pirogue, and Lopasuta fired again at the baleful yellow eyes of the giant saurian.

Once again there was that hideous, almost deafening roar, and in its frenzy, the huge alligator twisted and swung its tail, lashing the end of the pirogue. Eugene seemed paralyzed, his eyes staring at nothing. Suddenly the canoe turned over, and both men were precipitated into the stream. Lopasuta had just enough presence of mind to grab the one good Spencer and hold it over his head, but the other and the two Colts fell into the murky water and out of sight.

"The devil take it! There go our weapons," the Comanche lawyer groaned. "Get to shore! Eugene, get out of the way of that monster! I never imagined an alligator could get as big as that!"

They reached the relative safety of the levee, and they watched the alligator thrash about. Its struggles grew weaker, and then finally it turned over, floating with its belly upwards, a ghastly whitish gray.

"Thank God it's dead," Eugene panted. "I'll catch our pirogue. It hasn't gone far, thank Heaven for that."

He ran into the shallow water and, with both hands, righted the canoe. Then he grabbed for the nearest floating oar and threw it into the canoe as he hurried along to catch the other. "And without oars, we'd be just about helpless, too," he called, as he walked slowly back, holding tightly to the pirogue. Reaching the shore, Eugene nosed the bow toward Lopasuta, who grabbed it and hauled it onto the bank.

"Well, that's a fine mess. Our supplies are gone, and even if we fished them out, they wouldn't be fit to eat. All we can hope is that we find the slavers soon and get out of here as fast as we can."

Eugene emerged from the stream, thousands of tiny green duckweeds clinging to his boots and clothes up to his thighs.

"That was a close call! I'm still shaking, I can tell you that!" the Creole gasped.

After resting for a few minutes, the two men got back into the pirogue and continued the slow journey along the narrow tributary. The Spencer rifle was now their only weapon, apart from the hunting knives strapped to their belts; the ammunition, too, had gone to the bottom.

"We'll have to make every bullet in that Spencer count, Eugene," Lopasuta declared. "Our chances are not what they were, that's for certain."

Two hours later, Eugene pointed to the right bank. About a hundred yards ahead stood a group of thatched huts fortified by hewn timbers. Standing with their backs to the stream were two men, both black-bearded, one stout, the other lean and angular. Each of them carried an old Henry rifle, and they had hunting knives at their belts, as well. Just beyond them, coming out of a hut, were two black men and a black woman, manacled at wrists and ankles. One of the men was Malachi Evans.

Lopasuta and Eugene poled over to the right bank and drew the pirogue out of the water. Concealed by a thick group of palmetto trees, they knelt down and watched from this vantage point.

Almost an hour passed before Lopasuta ventured to murmur, "That looks to be all of them—just those two men."

"Yes, but they've got two rifles to our one, even if ours is a Spencer. I don't think we stand a chance."

"That's true, Eugene," Lopasuta whispered back. "Those poor devils—see how those manacles cut into their wrists and ankles? They can hardly walk without pain! What we've got to do is get back to New Orleans and talk to the authorities. We can lead a well-armed contingent out here, enough of them to free these people and take that pair of slavers to jail where they belong."

"Look—the fat slaver is telling the two black men to do something. Let's see what they're up to," Eugene whispered.

Crouching behind their screen of palmettos, the two lawyers waited to see what would happen. After conferring with his tall, cadaverous brother, the stout slaver took a whip made of alligator hide that was looped through his belt and lashed Malachi Evans across the shoulders, then pointed toward the sluggishly flowing tributary. With a cry of pain, the manacled captive stooped down to seize a long piece of rotted timber and moved reluctantly to the water's edge.

"Look! It's another huge alligator!" Eugene hissed, wide-eyed at the scene.

The black man gingerly held out the piece of timber, and

suddenly the alligator's jaws yawned to close on it, where-
upon the taller man, lifting his Henry rifle, fired point-blank.
The monster rolled over onto its side, swinging its tail savagely in its death throes, then slid back into the water.

"Catch him, you goddamned nigger! Catch him, or I'll
take your hide off in strips," the stout man bellowed.

Evans, sobbing under his breath, gingerly stepped into the
stream and seized the still-writhing tail of the alligator, then
began to drag him up onto the bank. Just then, another horrid
snout lifted from the water nearby, closing in on the mulatto.
The alligator opened its jaws to snap, and the taller brother
fired his Henry. The alligator jerked backwards, then thrashed
about in frenzy, lashing out with its tail as the blood oozed
along the surface of the murky water.

"You, nigger, get that one too, unless you also want to be
flayed!" the taller brother commanded, gesturing to the other
slave.

The two blacks dragged the lifeless bodies of the alligators
onto the bank, and the stout man turned to the black woman,
"All right, Willie Mae, help get those critters into the hut and
start gettin' the hides off. They're worth more than all three
of you niggers put together! Now git to work, or there won't
be any food tonight!"

"Yessir, master," the young black woman fearfully
stammered. She turned to the two manacled black men, and
trembling, she helped them to carry out the slaver's orders.

"That slaver's a damn good shot," Lopasuta whispered.
"Let's get out of here." Cautiously peering through their
living screen, he observed, "All right—the slavers are walking back to the huts. Now's our chance!" They lifted the
pirogue into the stream, dipped their oars into the shallow
water, and pushed off.

They had gone only a few yards back whence they had
come, when the tall man turned away from the hut. He put
his hand to his forehead, squinting, then cried out, "God-
dammit, Frank, we got some snoopers! Git your rifle, quick!"

The stout brother whirled, picked up his Henry, and leveled it at the pirogue. Eugene and Lopasuta dug their oars
again and again into the muck, frantically trying to get out of
range. There was a boom of the rifle, and a ball whistled over
Lopasuta's head.

"Missed, for Crissake!" the stout man growled in disgust. "Let's go after 'em, Amos!"

The taller slaver nodded and began to lope along the bank, while his brother ran into one of the huts.

Paddling with all their might, glancing back at their armed pursuer, Eugene and Lopasuta tried to put as much distance as they could between themselves and the slaver. They came to a bend, and turned to look back. The tall man was closing fast. He stopped and aimed his rifle, and then suddenly he uttered a hideous yowl. He dropped his rifle and sprawled onto the ground, both hands gripping his ankle. Eugene gasped, "It's a coral snake! He's been bitten by a coral snake! There's no hope for him!"

"Keep paddling, Eugene. Look—that other fellow's starting out after us in the pirogue he dragged out of one of the huts!"

Lopasuta glanced at the rifle, then decided that there was too much risk in stopping and trying a snap shot at the pursuer. If the shot were unsuccessful, the slaver might fire his Henry and kill Eugene, who was sitting in the rear of the canoe.

The Comanche lawyer remembered his training at the stronghold of how to overcome an enemy who had the advantage. Obviously, the slaver knew the swamp far better than either of them, he reasoned, and so the best course of action was to trick him. "Listen, Eugene, I just thought of something. See that big cypress tree about two hundred feet ahead on the right?"

"I see it."

"Now look. We'll head the pirogue over to the bank, and we'll run like the devil. You climb that tree and take the rifle. I'll stand there below you, unarmed. If he sees only me, he will think you've gone on ahead. If I'm any judge of character, he'll take his time and gloat awhile before he finishes me off. Needless to say, you'll shoot him before he has the chance."

"That's too dangerous for you, Lopasuta!" the Creole protested.

"Eugene, that's what we're going to do. I spent a good many years as a Comanche brave and several times I had to defend myself against renegades from some of the tribes who were out to kill me. Do as I say. Now, let's run!"

Suiting action to word, Lopasuta nimbly sprang out of the

229

canoe onto the bank and raced toward the huge cypress tree. With a groan, Eugene glanced back and saw the slaver's pirogue looming ever closer. He leaped out, and Lopasuta tossed him the rifle. The Creole hurried to the tree, secured a foothold, and laboriously began to hoist himself aloft, branch by branch.

Lopasuta stood with his back against the tree, his arms hanging at his side as if in submission. A few moments later, the slaver's pirogue drew up to the bank by the tree.

"Now then, you bastid, what the hell are you doin' snoopin' around here?" the man demanded, as he leaped out of the canoe and came lumbering toward Lopasuta, his Henry leveled at the Comanche.

"I was looking for a friend, mister," Lopasuta calmly assured him.

"Well, you found me instead. Take a good look, 'cause I'm the last sight you're ever gonna see!" The slaver slowly raised his Henry. At that moment, the Spencer barked from above.

The fat man dropped his rifle and clutched at his chest. With a look of incredulous surprise, he pitched forward and lay still.

"Great shot, Eugene! I guess we won't need any other help now! C'mon down, and let's go liberate those people."

Chapter Twenty-Three

"Lopasuta, I swear my heart's still in my mouth! I was sure that slaver was going to blow a hole through you and let kingdom come!" Eugene DuBois exhaled as he slowly climbed down the cypress tree. "Sorry I can't move any faster," he said with a grin, "but I'm a bit weak in the knees."

"I'll admit I'm no less shaky," Lopasuta declared, steadying himself up against the trunk of the tree, wiping sweat from his brow. "The next step is to get out of here with those three people. And it's going to take hours of paddling. Fortunately," he added sarcastically, "those two slavers were kind enough to furnish us with an extra pirogue."

Eugene laughed, then became serious. "These canoes are made to carry only two people, and one of them will be carrying an extra passenger. However, the woman is petite, so perhaps it won't be too difficult." He jumped down from the lowest tree limb and sat at the base of the cypress. "You know," he said, "it would probably be best if each of us pilots a separate pirogue, since we know these bayous pretty well now. I'm lighter than you, so the woman can ride with me and one of the men."

"Good idea, Eugene," Lopasuta declared. "And we may as well get started right now."

The two men walked quickly down the bank to where the two canoes were drawn up, and with a final look back to where the dead slaver lay, they pushed off and headed downstream for the encampment. They paddled alongside each other, each silent, thinking to themselves about the incredible adventure they had shared these last few days.

Suddenly Eugene uttered an oath, and when Lopasuta looked over at him quizzically, the young Creole exclaimed, "The key! We forgot to search the slaver's pockets for the key to the manacles!"

Lopasuta groaned. "I forgot all about it! I guess you might say my mind was somewhere else," he said with a rueful grin. "Look—there's the body of his brother. Over there, lying just ahead on the right. He probably carried a key with him, too. Let's check his pockets before we turn around and go back."

The taller man, who had fallen victim to a snakebite, lay in a position of contorted agony on the bank of the stream. The two lawyers peered carefully all around the area, but the coral snake that had inflicted the fatal bite was nowhere to be seen. Eugene shuddered. "What an awful way to die. Still, it was quick—which is probably more than he deserved, considering the horrible way he's been treating innocent people."

He maneuvered his pirogue over to the shore and gingerly stepped onto the levee while Lopasuta held on to the canoe. Quickly rifling through the dead man's pockets, Eugene suddenly smiled and triumphantly exclaimed, "I found it!" He held up the precious key for Lopasuta's inspection.

"Thank goodness," the Comanche declared. "Let's get going."

Eugene ran down the bank and was about to climb into the pirogue when he lost his footing, propelling the craft away, and slipped into the murky water. "Damn!" he said, laughing. "I thought I'd be able to keep dry this—"

A look of alarm swept over the young man's face and Lopasuta asked, "Eugene, what is it? What's— Oh, my God!" Lopasuta's voice rose in strident horror as he realized the Creole had stepped into quicksand. Eugene was sinking down slowly, flailing with his arms, desperately trying to get loose of the deadly mud.

The Comanche lawyer abandoned the pirogue, leaping as far as he could onto the shore beyond. He looked around frantically for a tree limb, a log, anything that his friend could grab hold of to pull him out, for Eugene was down now just past his waist.

"Try not to struggle, Eugene! I'll get you out! I'll get you out!" Lopasuta hoarsely cried.

Feverishly racing along the shore, he suddenly noticed a long, thick vine dangling just overhead. Reaching up, he yanked at the liana with all his strength, falling to his knees when the length of vine broke free of its grasp on the tree.

Racing back, he yelled, "Just hold still, Eugene! I'll get you out!"

Swiftly, with the imagination born of desperate endeavor, the Comanche lawyer tied one end of the fifteen-foot-long vine around the trunk of a cypress tree on the shore, knotting it as best as he could. Then slowly, on all fours, carrying the other end of the vine, he crawled down the embankment to where Eugene was mired, and handed him the other end. "Pull at it! Pull with all your strength! Hold on tight! I'll go back for the slaves and get them to help me!" Lopasuta cried.

"Wait! You'll need the key," Eugene exclaimed holding it up in one hand while clinging desperately to the vine with the other. He threw the key toward Lopasuta, and in one quick movement the Comanche lawyer caught it and turned to run in the direction of the encampment.

He raced along the shore like one possessed, and upon reaching the blacks, he shouted, "We've got to pull my friend out of quicksand!"

"Mr. Bouchard! Mr. Bouchard! God, am I ever glad to see you!" Malachi Evans exclaimed. "I thought I recognized you before! Are them bastids dead, Mr. Bouchard? Are we really free?"

"Yes, Malachi, but there's no time to talk now!" Lopasuta declared as he fumbled with the key in his haste. Finally he opened the manacles of the three slaves, and then all four ran back to where Eugene was trapped. He had continued to sink, and just his shoulders and head were visible now.

Lopasuta and the two black men crawled toward the Creole. Reaching out, seizing him under the shoulders, they pulled with all their strength. "Again!" Lopasuta commanded, and this time they dragged him loose of the sucking mire, hauling Eugene onto the levee.

He was gasping, covered with muck almost up to his chin. He opened his eyes and stared up at the black men, then gave them a wan smile. "I guess it's as they say: One good turn deserves another. Thank you both for saving my life." He looked over at the Comanche. "Lopasuta, how can I ever—"

"Just rest. Don't talk, Eugene." Lopasuta gently counseled. He turned to the middle-aged stevedore and clapped him on the shoulder. "I think you owe your friend Eddie Henry a good dinner, Malachi. It was he who suspected you were here."

"I owe him more than dinner, Mr. Bouchard. That's for sure," the man said, laughing. "And I guess bein' able to help save your friend's life is God's way of lettin' me say thanks for your savin' mine—ours." He gestured to the other two freed slaves.

"How did you ever get into a thing like this, Malachi?" Lopasuta asked out of curiosity.

The stevedore chuckled and shrugged. "Guess I was just a mite too greedy for my own good, Mr. Bouchard. See, Eddie Henry 'n me, we done been pals for a long spell, as probably he told you already. Anyhow, there wasn't much work down at the docks this season. And poor Eddie, he's older—'n lame, too. Got that limp from a real bad whippin' from a Louisiana cane-field overseer, that's how. But he gets along fine—only when most folks see he limps some, they don't want to hire him to do any real strong work. Anyway, he met some gal in a saloon 'bout a week ago, and she filled him up with stories 'bout how a man can get rich trappin' them big 'gators for two fellas, 'n they pay real good. Eddie thought I could do it better 'cause I don't limp none. So I went back to that saloon 'n found me that gal 'n she told me where in the bayou to go." He grinned and gestured expansively. "This wonderful place."

"What a terrible experience!"

"It sure was, Mr. Bouchard." The stevedore shook his head and exhaled a long breath. "Oh, this here's Johnny Kincaid and the woman, she's Willie Mae Thompson. They been here weeks 'n weeks. Done 'bout given up hope of ever gettin' free."

At this, the other black man bobbed his head in agreement, grinning thankfully. Lopasuta clapped him on the back. "You've nothing to worry about now. And Mr. DuBois and I will try to find all of you jobs."

Willie Mae had run back to the camp, and she now returned with some old rags. Kneeling by Eugene, she started to wipe away some of the slime clinging to his clothes. Eugene sat up and took the rags from her. "Thank you, Miss Thompson. But you don't have to do that—you're no one's slave now."

Tears ran down her face at this kindness, and she shyly reached out and touched Eugene's shoulder in silent thanks.

Eugene stood up, declaring he felt fine, and suggested they get started back to civilization. "For one thing," he said, grinning hugely, "I can't wait to get out of these disgusting clothes!"

The small band walked back to the encampment, where they bundled up food and other provisions for the journey home. They decided it would make sense to eat before they set out, and as they did so, Willie Mae told her story.

The daughter of a slave, she had been eleven at the time of the Emancipation Proclamation. Their white owner was a tyrant, so upon having their freedom granted, mother and daughter set out for New Orleans. Once there, her mother was killed by an enraged Confederate officer, but Willie Mae escaped his wrath and finally found work as a seamstress for a kindly woman who owned a dress shop. She had stayed there for ten years, happy in her work, until the shop owner died. She then took a job as a maid for an elderly brother and sister who owned a small, isolated house about thirty miles upriver from New Orleans. Though Willie Mae had been somewhat lonely, she had enjoyed the peace and tranquility of her new life. Then, when his sister died the year before, the brother had gone mad with grief and had been committed to an asylum. Willie Mae had decided her best chances of finding work were in New Orleans, so she came back to the Queen City. As a well-skilled, self-educated woman, she opted to hold out for a good job, living on her savings.

She met the same woman who had inveigled Malachi Evans into working for the slavers. The woman promised Willie Mae a job as a maid for a wealthy family, with the possibility of European travel. The woman had taken her to what appeared to be a respectable house, but once inside, the slavers bound and gagged her, and then took her out to the camp, where she had been captive for the past three months.

Lopasuta sat quietly after hearing the slave's story, but after a few minutes he said to his friend, "Eugene, I think perhaps Geraldine's prayers have been answered." He turned to Willie Mae and explained, "You see, Eugene's wife was my children's governess—until this handsome young man spirited her away. My wife was so fond of Mei Luong—that's Mrs. DuBois—that she never really felt anyone could ever take her place. But our children can be a handful, and deep down, Geraldine has been hoping the perfect person would somehow just come along. If you'd be willing to take such a position, I'd say you'd be that perfect person.''

''I sure would, Mr. Bouchard! Fact is, I know about you; I've read of you in the *Times-Picayune*—about how you stand up for poor folks and blacks, people who can't afford lawyers, and you help them. You're a good man. I'd certainly like to work for you. Besides, I owe you, getting me out of this place.'' She shivered reminiscently.

''Wonderful! Then it's settled. When we get back to New Orleans, I'll take you to our house and introduce you to Geraldine,'' Lopasuta proposed. Willie Mae, overcome by the whole turn of events, covered her face with her hands and cried softly.

''Malachi,'' Lopasuta went on, ''I'll personally go with you and Johnny to some shipping firms I deal with. I'll see if I can't do a bit of gentle arm twisting and get you men jobs right off. Certainly my employer's firm does enough business with them for the shippers to extend themselves somewhat. I'll recommend you highly, and I think the companies will take my word. And as far as your friend Eddie Henry goes, lame though he may be, he'd make a good watchman at one of the storage warehouses. Don't worry. We'll get you the decent jobs you men deserve.''

''I can't tell you how grateful I am, Mr. Bouchard, sir.'' The stevedore rubbed his knuckles over his eyes to hide the tears that had begun to form.

Willie Mae and Johnny Kincaid, the smaller of the two black men, rode in the pirogue with Eugene, while Malachi Evans paddled with Lopasuta in the one following as the travelers began their return from the junglelike bayous. Now that the danger was past, Lopasuta gave all his concentration to this remarkable region. The lush vegetation was riotous: Huge bald cypresses dotted the waters, their singular gnarled knees placed nearby, as if they were sentinels from a tribe of dwarfs sent to guard the lordly cypresses themselves. He could see Virginia creeper vines, air plants, ferns of every description, and everywhere, the ubiquitous Spanish moss garlanded the trees.

Night was coming on, and they had come to one of the

turns again, marked by a large tupelo-gum tree. Here the water was covered from bank to bank with the miniscule leaves of duckweed, which made the water look as if it were a carpet of lush green, solid enough to walk on.

From a distance, Lopasuta heard a coughing roar and called to Eugene, "Is that an alligator?"

"No, that's a cougar. There are red wolves and black bears in these parts, as well. Look, there's an armadillo!" Lopasuta followed Eugene's pointing finger. A bizarre-looking mammal about two-and-a-half feet long and eight inches high at its shoulder, with a foot-long tail, was ambling along the shoreline. Its protective covering of thick, rolled hide made it look as if it were armor plated. Seeing the intruders, it began to burrow with its strong claws, and soon disappeared from view.

Another turn, and the stagnant water became clear, reflecting the fan-shaped fronds of the palmettos dotting the banks. Ahead of them, a bull alligator slipped down into the water with a splash, emitting a thunderous roar. "Now that's an alligator for certain!" The Creole grinned and declared, "And we've all had enough to do with them to serve us for the rest of our lives."

"I agree with you there, sir," Malachi Evans nodded.

They made camp for the night on the same small island the Cajuns had recommended on their journey inland. The two black men insisted on taking the guard duty, saying Lopasuta and Eugene had done enough for them already.

The next morning, at first light, the band began their final trek out of the bayous.

After an hour on the water, the canoes passed by a column of fire ants, floating on the surface in this shallow subsidiary of the Blind River. They were tightly packed together, yet so light that their mass didn't sink below the water's surface. As a faint, humid breeze came up, they were propelled along. "That's something you wouldn't want to mess with!" Eugene vouchsafed. "They're probably looking for dry land because their old nest has been flooded."

It was indeed a world in which time seemed to have stopped. Lopasuta saw magnificent egrets and woodpeckers, and near his pirogue a dozen snapping turtles lay dozing in the sun. He broke off a branch from an overhanging tree and held it just below the water. Instantly one of the turtles leaped into the stream and clamped its jaws on it. Lopasuta drew it up, admiring its strength and tenacity, then let it fall back into the murky water.

"It would take great courage to live here most of the time," he commented to the Creole.

"Yes, it would. The people who live here, the ones we now call Cajuns, were once named Acadians. Their ancestors came here from Nova Scotia almost a hundred years ago. They were French, driven out of Canada by the British because the British thought they were disloyal to the Crown. So the Acadians sought refuge far across this continent in a place where they would not be found and where the civil and military authorities would hardly dare to venture."

"Yes, I remember reading something about that now—around the time I was studying law with my old mentor, Jedidiah Danforth," Lopasuta mused with a nostalgic sigh. He remembered the crotchety, keen-minded old man who had steadfastly helped him through the first difficult times of studying the law. There had been days when he was not certain he could grasp the fundamentals well enough to interpret them in a courtroom and help the downtrodden, but Jedidiah's patience and his illuminating mind had given inspiration to the tall Comanche. He would always revere that feisty old man who was not ashamed to voice his opinions, nor to fight for them, if need be. Jedidiah had died in just such a battle, against unscrupulous carpetbaggers who had sought to besmirch the Bouchard name.

"In a way," Eugene said, breaking his friend's reverie, "it's really surprising to find that some of these Cajuns would look the other way when it comes to slavery, because many of them intermarried with blacks after the Civil War. Still, they're a proud people, very self-reliant."

"I admire them. The men who gave us hospitality the other day at lunch, they impressed me. But come to think of it, tasty as that alligator steak was, I think that when I get home, I'd prefer to have Geraldine prepare me a chicken!"

238

Chapter Twenty-Four

It was June in Paris, a city that grew more exciting to Carla Bouchard with the dawn of each new day. Its size alone would have been enough to impress her: Two years earlier, the population of the City of Light had been reckoned at nearly five million, four times the size of New York City. But for an impressionable, intelligent young woman like Carla, it was not so much the size of Paris that interested her as the inexhaustible variety of Parisian culture, which kept her both exhilarated and bustling. To be sure, many of the discoveries she made in the fascinating, teeming metropolis could be attributed to her sponsor and chaperone, Cordelia Thornberg. Cordelia had entrée into virtually every soirée, as well as to private exhibitions of paintings and sculpture, workshops in which there flourished the fabrication of precious jewelry, hand-blown glassware, imaginative chinaware, and salons where one could rub elbows with an Émile Zola or a Victor Hugo. Here, the poets and prose writers brought their latest manuscripts to declaim them in loud voices for an enthralled audience, who crowded in to see their heroes. It was truly the dawn of a new day.

France in the Third Republic was weary of vain, despotic emperors on the one hand and the radical violence of mob rule on the other. People were determined to forget politics and live only for pleasure—and one result of this hedonistic impulse was an almost feverish cultivation of the arts.

Carla Bouchard, now twenty-two, had enrolled a few months earlier at the École des Beaux Arts. Here, the Impressionism that had begun roughly ten years before was exerting a growing influence, and expatriates as well as native French artists in great numbers were attracted to its premises.

Carla espoused the school of Impressionism because she felt that its tenets allowed for a liberalization of ideas, a protest against stuffiness and smug convention and all the pompous rules by which society ordained its many-tiered existence. Back in Texas, in the cloistered life—for Carla, at any rate—of Windhaven Range, she had lived exactly as her parents had expected her to do. She had been a dutiful daughter, loved her family, and accepted each new day as a link in the unending chain of inevitability. She had even thought, as recently as two or three years ago, that one day she would marry the son of some eminently successful rancher—like her father, Lucien Edmond—bear him several children, and concern herself mainly with the upbringing of these progeny.

To be sure, going to Chicago with her brother, Hugo, to study at the Chicago Academy of Fine Arts had been a total revelation to Carla. Still, without the influence of her chaperone, Cordelia Thornberg, she might not have been so boldly eager to cast away the traces of her former life and to take on adventure and new experiences. Thus, coming to Paris in the company of a truly sophisticated, worldly woman sent Carla even more deeply into the wonderful new world of discovering herself—what she thought and felt. It enabled her to understand that it was really important to know these things about herself, so that she could guide and direct her own life without feeling responsibility to others who might choose for her some alien way.

Until now, her only encounter with the expected norm of marriage and motherhood had come through her friendship with a young Bostonian, whom she had met while studying in Chicago. She had been very fond of him, but when he had unexpectedly returned to Boston to take over his father's affairs and had asked her to marry him, Carla had faced her own awareness that she was not yet ready to define her life for all time as the wife of a man whose family was greatly esteemed in the prim and proper setting of Boston. She would have been—although Carla did not quite put it in such terms—exchanging Windhaven Range for a new city, Boston, but the net effect would have been the same: the sacrifice of her own opportunity to explore the extent of her intellectual, artistic, and emotional capacity.

Thus, during her Parisian summer of 1882, Carla Bouchard

was more than usually open to inspiration, and the Impressionism that influenced her creativeness was inevitably bound to influence her lifestyle as well. . . .

The previous night, the second Thursday of June, Cordelia and Carla had gone to a performance of Offenbach's delightful operetta, *La Belle Hélène*. Then they had gone to a quiet, out-of-the-way bistro for coffee and petits fours and a glass of excellent Bordeaux.

Looking around the café, Carla's gaze had alighted on a young man in a paint-spattered smock and beret, sitting holding hands with a pretty young woman who obviously adored him and who was hanging upon his every word. Carla sighed wistfully and turned to Cordelia. "I like to see that, Cordy. Back home, nobody talked much about love, but still, everybody expected that I'd march up the aisle in a white gown and veil, marry some nice boy, and then have lots of children and live on a farm or a ranch. And maybe I would have, if I hadn't come to Chicago and met you!"

"I know, dear. And I know you're looking over at that young couple thinking that there's still something in life you haven't explored or experienced. It will come."

"But I'm all of twenty-two—by some standards an old woman already—and still a spinster," Carla complained, though sensible enough to see the humor in this and smiled at herself. However, seeing Cordelia smile in return at Carla's words and the expression on her face, she quickly flared, "Don't laugh, Cordy! At least, I'd like to meet someone who wasn't so conventional and who loved life and the arts and all the things I do just as much as I do."

Cordelia sympathetically nodded. "I understand exactly what you're trying to say, my dear. But, here in Paris, nobody judges you by your age. They judge you by your ability, the way you express yourself, the way you think. Look at me, in my forties, yet I haven't ruled out the possibility that I may one day, perhaps in this very city, meet someone that I'll adore as much as I once did my beloved Emile."

Carla looked once again at the young couple who were holding hands and staring at each other as if they had discovered that there were really angels in paradise. Then she turned back to her mentor. Cordelia wore a bright red silk dress this

241

evening and an imposing hat with feathers. She looked jaunty and youthful, and Carla commented, "It's just wonderful how young you look tonight, Cordy! And, for that matter, every day since we came to Paris."

"That's because Paris is a city of youthful memories, and it keeps one eternally young, my dear," Cordelia laughed. "Never mind, you'll learn that for yourself. You're a real beauty now. You dress well, you're not so maladroit as you were when I first introduced you to people, and you give off an aura of ease. I think it's because you know at last that you're doing exactly what you want to do."

"I'm sure that's true," Carla agreed. She looked intently at her chaperone and murmured, "It's so beautiful tonight that I feel like doing something entirely mad—like taking a walk along the Seine till dawn."

"That's a lovely idea—but ideally it should be with someone for whom you care very much, and not your chaperone."

"Oh, stuff and nonsense! We're dear friends, we communicate, we understand each other's thoughts. And you've put so many new thoughts into my mind that I'm practically a new woman," Carla insisted.

"You're very flattering, darling. I couldn't have asked for a more receptive, intelligent pupil. But I shan't take credit for it. I simply happened to be there when you needed me, when you were about to blossom. No—a walk along the Seine, or the Bois, or through Montmartre inspecting those darling bistros and cabarets nobody really knows anything about— that you should save for the company of some exciting young man who will see in you exactly what you want him to see."

"So far," Carla ruefully confessed, "I haven't found anyone like that at all."

"Who knows? In Paris, it might happen ten minutes from now, ten days from now, or ten months from now. Just keep an open mind and study people. If you're outgoing, they'll respond to you. One day there'll be a wave of sympathy between someone and you, and words won't be necessary. Oh, you'll know all right, Carla, when you've met someone of whom you could be entirely enamored, never fear! Well, now, let's have another glass of wine and then take a leisurely walk home."

* * *

242

As the two women walked slowly to their apartment house, Cordelia mentioned, "Tomorrow evening, we're going to the atelier of David Santos. He studied, you know, with Claude Monet."

"Oh, how wonderful! I've admired Monet's landscapes for as long as I can remember," Carla declared enthusiastically. "I wish I could have seen the Impressionist exhibition he organized in 1874 with Berthe Morisot and Sisley."

"What's interesting is that his school has been in disrepute all this while, and he's lived in extreme poverty. It's a shame, too, because he does such wonderful plein-air painting."

"I know. He has done some wonderful work at Argenteuil, depicting the Seine and its boats and such, and have you seen the remarkable series depicting a railroad station—the Gare St. Lazare, I believe? He is evidently fascinated by the play of light through steam and smoke. It's a wonderful idea, and he has carried it out so beautifully!"

"I must say, I obviously don't need to tell you anything about Monet, do I, my dear?" Cordelia laughed gaily. "Incidentally, when you're enthusiastic like this about an Impressionist painter, your face takes on a remarkable vivacity and piquant beauty. But a young man should say that to you, not an aging spinster."

"Oh, do stop! Anyway, I'll bet that, just as you think I can find someone overnight, your time may be near, too," Carla teased.

At this, Cordelia looked thoughtful. "Well," she admitted with a wistful smile, "if it should be the right sort of man, I certainly would never say no. Let's see what fate has in store for us."

Chapter Twenty-Five

The atelier of David Santos was just off the Boulevard des Capucines, a thoroughfare that Claude Monet himself had painted nine years before. As one climbed the stairs to the third floor of the red-brick building, one saw the original Monet of that street magnificently displayed in a gilt frame against a background of dark tapestry by Lurçat. Moreover, so that at night no visitor to the atelier should miss the beauty of this canvas, David Santos had installed two teakwood pedestals, one on each side of the painting, atop which reposed two gold candelabras, each with three red tapers. The illumination of these six candles intensified the almost mystic compulsion of the magnificent oil. One saw groups of houses, crossing carriages, and moving pedestrians—yet the viewer was never conscious of the wealth of detail. Instead, the beholder of this painting was struck by the overall sense of movement, conveyed in the dots of light projected by the many passersby. As Monet's closest friend, Gustave Jeffroy, once declared, ". . . his canvas is alive, agitated by the Paris which inspired it."

Cordelia and Carla paused almost in reverence, as their eyes fixed on the Monet masterpiece. Cordelia sighed and shook her head. "Would you believe that only four years ago, twelve of that master's works were sold at the Hoschedé auction, for an average price of one hundred eighty-four francs?"

"But it's unbelievable! How I wish I'd been there! I'd have bought all twelve of them," Carla raptly sighed.

"That's exactly what David Santos did. But he insisted on paying two hundred fifty for this oil—and he will treasure it for the rest of his life. I shall wager that by the time of his death, this oil will sell for at least twenty thousand francs, if not more," Cordelia predicted. "But now, let's go in! I want you to meet David, and he's certain to have some most congenial people here tonight."

Already, the two women could hear the buzz of conversation and the clinking of glasses, for the left-hand door of the atelier had been flung open. Carla brightened, for she felt herself on the brink of a remarkable new adventure. She told herself that for nothing in the world would she want to go back to the humdrum routine of life on a Texas ranch. There came into her mind the weighty question of how her parents would receive the news—which she was intending to send them in the next week or two—that she would like very much to spend at least another year, perhaps two or three, in Paris until she had developed the full potential of her artistic talents. She was going to ask Cordelia next week to marshal facts and figures that would compare living in Paris to living in the United States, to prove her point.

"There's David now," Cordelia excitedly whispered to Carla, pointing to a tall, gaunt-faced man in his early forties, with a Vandyke beard and pince-nez, the blue cord of which brushed against his thickly sideburned cheek. He was speaking animatedly to three women, beautifully dressed in the most elegant long gowns with full bodices, wearing feather boas and picturesque plumes in their curls. He took the hand of each woman in turn, kissed it, and then broke away to come toward Cordelia and Carla with a broad smile on his face. "My dear Cordy, you have made this evening memorable! And this is your protégée?"

"It is indeed. Carla Bouchard, this is David Santos."

"It's a distinct pleasure for me to meet you, M'sieu Santos," Carla declared, flushing self-consciously as he bent his head, brought her hand to his lips, and kissed it effusively. "I am most impressed by the fact that you studied with the great Monet."

"Ah, you appreciate that master? Then I forgive your being an American," Santos chuckled. "But of course, I myself was. I came here fifteen years ago. My parents in Dayton, Ohio, thought that I was mad because I didn't want to go into the harness shop when my father retired."

"There, you see?" Cordelia triumphantly avowed. "David is a perfect example of what I have been telling you all this

245

time, dear Carla. One must find oneself, even if it means a complete break with tradition and conventionality.''

"You don't need to sell me on that argument any longer, Cordy," was Carla's reply. David Santos was inspecting her with a genial and humorous look on his strikingly compelling face, when Carla—thinking that he would make a superb subject for a portrait in oil—said, "That painting outside is an absolute masterpiece. I'm sure that by the time I have grand-children, it will be worth a fortune.''

"Yes. But it isn't the monetary value that is important, Mam'selle Bouchard. It's the ethos of it. It represents, if I may say so, the very essence of the Impressionist movement. And that relates to music, to sculpture, to poetry as well. One is not so much absorbed with detail as one is with the composition of the whole—with the creation of an entity into which each little fragment seems miraculously to fit, as if it were a jigsaw puzzle. Only, of course, it isn't a jigsaw puzzle and mustn't be construed as one. The painter who believes only in detail is at best a copier, or if you will, a photographer. Impressionism—which I'm sure you've defined very well for yourself, judging from your feeling about my master—is really the art of translating the world through one's self and one's senses. That is why no two painters can ever see the same thing alike—nor should they.''

"I believe wholeheartedly in that, M'sieu Santos.''

"I like this protégée of yours, *ma belle dame.*" Santos turned to Cordelia and offered her his arm. "You shall both be my honored guests. There are a few distinguished persons I'd like you to meet. One, Mam'selle Bouchard, is a compatriot of yours—a very talented young painter named James Turner. He came from Minneapolis. His parents expected him to go into banking—what an abomination for a gifted artist!''

The atelier was a huge loft that David Santos had ingeniously converted into a magnificent studio apartment. The walls were covered with paintings, his own and others, and for curtains he had hung tapestries, contributed by friends who were weavers. The furniture was of a type Carla had never seen, the sinuous curves of some pieces intricately entwined into fantastic foliate designs, others having a disarming simplicity. These pieces were a far cry from the rococo couches, overstuffed chairs, and mirrors and dressers with their garish ornamentation that Carla was accustomed to seeing at home. Set at an angle in the ceiling at the very middle of the loft was a huge rectangular window that let in the beauty of the stars. When she looked upwards, her host noticed and explained, "The skylight faces north—which, as you know, is the truest of all possible light for painting."

Once again, as at the many soirées she and Cordelia had thus far attended, Carla saw men and women talking with the utmost lack of restraint, animatedly, with intimate smiles and gestures indicating that perhaps there was more than casual friendship to their encounters. The young artist found this bohemian lifestyle particularly satisfying, and inwardly praised herself for having had the capacity to reject the security of a conventional life in a stultifying atmosphere—as she felt she assuredly would have experienced with Thomas Lockwood's proper Boston family.

Cordelia suddenly exclaimed, "My dears, please excuse me for a few minutes. I see someone I know over there." With that, she walked off, leaving Carla with their host.

David Santos led Carla to a group of people who were standing admiring a Cézanne oil, "Three Bathers." He murmured, "He has just finished this. Cézanne, alas, is no more accepted today in our society than Claude Monet. I am told that one art dealer here offered Cézanne a hundred francs for his large canvases and forty for the small ones, so many francs per square foot—a disgusting way of appraising art. It is as if a man decided to buy books for the shelves of his cases, and ordered the book dealer to furnish so many in different colors and bindings and what have you. Appalling! Art is not to be reckoned in such grubby, materialistic terms."

"Oh, I quite agree with you, M'sieu Santos," Carla eagerly exclaimed.

"James Turner! I've someone I'd like you to meet," the painter called out. A man not quite six feet tall detached himself from the small group. He had unruly black hair and a wiry beard, and over a ruffled white shirt he wore an elaborate waistcoat and snug trousers. Carla's eyes widened, for he was extremely handsome.

"If you mean this young lady, *mon cher ami*, I'm in your debt," he said in a deep baritone voice to David, who apologized then for having to leave them to do their own introductions. Eyeing Carla more closely, James Turner grinned with an almost boyish, infectious enthusiasm. "You have to be an American!"

"I am," Carla confessed, unabashedly matching his close scrutiny. "I'm Carla Bouchard, from Texas, but I've just come from Chicago with my chaperone, Miss Cordelia Thornberg, and I'm very much enjoying Paris."

"I've a few years here on you, Miss Bouchard," James Turner confided. "Five, to be exact. And do you know, I can hardly remember what the winters were like in Minneapolis—except that they were very, very cold. That's something we rarely experience in Paris. Oh, yes, we get biting rains, but that's a wonderful time for work. I've always felt that the worse the weather, the more one can get done. When it's beautiful, when the sun's shining and the weather's warm and the air is an invitation to come out and stroll along, then you feel like procrastinating, like playing hookey from school."

"That's my feeling exactly." Carla was delighted to find a kindred spirit. "But all the same, I do believe in a certain amount of discipline. I mean, if you have a painting to do, you know that if you spend so many hours a day, you'll be that much closer—"

"Not exactly, if you'll forgive me for interrupting you, Miss Bouchard." His voice was low and vibrant now, as he moved her into a corner, just beyond a small Cézanne of a table with a bowl of fruit. "Once an artist regularizes his work schedule, then you can almost predict that his creativity will suffer. Not that I say one *has* to wait for flights of inspiration, not that at all. It's just that, as the mood seizes you, you work. You're not conscious of time or day or anything. And then, before you know it, you see something before you that couldn't have been done if you'd methodically painted away on the rate of so many hours a day, or so many brush strokes per minute. That's what I mean."

"This is really fascinating. What sort of work do you do, Mr. Turner?"

"I primarily do landscapes," he told her. "One that I'm very pleased with is of the countryside near Provence. It's really beautiful there in the summer. You can take a knapsack filled with a long, crisp loaf of French bread, a bottle of wine, and a fat sausage—perhaps a cheese, too, if you've a mind for it—then you go hiking across the fields. At noon, when the sun's hot, you sit in the shade of a barn or maybe a stack of hay. The smell of the earth is rich in your nostrils, and the sky is an impossible blue above you, and you watch the picturesque peasants in the fields. When you eat, every mouthful is a banquet because you're outdoors in the midst of nature, where everything is beauty and nothing is artificial.''

"That sounds wonderful!'' Carla breathed. She had never before met anyone who spoke to her with such exuberance and conviction. She was quite able to visualize the scene that James Turner had depicted with his enthusiastic words.

"May I get you a glass of wine, Miss Bouchard? And there's some very fine pâté that one of David's neighbors made for him. It's absolutely mouth-watering. There's also some of that crisp bread I was talking about. Why don't I bring you a plate?''

"That's very kind of you, Mr. Turner.''

"Please, it's James. And may I call you Carla? It's a lovely name. It sounds exotic, and it goes very well with your dark hair and lovely eyes.''

This time Carla blushed. Indeed, no man had ever before spoke to her so frankly, and the way he was looking at her made her tingle down to her toes. Yet, it wasn't what Cordelia might have called a "licentious appraisal''; quite the contrary, she felt as if this exciting young man were trying to peer into her very soul and understand her feelings so that he could communicate with her and share his enthusiasms. She felt a warm glow of flattery and delight. She finally remembered he was waiting for an answer, and, as airily as she could, managed to say, "Thank you. That would be very nice.''

"Fine. If you'll go to the very end of the room, over there to the left, you'll find two comfortable chairs. Fortunately, they're not occupied since everybody else seems to be walking about and looking at all the extraordinary paintings—David's as well as Monet's, Cézanne's, and Renoir's.''

As she moved slowly, looking all around the large room and making mental notes of the various types of people who were there, Cordelia Thornberg detached herself from a small group and came over to her. "Well, my dear, you certainly seem to be enjoying yourself. Didn't I tell you you'd find someone?''

"But I've only just met him,'' Carla protested for the sake of form, though inwardly she was vexed with herself because

249

she was blushing violently again. "He has some wonderful ideas about working and painting."

"That's very nice," Cordelia said simply, clearly seeing through the young woman's pragmatic words. "I want you to have a good time. David tells me in about an hour a group of amateur musicians will play some Offenbach, Rossini, and to end with, a Haydn quartet. He'll also have a grand collation. He has so many friends, and among them he numbers several chefs who like to come here and bring some of their concoctions with them. That way, everyone gets a good meal."

"It sounds like quite a communal get-together," Carla observed.

"Yes, it is. David has been lucky because his parents left him a small inheritance, which got him through the leanest years when he was studying with Monet. It's probably fortunate, in fact, that David didn't have too much money from his parents—that might have got in the way of his work. He still had to struggle a little, and that served him well. But now David has weathered the storm, and he's doing quite nicely. So, remembering how difficult it was when he started out, he sees to it that aspiring young artists—who probably have very little money and don't get many decent meals—at least have one good meal a week here. Sometimes two, because he's very gregarious."

"That's really wonderful! Oh, Cordy, I'm ever so glad you brought me here!" Carla's eyes were shining as she leaned forward and impulsively kissed the spinster, then made her way to the two chairs, which, with a sigh of relief, she saw were still unoccupied.

Seating herself, she waited patiently till she saw the handsome young man making his way carefully through the throng of guests, precariously balancing two plates with one hand and two glasses of red wine in the other. He sat down, transferring one of the plates to his lap while she took the other, then handed her a glass of wine. "There. I got you an assortment of everything that looked good. That pâté is just marvelous. And this is a young Beaujolais, not over a year old. It has a wonderful fruity bouquet to it, and you can drink a lot without getting too tipsy."

"That's very kind of you, Mr. Turner . . . I—I mean, James," Carla stammered, again vexed with herself because she was blushing now at the slightest provocation.

Sitting back, she sipped experimentally at the wine. It was really delicious, just as he had pronounced. Next, she took a small crusty piece of French bread, which was liberally smeared with the pâté, and bit into it. It was heavenly! The buzz of conversation grew now, and even more guests were arriving. James Turner pointed them out. "There's Laurence Duray, who does a column in *Le Figaro*. He thinks he's an art critic, but he's really a hanger-on. He hasn't got a *sou*, but fortunately a wealthy Austrian widow thinks he's the handsomest man alive and is seeing to all his expenses. So he can write to his heart's content and not worry about not making any money at it."

"My goodness, that sounds—I mean—that is, I don't want to tease you, but you sound the way women do when they discuss other people." Carla couldn't help giggling.

James broke out into a boisterous laugh. "You're very outspoken, Carla. I like that. Yes, I guess it did sound rather catty. But it's a well-known fact, and actually there's no shame in it. He's making her happy in her middle age, and she in turn is giving him the wherewithal to do the sort of writing that maybe one day will produce a novel—which he's threatening to start any day now. But he's not the most interesting character here. Over there, that man with the bald head and the goatee, he's Henri Robertin. He's a member of the Chamber of Deputies, and he daubs the most execrable watercolors. However, he has a reason for wanting to become involved with the artists. It seems he's head over heels in love with a pretty soubrette at the Comédie Française. She's a friend of David's, and she too thinks that the stage is not her milieu, but rather painting. And so the two of them meet under the guise of being passionately interested in art, when really she's hoping that he'll ask her to marry him. Oh, yes, he's very stuffy in that regard. He's twice been a widower, but he always offers marriage, and not a love nest."

"Gracious! I'm really learning a great deal tonight," Carla giggled again. The wine, actually, had gone to her head just a little, but the entire evening was so magical, and the attentions of this handsome young man so flattering, that these facets of the adventure intoxicated her equally as much as the Beaujolais. The stimulation of her personable companion and his attention toward her, the knowledge that she was here in Paris with no one to supervise her, or criticize her behavior,

251

and only Cordelia Thornberg to take benign charge of her and direct her to ever-new adventures, thoroughly exhilarated the beautiful young woman.

Cordelia had seen to it that this evening Carla had dressed with more than usual care. Only the day before, she had bought Carla an elegant dress in the shop of a young *midinette* two blocks away from their *pension*. Made of deep green satin, it had short puffed sleeves that left her slim arms exposed, with a flowing draped skirt and a mid-cut bodice. And, to give Carla a more worldly look, Cordelia had arranged the young woman's coiffure, drawing it up into an elaborate chignon twined with flowers and creating a row of curls all along her forehead. The result was bewitching, and it focused attention on Carla's soft, sweet mouth, her large, limpid blue eyes, and her small, classic nose.

"Have you sold any of your paintings, James?" she asked now, as her partner put his plate on the floor and finished his wine.

"Oh, yes, a few. Understand, that alone wouldn't keep me in wine and French bread, but my parents have been more than generous. They've resigned themselves to the fact that I don't want to go into banking, and since I'm their only son and heir, they feel that I should be allowed to live my own life, even if painting is what I decide I want to do permanently. I'm twenty-seven, by the way."

"I'm five years your junior."

"A perfect pairing," James frankly declared. "At any rate, you mustn't think I'm a mere dilettante with a stipend—although unfortunately a lot of people in this atelier are, more's the pity. You see, I have a part-time job. Since I learned French as a child from a private tutor—that's one aspect of my privileged upbringing that I don't regret—I speak and write it rather fluently, and because I like the language, I earn a few francs contributing feature articles to *Paris Temps* and also to *Le Figaro*. That's useful because I don't feel dependent on anyone, and when I want to paint, I can do so."

"That's really marvelous. I'd certainly like to see some of your work, James."

"I'd like to show it to you. And I'd like to see some of yours, too."

"I did a watercolor of the Seine when I first came to

Paris, and I have some things in my sketchbook. But I really haven't done any major work since I arrived."

"That's perfectly understandable. The first time one comes to Paris, one should just let the city take hold of you. It casts a magic spell, doesn't it?"

"Oh, yes!" Carla's eyes were shining with a faraway look in them. "And there's such freedom here, such a rapport between—well, even strangers."

"Like us, for example?" He smiled.

"Exactly! Only—" She blushed again and told herself in exasperation that she must really try to stop it. "Only, we're not really strangers any longer. Here we are chatting away like old friends."

"I feel that you're a kindred spirit, Carla."

"Thank you, James. I feel the same way."

"Well now, perhaps you and your friend, Miss Thornberg, would like to have dinner with me in a quaint Basque restaurant not far from my studio. Maybe tomorrow evening, unless you're booked for something else?"

"I—I don't think so. I'll ask Cordy—that's what all her friends call her, you see."

"That's a nice friendly nickname. She sounds like a wonderful woman—I know, because David told me all about her when he invited me here. She's a patroness of the arts, he tells me."

"Yes, she certainly is. Well, I'll ask her before the evening's over, James. I'd really love to dine with you, and I do want to see your work."

"Then it's settled—unless, of course, she's going to take you to the opera, or a play, or something like that. But there are other days—you're not going back to Texas right away, are you?"

Carla took a deep breath and faced him. "No, I don't want to go back at all, for now. I told Cordy just the other day that I'd like to spend at least a year here. Maybe more. I want to find myself, to see if my work is really good. I studied at the Chicago Academy of Fine Arts, and because my teacher was very much interested in the Impressionists, I fell in love with them. Now that I'm here and see so much of their work, I believe in what they're trying to do all the more."

"Then you're very perceptive. It's only a pity you can't be

253

an influential art critic or the owner of a famous gallery because then you could do these great artists a world of good. I'm afraid that some won't be, shall we say, discovered till after they're dead—then their canvases will bring a fortune."

"I don't know, James, but somehow I feel they'll have recognition before they're dead. They do such wonderful work!" Carla eagerly exclaimed. "I like them so much that—well, I'm afraid a lot of my work is imitative."

"That's essentially true of any artist, Carla," James earnestly responded. "I think that you have to experiment and imitate, until you finally discover your own style. And it's the same with all of the arts. Then, when you've mastered yourself and you know exactly how to express yourself, you can discard the tried and the true, the conventional and the traditional, and strike out on your own. You may not succeed commercially, but at least you'll have the satisfaction of knowing that what you've done is really you yourself, the very essence of you."

"That's a wonderful way to put it!" Carla looked at the handsome young man again, as if seeing him for the first time. Inwardly, she admitted to herself that he was extremely exciting, more than any other man she had ever known. Then she reprimanded herself: *But that's silly, to make a judgment like that, because what he's saying is true, and even if he were old and ugly, I'd still have to agree with it. I shouldn't let myself be so influenced because he's very good looking—and manly. He has such a pleasant voice . . . and he expresses himself so well. Oh, my! I wonder if this is what Cordy meant—that without expecting it, without any warning, I might find someone I could really care for. Oh, that's absurd, I've only just met him—but still and all, he certainly is nice. . . .*

They fell silent when the musicians began to tune their instruments in preparation for the musicale. James excused himself to Carla, saying he wished to speak with David Santos for a moment but would rejoin her in a few minutes for the concert. Seeing James walk away, Cordelia Thornberg detached herself from a group of men and women with whom she had been animatedly chatting and came over to sit next to her protégée. "Well, my dear, you two seem to have hit it off splendidly."

"Oh, we have! He's a wonderful person—probably very

talented!" Carla replied with a broad smile lighting up her face. "He's asked us both of dinner tomorrow evening, unless you've something planned—"

"I see—so that's the way the wind blows! Well now, Carla, we'll talk about that when we get home. I think as soon as the concert ends, we should bid our host goodbye and thank him for a lovely time."

"I shall hate to have to leave so soon," Carla wistfully declared.

Chapter Twenty-Six

No sooner had they come back to their apartment than Cordelia took Carla by the shoulders and sat her down on a chair. "Now I'm going to tell you something, Carla," she announced with a knowing smile. "James Turner is being very polite in inviting me to go along as chaperone. But honestly, if you were to say what's in your heart, Carla, you'd really prefer that I not accompany you tomorrow night. Isn't that true?"

Carla blushed violently, but before Cordelia's level gaze, she was forced to lower her eyes and finally nod her head.

"I thought so! Well now, you're going to do exactly that. You'll go to dinner, but you'll go without me. The fact is, I met someone myself tonight at David's, someone very, very nice. A bookseller. He's a charming man, and I think you may know him. After all, his shop is not far from the École des Beaux Arts. His name is Jules Berand."

"Oh, my goodness, yes, I do! It's a very nice bookstall, carrying all the latest magazines, newspapers, and journals, and, of course, wonderful books, too."

"Exactly. You've bought your copies of *Le Figaro* from him, I believe."

"So I have. You mean he was at the party this evening? I didn't recognize him."

"Probably because he was very elegantly dressed. He happens to be a descendant of a very old, famous Parisian family. It's quite a story, and I'll tell it to you—but not tonight, and not tomorrow, either."

"You mean you're going to go out with him?" Carla naively asked.

Cordelia tilted back her head and emitted a silvery peal of

laughter. "I shouldn't put it quite that way, but it'll do. Yes, dear Carla, I plan to spend the evening with him. He's invited me to the theater, actually to the Grand Guignol, and a very nice supper beforehand at Chez Dagobart, one of my favorite restaurants. No, you haven't been there yet, but I'll take you there next week, and that's a promise."

"My goodness, it seems that both of us were lucky this evening at M'sieu Santos's atelier," Carla giggled.

"That's quite possible. But do let nature take its course, and don't rush matters. Just go off and have a very nice evening with young Mr. Turner. It's what you really want to do, and you must do things without fearing what others might think about it. He seems a very decent sort, and if you're worried about any danger, there isn't any—unless you allow it. And that's all I'm going to say to you on that subject."

She paused a moment, then added, "You're your own mistress now, Carla Bouchard, and it's perfectly natural and normal to go out alone with a young man—and no one will look at you sideways and scold you for being so bold and daring, certainly not in Paris. If it's a friendship that's going to ripen, it will of its own accord. That's the only advice I'm going to give you because you're old enough to decide for yourself what you want. Though I may influence your mind, and I hope I've done that to some useful extent, I don't propose to influence your emotions one way or the other. Every woman has a right to her own decisions when it comes to friendship, whether it be a casual or a deep one. And now, I think we'd both better get our beauty sleep. Good night, my dear."

Carla sat musing as she watched her friend walk into the other room, and then uttered a soft sigh. It was uncanny how Cordy had penetrated right to her secret thoughts; Carla had really wished—after all was said and done—that she could be by herself and find out just how charming and delightful James really could be. . . .

As promised, James Turner took Carla Bouchard to the small Basque restaurant, where she had *tépinade* as an apéritif, and chicken with olives and grapes on a bed of wild rice with almonds browned in butter. A bottle of excellent Vouvray, that delicate, dry wine from the Loire, accompanied the meal, and fruit tarts with a strong chicory-based coffee ended it. As an afterthought, the young expatriate painter ordered two snifters of cognac. Carla watched in fascination as he took the huge glass goblet in both hands, bent his head to it to inhale the fragrance rising from the bottom of the bowl, and sloshed it to and fro before at last sipping it. "It's superb, Carla. Do as I do—you get more of the bouquet this way, and you can inhale the marvelous aroma," he instructed.

Once again, Carla felt a delicious tingle run through her. Secretly, she was quite happy that Cordelia had sent her off by herself, for that raised her own self-esteem: It signified that this woman of the world, a sophisticate on whose opinion she had so long and so often relied, believed that she was thoroughly capable of conducting her own affairs without the need of any supervision.

"That was a simply marvelous meal," Carla exulted as James gallantly came around to her chair and helped her rise. Her eyes met his and once again she couldn't help blushing. There was a magnetism to him, and his blue eyes were clear and without deception or deceit. She felt as if she had known him for a long, long time, and her pulses were swiftening as he took her arm and they strolled out to the boulevard, into the warm, moonlit June night.

His studio was on the third and top floor of a compact stone building whose ownership had changed hands, he explained to her, following the Franco-Prussian War. The original owners had been Prussian sympathizers, and during the terrible siege when the populace had been forced to eat rats and horses and exotic animals from the zoological gardens, these people had had plenty of food. At last, they had been taken out and shot as traitors, and a widow had purchased the building six years ago—an elderly woman whose husband had left her a good deal of money and who felt sympathetic toward young artists and especially expatriates. "I've really one of the cheapest rents in all Paris," he confided, as he helped her ascend the stairs.

The stairway was very narrow, and there was hardly any light. The concierge, who was the widow's sister—which reminded Carla of the two sisters at their own boardinghouse—bade James a most amicable and beaming *"Bonsoir, M'sieu Turner!"* to which he responded in voluble French. He graciously explained that the charming mademoiselle whom he was escorting was, like himself, an American. This produced an outburst of hospitable welcome and effusive compliments, till at last Carla and James were permitted to continue the rest of their ascent without further comment.

The wine and the liqueur had made Carla if not tipsy, at least imbued with a spirit of euphoria. Never had she been so conscious of her own well-being, of her physical senses. And to be squired by so personable a young man, who seemed to dwell on her every word and consider her opinions vital, was thrilling indeed.

James took out a key and opened the door, then moved to the nearest wall and turned on the gaslight and carefully lit it. It was a low-ceilinged, but rather spacious room. At one end of the garret was a small kitchen and, at the other end, a washbasin. There was no private bath, he explained, nor could he really expect one at such a low rent—only fifty francs a month. Carla gasped when James told her that the sloping front of the mansard roof was composed entirely of glass panes, although at the moment, shutters were drawn over them. Arrayed in the near end of the studio were an enormous couch, several comfortable chairs, and a table that served for work as well as for eating meals. On the walls he had pinned up some of his sketches and gouaches—a new medium for Carla—and she examined one with great attentiveness.

"It's a technique of painting using opaque watercolors prepared with gum, Carla," he explained.

"I like it very much. Will you show me how to do it?"

"Of course. It's really very simple, and it gives you a certain lovely haze, especially when you're doing foliage."

Over by the bank of windows, beyond the immense couch—which she correctly guessed served as a bed—there stood an easel. She hurried to it and exclaimed admiringly, "Oh, this is absolutely wonderful, James! Isn't this the Bois de Boulogne?"

"It is. And if you'll look to the lower right of the painting, you may recognize someone." He moved closer to her and stood with an expectant smile.

Carla bent to the painting on the easel and then let out a delighted gasp. "My gracious, that's me, isn't it? But how in the world—"

"It's easy. I had a lot of pedestrians in the picture, not unlike the Monet you saw at David Santos's atelier, and so

259

when I came home last night after meeting you, I just sketched in your lovely face.''

"I think it's absolutely marvelous—and you've caught me, you really have! Even though it's so tiny, you've put a certain eagerness in my face—the eagerness I've had since I've come to Paris, my joy in the city and in the life that's led here.'' She exuberantly turned to him, her eyes warm and receptive.

"You made an indelible impression on me, Carla. Someday I'd like to do a full-length portrait of you, if you'll sit for me.''

"Oh, yes, of course I will! I feel so honored, so flattered—nobody's ever painted me before,'' she breathed.

Once again, she felt her pulses racing, and the warm tingling glow that had pervaded her from the very outset of this evening—and, indeed, had begun last night when they had been introduced—become stronger than ever.

"I want to do full justice to you. You've the most exquisite nose, and your forehead should be chiseled in marble, Carla. But your eyes are the most expressive of all, those and your delicious mouth,'' he murmured. His left arm was suddenly around her shoulders, but not possessively, and Carla began to tremble. His lips were near hers and then, very gently and tenderly, almost like the touch of a butterfly's wings, she felt his mouth brush hers.

It was an electrifying kiss, nothing at all like the kisses of Thomas Lockwood, and now the tingling glow was almost a burning heat within her being.

"I wanted to do that the first moment I saw you last night,'' he murmured.

"Did you really? But don't you have a—isn't there a woman for whom you care? You said you've been in Paris about five years, so I supposed—'' Carla stammered, not exactly certain of her ground.

"I've no one now, Carla. And you?''

"There's no one. I just—I don't want you to think that—well—that I let any man I meet kiss me.'' She was flustered, for all her training had been to act as a model of maidenly propriety. Even now, in the corner of her mind, there rose the tiny, nagging thought: *I wonder what Father and Mother would say, if they'd seen this and how I let a virtual stranger kiss me. And coming up all alone to his apartment—how very bold! They'd probably think I was a fallen woman.*

"I'm not the sort of fellow who lies to a girl, Carla. I know it's quick, but we have a lot in common. We're both from America. We both have come to Paris to paint, to find ourselves, to express ourselves to the very fullest. So it's not unusual that, even at our first meeting, there should be a common ground between us."

"You make it seem so logical, James," she murmured.

His arm was still around her shoulders, and Carla, though at first gently trying to ease herself away from his embrace, now no longer resisted it. And once again, as he drew her to him, she felt that shivering, tingling glow, telling her that he was more than reasonably attractive to her.

Before she could think or say any more, his mouth had merged with hers, and this time she felt a furious excitement grow within her. Closing her eyes, she gave herself up completely to that kiss, her arms linked around his shoulders.

When the kiss ended, he very tactfully released her from his embrace and walked over to the table. "You remembered to bring your sketchbook, I see," he said. Carla had, indeed, wrapped it carefully in cloth—for there was always the danger of a sudden summer rain in Paris—and had brought it along.

"Oh! I forgot all about it. You know, James, I was so fascinated by—uh—seeing your work that I didn't remember I purposely brought the sketchbook so you could know what sort of things interest me," she explained. "Of course, since I don't have a space to work in just yet, I've not been able to do any oils. Our apartment isn't large enough to accommodate the clutter—not to mention the smell of turpentine and linseed oil! I'm hoping the school will have an available studio soon."

This done, she went over to the end of the couch where she had left the cloth-wrapped sketchbook containing a number of quick pastel studies, then brought it over to the table. She opened it slowly, and he nodded as she explained how and when this or that composition was done, until at the fourth sketch he put out a hand and said excitedly, "That one is particularly wonderful! I like the way you're handling colors, Carla. You're letting them make up the whole, and yet, collectively, there's something different in each little nuance. You've been very well taught. And you have a lot of talent, there's no doubt about it."

261

"Do you think it's talent enough for me to amount to something as a painter, like Mary Cassatt?"

"Well, not exactly like her." Again he gave her the boyish grin that had so endeared her to him at first meeting. "Don't forget, motherhood is becoming her favorite subject, and I don't think you've the interest in that, yet. Nevertheless, Cassatt has a refreshing simplicity and a pleasing color to her work, and she treats it vigorously. She's also quite good at pastels and etchings, and I personally am very fond of her dry points and color prints."

Carla had nearly blushed at that oblique reference to motherhood, which implied a sexual union. And yet, he had spoken of it so casually without showing the least self-consciousness. This, she told herself, was part and parcel of the Parisian lifestyle in which there need be no hypocrisy or euphemisms, but rather a forthright directness in discussions between the sexes. Indeed, in her late teens, when Maxine Bouchard had edified her somewhat on the role that a young wife is expected to play to her husband, Carla had been almost indignant at the thought that the man should be the dominant one. She had then and there resolved that this would never happen to her. And with someone like James Turner, she was sure that it never would.

He went on examining the sketches and extolled another one that depicted a sunset over a bridge. "This one I like very much. It's not quite a true Impressionistic piece, Carla, but it has a wonderful feeling for mood and atmosphere. I like the way the beginning of darkness in the sky touches the structure of the bridge itself, as well as the surface of the water," he commented.

"That's exactly what I was trying to show," she eagerly assented.

"There's a very nice feeling to this," he went on. "Yes, I'd say that, in a few years, if you go on working hard and dedicating yourself to it, you could become quite a good painter. But if you expect to earn your livelihood that way, you've only to study the examples of Paul Cézanne and Claude Monet—both almost penniless, and living from hand to mouth. However wonderful the creative work that they do is, the undeniable fact is that they're both making far less than if they were rural schoolteachers. That's my only criticism of the arts today—that the public isn't edified enough to accept it, to demand it, and most important of all, to pay for it."

When she had finished showing him the sketches, she wrapped up the sketchbook in the cloth and murmured, "I'd best go back now. Cordy will be worried about me."

"Are you sure? Do you really have to?" He took both her hands in his and looked longingly into her face. Then he kissed her again, very tenderly, on the lips.

"You—you really shouldn't—I shouldn't let you—oh, my!" Carla was totally flustered by the feeling welling within her, but nonetheless quite aware of what those feelings truly were. "I do want to see you again," she confessed, and thought that daring enough for their first time alone together.

"And I want to see you. A lot." He paused and looked at her intently. "What would you say if I suggested that we rent and share a studio together? I've considered looking for something bigger than this place because it cramps me too much. I want to be able to do much larger works than I can manage here. And you obviously need a place to work since you plan to stay in Paris for awhile."

"Yes, I do." She felt herself trembling again. What he had proposed was audacious, examined on the face of it: an unmarried man and woman working in close proximity for hours each day, with no one to chaperone them.

"I could be of great help to you," he went on. "I know some of the leading artists of the Impressionist school, and I'd introduce you to them. And besides your classes at the École des Beaux Arts, there are often symposiums on painting, where the great painters will lecture to us and show some of their own works in progress."

"That would be absolutely thrilling—but I'd like to take some time to think about your proposal. Right now I really must go back—it's been a wonderful evening, James. I've ever so enjoyed it!"

"It's mutual, Carla. And I do want to see you again."

She understood that he was interested in her as a woman, not only as a fellow artist. She realized also that now it was for her to make a decision that could take her to an exciting new crossroads of her life. Until this time, she had gone down a single thoroughfare in a definite direction. Now it was for her to choose in what direction she wanted to go, and she alone would make the choice and be the judge of what was proper for her and best calculated to develop all the perceptiveness and the affection and the creativity she felt innately within her.

"Do think about sharing a studio," he pursued.

"I—I will, James," she stammered. "We might work together very well."

"We'd have fun, too. There'd be parties at Montmartre, and you'd make lots of new friends, and we could have soirées just like David Santos's affairs. The exchange of ideas would make us better artists."

"That may be true, James. I—I will think about it, surely. And now I really must go," she weakly insisted.

"Of course, Carla. I'll go downstairs and call a fiacre," he proposed.

She lifted the sketchbook in its cloth wrapping and went slowly down the stairs, with James Turner at her side. She felt a shivering, as if she had just experienced a crisis and solved it, though she was not at this moment certain of how satisfactorily she had done it. One thing was certain: She was greatly attracted to him. Their minds met on a plane highly congenial to her and certainly inspirational for the future. That was much more than she had derived from any male she had ever met—either in Chicago or, before that, on Windhaven Range. For better or for worse, Carla knew that the next step would be up to her. And before she took it, she felt an urgent need to talk it over with Cordelia Thornberg.

Chapter Twenty-Seven

Carla Bouchard came back to the *pension* and was informed by the solicitous younger sister, who acted as concierge, that Cordelia Thornberg had not yet returned. Once by herself in her room, Carla made a wry face: She was annoyed to find Cordelia still out after she herself had made a special effort to return early. She wondered if her chaperone's own sense of propriety would lead her, as Carla's had, to terminate the evening before a daring and exciting finale took place.

There could be no doubt that James Turner had wanted to make love to her—and being honest with herself, she would not have been resentful if he had made an overt attempt. Carla realized that in all the months she had been courted by Thomas Lockwood, never once did he make any improper advances—nor did she ever want him to. He had never stirred her as James so quickly had done.

She blushed, thinking herself completely shameless. She was still a virgin and as such was supposed to put all thoughts of physical love from her mind until the day when her husband-to-be came upon the scene. Only this was Paris, not Texas or even Chicago. Here in Paris, far away from her parents' supervision, she could choose the sort of life she wanted for herself.

Still, she impatiently awaited Cordelia's return because she wanted to tell her of the proposal that James had made—that both of them share the expense of a studio where they could paint and exchange ideas . . .

. . . *And make love*, Carla thought to herself with a warm glow suffusing her features.

She wanted very much to know exactly what Cordelia thought about James's startling proposal, and whether it was customary for a young man who had met a girl just the day before to make such an offer to her—and also whether she was right in assuming that it implied what she thought it did.

Carla paced the room impatiently, waiting for Cordelia's return. At the soirée, someone had given her a package of French cigarettes, and now for the first time in her life she lit one. Inhaling, she immediately choked and coughed, grimacing into the mirror at herself, and then considered the cigarette. The blue smoke rising slowly in whorls to the ceiling made a fanciful pattern. She thought to herself that it was very much like the way of life she had seen in this city since she had come here with Cordelia—was it an illusion . . . or was it reality? How far did the artistic freedom go, and was such freedom to be carried over from work into actual life itself, or was it simply necessary to accept it intellectually, without practicing it? For Carla Bouchard, these were momentous thoughts, for she knew them to be entirely at variance with all the tenets her parents had instilled in her from infancy to young womanhood.

She finished the cigarette and then lit another. Now, practicing, she found it easier, and soon she was holding it at a rakish angle, observing herself in the mirror and smiling back, tilting her head to give herself an insouciant air, resembling that of the women she had seen at so many cultural gatherings. She was pleased with herself, and yet inwardly troubled. Was it right to find herself infatuated with this handsome young man, this artist who had so much in common with her? And was the fact that he attracted her physically also a vital consideration? She knew nothing about him, except what he had vouchsafed about his parents back in Minneapolis. He might have a dozen mistresses—or he might be addicted to opium or absinthe, two formidable illusory escapes that, as Cordelia had told her, many bored, jaded, or disgruntled people took in order to color their lives, which had become drearily unacceptable to them.

It was not till nearly five in the morning that Cordelia returned, and she was startled to find her protégée still up, the small salon wreathed in heavy smoke.

"Why, Carla, whatever made you wait up for me?" she laughed.

"I—I have to talk to you, Cordy. It's very important."

"I see." Cordelia at once sobered, observing the intensity

of Carla's expression. "Well, wait until I get off my evening gown and slip into a wrapper. Also, if you want to be a darling, go pour me a Pernod—and have one yourself. I rather think you need it. I see you've been smoking cigarettes. This is the new Carla Bouchard, I take it?"

"Please don't patronize or tease me!" Carla petulently broke out, almost bursting into tears. "It's really important, and it's not a joke, and I'm very much upset. I need your advice—after all, you *are* my chaperone, Cordy."

"Yes, darling. I'm sorry. I suppose I was so carried away by the lovely time I had this evening—or should I say this morning—that I quite forgot your experience at David Santos's little affair last night—night before last, I mean. Dear me, I really must be more conscious of time, mustn't I?" Airily, she went off to her bedroom to come back in a cream-colored silk wrapper and sandals, while Carla went to the tiny convenience kitchen, uncorked the bottle of Pernod, and poured two generous glassfuls.

"That's better." Cordelia took a generous sip and licked her lips. "Now I can think clearly, and I'm ready for your problem."

"I—I dined with James Turner."

"I know that. Go on."

"Well, after that, he took me to his place, and he showed me his work. He does wonderful gouaches, Cordy!"

"I've heard that he did. But that's not what's on your mind, is it?"

"No." Carla hung her head, bit her lip, and then blurted out, "He—he asked me if I'd like to share a studio with him, so we could both work together. He said it would be near Montmartre, that we could meet many people who would have similar views on art, and that it would improve our work, our outlook on life, and our thinking in general."

"So that's the way the wind blows. . . . Carla, James is very much taken with you. And I learned enough about his background from David Santos to tell you that if you're worried that he's a wolf in sheep's clothing, you can put your mind at ease. He's a very decent chap, and actually, David tells me, he's only had one sweetheart in all the five years he's been here. He even wanted to marry her, but she chose to marry an elderly and very wealthy banker in Lyons."

"Oh. Well, that doesn't sound too awful."

267

"What you must realize, my darling, is that it's not at all unusual for a single man to have a lover with whom he has a very tender and enduring relationship. When he marries, if he is somewhat staid, he bids the mistress farewell. They remain good friends, and he is faithful to his wife. On the other hand, there are plenty of men in Paris, I've no doubt—for I know quite a few myself—who maintain their mistresses after they are married. And in some instances, the wives know about it and are even good friends with the mistresses. We call that a *ménage à trois*."

"My gracious!" Carla's eyes were wide, and her tone was one of utter incredulity.

"I am simply stating what goes on all the time here, my dear. And not only in Paris. You see, Europe is somewhat more emancipated about the matter of physical relationships between the sexes than we are back across the seas. We suffer from a very definite Puritanism, bequeathed to us by our illustrious forefathers on Plymouth Rock. Here, a young man is brought up to believe that the world is his oyster, and if he is well-to-do enough—or his parents are, which is the same thing—his mother or his father generally finds a complacent widow or a mature spinster who has no interest in marriage to initiate him into the tender mysteries of Cythera. This provides him with assurance and eliminates his anxiety so that when he is really ready to mate with the proper woman and procreate, he is quite competent, and there is no problem for the wife. Now that's a sensible outlook. Alas, it's hardly the same back where we come from, Carla."

"I—I guess I understand something about that. But—but—" Carla faltered, trying to find exactly the right phrase.

"But what you really want to know, Carla, is whether young Mr. Turner will want to go to bed with you—especially if you share a studio—isn't that it?"

Carla's blushes were the most violent of the entire evening as she turned slightly away and then nodded.

"I would think so, unless he is a eunuch or has given up lovemaking as a penance—"

"Oh, for heaven's sake, Cordy!" Carla stamped her foot and was almost in tears again. "Don't make a joke about such an important thing!"

"Forgive me again. Come here and sit down beside me." As Carla reluctantly obeyed, the auburn-haired spinster put her arm around the young woman's shoulders and drew her closer, then kissed her on the cheek and said, "Carla, I told you that you should come to Paris to find yourself. I'm not advising you to go to extremes or excesses—and even if I did, you probably wouldn't take my advice, for you have a pretty level head. You're neither promiscuous nor given to seeking escape from the world in either drugs or liqueurs, or spiritualism, or any of the new fads that are popping up every day to distract people from the routine business of living. If you're drawn to this young man, and you want him and he wants you, there's nothing healthier in the world than a good love affair. And if he's the decent sort I rather sense he is, he'll see to it that you have no problems about—I mean—well, to put it bluntly, having a child outside of wedlock, which would of course scandalize your parents and leave me open to a good deal of blame for having lured you down the crimson path."

"Oh, my goodness!" Carla ejaculated, for such candid talk was rather more than she had bargained for.

"Well, my dear, if I'm to be your chaperone in more than name only, I should think that you and I had best be frank with each other. And the facts of life, dear girl, are certainly what every young woman should know—especially if she has never before had a man make love to her. I know you haven't, and so it's a matter of your own decision. Just remember that it's not a mortal sin. A man can love a woman without marrying her, and if he's considerate and tender, the two of them can be sometimes more blissfully united than by all the ritual that passes for holy matrimony."

"I see. What else do you know about James?"

"Just what David told me. But David never lies, not about such matters as that. He's known James for almost as long as he's been in Paris, and he was the one who told me about the sweetheart who married the banker. I'd say that's a fairly good track record, darling. After all, he's at least four or five years older than you, and it would be peculiar if he hadn't had a lover by this time."

Once again, Carla could not help blushing. Such candor was taking her farther along the emotional path she had hoped somehow to bypass until she could be alone by herself and single out her own feelings to determine what course of action to take.

Cordelia looked at her for a long moment without speaking, then, to ease Carla's troubled mind, said, "But let me tell you about my *own* little adventure this evening. As you know, I went to dinner with that nice bookseller, Jules Berand. He's a descendant of, as I think I told you earlier, a very fine family, part of the minor nobility of France, whose fortune was wiped out during the French Revolution. When it was over—since they were never convicted of any acts against the Republic, and since his forebears had the presence of mind to go to England during the Terror—they were able to get a restoration of their estate, a magnificent house in the finest section of Paris. However, during the Franco-Prussian War, the house was stolen from them by a corrupt government functionary. It was done by means of some forged papers that purported to show taxes had not been paid since the restoration despite several notices sent to Jules's parents. Both of them are dead now, by the way. It was tragic, too, for his mother was ailing and ended her life with gas. When his father discovered it, he put a bullet through his temple."

"How dreadful! The poor man!" Carla sympathetically exclaimed.

"However, I have a few influential friends in Paris, one of them being a deputy. Jules and I plan to have an interview with this man in the next week or so and see if we can't do something about restoring the house to Jules, since it's his rightful due."

"That sounds very romantic! I guess you like him very much, don't you?"

"Very much indeed. He's cultured, not so much older than I am, and with a maturity that makes a man of his years appreciate a woman for her mind, as well as for her body. I must say," Cordelia now rose and moved over to contemplate herself in the mirror, with an arch smile, "that happily, Old Man Time has been very good to me. Because I've been sensible about my diet, never used tobacco or liquor to excess, I think I can still capture a man's interest when his thoughts move to the birds, the bees, and the flowers, instead of the paintings in the Louvre."

"My gracious, Cordy," Carla expostulated, "you're certainly beautiful, and I don't ever think of you as being old—just wiser and more experienced."

"And I want to share my experience with you, pet. But

270

now, I'd say it's time we both got our beauty sleep, and I need mine more than you do because, let's face it, I've a good many years on you. As for James Turner, you'll cope with that problem when the time comes to cope with it, and I'm sure you'll make the right decision. Remember, don't be influenced by what I say or what anybody else says. If it's what you want, do it. And don't regret it once you've decided because there's nothing worse than someone who goes around moping and saying, 'If only I had done this,' or 'If only I had not done that.' Have the courage to stand by your convictions, no matter what they may cost you, once you've made them. And now, good night.''

Chapter Twenty-Eight

A week after Carla Bouchard had met James Turner, the young expatriate painter invited both her and Cordelia Thornberg to attend a soirée at which a former member of the Chamber of Deputies was to be an honored guest and principal speaker. Two minor poets would precede him, reading from their works, and there would also be an exhibition of paintings by Nadine Cochard, a gifted, eccentric, and licentious minor Impressionist who, according to James, was far too imitative of her god, Paul Cézanne.

David Santos was present at the reception and greeted Carla and Cordelia when they arrived. As they walked near the wall on which Cochard's oils were displayed, David mockingly murmured, "There is an old adage to the effect that when someone associates with a genius, the former hopes that the latter's gifts will rub off through osmosis. In Nadine's case, alas, she naively believes that by sleeping with as many Impressionist painters as she can, she will become a great painter herself. As you see, this rendering of a kitchen table is almost a copy of one of Cézanne's most famous works."

At the end of the huge loftlike room where the soirée was being held, in a building located on the Rue des Belles Amies, coppery-haired Nadine Cochard herself presided. She stood in a corner, with a glass of wine in one hand and a long ivory cigarette holder in the other, blowing wreaths of smoke around a group of young men—all of whom, as David again mockingly pointed out, were painters of no particular talent, all hoping that Nadine would favor them with her full-blown charms.

The works of the two poets were not particularly interesting to Carla, for these were predominantly sentimental effusions on love and idealism. But the deputy, a balding, wiry man names Louis Montfassier, brought her up short by forcing her to realize that there was much more to Paris than the flowering of the arts.

Montfassier had just lost his seat in the Chamber of Deputies, having been voted out of office in one of the many parliamentary elections occurring during these years. But his political enthusiams had in no way diminished, nor had his fervor as a French patriot. His message on this evening was that, with the shameful legacy of the events of 1870-71, the one great cause that should bring together all loyal Frenchmen, now and in the future, was *revanche*—revenge upon Germany, for the humiliation inflicted on France.

"You here are the flower of our intellectual and cultural life, *mes amis*," he thundered, bringing his fist down upon the lectern for emphasis. "It is not to the masses that I appeal for what must be in every native Frenchman's blood a burning, unquenchable desire. It is to you, who are the thinking people and whose decisions will surely affect our spurned and suborned nation. No, do not misunderstand me; I do not call upon you to answer the summons of military drums and fifes and to enlist in an army that will one day make the detested Prussians regret their action of a dozen years ago. Instead, I ask you all to be rational and practical, and to realize that the only way for your own culture to thrive is in a society made safe against usurpation and tyranny by a foreign power. Then you will be free to realize your own individual genius in the creation of your paintings, your poems, your novels and dramas, all the forms by which you express the noblest of your thoughts. And such nobility will again flourish under a strong French regime, unassailable by such warmongers as the Prussians."

He paused dramatically, looking here and there among the audience, and then leaned forward, pointing a long forefinger at Carla herself. "Mademoiselle, I address myself to you, who represents the very flower of French womanhood." Carla was hard put not to giggle, and still more so not to speak out that she was an American. "You who are undoubtedly an artist will one day allow yourself to unite with a gifted young man. The two of you will create beautiful children in whom the future of France rests. Think of how much happier you and your husband and those children will be if all of you live

273

in a strong, secure France that, because it has nothing to fear from destructive people such as the Prussians, can concentrate all its energy and its wealth and its planning upon bringing to fruition the creativity of people like yourself."

He paused again, and then resumed. "There is a man alive today in France, a man on whom I for one would place my trust for the guarantee of this glorious future France must and shall have. He is a man who displayed brilliant military abilities in North Africa and Indochina, and it was he who almost single-handedly suppressed the Commune of Paris eleven years ago."

There was a murmur in the audience as his listeners turned to one another and began to whisper. He waited again, then held up a hand and, with a broad smile, went on. "I can tell that you already know his name. It will be better known before much longer, of this I am certain. He is Georges Ernest Boulanger. Here is a man of forty-five, with brilliant military experience as well as governmental understanding. He is an organizer, a man who makes friends, a man who can appeal to intellectuals like yourselves, as well as to the masses. And he has a single theme: Restore France to its glory, as it was in the days of Charlemagne and the great kings, when France was known throughout the world for its colonization, its strength, its military prowess, and its patronage of the arts. Georges Ernest Boulanger is a man who will bring France its vengeance against the hated Prussians. Think of him, remember him, and above all else, remember his lofty ideal. If all of you help him realize it, you will sustain this era of the greatest creativity and intellectual freedom France has ever known."

He bowed his head to scattered applause, and then went off to one side, where he conferred with his host, Marc Loralier. A middle-aged romantic painter who had of late begun to espouse the Impressionist movement, Loralier was, unlike most of the young artists gathered under his roof tonight, wealthy not only by inheritance, but also by his previous success as a portrait painter for the elite of Paris.

James Turner excused himself for a moment, went off to the sideboard where a buffet of refreshments was offered, and came back with a plate of hors d'oeuvres—some melon, prosciutto, and a wedge of Reblochon cheese. In his other hand, he had a glass of chilled Chablis, and Carla thanked him for his attentiveness. He went back to get a plate and some wine for himself, then took the chair beside hers in a corner of the huge loft. Some of the guests had already left, a few of them doubtless disturbed by the bold declaration of the former deputy.

The young expatriate turned to Carla. "What did you think of our speaker?"

"He was really very strong on the subject of making France powerful again and punishing Germany," she observed. "It sounds rather ominous. Doesn't that sort of talk and activity lead to war?"

"It could very easily, but not for a good long time. France was left practically decimated by the Franco-Prussian War, Carla. It would take many years to rearm the nation and to build up a line of supplies and defenses for another war. No, I don't think we'll see war in this century," he philosophically remarked.

"I don't know anything about General Boulanger, but the way this deputy was speaking, he made him sound as if he were the new messiah who would cure all France's ills," was Carla's comment.

"You're absolutely correct. There's a certain fascination even for a great many intellectuals over the idea of uniforms and parades and the drums beating and artillery and guns. It gives people the illusion that they are being well guarded and safe, that nothing can touch them. But it's also an invitation to imperialism, in my opinion," James said as he sipped his wine.

"I feel that way, too. But I'm relieved, James, that you don't foresee another war in the near future. Perhaps by then, both of us will be far too old to have it affect us."

"Let's hope it never happens. Nobody wins a war—and only the munitions makers, the generals, the politicians, and the diplomats profit. Certainly not the common people. And no one cares a hoot about the people who lay down their lives in the trenches. They're the glorious dead, the heroes, and they're very easily forgotten that way. No, I'm certainly not a warmonger the way our friend was this evening. After all, I was born five years before the Civil War, and the thought of what happened in our own country still horrifies me. The South is *still* suffering from the effects of that war. No, when one thinks of war, one should really think about the aftereffects in the years ahead.''

"You sound so wise, James," Carla smiled.

"I'm just a simple man from Minneapolis who came to Paris because I would rather paint than count people's money, and I hope someday to make a success at it. Also, I hope that I can share my life with someone very exuberant and lovely and warmhearted and sensitive—like you, Carla. Have you thought about our taking a studio together? Please don't think I want to hurry you into anything. It's an important step for both of us.''

Her heart swelled at this, for the way he was talking to her had no intimation of his being simply a young philanderer who sought a quick conquest. And the fact was, having heard him express his views on war, she was more than ever convinced that she would find in James Turner someone with whom she could readily communicate her innermost feelings, and that he would not disparage or denigrate them, either on their own merit or because she happened to be a woman.

She tried to choose her words with care, hesitating a moment, and then said, "Yes, I have been thinking about it, James. I—well, I've never considered anything like this before. I also have to think about what my parents would say.''

"You're certainly of age, so they would have to respect your decision. Besides, I'm sure they know you're intelligent enough to do what's best for yourself.''

Impulsively, she put out a hand to touch his wrist, and they exchanged a long look. He was smiling, and she felt a warm rapport. "I do like the idea very much," she murmured. "Maybe we can talk about it this evening, when we leave here?''

"I'd like that, too, dearest Carla.''

She was shivering now, for she caught the intimation that tonight, if she went back with him to his place, he would certainly try to make love to her. And she felt also that this time she might very well respond. It was a Rubicon to cross. Should she decide to take that final, irrevocable step? She knew that she longed to, and that she would not be afraid to take it once she decided to do so.

It was nearly midnight when James Turner and Carla Bouchard finished their collation, enjoyed a second glass of wine, said good-bye to their host and some of the friends they had made this evening, and then went out into the street. Cordelia had left hours earlier, on the arm of Jules Berand, who had unexpectedly appeared at the atelier.

There was a faint rumble of thunder, yet the sky was only slightly overcast, barely dimming the full moon. "That's not the rumble of guns, I hope," Carla quipped.

"No, that's really thunder, off to the west. But it's not far to my place, Carla, and I'm sure we can reach there before we're drenched—do you want to try?"

She began to shiver a little again, because he had inferred that she would want to go to his place, instead of returning to her *pension* at this late hour. She quickly wondered to herself that if she asked him to call her a fiacre to go back home, would he take her for a silly American prude? On the other hand, she didn't want him to think that she was a girl of easy virtue. It was an emotional quandary that she faced for the very first time in her life, and she had to admit to herself that, in spite of her twenty-two years, her knowledge of art, and her now intense familiarity with Paris, she still knew very little about men and, specifically, how to relate to them.

There was a certain amount of defiance to her as she tilted up her chin and, with almost a provocative small smile, replied, "I'm not made of sugar, and I shan't melt from a little rain, James. By all means, let's walk to your place. I don't feel the least bit sleepy."

"I don't either. One never does when one is stimulated by good ideas, good friends, and good food and wine," he chuckled, taking her arm. As they walked along the boulevard, another couple passed them, arm in arm, intent in conversation, the girl boldly insinuating her hip against her companion's. Carla guessed that they were lovers, or would soon be. Or perhaps, she suddenly realized, as there were girls who had to earn their livelihood by accepting any man who would pay for their favors, that girl might well be a *putain* who would have to pretend to this man she had selected on a Paris street that he was a handsome, wonderful lover—but whom she would promptly forget the next morning. Carla found herself wondering how a girl could come to accept love on such transient terms, and whether it did not indelibly scar her psyche.

She was amazed at her own reactions and her own philosophizing as she walked along with James. She scarcely heard what he was saying to her, except that it was very flattering: that in the moonlight her hair looked particularly dark sheened and lovely, that she had beautiful eyes, and that he was intensely fond of her.

An aura of romance had been evoked tonight, stirred by the ominous speech of the former deputy who seemed to prophesy a militaristic glory for downtrodden France . . . one that would involve thousands of as yet unsuspecting men, women, and children. But out of the evening had come a strengthening of her bond with James because his reaction to the man's speech had been precisely what she herself had been feeling. Their shared reaction was important, for if she accepted the handsome young man, it would be because his mind and hers had communion, not only their bodies. And when she thought of this, she felt herself shivering again, and she was almost giddy with titillated expectation as she reached the door of the building where he lived.

He unlocked it and held it open for her, and the gesture pleased her. In every way, thus far, he had rung true—most of all in his mind and his work and his respect for art. This she would cling to, as she did to Cordy's revelation that in five years James Turner had had only one known sweetheart. She wondered if he were a skillful lover, a man who would be gentle and considerate. . . .

She expected that he would stop her on the landing and take her in his arms and kiss her. She was ready for it—yet he did not. Very courteously, he took hold of her elbow to guide her up the darkened turn at the landing. Reaching the floor where he lived, he swiftly unlocked the door, went in, and turned on the gas. He said, "Now you won't trip over things. I confess I'm not the world's best housekeeper."

"I'm not, either," she laughed, and there was a vibrance to her laughter, a nervous exhilaration because of the impending momentous step she had decided to take . . . the step across the Rubicon.

The door closed, but again to her secret delight, he did not thrust the bolt home. If he had done that, she reasoned, there would have been a kind of finality to it, as if declaring to her that she was there to stay. The titillation of all this conjecture stirred her more than she knew. Her breath came quickly, and

278

there was a rosy flush to her cheeks, and her eyes were large and humid with a quivering expectancy.

He took her hat and cloak and then offered her a glass of wine. She considered a moment, and then agreed. It would give her greater courage, and besides, she hadn't had all that much tonight, so it wouldn't influence either her judgment or her reactions.

She seated herself on the large studio couch, leaned back, and watched him go to the sideboard to take a bottle of Beaujolais, uncork it, and pour out two glasses. He brought them back to her, handed her one, then clinked his to hers. "Here's to the two of us as a team of painters who I hope will make Impressionist history, Carla," he proposed.

"That's a toast I can drink to with enthusiasm, James," she laughed.

"Carla, I know we've known each other only a little more than a week, yet I feel as if we've been friends for a long time."

"I—I feel the same way about you, James." She felt a stirring, a curious, sensual tingle rise along her thighs and her stomach, and her bosom rose and fell more quickly. Bringing his glass to her lips, his arm brushed her breast, and there was a sensitivity to her nipple of which she had never before been conscious. At the same time, she felt herself blushing and damned herself—he must really think her a very silly, naive child to be so affected. After all, what was so wrong or immoral about being alone with a nice young man who painted the way she did and who thought the way she thought? They were both of age, and they were in Paris, where people acted as they wished so long as they didn't hurt anyone or themselves—there *couldn't* be anything wrong about it.

The thought emboldened her and made her decide that she would not flinch if he made the slightest overt caress. Overcoming all other speculations and doubts and hesitations was the awareness that, till this moment, she had never before been alone with a young man to whom she had been so attracted physically—yes, that most of all—and she did not even know how her own body would respond. It was important that she learn. This was her time for development, not only of her skills and talents and potential, but also of her awareness of herself as a full-fledged woman.

He finished his wine and set the glass down on a small

taboret. She took a while longer with hers, wanting to prolong the moment, wanting to be more certain of herself and not appear so gauche and uninitiated. Yet at the same time, out of her own sense of values and the propriety inculcated in her since her childhood, she did not wish him to think that she was wantonly awaiting his declaration of physical desire for her.

"This is really very nice wine, James." She felt it necessary to make some sort of conversation, to indicate to him that she was completely at her ease and not the least fearful. Nonetheless, she was more conscious than ever of the continued and increased tingling, and her thighs almost instinctively pressed together. It was, though she had no way of understanding it, the subconscious proclamation of her vulnerability, of her hitherto unprofaned virginity. She had never been prepared for this moment.

At last, she set down the glass, trying to make it a casual gesture, though nonetheless she could not help looking at him, for he had turned to her. She moistened her lips, which had suddenly gone dry, and then his left arm was around her shoulders and his right palm cupped her chin as he murmured, "You're so very beautiful, Carla." And before she could reply to this, his mouth sealed hers with a gentle pressure that was at the same time both gentle and exciting. It was a kiss that demanded only an acceptance of its camaraderie and tenderness, and it did not importune her with overtones of overwhelming passion or lust.

Her eyes closed, she put one hand around his shoulders as she gave herself to the kiss. And when it was over, her senses were swimming in euphoric delight, and the trembling and the tingling had redoubled. But now they were not nearly so alarming as they had been at the outset, when they had been a cerebral concern and not a growing awareness of her body's yearning—for such it was, and as such she now recognized it, perhaps dimly because she was virginal, but she recognized it all the same.

"I hope you don't think I do this with every woman I meet, Carla," he said with a slight hoarseness, as his arm slid away from her shoulder. "I have a need to be absolutely honest with you, as I hope you will be with me. I want you—I want you terribly. I don't have other lovers, and I'm not looking for any. Of course, you know I'm not married—

David must have told you that—but I did have an affair with someone. I wanted to marry her, but she preferred an older man who was far wealthier than I'll probably ever be. I tell you this so you know that I'm not trying to deceive you or get you to like me on false pretenses.''

"You're very sweet, James, and I know you're honest. I did know about that other woman. As for myself—well, there's very little to tell because other than one brief and chaste romance, you're the only other man I've ever kissed apart from my father or my relatives.'' She paused and looked down at her lap. "I trust you, James.''

She faced him now, her lips quivering, and her eyes were moist with tears of an almost ineffable yearning, caused by his surprising and disarming candor and gentleness with her. If he had been cynical or callous or exhibited an impatience, she would have repulsed him at once and been indignant. Under these circumstances, however, she would not deny an experience that she knew inevitably she must have to complete her fulfillment as a woman, to complete her virtual self-declaration of independence in this emancipated Paris—a world of which those on Windhaven Range could have no possible understanding or knowledge.

"I know how sweet and innocent you are, Carla. You can trust me. I want us to be together—but I want it to be your choice, and I want you to be sure. If you feel you shouldn't, if there's any reason you can't, tell me.''

"I—I do want to . . . and I'm not afraid.''

"Oh, Carla! Carla darling!'' he murmured. His arms were around her, his hands against her shoulder blades as he drew her to him, and his mouth came down on hers in an eager, joyous fusion that made her shudder with the intimations of a physical rapture hitherto unknown and undivined and yet, she was certain, monumentally vital to her entire life and being.

When the kiss was over, he released her and moved away to draw the shutters. This too gave her greater reassurance. He was thoughtful of her, he did not wish people across the way to look in upon their privacy. At the same time, he was giving her ample time to consider every ramification of her decision.

He moved from the huge window to the sideboard and lit a large red candle in a single silver-plated candlestick holder. Then, glancing back at her, he turned off the gaslight, and only the single candle illuminated the room. The eerie shadows on the wall created a kind of phantasmagoria, and the room took on a mystical aura of nebulous dreams and delicately hidden illusions, the perfect setting for a night of idyllic, virginal love—for such a night it would be for Carla Bouchard.

He came back slowly to her, and of her own accord, she slid forward to the edge of the couch, holding up her arms to him, her face wreathed in joyous expectancy. He knelt down, his hands against her waist, and his lips pressed against her soft, pulsing throat. Carla uttered a choking little cry, tilting back her head, closing her eyes, and her hands pressed against the top of his curly head as she surrendered herself to the sheer hedonistic sensation of this amorous prelude. The very tenderness and the prolongation enchanted her: All that had taken place thus far had been the fullfillment of a dream-wish of which she had not been really conscious all these past years, but which now seemed what had always been intended for her wakening into womanhood.

There was no grossness, nothing offensive, and although her complete naiveté deterred her from a full realization, she was nonetheless dimly aware that he obviously must have had either a marvelously intuitive gift for lovemaking, or else sufficient experience to be able to evoke such delicate and gentle sensations. For an instant, there flared into her mind a sense that it had been that other woman—now far out of his life and doubtless gone forever because of her marriage to an elderly banker—who had prepared him for initiating her, Carla Bouchard, into the awesome, exquisite mysteries of passionate love and sweet fulfillment.

She felt his hands glide slowly along her sides, till they brushed the outer curves of her swelling young breasts. The tingling and stiffening of her nipples was a sudden swift, keen, almost excruciating sensation. The secrets of her body were being unlocked; in this almost complete darkness, touched only by the flickering candle in that one far-off corner of the room, it was as if an invisible lover was paying homage to her body, to her beauty. It was so tantalizing and arousing that she felt almost on the verge of swooning—yet she had never been more alive, never more vibrantly conscious of each mote, each nuance, each infinitessimal gradation of her sexuality.

When at last his hands almost reverently brushed the undercurves of her ripe, firm breasts and then his lips pressed insistently but lightly on the bodice of her blouse to touch the soft deepening cleft between them, she uttered an incoherent little moan of sheer pleasure and delight.

She felt herself completely eager, without the least shyness or fear; she felt, in a word, liberated from conventions she had been brought up with and which, till now, she never had reason to doubt as to their wisdom in channeling her life. There was no wantonness to this, for Carla Bouchard was conscious only of the poetic blending of all her senses and of the patiently gentle initiative of her handsome lover. Not one jarring chord had been sounded in this tone poem of surging desire, which would culminate in her ultimate fulfillment.

"Oh, James! How lovely it is—" she brokenly whispered, wanting to express her feelings so that he would know and share the excitement and the growing wonder of what he was doing to her and how he was reshaping her emotions and feelings and cogent yearnings.

"Carla, my darling, you're so beautiful! I want you so very much—we'll be so happy—oh, Carla!" he murmured back.

She felt his fingers begin to unbutton her blouse, and almost without knowing it, she aided him, her own fingers more adept in such intimate matters as a woman's garments. And as she did so, his fingertips stroked her wrists and forearms and elbows, then rose to caress her upper arms.

He drew off her blouse, then her long skirt, carefully placing her clothes on a chair. Coming back to the couch, he ever so slowly removed her chemise and her petticoat, staring almost reverently at her nearly naked body. With infinite care, he removed first one, then the other, of her silk stockings, then her garters, and finally, as Carla averted her face, he drew off her panties. She kept her face averted as he swiftly undressed, dropping his clothes in a heap on the floor.

The candlelight played upon the symmetry and beauty and satiny sheen of her nudity as she lay on the couch, trembling in every limb, dazed by the wonder and the power and the unforeseen onrush of all these sensations that crowded in, one upon the other, taking her from stage to stage, from ethereal plane to plane, until she did not think she could bear it and still remain in full possession of all her faculties.

"Oh, Carla! How beautiful you are—my darling Carla—"

She faintly gasped as he lightly stroked her naked body. When he finally entered her, the swift, momentary pang of virginal loss was almost a welcome relief from the nearly unbearable arousal of his caresses. Merged with him, fused in ardor, eager to go beyond the bounds of what had been her own trepidations, Carla found herself uplifted into the final transports of passion.

As they lay entwined on the couch, his hands gently stroking her still-quivering body, the touch of which was almost painful to her heightened, stimulated nerve endings, she hoarsely whispered, "James, oh, James, I never dreamed it could be like this! It was just wonderful. . . ."

"I'm so glad. I hope I didn't—that is, I didn't want you to have the least hurt, sweetheart," he murmured, as he stroked her thighs and leaned solicitously over her, peering into her rapt, smiling face.

"And I didn't. Oh, what a wonderful lover you are, my darling—I'm so happy. I want to take a studio together, and we'll work together—"

"And always be like this," he finished.

"Yes," Carla drowsily murmured, "and it will be heaven. But now, I just want to sleep in your arms and dream about how wonderful it is that we met. It seems that Fate brought me all the way from Texas and Chicago to meet you at last, my dearest, wonderful James!"

Chapter Twenty-Nine

It was the sixth of August, but on Windhaven Range, though the vaqueros were preparing a fiesta for the next day in honor of their *patrón*'s birthday, the prevailing mood was hardly one of celebration—certainly not so far as Lucien Edmond and Maxine Bouchard were concerned. For the day before they had received a long letter from Carla in which, along with her birthday greetings to her father, she had with a spirited and almost joyous defiance not only detailed her decision to remain in Paris at least for the rest of this year but also given them a new address at which to write her: the address of the studio that she was sharing with young James Turner.

She had gone so far as to declare, in a manner flagrantly shocking for a young woman in this epoch:

> We are living together because we are one in our beliefs and our craftsmanship in the art of painting, and because we want to be with each other all the time. He is a fine, good man, with a background that would meet with anyone's approval. He is the first man I have truly loved, and I know that he cares for me very deeply. Do not think badly of me, Mother, Father, because I have acted on my own convictions and with the knowledge that I feel the relationship is best for me.

"I can't believe what the girl wrote us, Maxine!" Lucien Edmond uttered a groan and leaned back in his chair at the breakfast table. Carla's letter, reread at least a dozen times since its receipt, lay on the table beside him. "And I hold that Thornberg woman chiefly responsible. We believed her to be a true friend, and from what Hugo and Carla wrote us from Chicago, she was one. Now she betrays our trust by leading our daughter to Paris and then standing by while Carla enters into an illicit liaison with a man about whom we know nothing!''

''Darling, she *is* of age,'' Maxine gently reminded him, though her eyes were swollen from having wept most of the previous night while he lay asleep. ''And I for one can't really blame Cordelia Thornberg.''

''We should have made further investigations about where she was going to live in Paris, what sort of companions she would have. And now it begins to look as if that Thornberg woman steered Carla into this. She probably told her it was the modern thing to do. Modern, indeed!'' Lucien Edmond snorted, taking up the letter, then crumpling it and flinging it down to the floor. ''I don't know what to do! I've half a mind to go to New York, take the first steamship to Paris, and bring her back—whether she likes it or not!''

''You really can't, Lucien Edmond. And she would hate you for it.'' Maxine sighed poignantly. ''But how could she be so misguided? Couldn't she have thought about how *we* would feel about this, our daughter brought up in the Catholic faith that professes the sanctity of marriage and holds that the only true union is a love that is blessed in God's church?'' she asked in a pained voice. Then she shook her head. ''It's beyond me. I thought she was sensible enough to realize that what she's chosen to do is not only immoral, but may actually be dangerous for her. You know yourself, Lucien Edmond, we've read stories of how many of those Left Bank artists drink horrible stuff like absinthe and even experiment with opium and the like. It could destroy her!''

''Well, for one thing, I intend to send off a letter immediately to let her know how both of us feel,'' Lucien Edmond angrily declared, banging his clenched fists on the table to emphasize his indignant disapproval.

''I'll write her, too, darling. After all, as her mother, I should be closer to her, and perhaps when she understands what despair she's causing both of us, she may stop to reflect that she's acted very unwisely. Fortunately, at least so far, there's no hint of a scandal—it would be dreadful if she should do anything that would disgrace the name of Bouchard—''

"No, I won't go so far as to say that she would do that," Lucien Edmond grumbled. "She's never given us any trouble before."

"But then, she's never been to Paris before. I just don't know, Lucien Edmond, I just don't know where to turn or what to do. I think I'll have a talk with Mara. Your sister knows her well; maybe she has some suggestions. But I feel so helpless—"

"So do I, Maxine." He rose and kissed his wife's forehead. "Well, I'll go to my study and write that letter."

"I'll write my own, later. If she hears from us at once, both of us, it may make her come to her senses." Maxine slowly rose from the table, her face drawn and anxious.

"I really am at a loss to understand all this," Lucien Edmond sighed, shaking his head. "What was it King Lear said about how sharper than a serpent's tooth it is to have a thankless child—?"

"Oh, no, please, Lucien Edmond, you shouldn't be so harsh on Carla. I know it's upsetting, but we mustn't pass judgment so severely before we know all the facts."

Lucien Edmond turned to his wife and spread out his hands in a helpless gesture. "In God's name, Maxine, what facts are we missing? They're plainly expressed in her letter. She's met a young man, and she's moving in with him, which means of course that they're lovers. What other facts are we to assume she hasn't told us?"

"I don't know, Lucien Edmond," Maxine sighed distractedly. "But you know that Carla isn't a flighty girl, and she's never shown any inclination to go against our wishes in the past. Give her the benefit of the doubt, and let's assume that she's truly fallen in love. In itself, that's not objectionable, for after all she's twenty-two."

"I know that very well. What I'm objecting to is this inclination to accept physical love without the guarantee of an eventual marriage. And without wanting to be indecent about the matter, what would happen if Carla should become pregnant?"

"Oh, God, I certainly hope not—" Maxine couldn't help exclaiming, putting a hand to her cheek and noticeably paling.

"There, you see? That's something that neither of them might think about, and yet it could happen. And then she would truly be disgraced. No, I'm not happy about the whole situation, and I'm going to express myself to her as strongly as I can. I only hope that, when she realizes the grief and anxiety she's causing us by her headstrong action, she'll think twice about perpetuating it. And I'll insist that she be back here for Christmas."

"That, to be certain, Lucien Edmond. Well, I'm going to have a chat with Mara—after I try to calm down a bit."

"As you like," he shrugged, again shaking his head, and walked off to the study.

Maxine Bouchard went back to the kitchen and made herself a cup of chamomile tea. She needed it, for her nerves were shaken by this domestic altercation. She had never dreamed that Carla would go quite so far, take such an initiative, and make so momentous a decision that might very well alter the course of her promising young life. It was not only the morality that concerned her, but also the risk and the danger: If Carla was thought to be so accessible, there would be other young men who would seek to replace this man whom she had chosen as her first lover—and heaven alone knew what consequences might follow.

After finishing her tea, she walked out of the hacienda and went across the way to Ramón's house. The children were in school, and Mara was in the kitchen washing breakfast dishes. When her sister-in-law called out to signify her presence, Mara dried her hands with a dishcloth and answered, "Oh, Maxine dear, come in, please!"

"Thank you, Mara."

"You look upset—is anything wrong?"

"Yes, I—oh, Mara! We've had a letter from Carla, and it brought the most dreadful news! You just can't imagine. Lucien Edmond and I are both very much distressed about it. It seems that she's met a young man there—a painter like herself and an American, too, who's been living in Paris some years now—and they've decided to share a studio together and . . . and live together. It's scandalous—there's no mention of marriage!"

"I see," Mara coolly replied with a frown. She then turned to face Maxine and bitterly retorted, "At least you know that your daughter is well and, in her own way, enjoying her life. To me, your problem is really not so significant as you and Lucien Edmond want to make it, simply because of a moral judgment. Consider me. I don't even know if Gatita's still

alive—nor, for that matter, if *Ramón* is still alive. I'm beginning to doubt that I'll ever see either one of them again. It's
been a long time now, and not a word from him. Not a single
letter, not even a courier—nothing to let me know whether
he's well or ill . . . he might even be dead. So I'm afraid that
I can't have too much sympathy for the effect of Carla's letter
on you both.'' She had maintained an almost angry glare
during this declaration, but now, seeing the shocked and
chagrined look on Maxine's face, she burst into tears.

Maxine took her sister-in-law into her arms, crooning to
her as if she were a child. ''There, there, Mara, I'm sorry.
Forgive me; it was unfair of me. I didn't mean to distress you
so. You're right, of course—you have a far greater hardship
to bear. And as you say, Carla is alive and apparently enjoying life. Please, I didn't mean to make you cry— It was
stupid, clumsy, inappropriate of me to be bewailing my
daughter's behavior, when you've shown so much courage
through this ordeal of yours.''

''Maxine—'' Mara straightened, took off her apron, and
mopped her eyes with it. ''I'm the one who should be forgiven.
I was too harsh. But Carla was always a sweet, obedient girl,
and I'm sure that by taking matters into her own hands, she's
merely testing her newly found independence, as it were.
Nonetheless, I don't agree with her behavior, either. If I can
be of any help—''

''You've helped me already by taking a calmer perspective
on this whole matter. Lucien Edmond is writing a letter right
now telling Carla how thoroughly he disapproves of what
she's done—but I think when I write my own letter, and I'll
do it this afternoon, I'm going to put a lot of compassion and
understanding and love into it. I am her mother, and I do love
her. She's very talented and very beautiful, and because of
that, she's vulnerable. Perhaps I can make some suggestions
that will help her show a little more common sense and not
act rashly simply because of an infatuation.''

''I'm sure you'll know what to say to her, dear.'' She
smiled and kissed her sister-in-law's cheek. ''Well now, maybe
we could both stand some coffee.''

''Oh, no, thank you, Mara. I had some tea before I came
over here. But if you'd like, maybe I can help you with the
dishes—I feel the need to do something concrete and positive.''

''Do you know, Maxine,'' Mara almost giggled now, ''I

think I'll take you up on your offer. I haven't had maid service in longer than I care to remember. And it's a little harassing to have the children ask all the time when Gatita and Papa are coming back home. Come along then—I'll put you to work, and we'll both forget this little tantrum of mine."

"And of mine too, dear Mara," Maxine responded, more grateful than ever for her friendship with this strong, caring woman.

Chapter Thirty

He had lost all track of time, all knowledge of where he had been and where he was going. For Ramón Hernandez, the days and nights had followed an inexorable, agonizing pattern: Doggedly mounted on Magdalena—a canteen full of water and another of tequila tied to the saddle—he had passed through unending stretches of desert, through steep mountain passes and along verdant river valleys. With a jaundiced eye, he would glare at passersby—riding singly or in pairs, others walking as they led burros that were harnessed to wagons laden with supplies or produce for the nearest hamlet where the goods would be sold—and stare at them as if willing that somehow, by some miracle, those bland, bearded, suntanned faces would turn into the visage of that accursed woman and the exquisite face of his beloved daughter, Gatita.

At night, he would invariably make a haunted entry into this or that cantina or *posada*, accustoming himself to the relative darkness and coolness after a torturing day under the Mexican sun. He would move up to the bar, make his inquiries, receive the usual answer, and then turn to stare at each of the patrons. Then he would take a long swig from the canteen that held tequila, and as his speech slurred and his senses grew more jumbled, Ramón Hernandez would shout out, "Attention, *hombres*! You must tell me the truth now, or it will go hard with you. I look for a *gringa*, a black-haired *gringa* with a little girl, also with black hair. She would be about five now, this *niña*. She is mine. She was stolen away from me almost two years ago. I command you to tell me you have seen these two."

And, inevitably, there would be shakes of the head all around, mumbled words, whispered conversations as one customer asked another if this madman were really serious. Then someone would twist his sombrero between his hands, shuffle his feet nervously because of the glare in Ramón's eyes, which seemed unusually menacing, and stammer, "Forgive me, señor, but no one has seen the people you have just described. We are sorry, but no, we have seen no one like that at all."

In June, four long months after leaving Windhaven Range, Ramón went from Guadalajara to Rosamorada after attacking a man. In his drunken fury, he had believed that the man was insulting him and thought that he wished to find a prostitute rather than his little girl. Ramón had been beaten, left unconscious, and flung out into the night, his money taken from his pockets. Only his mare, Magdalena, had been loyal to him in these the blackest hours he had ever known.

In Rosamorada, a small town close to the Gulf of California, he so offended a *sergente* that he was clapped into jail, brought before a yawning, bearded, ill-kempt judge the next morning, and sentenced to three weeks of hard labor in a salt mine.

In vain, the crazed man drunkenly protested that he was Ramón Hernandez, partner of the Texas ranch Windhaven Range. The judge merely laughed and called him an imaginative madman in response.

By the beginning of July of this year of 1882, released from prison and temporarily purged of his drunken stupors, he was leaner and wirier than ever. But his hair was now completely gray, and there were pockets under his eyes, pools of the darkest, most cynical despair. He had forgotten how to smile, how to laugh, how to cry; most of all, he had forgotten—or else denied—that God existed.

He had worked assiduously during his time in prison, and the judge had been sufficiently impressed to order that upon his liberation he be given thirty *pesos* and told to go back to his home in Texas, if that was where he truly came from.

But Ramón knew he could not—he would not—return to Windhaven Range until he brought Gatita back with him. Though he was stronger now because of the enforced labor at the prison farm, his mind was still clouded with an obsessive hatred, an almost demonic rage, whenever he thought of Rita Galloway and how she had tricked him and Lucien Edmond.

After leaving Rosamorada, he went farther up along the

coast. He had met someone along the road who had seen a *gringa*—and although Ramón had been told she had two children with her, his hopes had been quickened. Feverishly, he rode Magdalena some forty miles northwest to the town, only to learn that the woman was a nun and the two little girls orphans whom she was taking to a nearby convent. Not satisfied with this, Ramón insisted on visiting the convent, and the nun herself, a woman in her mid-fifties, came out into the garden to speak with him.

When he poured forth his story, she sighed, put her hand on his shoulder, and said, "It tears my heart to hear what you have said to me, my son. I cannot help you. But I will pray for you."

Ramón looked at her and then said, "I have prayed myself, Sister, but it does no good. I do not believe in God any longer. Neither I nor my dear wife has sinned so much as to deserve what has happened to our daughter. No, if He truly existed, He would not inflict such needless punishment upon the innocent." Then he turned on his heel and left the convent garden, while the sister wept and made the sign of the cross after him.

From there, he found a cantina two miles to the north and spent nearly all of the *pesos* he had earned at the prison farm in buying tequila for himself and for the gaping, curious customers he found there. Then, as was inevitable, when the liquor took possession of him and drove away all reason, he began to harangue them, calling them liars and thieves, calling them assassins of an innocent little child, till at last, as had happened at Guadalajara, he was beaten and thrown out of the *posada*. What money he had left, the owner righteously appropriated, asking his patrons if he was not entitled to it, considering that this *loco* had bought drinks for everyone and had not yet paid for all of them.

When Ramón wakened, it was again to find the mare standing patiently by, nuzzling him, whinnying to rouse him. She alone was faithful to him; she alone could be depended on—and he needed her, for he had to find Gatita. He did not know where he would go, only that he would go on and ever on, until at last he confronted that hellcat who had robbed him of all peace and dignity and manhood, who had destroyed his marriage, who was destroying him by keeping the child hidden away and undoubtedly debauching her.

Penniless, he tried to beg for food at a ranch where the elderly owner, recognizing from the way he spoke that this was no mere crazed vagrant or drunkard, shrewdly wheedled him into working for him. "Señor, some of my *peones* have run away. Some have even crossed the border into *Los Estados Unidos*. I am short of help, and you seem like a strong man who knows how to work in the fields. I will pay you well if you'll stay with me through the fall, till the crops are in. Till November, at least."

Ramón hesitated, not wanting to commit himself. Then the old man, Carlos Abierto, craftily proposed. "Think it over, señor. Let us drink together in friendship, at any rate. I have some fine old tequila. It will go down very well. Let us salute each other."

Ramón wordlessly nodded. Then he drank avidly, until the strong tequila began to cloud his reason and make his speech slurred and his actions inchoate.

The tequila was powerful indeed, and after two glasses of it, the *hacendado* slyly slipped a paper beside Ramón and a pen. "It is a gentleman's agreement between us, señor. You will work for me till November, and I agree to pay you fifteen silver *pesos* a week. That is a very generous wage— for a stranger especially."

And so Ramón acquiesced, after downing a third glass of tequila, and he scrawled his signature on the document. The old man pocketed it, chuckling softly to himself.

Magdalena had been put into a stall in the stable, where Ramón, too, was expected to sleep. The next morning, after he had been rudely awakened by the majordomo—who poured a bucket of cold water over his head, making him sit up with a start and utter a hoarse cry of distress—he was informed that he was to report to the fields, under the direction of the *capataz*, one Sancho Lormego.

Grumblingly, Ramón assented and found himself confronted by a foreman who had once been an officer of the *federalistas*. The man liked nothing better than to browbeat his *peones*, to swagger among them with threats of cruel punishment if they did not finish their chores.

Ramón worked there for two weeks, loathing every moment of it but desperately needing the money. For in his maddened, confused state, his ability to perform any logical action was completely undermined, and he never once realized that he could have simply wired his bank in San Antonio for a draft.

At the beginning of the third week, the old man sent for him. He counted out silver *pesos,* and then mockingly added, "Señor Hernandez, you have been drunk at least five times during your stay with us. Sancho has informed me of this. Therefore, I am releasing you from our contract—however I shall have to debit your wages, since you cost me a good deal of time, and time has been of the essence with me. I therefore only owe you five *pesos.*"

"What the devil—what game do you play with me, señor?" Ramón angrily demanded.

"Oh, so you wish to cause trouble, do you? Sancho will know how to deal with a *borrachón* like you, Hernandez," the old man sneered, then clapped his hands. Before Ramón could turn, he felt himself seized from behind by two sturdy *peones.* Then the *capataz* approached him, swaggering and smirking. He began to beat Ramón across the cheeks, the mouth, the forehead, the chest, and the ribs. Finally, exhausted and weakened, his head bowed, panting hoarsely, Ramón sagged to his knees while the two *peones* held him from falling.

"Now then, *amigo,*" the *capataz* mockingly suggested, "are you going to accept the *patrón*'s offer? It is a very fair one. If you say no, I shall beat you until you do, and you will take back no silver at all for your work. Quickly now, it is a hot day, and I have very little time to waste on you."

Ramón accepted the pittance for his hard labor, and he set forth on Magdalena again, still undaunted in his obsessive determination to find Gatita.

He headed north once more, and along the roads by now he was known as *El Loco* or *El Borrachón.* To everyone he passed, the lone, bearded, disconsolate man was an object of both ridicule and pity. By now, most of them too had learned what prompted him to search so endlessly and fruitlessly throughout Mexico. Most of these people declared that they considered him deranged, compelled by an idea that would not be purged from his unbalanced mind.

In Rosario, nearly penniless again, he entered a *posada* on the edge of town and there, curiously enough, the owner—a widow in her early sixties—took a liking to him. Perhaps he sensed in Ramón's dark, bloodshot eyes the vestige of what had once been a man of influence and power. At any rate, after standing Ramón a drink, he leaned forward across the counter and said, "I know nothing about you, señor, except that you seem strong and somehow distinguished. I need someone like you when my customers give me trouble and start fights and need to be taught a lesson. I will give you a room at the back of this *posada*, all the food you can eat, and all the tequila you can drink. Also, I will give you five *pesos* a week."

Ramón had no choice but to accept this lowly post, dealing with coarse, irascible men. Most of them worked either at a tannery or in the small nitrate factory two miles outside the town that made gunpowder and bullets on commission from the fort of *federalista* soldiers.

Ramón worked there for only a few days before becoming more of a burden than a help to the *posada* owner. Whenever a new customer came in, he would sneak out from behind the counter of the bar and ask the man, "Have you seen my Gatita? She was taken from my nearly two years ago by a *gringa*, a young one, who was a devil out of hell and the worst *puta* this side of the Rio Grande." And, of course, they had seen no one, and they told him so, and then he would fly into a mad, senseless rage.

Finally, as might have been expected, he got in so violent a fight with two of the customers that his employer took him by the scruff of the neck and shoved him outside the *posada*. Throwing a few *pesos* into the dirt, he sneered at Ramón, "There is your pay, *Señor Loco*. I need no more help like yours."

Once again the cycle of drunkenness, despair, and vengeful hatred took hold of Ramón Hernandez. Aimlessly, he mounted his mare and headed east into the mountains again, toward El Salto in the province of Durango. He lived for an entire week on *frijoles*, a bit of meat, some soup, and a few tortillas. Yes, singularly enough, he did not neglect Magdalena and haggled with the owner of a small stable outside the town to board her while he went to look for some kind of work. By now, Ramón had only two *pesos* left, and he was again scraggly and unkempt, his clothes torn and dirty, and the gaunt, despairing look seemed to have been engraved on his face with an indelible chisel.

There was work, he was informed, in a silver mine. Ramón

shuddered when he was told of this kind of work; it reminded him only too well of his boyhood, when his father had worked in just such a mine before being flogged to death at the orders of the cruel, arrogant owner. And yet, perhaps with an obscure and subconscious sense of aptness, he told himself, "You are lower than the low now, and even your father would be ashamed of you, Ramón Hernandez. Go you then and work like a dog for this *rico* and feel perhaps the lash of his *capataz* and hear the slurs upon your ancestry that he and his fellows will surely heap upon you. Perhaps it will do you good. Perhaps this is what the devil requires of you, before he will let you find Gatita and that whore!"

Under the guise of a self-inflicted penance, Ramón had obstinately gone to work in the silver mine—underground, in the intense heat, with coarse food and only enough water to survive, and for only a few *pesos* a week. At least, he told himself, he was not a *peón* like the others, and again this hard work drained him of the sickness the tequila had brought upon him.

But one day the *capataz* went too far. He rebuked Ramón for not having completely filled his basket with the silver ore, as was demanded, and he took his quirt and lashed Ramón across the shoulders.

Blind with furious rage, remembering what had happened to his father and how he had avenged him, Ramón took the man by the throat, shoved him against the wall, and snarled, "I should kill you, for you are not fit to live. But I will instead let you live, and let the devil have you. For you will do worse to others, and *they* will kill you. I spit upon your mine, your *patrón*, and on you." Then, suiting action to word, he spat forcefully at the *capataz*'s contorted face, shoved him rudely onto the ground, and stalked off in the direction of the stable of the *hacendado*, where he found Magdalena patiently awaiting her master. He did not even bother to collect his wages for the last week but merely rode onward.

And this time his wanderings took him to Mazatlán, back in the province of Sinaloa, where the Pacific Ocean rolled its gentle waters along the shore. He had been told that it was a fishing town as well as a seaport for much trade. Perhaps here he would find Gatita and that damned woman who had carried her off.

As he entered the outskirts of the town, he could see dozens of small skiffs and boats out in the harbor. It was a dusty road, and the August heat was oppressive. Magdalena began to whinny a good deal, uttering guttural noises. Ramón dismounted, and out of solicitude and anxiety, stroked her muzzle and crooned to her. She was the only friend he had. No one else cared whether he lived or died.

Suddenly she began to shudder violently, a fit of the dry heaves, and then, before his disbelieving eyes, she collapsed on the dusty road, kicked several times, her eyes rolling upward, and then lay still.

"Oh, no, not this! Is this more of Your work, Your 'good' work, *Señor Dios*?" he cried, shaking his fist at the sky. Tears ran down his dusty cheeks, and he drove his filthy fingernails into his palms as he stared down at the dead mare.

He stood weeping until he was hoarse, then he unfastened the saddlebag, flung it over his shoulder, and began to trudge wearily into the town of Mazatlán.

Chapter Thirty-One

When Lucien Bouchard had made up his mind not to return to New York for the summer holiday, his letters home had indicated his intention as strongly as he could put it. His mother, Laure, to be sure, had been distressed to have that news so frequently repeated. On this mid-August evening, as she and Leland dressed for dinner, which they would be having with the Cohen family, Laure said, "I have the distinct feeling that he'd simply *rather* be over there than be with his family—despite what he implied about schoolwork in his letters. And, naturally, a mother wants to see her son as often as she can, especially when he's going to school across the Atlantic."

"I know, Laure dear." Leland came over to his wife, who was seated at her dressing table, applying the finishing touches of her makeup. "I can understand his love of the Irish countryside and Dublin, of his classmates, and particularly of that charming colleen, Mary Eileen Brennert, of whom he writes so rhapsodically. That's all to the good. What disturbs me is that his letters are filled with braggadocio, as if he wants to impress me by boasting of his exploits with the constabulary and the military. I'm beginning to think he sees himself as a kind of young Hercules who hopes to clean out the Augean Stables—and a teenaged boy can hardly undertake so monumental a task, certainly not without getting himself into a great deal of trouble, as well as physical danger."

"I know." Laure distractedly dabbed a stopper of perfume to her neck. "No, I don't like some of the things he says, either. What are we to do?"

"I had hoped to send Paul to that school, perhaps next

299

year," Leland continued. "Now I'm not so certain that it would be a good idea. The influence of this man Sean Flannery seems to be extremely powerful—though, from what Lucien writes, Flannery does advise caution and discretion. Still, I think that this instructor may have been feeding Lucien a few too many of the Irish legends and preaching too much about the passion for freedom at all costs, so that even if he advises caution, Lucien—young as he is and romantically inclined— will ignore the warning part of the lectures."

"Well, darling, I feel as you do, and— Oh, good heavens! Look at the time! The Cohens are probably waiting for us at the restaurant already. We'd best not talk of this any longer and finish dressing instead."

Leland, Laure, and the children bustled into the crowded restaurant where the Cohens frequently dined. Catching sight of their good friends now, the Kennistons waved and then threaded their way to the Cohens' table, where they greeted their friends warmly. After they had all sat down and the waiter had taken their orders, Miriam turned to the handsome Irishman and said, "I'm so pleased, Leland, that Laure and I were able to get that building we wanted for our extended settlement project."

"So am I. Incidentally, as I promised you, my solicitors looked into it, and they think it's an exceptional value. And that, my dear," he said, turning to Laure, "is why I wish you'd let me contribute part of purchase price. I understand you're going to rent it with an option to buy. That's very sensible. It shouldn't take long before you know whether it will suit the project, or whether you'll need ever larger quarters, if all goes well."

"Indeed!" Miriam Cohen broke in, a broad smile on her face. "We've already had applications from some forty families since they had the news from us that we were going to have another location to serve them. Oh, it's been so rewarding for me to be able to help my fellow countrymen—and women."

"It's also been helping Laure," Leland responded. "It's given her life a whole new dimension. I'm very proud of both of you. Ah, here comes our dinner. What excellent service. I'm glad you invited us here, Jacob. The food looks delicious."

Two waiters bore huge trays to the table and set them down

on nearby stands. After having served everyone, one of the waiters turned to Jacob and asked, "Will there be anything else, sir?"

"No, this is fine, just fine," Jacob Cohen murmured. He shook his head and glanced at Miriam beside him. "I must say, two-and-a-half years ago, I never would have dreamed that we would ever again be dining with good friends in such comfortable surroundings."

"That must have been a terribly difficult adjustment for all of you—to have gone from a position of wealth and respect to one of utter poverty." Leland shook his head, then said to Jacob, "I'm very pleased with the way our association has worked out—and I count you as a good friend, which is even more vital to me."

It was after ten o'clock when they got back home that evening. The children had immediately gone to bed, and Laure and Leland were alone together in the study. Outside, there was the faint rumble of thunder, presaging a summer storm. Laure turned to her husband, her forehead lined with concern. "I really am beginning to worry about Lucien, darling," she said.

"I am, too. It's all very well to be a romantic idealist—I'm one myself, heaven knows, and that's a side of me you like—"

"It certainly is. I loved that wonderful madcap charade of yours during Mardi Gras in New Orleans that made me yours," she said very softly, as she put her arm around his waist and turned up her face to be kissed.

"I intend to keep you mine for the rest of my life and yours, God willing," he chuckled. "And I want it to be an incredibly happy life, with nothing but joy and harmony among all of us."

"So do I, Leland. It's my fondest wish. But I'm really concerned about Lucien. I haven't said anything, because his progress in school has been quite excellent. However, lately, with these upsetting letters about his taking part in the struggle for Irish independence, I'm beginning to have grave doubts about his being there."

"I share your concern, dear Laure," he solemnly assured her. "I don't know where he got the idea that he could be a one-man army, or a band of crusaders all rolled into one

301

teenaged boy. But from the tone of his letters lately, it seems that he's trying to do exactly that. It's somewhat alarming, to say the least.''

"What can we do? You did write him that you didn't approve of his public escapades, didn't you, dear?" he asked.

"Of course I did. Probably our letters have crossed. Maybe we'll have another one from him in the next few days, since it's been about two weeks since the last one. Don't look so worried, darling. I'll be able to handle it, you'll see. He's alone in a strange country, we have to allow for that, and he's impressionable—then, too, he's head-over-heels in love with that pretty young girl who goes to the school nearby. All of these things converge upon him, and they make him perhaps a bit more impulsive than he'd normally be.''

"You always put things so well—I feel reassured already.'' She put both arms around his shoulders, pressed herself against him, and kissed him tenderly. "That's to remind you that I'm just as much in love with you as ever.''

"I pray you always will be, darling.''

She glanced down the hallway and then mischievously whispered to him, "I'll come to your room tonight, dear Leland. . . .'' She kissed him again, this time passionately. "I love you so. It's thrilling to pretend that we're still secret lovers.''

"In that way, the honeymoon can never be over. And as Shakespeare would say, ' 'Tis a consummation devoutly to be wish'd.' ''

On the following Monday, a letter arrived from Lucien. Since it was addressed to Leland, Laure did not open it, but all day long she found herself looking at the silver salver atop the table in the foyer on which it had been placed, her fingers itching to break the seal. She had a presentiment that all would not be well after she finally did read it.

The day wearily dragged on for her. Her mind was totally preoccupied with the letter, and she could hardly wait till Leland returned from his office. When he finally arrived home, she forced herself not to demand the letter be opened at once, but instead—as calmly as she could—sat down to dinner with Leland and the children. Her husband had the letter under his saucer, and her heart bounded in her anxiety. Nevertheless, she said nothing about it, wanting to let him decide when the proper moment had come for reading it to her.

After dessert, the children were excused. As soon as they had left the dining room, Leland deliberately moved aside his saucer, took up the letter, slowly opened it, and scanned the lengthy, handwritten pages. Presently he said, "I might write Father O'Mara that our son should learn a better style of handwriting. Myself, I like the Palmer method, or, if one wishes to be fancier, Spencerian script."

Laure rolled her eyes ceilingward, wishing desperately to let him know how very much she wanted to read the letter, but she patiently waited until he had finished his coffee and then leaned back to peruse it.

He read it quickly, and as she leaned forward to watch the interplay of his emotions on his face, she saw that he was controlling himself with difficulty. "Leland, is anything wrong?"

"Judge for yourself, Laure. Here you are."

She nodded her head in thanks as she accepted the neatly folded letter, unfolded it, and began to read. Almost at once she uttered a startled cry. "Good heavens! He's going from bad to worse—and he boasts about it!"

"Precisely. I told you that he expects us to look upon him as a hero—but unfortunately he's created quite the opposite reaction."

"He—he might have gone to jail!" Laure gasped, her face coloring furiously. "But how could he do such a thing? Doesn't he have any consideration for *us*?" She put the letter down on the table without finishing it and stared at it in disbelief.

"Apparently not." Leland picked up the folded sheet, asking, "Did you reach the part where he tells how he and his friend, young Riordan, went into Dublin of a Sunday and saw a group of British soldiers accosting some young local girls? No? Well, apparently the men were being obscene—which can be expected, I daresay, from those soldiers—but the girls ignored them. Then Lucien had to go and stick his two cents in, and he got trounced for his pains. He writes here that he went up to the soldiers and boldly told them to stop pestering the girls. One of them took a punch at him, and Lucien retaliated and sent the man sprawling. The boys got away before being spotted by a constable—otherwise, Lucien says, they surely would have been arrested again and hauled up before a magistrate. And Father O'Mara would have had no choice but to expel him!"

"This is really frightening, Leland," Laure anxiously responded. "Why does he choose to socialize with that sort of boy, boys who incite him and egg him on to do still more heroic deeds? He's going to get into terrible trouble."

"I feel the same way, Laure. Lucien must be made to realize that he's worrying us considerably. I may have to do something very drastic."

"Wait a minute, Leland . . . please, dear. What do you mean by drastic?"

"Go over there and bring him back from his school" was Leland's terse reply. He reached for the letter again and continued reading to himself, his brows knitting as he studied the pages. Suddenly he flung the letter down with an imprecation. "He's *really* going to get himself into hot water!"

"Oh, dear!" Laure wrung her hands and stared hopelessly at her handsome husband. "I don't like to have you angry with him. He is my oldest son, and I've always admired and respected his integrity. I'm sure there must be extenuating circumstances that would explain all this if we only had the opportunity to learn them."

"We're more likely to learn that an English magistrate has sentenced our young would-be hero to jail! An Irish policeman might esteem him and look the other way, but they don't have control of Irish cities. The British do, and by this time, Lucien must be a marked man in their books. That isn't encouraging at all. Listen to some of the later sections of the letter:

"I told Father O'Mara that I couldn't help my feelings, and that it's very hard for me—even though I'm an American—to stand by and watch innocent, helpless people brutalized by British soldiers.

"Father O'Mara said that he privately agreed with me, but that I must continue to play the role of passive onlooker, reserving my feelings and my comments for school discussion, perhaps, or with my friends. He urged me also to come to him for such discussions and said that it would be far better for me to take this intellectually than to try to show my feelings by violent physical action.

"And of course, he's right," Leland interjected, "but the young fool won't pay any mind to *that*. He writes us detailing what Father O'Mara said, and then he has the effrontery to challenge it—just listen to this, Laure!

"I told him that it was hard for me to take an intellectual view of something so tyrannical and oppressive, and that when I saw it in front of my own eyes, it was almost impossible for me not to react and try to stop it. So he warned me again, Father, but I have a feeling that he secretly thinks I am a very patriotic transplant. I certainly don't see anything wrong with it.

"But I do!" Leland fiercely declared, looking up at Laure and scowling. "If he keeps on this way, he's surely going to force Father O'Mara's patience to an abrupt end and be sent packing back to us. Indeed, I'm surprised Father O'Mara has allowed Lucien to stay—luckily for us. With a record like his, it would be difficult to enroll him in any other decent school. He just doesn't see the risk he's taking, not only for his physical safety but also in the furtherance of his education."

"But wait a minute, Leland," Laure put in. "It was *you* who convinced us both—Lucien and me—that by sending him to this fine school in Ireland, he would have far more opportunity than in the schools either in Alabama or here in New York. I had implicit belief in you, and that was why I agreed unhesitatingly to send him off to Dublin. So, in a sense, it was your influence that put him there and exposed him to all this."

Leland looked at her sharply and then was silent for a moment as he pondered the reproach in her words. Irritated that he was now being blamed for what at the time had been a decision applauded by all, he now retorted with some asperity, "Now wait just a moment, Laure, let's be realistic." Leland leaned back in his chair and tried to choose his words carefully, for he saw by the brightness of her eyes and the animation of her face that she was becoming incensed over his anger with her son. "It's true that I recommended Father O'Mara's school highly because I was familiar with it—I still think it's an excellent place. Lucien did well from the outset, he adapted himself, and he made friends. How could we have foreseen that he would embroil himself in a senseless defense of

English oppression against the Irish? Not in my wildest moments did I think your son would react this way."

"So now it's 'your son,' is it, Leland?" she frostily responded. "Well, as far as being realistic goes, I'm being extremely realistic—and rational. The fact is, he's where we can't reach him quickly, and he can get into all sorts of trouble—he already has. I'm beginning to wish that I hadn't sent him across the Atlantic for schooling. Surely there must have been some fine private school either here in New York, or perhaps New Orleans—"

"We've been over that, Laure," he patiently interrupted. "I still say if the boy had any common sense to him, if he had a leavening of humility to go along with his keen mind, all these problems wouldn't have arisen. I really don't hold the school responsible for them."

"Don't you? It seems to me, Leland, you're dismissing this very summarily. He's my son, my flesh and blood, and I'm beholden to try to do what's best for him and his welfare. I realize that you're concerned, too, dear, but you mustn't be so critical and so severe when you discuss him. He isn't a statistic—he's a human being."

"I know he is." Leland uttered a sigh of weariness. "All I'm saying is that since my letters of advice seem to be ignored by the boy, I'm going to have to appeal to him directly—in person. I'll sail for Ireland and closet myself with Lucien and show him what an erroneous course he's pursuing."

"You would do that for him?"

"Of course, I would. He's my son as much as yours now, so we won't confuse our priority by saying that I'm to blame or you're to blame. No one's to blame. I guess we expected too much from Lucien. He's at an age when boys are at their most rebellious and want to show off their knowledge and abilities and the like, so Lucien has rushed off on a tangent during the last several weeks."

"It's so easy for you so sit there and make pronouncements on his character," she angrily attacked him. "You have to give some heed to the fact that he's certainly bound to be homesick—"

"Homesick?" Leland retorted, his eyes widening with surprise. "I don't read homesickness in any of these letters, certainly not for the last several months. All he does is talk about wanting to stay there, to miss all summer with us and his brothers and sisters. No, Laure, there's no homesickness to this. Rather, there's a disobedient bravado. You may find it romantic and charming—and I do, too, in theory—but, when it comes to defying the law openly, when it comes to going out of his way to physically express his dislike of English law and order, then he is going too far for a boy of his tender years.''

He paused for a moment to let his words sink in, then continued, ''And, finally, all our children bear the Bouchard name, and it seems to me he might very well sully that respected name. For I wonder how long he will be looked upon as a champion of the Irish when, in reality, he may turn out to be nothing more than the bully who enjoys picking a fight for the sheer exhilaration of it.''

''Now that's unfair, Leland Kenniston!'' Laure's green eyes were sparkling with anger as she rose from the table. ''I also detect a note of threat in your words, Leland—and that's a side of you I'd never dreamed you had! Not content with influencing me to enroll Lucien far away from home, now you take no responsibility whatever for the danger he may be in—when that danger, at least so far as I can tell from my son's letters, stems from his accepting your theories about Irish freedom. He respected you, he gave great weight to your opinions, and he also understood that it would please you for him to study in Ireland. Very well. He studied. And he came under the influence of an instructor who filled him with even more ideas of Irish independence, even granted that this instructor tempers his fantasies with words of caution—''

''Now you are indulging in a fit of semantics, my dear Laure,'' Leland coldly interrupted, ''and I don't want us to regret what we may say to each other over this. You know perfectly well that my enthusiasm for St. Timothy's stemmed from my knowledge of what Father O'Mara could do for an enlightened, sensitive boy like Lucien. You must admit, Laure, that the school's reputation is absolutely first rate.''

''Of course I admit that, but that's not the question at all. Now it's *you* who is indulging in semantics, to quote you, Leland Kenniston,'' Laure snapped. ''What I'm getting at— and it should be very plain to you—is that he has accepted so many of your theories as gospel, but you're the first to rebuke him when he understandably tries to stand up for justice and for freedom, the very qualities which you hold so dear.''

"I do, for God's sake, Laure," he shouted in exasperation, "but I also believe in common sense. At sixteen, your son is old enough to know the difference between right and wrong, to know the difference between theory and practice, and to be a realist."

He rose and went to the window. "Of course I want Ireland free. Of course I want Ireland away from English oppression. Everyone in his right mind wants that—but without bloodshed, and certainly without violent incidents that don't really advance the cause of Irish freedom, but only get a single boy, an American at that, into trouble and jeopardize everything that he's working for, jeopardize the reason that you and I *agreed* he should study abroad! Don't you understand that?"

"You have quite a way with words, Leland," she said softly, "but this isn't the time for words. This concerns my son. *Your* son, too, as you're so fond of saying all the time."

"That's unkind!" Color mounted in his cheeks.

"But it's true. I'm angry with Lucien myself. I think he's being quite the young rowdy. Or at best like a Don Quixote, tilting against windmills. But we cannot ignore the fact that it was really you who were and are responsible for putting my oldest son into such danger."

"I?" he echoed, his color deepening and his eyes narrowing with anger. "Laure, you go a little too far now. I have written him repeatedly, urging him to give up this useless crusade, this business of playing the hero. But he's obstinate. He takes pleasure in it now, and that's his own idea entirely. I'm not responsible for that."

"If he'd never gone to Dublin, this wouldn't have happened," she stubbornly, irrationally insisted.

"I see," he said after a long pause, "that there's no sense pursuing this discussion. It will only lead to angry words, shouting. I love you too much to want to do that. Of course this is trying to both of us, but by now you should know enough of how much I love you to realize that the last thing in the world I want is to put *our* son in danger. Let's end this conversation *now* and discuss it again at another time, when we can both be less impassioned about it. I bid you good night." With this, he turned and walked out of the room.

Laure stared after him and then, with a sob, covered her face with her hands and began to weep.

*　　*　　*

Dressed only in her nightgown and slippers, Laure paced the floor of her bedroom, heedless of the lateness of the hour, which was well past midnight. She had sat down at her desk and twice begun a letter to Lucien, twice torn it up, and then burst into tears as she crumpled the pages and flung them into the wastebasket beside her. Now, looking at herself in the full-length mirror, she saw that her eyes were red and swollen from tears, and she took her handkerchief to a vial of cologne and dabbed it over her cheeks and nape and then the cleft of her bosom. Then, taking another handkerchief, she dipped it into a basin of water and pressed it to her eyes, closing them and sinking back against her chair as she tried to compose herself.

They had come very close to the brink this evening, a dangerous brink. She loved Leland, in a far different way from that in which she loved her martyred Luke. And yet each man had a power and an integrity that compelled her, however reluctantly, to admit wrong when there was wrong on her part, and to respect and to admire even when she could not always accept.

What could she say to her son that would make him abandon his folly? What was the proper course of action? Should she insist that he be removed from the school and brought back home, where no doubt some excellent private institution in New York City could readily replace St. Timothy's? And would Leland stand beside her in making such a decision?

She felt better now, and when she looked at herself in the mirror, her eyes looked less swollen. She rose and went to her door, staring at the closed door of Leland's bedchamber across the hall. She thought to herself for a moment that she should knock and enter, and seek a reconciliation. But then, proud and defiant as had always been her nature, she said to herself, *No, that way solves nothing. Of course I want him—I love him. But we can't make up over so strong an issue as this just by making love. Besides, it's his place to come to me, not I to him.*

And so, weeping again, she got into bed and tried to fall asleep. She had strange dreams, fitful episodes that frightened her, in which she saw Lucien surrounded by a crowd of soldiers, mocking and jeering him, some of them striking him, as his fists flailed and he tried to withstand them all. She woke before dawn, her head aching, her heart pounding. *Oh God,* she thought to herself, *I hope it isn't a prophetic dream! Oh, please, dear God, don't let any harm come to Lucien!*

At breakfast later that morning she was cool and efficient and pleasant, and made a special point of chatting with Paul about his outing that day with David Cohen. They would explore the Central Park Zoo, and then they would go to the Metropolitan Museum of Art, after which they would take a hansom cab back home. Gulping down the last of his orange juice, Paul kissed his mother goodbye. Celestine and Clarissa also went out to play, and Clarabelle Hendry took five-year-old John off for his reading lessons.

At last Laure and Leland were alone. She eyed him, waiting for him to speak, as the cook came out to fill her coffee cup and then his. After Mrs. Emmons had gone back to the kitchen, Laure lifted her cup and murmured, "I started a letter to Lucien last night, but I couldn't finish it."

"I almost did the same, Laure," he said. "Forgive me if I seemed to ride over you roughshod last night—it wasn't my intention."

"I understand. But what *are* we going to do about Lucien?"

"I think the only solution is for me to arrange my business affairs so I can take off time to sail to Ireland and bring him back."

"You—you'd actually do that, Leland?"

"Yes, I would. I want peace between us, Laure—no, damnation, that's not the word at all, because that implies that we're at war with each other. I love you, and I certainly have no wish to quarrel with you, not over the children. And since you and I both agree that Lucien is behaving very badly, I see that the only option I have is to bring him back."

"That probably is the best course," she guardedly ventured, "but he may be very resentful. And what about that girl he likes so much? He might refuse to leave."

"He's still a minor and dependent upon both of us. Parental wishes come ahead of a teenager's inclinations, and though it won't come to that, I'm sure, a court of law would agree that you and I have every right to bring him back, whether he likes it or not."

"But you must be tactful, Leland. He may be only sixteen,

but all the same, he has such a quick mind, and he's really brilliant—''

"I know that very well from Father O'Mara's earlier reports," Leland interrupted. "But this brilliance is intellectual; it isn't emotional and it isn't related to common sense. Till he learns how to cope with reality, all his brilliance may do nothing more than precipitate him into dangerous situations from which, having no worldly wisdom, he might not be able to extricate himself. I know—you think I'm indulging in semantics again. . . ."

"I wish I hadn't said that last night." Laure impulsively put out her hand in a gesture of contrition. "And I'm grateful that you would go to such trouble to bring him back. It shows me that you're as deeply concerned about him as I am."

"I'm glad that you understand it as such, dear Laure. I'm sorry, too, for all my harshness and bitterness last night."

She rose and came to him, putting an arm around his shoulders. "I was wrong to blame you, Leland." She looked at him with a fond tenderness, for now she had swallowed her pride, having feared that she might have estranged him. "The unfortunate thing is, my darling, Lucien is displaying exactly the same idealistic traits that Luke always did. I've no doubt that, had Luke been exposed to the fight waged by Irish patriots, he too would have wanted to fight on their side, just as Lucien does now. He was always a battler against injustice and oppression, and very likely his son has inherited that quality."

"Undeniably, darling." He looked up at her and put his arms around her waist.

She bent to him, cupped his face between her hands, and looked deeply into his eyes. "Needless to say, that was one of the things that attracted me so much to *you*—that same wonderful, idealistic spirit. Yes, all that is true. But when I say it's unfortunate, I mean that Lucien is still far too young to follow in his father's and your footsteps. I'll be most grateful to you if you can get him to return to the safety of our home."

With this, she kissed him, and Leland sighed happily at the tranquil end of their conjugal storm. He kissed her tenderly, and then he rose, holding her in his arms. "I'll start making arrangements immediately, and I'll take the very first steamship to Ireland that I can, my darling. Say you forgive me for all the harsh things I said."

"Of course I do. And you must forgive me for being angry with you—and also for blaming you. I'm just so worried about him. . . ."

"I've forgotten it already. Let there be peace and love and harmony between us always, my dearest."

They stood embracing a long moment, and then at last, reluctantly, he disengaged himself. "I'm going to get down to things quickly and arrange for Jacob to look after the office while I'm gone. There are some matters I must attend to, but as soon as they're cleared up I'll be free to leave for a few weeks. Meanwhile, I'll send a cable to Lucien to tell him that I'm coming over on business and I'll stop in at the school to see him. I think it would be a mistake to tell him in that cable that I plan to bring him back—because that would give him a chance to get his guard up, and I want to avoid any painful scene with him. I love him too much for that."

"I think that is the best way to handle it, my darling. I'm so happy that we can forget last night's unpleasantness," Laure murmured.

"I don't remember any unpleasantness, not ever with you, sweetheart."

Two mornings later, when Leland Kenniston arrived at his office, Jacob Cohen was waiting in the reception room of the suite. As his employer entered, Jacob said, "Leland, there's a cable from Hong Kong for you. I came in this morning and found that a messenger had slipped it under the door. It may be terribly important, and I wanted to be certain that you'd have it first thing."

"That was thoughtful of you, Jacob." Leland slit open the envelope, took out the cable, and then uttered a startled, "Oh, my God!"

"What's wrong, Leland? Bad news?" Jacob solicitously asked.

"The very worst kind. My office manager in Hong Kong has been murdered! My God, this is terrible!"

"*Gottenyu!* Murdered—why, that's horrible!"

"The cable is from my assistant manager, a very trustworthy man named Wong Fu. According to this, though of course he doesn't give any lengthy details, James Parker, my manager, somehow stumbled onto some opium smuggling and was killed for his pains. My guess is that one of the cargo firms my company employs was shipping a little contraband on the side and Parker found out about it and was prepared to go to the authorities—but I won't know till I get to Hong Kong. I'll have to leave at once. What a tragedy! Parker was a fine, gifted young man with a great future—only thirty-four years old and extremely dedicated and imaginative!''

"It *is* terrible, indeed. How long will you be in Hong Kong?''

"As long as is necessary,'' Leland philosophically shrugged, shaking his head. "I'll have to find a replacement—I could appoint Wong Fu, except that he isn't all that fluent in English and isn't too familiar with some of the intricacies of our billing and purchasing methods. Well, Jacob, I'd best contact the steamship line and reserve passage from San Francisco. Then I'll have to take the fastest train—this evening, more than likely—to make connections. This is really unfortunate. As for Lucien, well, obviously I'll have to cancel my plans to go to Ireland now. Laure will be terribly disappointed, of course, but I'm sure she'll understand. All that will just have to wait until after I get back.''

Chapter Thirty-Two

On the same day that Leland Kenniston received the cable from Hong Kong, young Lucien Bouchard faced his own crisis.

His last scolding from Father O'Mara had still not made him fully realize that further continuance of his "one-man battle"—as St. Timothy's headmaster had irascibly described it—would lead to his expulsion from the school that he had come to love. His friends Edward Cordovan and Ned Riordan—who had also chosen to stay at St. Timothy's for the summer—had been considerably abashed by their own confrontations with the irate priest. They had both told Lucien that they were going to forego going into Dublin on Sundays for at least a month or so, "until things cool off a bit," to use Ned's phrase.

This alone did not give Lucien considerable pause, and it was Mary Eileen Brennert who indirectly convinced him that he should content himself with an intellectual view of the English-Irish conflict, without taking a physical role in it. Lucien had been disconsolately walking back to his dormitory in the afternoon after a soccer game when he saw Mary Eileen hurrying toward him.

"Mary Eileen! What a nice surprise! I was thinking of you, and I wanted to see you and find out if—" he began.

"Oh, Lucien, I'm afraid—well, my father says I mustn't go out with you anymore. You see, he's heard about the fights you've been in, and he told me that associating with you would be harmful for my own reputation, as well as his. Not that he doesn't admire you, in a way, for your stand against the British," she hastily added by way of propitiation, "but he just thinks that it's highly improper for a mere schoolboy, as he puts it, to go up against soldiers and constables and magistrates. He says probably all that'll come of it is you'll get expelled—and I wouldn't ever want that to happen!''

"I—I understand, Mary Eileen. Does that mean—surely, your father doesn't mean he *never* wants me to see you again!''

"I don't know." She shook her head and looked down, her lips trembling. "I just think—at least, for a while, until he says it's all right.''

"I was going to ask you to go out with me this evening, Mary Eileen. But now I suppose we can't.''

"Oh, no!''

"Well, then, I guess all I can do is just see you when you can get away without your father knowing it—you know I want to see you a lot, Mary Eileen.''

She blushed exquisitely, looking away, then said in a soft, vibrant voice, "I want to see you too, Lucien, but I really should do what my father tells me. He's very stern and strict with me because I don't have a mother, so he thinks he has to be all the more protective.''

"I know. I can understand that. It's just a shame. . . . Well, there's no hope for it then, is there? But I don't know how I'll be able to stand not seeing you the rest of the summer,'' he declared.

Again she blushed and looked away. Then, in a tremulous whisper, she murmured, "It—it will be hard for me, too. Maybe we can meet sometime. Oh, Lucien, please don't get into any more trouble.''

"I'll do it for your sake, Mary Eileen.''

She glanced around quickly, and then, impulsively and to his ecstatic delight, gave him a hasty kiss on the cheek. After that bold action she turned and ran back toward her house.

Since that day, Lucien and Mary Eileen had met infrequently. At St. Eulalie's, a few courses were held during the summer, one of them being a cooking class. Mary Eileen cooked her father's meals, but she was anxious to improve her skill in the kitchen and so had registered for the class, which met twice a week. As for Lucien, he had also decided to take a summer class, this one being a forum type of instruction, presided over by Sean Flannery. The Irish instructor had, at the conclusion of the spring term, mentioned that he proposed to offer, to students whom he would personally select, a small participation group. They would discuss Irish literature and history, and there would be lengthy discussions and projects such as essays and short stories inspired by the themes.

Lucien and Mary Eileen managed to meet at the conclusion of their classes. This afternoon—the day his stepfather left for Hong Kong—Lucien hurried to wait for Mary Eileen near a huge chestnut tree located on a grassy knoll midway between the two schools. He saw her walking with several other girls, her head bowed, and observed that she was withholding herself from their conversation. Impatient to see her, he called out, "Mary Eileen!" and saw her stop, turn, and shake her head. Then, quickening her footsteps, she walked farther away from him, leaving her classmates behind her.

Startled by this rejection, Lucien hurried to catch up with her, finally doing so. "What's the matter, Mary Eileen? Are you angry with me or something?"

She turned to face him, and he saw that her face was streaked with tears. "N-no, L-Lucien," she faltered in a tiny, unsteady voice. "But you see, somebody—somebody saw us meeting like this and told my father. Last night, he—he gave me the cane."

"Oh, no! Oh, Mary Eileen, that's awful!" he blurted.

"He said that I was going against his wishes, and that he had to punish me for disobedience. And he warned me not even to write a note to you until further notice."

"I'm so sorry, Mary Eileen. It was terrible what he did—and I—and I was responsible. . . ."

"You—you mustn't feel that way! It was my choice to keep seeing you. But—please go, Lucien—I don't want Rosemary and Alice to see—maybe they were the ones who told my father. Goodbye, Lucien!" There were tears in her eyes as she turned away and ran. Lucien stared after her, hands in his pockets, his face gloomy and despondent.

He was absolutely disconcerted. He had not envisioned that his friendship with Mary Eileen Brennert could possibly have resulted in corporal chastisement of her. But he was aware that some of the masters at St. Timothy's and some of the nuns at St. Eulalie's occasionally resorted to physical punishment for extreme cases, though he was personally ignorant of the details of such a procedure. It seemed to him cruel and inhumane, even though the games master was her father and had, to be sure, disciplinary rights over her. But at her age, nearly his own, to be humiliated in that way . . .

He walked slowly back to the dormitory, brooding over what she had just told him. Caned! He had the image of her bending over the back of a chair as a thin, swishy rattan was stingingly applied. How brave she must have been—more than brave—to suffer such pain and shame all because of him!

He imagined that he could even hear her cries and plaints, her pleas to be forgiven, to be spared the indignity and the burning torment of that cane—oh, it was absolutely dreadful even to think about it!

Lucien dug his nails into his palms and angrily shook his head. Inescapably, his mind filled with the awareness that, if he had not continued to behave so rashly after first being reprimanded by Father O'Mara, this would never have happened to Mary Eileen.

Not to see her again—that was the worst thing of all. The days, weeks would now be long and dreary without the chance of meeting her, exchanging ideas, feeling the pressure of her hand on his, and seeing her adorable dimpled smile.

He would have, he concluded, to take a very different view of his extracurricular activities in Dublin from now on. The thought of expulsion had not really concerned him, but now he saw it as a deterrent to any further relationship with the girl with whom he was so deeply infatuated. He wanted to stay in Ireland until she had finished her schooling, at which time, he told himself, he would propose marriage to her. By then he would be almost nineteen, and surely there could be no opposition to such a marriage. He dared not jeopardize her by having some of his classmates or some of her friends at the other school pass notes to her, for there was the same danger of detection and punishment. No, there was no help for it; he would just have to change the games master's opinion about him so that, eventually, he would be permitted to see Mary Ellen.

Sitting alone in his dormitory room—for his roommate had gone to Belfast for the summer—Lucien began a new letter to his father and mother:

Dear Mother and Father,
   I have done a lot of thinking, and it isn't just Father O'Mara's sermons and warnings that make me think of this Irish question in a different light. Mary Eileen told

me today that she had been punished by her father for seeing me, after he had expressly forbidden it when he found out about the trouble I've gotten into.

Because of what happened to her, I see clearly now that I've behaved badly. I apologize most sincerely, for I know I've upset you. I want to stay here very much indeed, and since I shan't be allowed to see Mary Eileen until my conduct is satisfactory to Father O'Mara and to Mr. Brennert, I shall just have to work at it and try to curb my irritation when I see British soldiers domineering elderly people or women who can't defend themselves. I guess the wisest thing for me to do is take all that energy I've been expending in fighting and apply it to my schoolwork.

I shall write again soon and tell you if my attempts to better my record have proved fruitful. I surely hope they will because the prospect of not seeing Mary Eileen for weeks or maybe even months really upsets me.

I'm going to tackle my books and write a few essays about my visits to Dublin. Maybe, as Sean Flannery suggested, I can contribute a few ideas to the cause of Irish freedom without breaking any heads—or getting my own severely rapped. I'll conclude this letter by saying that I've enough pocket money for the time being, especially since I don't plan to go into Dublin for the next few Sundays. It's so lovely around here, I'll make up for it by taking long walks and thinking about my writing.

Please give my love to Paul, Celestine, Clarissa, and John.

I love you both,
Lucien

It was Laure who read this letter, for Leland was on his way to Hong Kong, where it was necessary for him to remain till nearly the middle of September. The murder of James Parker had, as Leland had guessed, been engineered by an unscrupulous sea captain. Believing himself to be beyond suspicion as the master of a vessel on which much of the Kenniston cargo was shipped between Hong Kong and San

318

Francisco, the captain had decided to enter the opium trade on his own. During the course of a routine inventory check, the unfortunate Parker had discovered a secret cache of raw opium destined for San Francisco's Chinatown, and had confiscated it, reporting the matter to the authorities.

After being questioned by the police, the sea captain had arranged for hired thugs to waylay the young office manager on his way home. Wong Fu, the assistant office manager, had been instrumental in bringing the two assassins and the captain himself to justice. All three of them were scheduled to be hanged at dawn a few weeks hence.

Leland left Hong Kong some ten days before the execution, and when he arrived at his Gramercy Park house, Laure received him with tearful joy and the news that her fears for Lucien had been greatly alleviated by the boy's last letters home.

There had been one further letter after the one in which Lucien had related Mary Eileen's punishment and its effect upon him. In it he described his "simple pleasures of hiking and rowing and some fishing, and Father O'Mara has told me that he is greatly pleased with the way I have, to use his expression, brought myself up short. He also promised to tell the games master about my good conduct. I do hope this will mean that I'll be permitted to see Mary Eileen again."

"That's a great relief, I'll admit," Leland said as he dined with Laure and the children on this summery mid-September evening. "He's obviously trying to make amends, and evidently his friendship with Mary Eileen was instrumental in enabling him to realize—more than severe lectures ever have done—how dangerously close he was to ruining all his chances at a fine and liberal education. Well then, Laure dear, I suggest we let him stay on—but we'll continue to read his letters with greater attention than ever. I can only hope that this new outlook of his is more than temporary. I know for a fact, from the news going around Hong Kong, that there have been violent outbursts of hostility against British soldiers in various parts of Ireland. I pray to God that Lucien will never be involved in anything so terrifying and brutal."

Chapter Thirty-Three

Carla Bouchard in no way regretted her decision to share a Paris studio with James Turner. In the little more than two months they had known each other, he had fulfilled her ideal as companion, lover, confidant, and friend, and—what was equally important to her—as an adviser in her work. Under his guidance, she had begun an oil of the gardens at Fontainebleau, a pastiche with delicate, subtle coloring, and Impressionistic forms. Once a private palace, Fontainebleau was where the great Bourbon kings of France had sequestered themselves, impervious to the growing unrest of the populace of Paris. They lived as sovereign lords who brooked no challenge to the status quo—the norm of affluence, extravagance, and insolent monarchical power.

James had complimented her on the depth and imagination she had shown. "Carla, this is by far the most important thing you've ever done. True, it's a bit imitative, but then what artist isn't at the outset of his or her career? But see here—in your merging of the horizon with the rooftop of the palace, there's a definite advance in technique and a subtler form of expression than you've ever exhibited until now. You're coming of age, my darling. And if I can contribute just a little, I'll be very proud."

By the end of August, the canvas had been halfway completed, and James's praise spurred her to work long hours into the night, driven by a compulsion to fulfill her own expectations, not merely his.

Indeed, the only cloud on Carla's bright horizon was the content of the letters she had received from her parents. She had heard from both her father and mother, and she had been surprised at their wholly indignant reaction to her forthright declaration of self-dependence. Between the lines, she could read that they considered her immoral, even a deviate, and both of them had pleaded with her to reconsider so drastic a decision—one they felt would severely damage the reputation by which, they pointed out, society inevitably judges the iconoclast and the nonconformist.

After receiving these letters, Carla decided to write to Hugo in Wyoming. She remembered how he had almost scornfully derided her determination to pursue a career, not understanding it at all. He—a typical male, in her opinion—had believed that her true vocation was a happy marriage with plenty of children. But now that he was married himself and working with his wife as a team of doctors in an isolated community, Carla believed that perhaps her brother might not be quite so critical of her choice of lifestyles. Accordingly, she wrote him a long letter, frankly detailing her experiences in Paris, her meeting with James Turner, and her decision to live with him and remain in Paris until she felt that she had exhausted its potential, so far as creativity was concerned.

When Hugo received his sister's letter, sometime toward the middle of September, he waited until late at night to read it. His lovely wife, Cecily, had gone to sleep, having had an arduous day calling on three different patients. His first reaction was one of incredulity and surprise: He had never dreamed that Carla, hitherto so docile and obedient, could of her own accord undertake a liaison whose illicit overtones would expose her to parental as well as public censure. And yet, the lengthy letter was so forthright and candid that Hugo began at last to understand the difference between his sister and himself. Certain passages in particular made a distinct impression on him:

Hugo, Father and Mother don't approve of my decision at all. They've written me that I'm a "fallen woman," on the "primrose path to ruin and perdition" and so on, and so on. But I don't feel that way at all. And as for my painting, I know that you never really liked it, but I can tell you that art dealers and respected artists have told me that I have a good deal of talent and that I'm improving from day to day. That's very heartening, my dear brother. It's as if some of your patients got well quickly and praised you to the skies. It's a wonderful feeling, Hugo.

So please try to understand what I'm going to say to you now. . . .

While you and I were growing up together, of course we had our differences—and in Chicago I thought you were an insufferable prig. I don't now. I really respect and admire you for going out to a godforsaken part of the country and trying to make a living by taking care of patients who probably don't have much money to start with, and who probably will wind up resenting you to end with, just because you're so different. You're no doubt far in advance of them, Hugo, what with your mind and the way you think, so you've probably had by now a certain amount of hostility—just as I've had from Mother and Father.

I'm writing this to you at about three in the morning. James is sleeping, and we've just made love—there, you see already how bold I've become—and if I wrote this to Mother and Father, they'd probably cable me to come back before I become an utter Jezebel! But somehow, I don't think you're going to feel that way about me. It hurts to see the rift that has developed between me and them, but that's because they're part of the past. They had their ideals and hopes and dreams, and they've achieved what they wanted, and so they judge life by what it was for them—not by what it is for you and for me, Hugo.

The way I look at it, you and I belong to the new generation, and we have new ideas and ideals. What was considered immoral or wrong a generation ago isn't necessarily so today—don't you feel the same way, really? For example, consider your wife's profession. Only a few years ago, it was thought terribly immoral for a woman to be a doctor, to view naked bodies. And I'm sure that even today where you are, there are men who would be horrified at the idea of letting your wife look at them without their clothes on, even if they were dying. Isn't that so, too?

Hugo read that last paragraph over and over again, and then he chuckled softly and said to himself, *It's true. I remember that man whose wife had a tumor in her leg—her husband insisted on calling it a limb—refused to have Cecily treat her because he felt it was practically sinful for a woman to be a physician. Yes, Carla dear, I can see exactly what you're driving at.*

Her letter went on:

But you know, as well as I do, that your wife is an honorable woman doing honorable work. The human body was made by God, so how can it be immoral or obscene or unclean or whatever? It's the way people look at it, the way they've been brought up. Now take my age, twenty-two. By all the standards back in Texas, I'd be considered an old maid, a spinster like Cordelia—Cordy, as I call her. But it's not that way at all. And why shouldn't a woman live with a man and find out if the two of them are compatible before they marry and have children? I'm sure there are many marriages throughout the United States hanging together only because there are children, or maybe the man and wife hate each other but don't do anything about it because of their religious background and their upbringing as children. It's secret hatred, and often they take it out on the children. That's not going to happen with James and me. I don't know that I'm going to marry him—and I'm not sure that he wants to marry me. But, meanwhile, we're happy together, we're working together, I can feel myself improving in my work, and I'm intelligent enough to select which way I'm going to go when the right time comes. If we marry and if we have children, it'll be because both of us want exactly that.

So you see, dear Hugo, I'm asking for your understanding. I'd like to have one friendly letter telling me that I'm not so bad as Father and Mother seem to think. Write me what you feel—be honest with me. Please convey my very best wishes to Cecily, and tell her I think she has a wonderful fellow for a husband. Maybe you and I got off on the wrong track in Chicago, Hugo, but I hope we can change that now.

Your loving sister,
Carla

The day after Hugo had received this letter, he decided to tell Cecily about it while they were having breakfast together. Casually, he announced, "I had a letter from Carla in Paris. I want you to read it all the way through, and then tell me what you honestly think."

"Paris—I've always wanted to see that city! Maybe someday you and I shall, once our practice has been established. What a wonderful place for a second honeymoon! Oh—I'm sorry, Hugo, I'm ignoring your request. I must say, I'm surprised you've heard from Carla after the differences you two had."

"I've changed from the way I was in Chicago. And now she's reaching out for my friendship, and I'd like to give it to her."

"Yes, I remember how talented and how spirited she was. I thought she could have gone on to do great things."

"She apparently is doing quite well—but there's more, Cecily. Go ahead, read the letter. I'll just sit here till you're finished."

He handed it to Cecily, then leaned back and watched as his attractive young wife carefully perused the lengthy letter. There was a long silence, and finally Cecily looked up and smiled. "Hugo, she's quite a woman! Some people would say she's feeling her oats, the way a frisky filly might. I think it's more than that. And I agree with her remarks about the difference in generations. She really loves you, Hugo—I can read all that between the lines. She wants your opinion so badly, though she hopes that you'll have some kind things to say."

"And I will, too, Cecily. When we were living with Cordelia Thornberg in Chicago, I annoyed Carla by looking down my nose at her painting—just because I didn't understand the Impressionist paintings she was so fond of. But she was trying to find herself, and I don't really think that she's done anything wrong."

"You're not condemning her then because—to use one of those old-fashioned phrases—she's 'living in sin'?" Cecily asked, an amused look on her face.

"No. And I suppose trial marriage isn't so immoral as it may sound at first blush, darling."

"Well, now," she twitted him, "would you have liked to

have tried that, instead of making an honorable woman out of me?"

"I didn't say that," he hedged with a happy chuckle. "The fact is, Cecily, I knew almost immediately that I wanted you for life, and I didn't think you'd settle for anything less than marriage. I wouldn't have dared propose that we live together and try it out."

"Young man, there are times when you have an unerring instinct for saying just the right thing," she laughed, then got up from the table and went around to kiss him very passionately.

"You know, Cecily, you've done wonders for me. I can see now what a pest I must have been and what an obnoxious brat I was when Carla and I were growing up. Now she wants to make a life for herself, and who am I to judge?"

"You know, Hugo, there's a lot of hope for you, if you can say a thing like that. And maybe one day, you'll understand my feelings about sheep ranchers and cattlemen. I believe that both sides ought to be able to live together in peace, without bloodshed and bigotry and hatred. Maybe we can spread the doctrine, possibly make a few advances, and end some old feuds. I know my aunt Margaret would love to see that."

"Cecily, now that I've lived here in Wyoming for a spell with you, I understand a lot more about people than I used to. I was sheltered. I had a happy childhood, and my parents cared for me, but it was sort of expected that I become the head of the ranch when my father decided he'd call it quits. Only, when I went on that drive, when I saw that there were more things in life than driving cattle to market and pocketing the money, when I actually helped save a human life, I felt good about it."

"That's when you began to grow up, Hugo," Cecily observed.

"Exactly. And Carla's doing the same thing. You know, I can see how there can be a lot of rivalry between brother and sister. We both were very young then, and we wanted to assert our own personalities. Because I was a male—and I supposed the logical heir to the Windhaven estate—Carla naturally resented me. And I resented her because she was so outspoken about my shortcomings."

"Honey, I can be just as outspoken about yours now," Cecily teased him, and Hugo laughed and took her on his lap and kissed her very tenderly as her arms clung around his neck.

"That you can, Dr. Bouchard," he joshed her.

"I'm glad you realize that, Dr. Bouchard, sir," she mocked him and gave him a kiss on the tip of his nose, then sprang up from his lap and went back to her own chair. "It's a time for seriousness. What are you going to write to your sister?"

"That I think she has every right to make her own choice, that I think she's got brains enough to decide what's good for her. Even if our parents don't understand, Carla should stick to her guns. That's the most important thing of all. Of course, I don't want her to get hurt, so I can only hope this James Turner she writes about is a decent fellow and won't leave her in the lurch."

"You know I wish that for her, too. Anyway, Hugo, I'm very proud of you. You have done a lot of growing up the last year—and I won't even take all the credit for it," Cecily declared with a wry smile.

"Well, then, shall I add your sentiments in my letter?" he asked.

"Of course. Tell her it's her life. Tell her that I wish her happiness and hope that everything will work out just wonderfully for her."

"I'll do just that, and I'll send it off tomorrow when I go to town for supplies," Hugo said.

"Wonderful. Well," she said as she stood up, "I've got to go out and call on old Mr. Persinger, the one who sprained his back." Cecily put on her light coat and a nondescript hat to protect her from the sun. In Levi's and shirt, booted and dressed very much like a man, she took her satchel, blew Hugo a kiss, and left the house.

Hugo went to the small study, took a piece of foolscap, dipped the pen in the inkwell, and after musing a moment, began to write:

Dear Carla,

I've tried to see Paris exactly as you've described it—your feelings and reactions to it. You have a good way with words, and you're direct. I now understand that I was quite wrong in saying what I did about your painting. In case you think there's still some hope that I might learn something new—and you can teach me—I'd like very much to own one of your paintings. Why don't you do one for me showing the Seine, either at early dawn, or just before the sun sets? I'm sure you could use a little extra money, and I've put away some from my practice the last few months. We're beginning to turn the tide here, and it's a good feeling.

Our house is way out in the middle of nowhere, but it's wonderful. There's peace and isolation right amid nature, and it's good for the soul. I think you could do a lot of work here. If you ever have a notion you'd like to come out West, we'd love to have you stay with us—you and James, both.

Now about what you said to me in your letter. First off, Cecily sends you her love and her best wishes. She says she's on your side. So am I. I think you've a perfect right to live your own life, so long as nobody gets hurt. My only impartial suggestion would be don't have a baby till you get married. I say that simply because it would be a hindrance unless you planned to concentrate on being a wife and mother. And since I have the feeling that you don't want that right now, I just think that the two of you should take special pains to have love and tenderness and all the things that go with it, without any unpleasant consequences.

With that lumbering sentiment out of the way, I'll say only that I think you've found yourself, and you know pretty clearly what you want out of life. I know what I want, and I'm glad I made the decision I did. You mustn't be too disheartened by what Father and Mother tell you. They don't know what you've been through, they don't know what's really in you—for that matter, you still have to find out for yourself. We all do, and it's part of growing up and taking on more responsibilities.

I'm envious of you, Carla. A doctor has his rewards when he cures a patient, or prevents pain or eases suffering or helps bring a child into the world. And there are a lot of other ways in which he feels rewarded. But, when he's gone from practice, either through death or retirement, he's lucky if a few people remember that he had compassion for them during his lifetime. With you, you can leave something to posterity. I have a feeling that, one day, your pictures are going to hang in a museum, and Cecily and I will walk through it and say, "We know her very well, and she deserves this."

Do keep in touch with me. Cecily would like to have a personal letter from you, too, by the by. I wouldn't get too down in the mouth about news from home. You're of age, as I am, and you know what you want to do. I've begun to think that maybe there isn't any such thing as morality, except one's own code of ethics and behavior. If you're true to yourself, the way Shakespeare puts it, you can't be false to anybody else. That's as good a maxim to follow as I can think of. And so, Carla, I wish you all the luck in the world and all the happiness there can be. I want to be friends, and I want to hear from you regularly.

Hugo

When Cecily returned from treating her elderly patient and Hugo showed her the letter to his sister, his young wife smiled and nodded. "You might say this is just what the doctor ordered, Hugo. I think it's going to cheer her up, and I hope it'll chase away the blues she's bound to have after those letters from your folks. Well, I actually got a fee for my call today, and it's going into the kitty. We've done very well the last month or two, and the future looks very bright."

"That's because not only are you a wonderful doctor, but you've also got the knack of making people like you the very first time they lay eyes on you," Hugo averred.

"Thank you very much. That's a very sweet thing to say. Well, I'm going to make lunch for us now. But, before I do, I want a hug and a kiss."

"Always happy to fill the prescription of a beautiful doctor like you," Hugo quipped as he rose and took Cecily in his arms.

Early Friday morning in the last week of September, a wiry young horseman reined in his mustang in front of the Bouchard house, tethered the reins to the porch railing, and knocked at the door. Having just finished breakfast, Hugo was proving how thoroughly domesticated a husband he was by helping Cecily with the dishes. "Wonder who that could be?" he hazarded. "I was looking forward to a nice long weekend of rest and maybe some old-fashioned spooning with my beautiful wife, so I hope it's not a patient with a complicated disorder."

"Don't forget you took the Hippocratic Oath, my darling—and I think good old Hippocrates didn't take marriage into consideration," Cecily brightly responded, making a face at him. "Anyway, you'd better answer the door."

Hugo promptly obeyed and eyed with some curiosity the cowboy who stood there, Stetson in hand. "Good morning. What can I do for you?"

"You're Hugo Bouchard, aren't you?"

"That's right. Dr. Hugo Bouchard, to be exact."

"That's it. My boss, Maxwell Grantham, he got word that you settled out this way, and he sent me riding to invite you out to dinner at his place."

"Well, that's very neighborly of him. Yes, I remember, I met him three years ago when I went on a cattle drive with my uncle, Ramón Hernandez. We took out some prime cattle and met him in Colorado."

"You're definitely the right man, Doc," the cowboy grinned. "He'd like it mighty fine if you'd ride back with me."

"Wait a minute." Hugo was remembering. "His ranch is near Cheyenne, isn't it?"

"That's the same Mr. Grantham I work for, Doc," the cowboy chuckled and nodded.

"That's about a hundred miles from here, and there's a little matter of the Medicine Bow Range in between where we are and he is!"

"Well, it ain't as bad as that, Doc. He's actually a good forty miles northwest of Cheyenne—just east of a little town called Rock River. Hell—oh, 'scuse me, Doc—anyway, it's only sixty miles or so to the Grantham spread."

"I see." Hugo pondered a moment. "I wonder if he's heard that I'm married, and that my wife is a doctor, too?"

"Sure. Like I said, he wants you to come to have dinner with him and chew the fat a little. That invitation includes your wife, of course. So, if you want to pack a few things . . ."

"You mean you want us to go *now*? Today?" Hugo incredulously asked.

" 'Pears so. I mean, you don't want me to ride back and

say you're coming some other time and then have to go through all of it again, do you?" The cowboy grinned again.

Hugo couldn't help laughing at the direct simplicity of this courtesy call. And, if truth be told, he found himself suddenly anxious to see Maxwell Grantham again because he was a cattleman who had greatly helped his father in buying that lot of two thousand head. Undoubtedly, a part of the money from that sale had helped pay for his schooling at Rush Medical College. "Well, as luck has it, my wife and I don't have any patients on the critical list this weekend. So I guess we could go, at that. However, I'd best confer with Cecily." He turned to call to his wife, "Cecily honey, would you come here a second?"

Cecily hurried out from the kitchen, wiping her hands on her apron. She glanced at the freckle-faced, lanky cowboy, then at her husband, and waited for an explanation.

"He works for Maxwell Grantham, honey," Hugo explained to her. "You remember, I told you about him—it was during that drive that I decided to become a doctor. You might say Mr. Grantham grubstaked me. Well, this man has ridden all the way from near Rock River to invite us out to Mr. Grantham's ranch to have dinner with him."

"Dinner? But Rock River's at least sixty miles away!" Cecily protested. Then she frowned. "He has a big ranch, doesn't he? He'd have to, if he bought thousands of head of cattle for breeding stock."

"That's right, ma'am," the cowboy put in. "Fact is, he's one of the biggest cattle ranchers in this territory."

"I see," Cecily replied. She turned to Hugo and, still frowning, declared, "Well, it would take nearly two days each way to ride there and back, wouldn't it?"

"Yes, I guess it would. But, as matters stand right now, honey, all our patients are getting along fine, and I think they can spare us. Besides, it would be a kind of change of pace for us both, seeing how busy we've been the last few months. A vacation. And the weather's wonderful for traveling."

"That's a fact, Doc," the friendly cowboy genially interrupted.

"Hugo, I—I'd like to talk to you for a minute in private—if this gentleman doesn't mind?" She raised her voice, looking at the cowboy.

330

"Take all the time you want, ma'am. No offense taken at all. You go and have a palaver, if you've a mind to."

"I will." She watched as the cowboy turned back to his horse, and then she said in a low, intense tone throbbing with indignation, "Hugo, don't you know my feelings about cattlemen? How do you think I'd feel going off to a big rancher's place, remembering that it was cattlemen who murdered my uncle over sheep?"

"Wait a minute, honey," he soberly replied, taking her hands in his and looking directly into her eyes. "You remember that you used to take me to task a lot because I was so set in my opinions. Seems to me you're showing exactly the same contrariness. You get mad at me when I look at things a certain way that you don't like, but you've noticed that I never have gotten mad at you when you do it—and I'm certainly not now."

Cecily glanced down at her hands, then giggled softly. "You're right, Hugo. I guess I was jumping to conclusions. I don't think Mr. Grantham, from all you've told me, is the same sort of man as the one who killed my uncle. So I'll tell you this—I'll go there with an open mind, and I won't prejudge him just because he's a cattle rancher."

"I couldn't ask for anything better than that. It'll be fun. Just think, getting away from preparing regular meals and all, and riding out there in the fine, pure air and the sun and the blue sky," Hugo grinned at her.

"You've sold me." She wrinkled her nose at him. "You'd best go tell that nice cowboy that we're going to accept his invitation. Furthermore, the poor man must be hungry and tired, so tell him I insist he has some breakfast and a rest before we start off. Doctor's orders!"

"You're wonderful, Cecily," Hugo laughed. "Now then, I'll go find a knapsack. We'll need changes of clothes and warm jackets. It turns cool in the evenings, I'm sure. I shouldn't be surprised if there is still some snow up at the top of Medicine Bow Range. And, of course, we'll need provisions, Cecily. We'll take the buckboard and carry enough food for three days."

"You know, this might be fun, at that. And, as I said, I'll suspend judgment. If Mr. Grantham is a nice man, I'll certainly be friendly."

331

"I can't ask for any more than that. I'll tell the cowboy to go sit down in the kitchen."

"Fine. I'll start breakfast for him."

Hugo went outside the house and nodded pleasantly to the cowboy who was stroking the muzzle of his horse and talking to it. "We've a buckboard that we'll drive there, if you've no objection. Incidentally, my wife insists you eat and rest a bit before we start off."

"That's mighty nice, Doc. By the way, I've got food in my saddlebags, but I'm sort of running low on beans and coffee. If you've got some extra to spare, I'd be much obliged."

"That's no problem at all. You go in and eat, and I'll pack the food for all of us."

"Thanks, Doc. Incidentally, Mr. Grantham said to tell you that he'd like you to be his guests for a couple of days, if you've no objection. Seems hardly worthwhile ridin' all that long way there and back for just one measly meal."

"I guess you're right," Hugo grinned. "I don't know your name, by the way."

"I'm Hank Johnson. Just call me Hank. I can tell we'll get along just fine, Doc," the cowboy grinned.

It was late morning when they set off. The young Bouchard couple was ready, and Cecily had packed food in a large gunnysack and put it to one side on the floor of the buckboard. Hugo clambered into the driver's seat, took up the reins, and called to Hank Johnson, "You lead the way. We'll follow your trail."

"Sounds fair enough, Doc. Let's go, then!"

Chapter Thirty-Four

Late Saturday afternoon, Hugo slackened the reins of his horse as they passed through the gate of the Grantham ranch. Hank Johnson rode alongside them, waving his Stetson and calling out, "Tell the boss we've come. Tell him now, Rusty!" A tall, thin wrangler, who had been coiling a lariat, nodded back. He dropped the rope and hastened to the large frame house, imposing with its white-painted columns that in some ways resembled a Southern mansion of antebellum days.

They had made better time than Hugo would have believed, but Hank Johnson had taken, as he put it, "a shortcut, but only if you know where to turn back to the main road, once you've made it." Around the campfire on Friday night, Hank had proved a most amiable companion, relating anecdotes of his trail-driving days and had, to Hugo's pleasure, enlightened him and Cecily on "what makes the big boss tick." Hugo was glad of this, for he wanted Cecily to have an accurate picture of the man whom he had met three years ago and whom he could not believe capable of leading a war against sheep ranchers. For her part, Cecily had enjoyed the outdoors journey, and she had eaten with ravenous hunger even though the meal was not much more than beans and bacon, biscuits and coffee. "It's probably not the most nutritious diet in the world," she had quipped the previous night, "but when you're riding out in the fresh air all day long, just about anything tastes heavenly!"

The wrangler who had run into the ranch house to tell Maxwell Grantham that his guests had arrived now emerged and, cupping his hands to his mouth, bawled out, "Tell 'em to come right on in, Hank!"

"There, you see, Cecily?" Hugo quipped. "That's most

hospitable. You just wait and see if you don't think Maxwell Grantham is a fair-minded, decent man. That's the way he impressed me when I met him."

"Hugo dear," Cecily patiently rejoined, "he may very well be. But I'm certainly not going to gush over him, and the fact that he owns this huge spread doesn't impress me at all. It's how he treats his people, how he behaves to his neighbors, that counts with me."

"All right, honey. Let's just enjoy the outing and the hospitality we're certain to get. At least," Hugo leaned over to whisper, "you're bound to get a lot more to eat here than we had on the trail."

"Well, I should certainly hope so." Cecily drew herself up and gave him a mock-indignant look. "The fact is, I'm hungry already—and I certainly hope we'll eat something other than beans and bacon and biscuits. Especially since we'll probably have the same thing going back home."

Hank Johnson took the reins from Hugo. "I'll take your buckboard to the stable, Doc, and unharness the horse. But don't you plan on goin' back for a spell. Mr. Grantham, he does things in style. Anyhow, I just want to let you know I had a lot of fun riding with you and camping out. You're reg'lar folks, Doc—both of you docs."

"Thank you, Hank, that's very nice of you to say." Cecily smiled and acknowledged the cowboy's praise. "Well, Hugo, we'd best go on into the house. I'm sure Mr. Grantham is waiting for us."

The young couple ascended the steps of the colonnaded porch, and Hugo reached out to rap the huge brass knocker, which was in the form of a bronze long-horned steer. It was opened by Maxwell Grantham himself, tall, gray haired, now fifty-three, with a frank, expressive face, dark-blue eyes, and a firm mouth. "I'm glad you could accept my invitation, Dr. Bouchard, Mrs. Bouchard—I hear I should say doctor to you, too, ma'am."

"That's true. It's a pleasure to meet you, Mr. Grantham." Cecily extended her hand, and the rancher heartily shook it.

"Come in. Make yourselves at home. I had a feeling you'd make it by this evening, knowing Hank's familiarity with this territory, so I held supper up for you. I've a Chinese cook, and he does wonders not only with beef but also with chicken. We raise our own poultry here, too, by the way."

334

He led them inside, into a huge living room with a stone fireplace. Cecily looked around and was surprised to see bookcases filled with leather-bound volumes and was even more surprised to see fine paintings on the walls. Maxwell Grantham eyed her with amusement as she made this mental tour of inspection, and then slyly remarked, "I suppose maybe you thought because I was a cattle rancher, Dr. Bouchard, I had to be a bumpkin. The fact is, I was born in Utica, New York, lived in New York City a good part of my life, and finally came out here about five years ago. I decided I'd had enough of society life back East and so I hired myself a top foreman and the best crew of cowhands money could buy. Of course, I also had to rely on my neighbors who had preceded me here, but they gave me pretty good advice." He chuckled expansively. "Well now, I should let you two freshen up. Then, how about a bit of bourbon before supper?"

"You know," Cecily said with a piquant sparkle in her eyes, "I think that would be a treat. It would certainly help settle some of the trail dust we swallowed all the way from Rawlins."

"It would, indeed. I have to apologize for rousting you out and asking you to take a trip like that, but I wanted to meet you and spend some time with you both. It's good to know that there's another doctor—I mean, a pair of doctors—in the territory. I'll get your bourbon right away. And a little branch water, I should judge?"

"That would be fine, thank you, Mr. Grantham," Cecily smiled and nodded.

Hugo was pleased to see that his young wife hadn't got her hackles up against Grantham and that they were getting off to a good start their first few minutes here.

After they had freshened up and sipped bourbon with their host, a Chinese with a long queue appeared and, holding a gong in his left hand, tapped it with what looked like a huge cotton ball at the end of a thin stick.

"Kee Dan wants to let us know that dinner is waiting, and we'd better not be late. There's nothing worse than a temperamental Chinese chef," Maxwell quipped as he rose from his comfortable armchair.

Cecily and Hugo had sat opposite him on a stuffed couch, and Cecily now whispered to her husband, "This is so comfy after that long ride we had in the buckboard, I'm not sure I want to get up, even if dinner's ready." Nonetheless, with Hugo to offer her his arm, Cecily rose in one quick and fluid movement from the couch and brightly walked into the sumptuously decorated dining room.

"I know it's large, but sometimes I have meetings here, and I like to give my neighbors a good spread," Maxwell explained. "I took the liberty of asking my foreman, Chuck Denby, to have supper with us—I hope you don't mind."

"Not at all." Cecily looked around. Against one wall stood a cherrywood sideboard on which were placed several decanters of wines and liqueurs, and the magnificent matching table was set with elegant silverware, a fine linen tablecloth, and monogrammed napkins in holders. Noticing her studied gaze, Maxwell humorously explained, "I guess I got used to the good life back East, so when I came out here, I brought a lot of fine things with me. The ranch has paid off very nicely, and my investments back East keep growing, so why not have as many creature comforts as one can, especially in a rough-and-ready place like Wyoming? It makes an otherwise hard life quite tolerable."

"That's very logical and sensible, Mr. Grantham. I was admiring your good taste. That's a beautiful sideboard," Cecily exclaimed.

"Thank you. Ah, here's Chuck Denby now." The gray-haired rancher turned as a tall, black-haired, square-jawed man in his mid-thirties entered. His hair was slicked down, and it was plain to see that he was uncomfortable in the dress shirt and cravat and waistcoat in which he was attired.

"Chuck, these are my special guests, Drs. Hugo and Cecily Bouchard."

"It's a pleasure to meet you, Doc—and you, Doctor, ma'am," the foreman stammered, grimacing a little as he surreptitiously tried to loosen the tight knot of his cravat.

"I'll admit, Chuck, you look much more comfortable in your chaps and Levis astride a horse—but after all, this is an occasion that calls for something fancier," his employer told him. "Sit down. Dinner will be served in a jiffy."

"Thanks, Mr. Grantham." The foreman seated himself across from the Bouchards, at his employer's left.

Cecily asked, "How many cattle do you handle on this ranch, Mr. Denby?"

"Around twelve thousand, give or take a few, ma'am," he

336

stiffly replied, still not entirely at ease in what he privately termed a fancy-dress rig.

"Loosen your cravat, if you have to, Chuck," Maxwell interposed. "You're making me nervous fiddling with it all the time. I think our guests won't hold it against you if you make yourself comfortable."

"Thanks, boss." Chuck Denby lost no time in taking his employer at his word and immediately loosened the cravat and then exhaled a gusty sigh of relief. "That's sure a mite better, that is!" he pronounced.

"Well now, Chuck, with that out of the way, perhaps we can enjoy our dinner. I see that Kee Dan is peering in with a worried look on his face. We don't want to change it into a scowl, or we might have to take potluck instead of the wonderful chicken I know he's cooked for us tonight," the rancher humorously declared. Then he made a sign to the cook, who bowed and hurried back into his kitchen.

The dinner began with a soup that Cecily could not identify. It had snow peas and bean sprouts, bits of egg, and some herbs and spices that made it marvelously savory. Then followed a salad, with snap beans that had been soaked in a light, salty vinaigrette, combined with lettuce, tomatoes, and baby carrots.

Maxwell Grantham rose, went to the cherrywood sideboard, and brought back a decanter of red wine. "This is an excellent wine from Medoc, in France. I think it will go splendidly with the chicken. In the East, they're learning to drink white wine, chilled, but in my book, one drinks what one finds best for one's palate. I hope I can convince you that the red wine and the chicken will blend very delightfully."

So saying, he filled glasses for all of them, and then seated himself just as the Chinese cook brought out a huge platter on which reposed three roasted young chickens on a bed of rice with almonds. Maxwell praised the cook, whose stolid, unemotional face broke into a radiant smile when the gray-haired cattleman interpolated a few words of Chinese.

"What did you say to him that made him smile like that?" Cecily couldn't help asking, with a silvery little laugh.

"Why, I told him that his ancestors could hardly wait to collect him so that he could prepare just such an exceptional dish for them in heaven, with Buddha looking on benevolently."

"But that's wonderful! I didn't know you knew Chinese— and after what Hugo and I have read about the way some people are trying to ban their coming into this country, I think it's admirable that you have employed a Chinese cook, Mr. Grantham," Cecily declared.

Hugo sent a smile of pleasure to his lovely young wife, quite happy with the way she was comporting herself. The resentment and enmity he had feared she would display because of her uncle's unfortunate death at the hands of a cattleman had not at all materialized. Indeed, the evening augured well.

"I'll carve, if you'll pass me your plates," Maxwell suggested.

Soon they settled down to the serious business of eating, and Chuck Denby smacked his lips as he tried the first bite of chicken. "Damn, but that's good—sorry, folks, Mr. Grantham—boss—I mean, we don't get served anything like this over in the mess hall, you can bet on that!"

"Maybe I'll have to get after your cook and ask her to be a little more creative. I'll tell Kee Dan that you praised him highly," his employer chuckled. "More wine, Chuck? Help yourself to the decanter. There's another one on the sideboard if we empty this one. What do you think of the Medoc, Dr. Bouchard?" He addressed himself to Cecily.

"It has a lovely bouquet, and just as you say, it's light and delicate—I think it goes wonderfully with the chicken, Mr. Grantham." Cecily was obviously enjoying herself.

"Well now, Hugo," Maxwell paused with his fork midway to his mouth, "how do you like Wyoming?"

"Wide open spaces, pure air, fine beef, a cozy house, and a beautiful bride—I'd say it's paradise, Mr. Grantham," Hugo at once responded with a wink at Cecily, who made a little face at him, as she took another sip of her wine. "Seriously, though, I came out to Wyoming because when I met Cecily in Chicago, at Rush Medical College, she said she wanted to become a doctor in an area where there weren't too many people who could help out when their neighbors got sick. Of course, it's not an area where you expect to make money, but we didn't become doctors for that purpose. We feel we're needed here and that we're making a contribution. I think that's the most important goal of all—finding yourself and doing what you really enjoy."

"Your father wrote me last year that you were finishing your studies and getting married, and had decided to come out to Wyoming. I said to myself then that you'd be a great addition, and obviously you both are. Do your patients keep you busy much of the time?"

"We don't have as many as we'd like, to be honest with you, Mr. Grantham," Hugo responded. "I think in any new area, whether it's the East, West, South, or North, people are going to be a little careful about you until they're sure you'll fit in. They're naturally suspicious, and I will say, so far as my wife is concerned, most of the residents in our area never in the world expected that a woman could be a doctor. On the other hand, there have been a few instances where her being a woman has given her a patient or two—where a woman preferred to be examined by another woman."

Maxwell Grantham smiled warmly at Hugo. "I think you've a very refreshing and practical outlook, and I predict you're going to do very well, the two of you. I'm sure being married and working together like this gives you an additional incentive."

"We like it that way, Mr. Grantham," Cecily said softly with a fond glance at her husband. "But what about yourself? Don't you find living by yourself in a big house like this gets a bit lonely at times?"

A momentary shadow crossed the rancher's rugged face. "I was married once, as perhaps Hugo's father may have told him, for he knew in some detail about my background. You see, Dr. Bouchard,"—this to Cecily—"I was married when I was twenty-seven—to a debutante, actually. But I soon found that she preferred sophisticated city gigolos and the fashionable rendezvous of what we call high society to the domestic bliss of a home. So we agreed to disagree, and actually she made the first move by going off with one of her preferred friends. I didn't contest the divorce. I decided that I was fed up with city living, and besides, my doctor told me that I would benefit from outdoor life. So I took his advice, and I came out here, and I don't regret it a bit."

"I see," Cecily said noncommittally.

"But, to answer your question directly—yes, of course, I get a bit lonesome at times. And now, seeing the two of you—so young and attractive and both so talented—I admit that there are times when I wish I were married again. I'm not ruling it out—don't misunderstand me, for I'm not a misogynist. And, too, with each new year, more women come out this way, though usually they're not single. Oh, there's the usual number of mail-order brides, of course, and then there are the painted women who work in the Cheyenne saloons and dance halls—but they don't appeal to me in the least. However, if it happens that I meet someone who's congenial and who likes this kind of life, I'd like very much to marry and have children, even though I'm in my fifties.''

"Thank you for being so frank, Mr. Grantham, and I think you've every chance. I'm sure it won't be in the distant future, either,'' Cecily offered with a warm smile.

"I hope you're right. Well, now, there's more chicken. How about you, Chuck?''

"Gawd no, boss, I'm stuffed for fair.'' The foreman put a hand over his stomach and groaned.

"You, Hugo?'' He shook his head.

Cecily, however, decided that she would have another helping, and Maxwell piled her plate high with chicken and some of the vegetables, against her protests. "Now, Dr. Bouchard, let me pour you another glass of wine,'' he prompted.

"You really would make a wonderful husband,'' Cecily giggled, as the rancher reached over and filled her glass.

"Let's hope your words are prophetic, Dr. Bouchard.'' He nodded pleasantly at her, and then cut into his own second helping of chicken and began to eat. Then suddenly, without warning, his hands went to his throat, and he stumbled up from his seat, and pitched forward onto his plate, gasping for air.

"My Gawd, boss, what's the matter?'' Chuck Denby was paralyzed with apprehension as he stared at the rancher.

Hugo quickly rose, but it was Cecily who immediately realized that their host was choking to death. She sprang up from her chair and hurried around behind Maxwell Grantham, whose face was turning bluish, his eyes hugely dilated. Then, making a fist, she hit him soundly between the shoulderblades. She had to repeat this process two more times before the paroxysm ceased, indicating that the obstruction had been dislodged. Slumping to the floor, Maxwell began to draw in great gulps of irregular breath. "That's right, Mr. Grantham, you're all right now," Cecily exclaimed. "Just breathe in normally, and you'll be fine in a jiffy."

His eyes were watery with tears as he looked around the room and finally panted, "My God, I thought I was a goner! A chicken bone—that's what I get for being so greedy—"

"Don't try to talk for a bit," Cecily warned. "Just breathe in and out. You feel somewhat giddy now, but that's only natural. You really could have choked to death if we hadn't dislodged the bone. There now, are you feeling better?"

His complexion still wan from his narrow escape, Maxwell nodded. Denby, his mouth agape, stared as if he could not believe his eyes. Then he swore under his breath, "Goddamn, that was a close one, boss! This lady doc sure knew what she was doing! I wouldn't have ever thought of a thing like that.—. . ."

"She had great presence of mind—ah, that's better; I'm getting my strength back—and next time, I won't try to eat so fast," Maxwell promised. Then he slowly seated himself, put his palms flat on the table before him, and leaned back and breathed in and out for a few minutes until he had completely recovered. "That was incredible—I owe you my life, Dr. Bouchard."

"It's a simple procedure. Anybody can do it, even a layman. That was one of the things that I learned at Rush," Cecily explained.

The rancher looked at her with a mute gratitude that transcended words. Finally, he said, "I thank God you learned what you did, Dr. Bouchard. You know, there's an old superstition that when you save somebody's life, that person owes you a debt. I want to do whatever I can, till the debt's paid."

"I—I did only what any doctor would have done, Mr. Grantham."

"That may be, but you had the presence of mind to act quickly. A few minutes more, and I would have died. I couldn't get my breath . . . everything was clogged up. It was a horrible feeling."

"I'm glad that I was trained to help you. And you don't owe me anything."

"Well, I feel that I do." He paused, watching Cecily. "You know, when I first met you this evening, I had the feeling that you were prepared not to like me. Won't you tell me why?''

Cecily exchanged a look with her husband, who nodded and made a gesture with his hand as if to say, ''Go ahead, get it off your chest, for once and for all.''

''All right, then, Mr. Grantham. Hugo and I have had disagreements in the past because he's the son of a cattleman. One of the main reasons I came out here was to be with my aunt, Margaret. She's been almost single-handedly running a sheep ranch ever since her husband—my uncle—was murdered in a fight between cattlemen and sheep ranchers. I naturally feel a certain degree of enmity toward cattlemen. That's what bothers me. I understand why cattlemen don't like sheep, but I object to this warring and feuding. Isn't there any way to stop it?''

Maxwell Grantham looked intently at the lovely young woman for a long moment. ''What's your aunt's name, Dr. Bouchard?''

''It's Margaret Denton. She's fifty-six now, doing all the work with just a few helpers. And she's worried sick that someday the cattlemen of Wyoming will decide that she has to be dealt with the way my uncle was.''

''Dr. Bouchard, how long ago was your uncle killed?''

Cecily thought a moment. ''At least ten years ago.''

''Well, Dr. Bouchard, I came out here only five years ago, so I personally have no knowledge of the incident. But as it happens, I have from ten to twelve thousand head of cattle, and my ranch is growing in importance every day—thanks in part to your husband's father, who sold me two thousand head of really superb breeding stock. That means I have no little influence with the cattlemen of Wyoming. I'll promise you this: One of these days, very shortly, I'll call them all together for a meeting. I, for one, don't believe in useless killing for intimidation. To my mind, if the sheepmen keep their animals away from where cattle graze, we cattlemen don't need to make things too tough for them. We need water rights and grazing rights, but if the sheepmen can compromise with us, I think it can work out.''

''Would you really do that? Would you really investigate the situation and see what you could do so that there won't be any more killings, Mr. Grantham? Then you'd pay the debt that you feel you owe me. I still say you don't, but you'd be saving human life, just as I saved yours."

"You're a fine, warmhearted woman, and your husband is a very fortunate young man. Yes, I give you my word of honor that I'll see to it that all the principal cattle ranchers come to my place for a pow-wow."

"Thank you, and God bless you, Mr. Grantham."

"These are needless feuds," the rancher continued, "and they come out of anger and the fact that, because this is such a big territory with so few lawmen, people take matters into their own hands. I promise you I'll do all I can. Now then, let's have Kee Dan bring in the dessert. He's made something with apples and lichee nuts and caramel, and it's the tastiest thing you've ever put a spoon to."

Cecily looked at her husband and smiled broadly. "You've given me quite an appetite, Mr. Grantham. I'm glad you invited us here. And by the way, if you don't have a regular doctor, I'd like to be yours whenever you need me."

"I'll just take you up on that, Dr. Bouchard," the cattle rancher grinned.

Chapter Thirty-Five

On his way into the tiny Mexican village of Mazatlán, Ramón Hernandez passed a small cantina, just at the beginning of the main thoroughfare. *"Bueno,"* he had said half aloud, "here I can fill my canteen with more tequila." Perhaps, he thought, in this obscure, out-of-the-way little place, if there were a miracle and if *El Diablo* had finally heard his prayer and decided to perform the miracle that *El Señor Dios* was not willing to do, perhaps here he would learn news of Gatita and that damned, hell-born woman.

He could hardly stand, for his exhaustion, his debauchery, and the murderous heat of the full sun, intensified by its reflection back from the ocean beyond, had sapped him of what little energy he had left. And the death of Magdalena had seemed like a symbol of complete annihilation and denial of his interminable search for his daughter. In his enervated, deranged mind, it had been one more monumental proof that God had cast Ramón Hernandez aside and would never consider him or his prayers.

Mumbling to himself, Ramón reached out a hand and pushed open the door of the little cantina. He blinked his eyes several times to adjust them to the sudden, cooler darkness, a stark contrast to the dust and the blue sky and water and the blazing sun. With a groan, he eased off the strap of the saddlebag and slumped down into a chair at the nearest table.

There were three young fishermen at the bar, and two others, in their late thirties, occupied a table at the very back of the cantina. They looked up and regarded him with curiosity, then went back to their drinking and their conversation. Behind the bar, there was a pleasant-faced, black-haired woman in a red cotton blouse and green skirt, who was busy polishing glasses. She eyed Ramón as he sat slumped over in his chair, and then she went on with her work. Gradually, Ramón became conscious of her and, stiffening, pounded on the table. *"¡Tequila, por favor!"* he demanded in a hoarse, unsteady voice.

"At once, señor," the woman said, as she turned to the rows of bottles behind her, chose one of them, took one of the glasses she had just dried, and came over toward the table. She was about to pour it for him when he stopped her.

"Leave it, woman!" he growled. "I am not yet that feeble that I need you to pour my tequila for me!" And then, seeing her standing there nonplussed, he scowled at her, fumbled in his pocket till he found what he was looking for, and extracted a coin. He tossed it onto the table. "There, in case you think I can't pay for the tequila!"

"I will bring you your change, señor," she answered in a low, vibrant voice.

"Keep it. I may want more to drink." He poured himself out a full glass of tequila, put it to his lips, and drank nearly half of it at a gulp, then set the glass down with a clatter. "Now—I need information, and you must give it to me."

"If I can, señor."

"We will see." He gave her a suspicious look. "My little daughter, my Gatita, was stolen from me. She was taken by a *gringa* who called herself Rita Galloway. Do you know these two? Have you seen them?"

"No, señor, no one like that has come to Mazatlán—or at least, if they have, I have not seen them here in my cantina," the woman responded.

Ramón struggled to his feet, lifted his fist, and banged it down on the table till the bottle almost toppled. The woman caught it just in time, giving him a scared look and then moving back a little, not quite certain what to make of this unkempt, nasty man, who all the same had given her a five-*peso* coin for a bottle that only cost three *pesos*.

"Listen to me, all of you!" he shouted. The men at the bar and the two at the table turned to look at him. "I have come here in search of my daughter, do you understand me? She was stolen from me, from my ranch in Texas last year—no, no, longer than that—nearly two years—by a *gringa*. Tell me if you have seen these two! You must tell me! I have gone all through Mexico trying to find them."

"No, señor, we have not seen those two," one of the men at the bar spoke up, giving his two companions a puzzled look. The one in the middle put his finger to his head and described a circle, whispering, "*Es muy loco, el borrachón.*"

"So you say," Ramón growled, glaring at the man. He reached for the bottle of tequila, then realized that his glass was still half filled, seized it, and gulped the rest down. Then, lifting the glass, he flung it on the floor, shattering it. There was a gasp from the woman, who shook her head and hurried back behind the bar to find a broom. Ramón didn't notice, for he had been too busy pouring the fiery contents of the bottle down his throat.

"All of you are liars! Liars and criminals, for if you conceal information about my stolen child, you are as bad as the woman who took her. Do you understand me?" Ramón shouted. His bloodshot eyes fixed the men at the table and men at the bar with a baleful look.

"A moment, señor." The tall man at the table rose now and politely addressed Ramón. "You are making yourself unpleasant. All of us have told you that we know nothing about your daughter and this *gringa*, this Rita Galloway, as you call her. Now be a good fellow. Just drink your tequila—and pray. Perhaps *El Señor Dios* will help you—"

"To hell with *El Señor Dios!*" Ramón almost shrieked. He lifted the bottle of tequila and flung it at the friendly man, who ducked as the bottle went sailing past his head and smashed against the opposite wall. "I have prayed to Him, ever since my Gatita was first stolen—and He has done nothing. I have renounced him. Now I believe in *El Diablo!* And I still say that all of you are liars. I will go to the authorities, to the *policía*, and we will see if it is true that you know nothing."

"Juana, this has gone far enough." The tall man turned to the woman who had come forward with a broom and was sweeping away the shards of broken glass. "*Con su permiso*, I will get rid of him." He moved slowly and purposefully toward Ramón's table.

Lucien Edmond's brother-in-law chuckled thickly. "So, now, you want to challenge me, do you? I will have your *cojones*. I will cut them off with a knife and hang them up to dry—you and your *El Señor Dios*. . . ." With this he doubled his fist and lunged forward, but the younger man stepped aside and, with a single blow, knocked Ramón backwards, where he sprawled on the floor of the cantina, unconscious.

"Shall I throw this *borrachón* outside, Juana?" the man asked.

"No, no, *gracias*, Paco. I—I feel sorry for him. He has had a great loss—his daughter stolen from him—and I know what a loss is. . . ."

"Yes, Juana, I understand," the tall man said sympathetically, glancing at the others, who nodded. "Your husband, that fine man Alonso—may his soul rest among the angels!"

"*Gracias*, Paco." The woman bowed her head a moment. "Leave him to me. He is exhausted, one can see that. I feel certain that he has not eaten in a long time. And his smell—surely he has not bathed for even longer. You heard him say it has been two years since his child was taken, and still he looks for her—no, Paco, I would not throw such a man out into the street. It would not be Christian."

"You have a heart of gold, Juana," Paco declared. "We will leave now, but I shall come back tomorrow to see if all is well. Be careful. He has a very bad temper—and he does not even believe in God! He is a lawless, soulless one!"

"I do not think he is quite as bad as you make out, Paco. And I do not think I am in any danger. Of course, he is drunk—that is undeniable. But you have only to look at him and see how exhausted he is to know what this long search must have cost him."

"Very well. Come, *mis compañeros*, we've had enough to drink anyway. It is time for a siesta. Perhaps this evening, when the sun has gone down, we will be lucky at fishing and make more *dinero* so we can come back here and spend it with Juana," Paco chuckled.

Ramón Hernández groaned, vaguely groped his hand toward his forehead, then turned over onto his side. Every muscle in his body seemed to ache, and there was a throbbing in his head that threatened to blow off his skull. He winced and moaned and slowly rolled over to the other side.

"So, you are coming back to life." Dimly he heard a throaty, gentle voice. He blinked his eyes, but the vision had not yet returned to them. It was as if he were blind and partially deaf, but perceptive of all those things that filtered through his reawakening senses.

There was a coolness and a gentle pressure along his forehead, and he moaned softly. Fingers touched his ears, his cheeks, his chin. He groped to meet that touch, blinking his eyes again and finally opening them. He had felt no beard, no sideburns, and the greasy, sweaty slickness that the hot Mexican summer sun had brought to his skin seemed to have disappeared.

"I—I don't know who you are—where am I? *¡Dios!*" he groaned aloud.

"Hush, *hombre*. You are at the back of my cantina. I am Juana Perez."

"J-Juana—P-P-Perez? I do not know the name—" he stammered hoarsely.

"You are in Mazatlán, señor. You came into my cantina two days ago, and you got very drunk."

"*Dios Grande*—now I remember—two days ago, you say?" he asked in astonishment.

"*Sí*, señor. Lie still. Do not try to get up yet. You are very weak, and I was afraid that you would die."

"Perhaps it would have been better for all of you, if I had—for my family, for those who cared for me. Nothing matters now. . . ."

"You must not speak like that, señor. I am very sorry that you do not like the world, and still more concerned that you deny *El Señor Dios*. But we will talk of that another time. Rest now, because I am making you some nourishing soup. In about half an hour it will be ready, and I will feed you. Then you will sleep again, till your vitality comes back to you. You are a strong *hombre*."

He groaned again and tried to rise, but her soft hands pushed him gently back. "No! You must rest. You are still very weak."

"But I must find Gatita. I have to find her—I've gone so far—" he began.

"*Comprendo. Comprendo mucho, señor.*" Her voice was softly compassionate. "But it will not hurt you to lie still and gain your strength. Soon, when you feel the need for it, I will make you some more substantial food—beans to give you lots of energy, and tortillas made of the best cornmeal. Do you like fish?"

"I have not had very much—in Texas, I lived on a ranch and—" His voice trailed off, as a lucid flash of sanity came

348

back to him through the laborious, tortured nightmare of these long, endless months of searching.

"Here in Mazatlán, señor, there is much good fish from the ocean. The men who come to my cantina are fishermen, most of them. And when they do not have *dinero* for tequila or *cerveza*, they pay me back in fish from the sea. It is a good trade."

"You are very kind. Why do you do this for me?"

"Because you are a man in need, with much sorrow. I understand this."

"*Gracias, señora.*"

"*De nada, señor.* What is your name?"

He blinked his eyes again, trying to accustom himself to the soft light cast by an oil lamp. His eyes were no longer swollen, but there was a penumbra about her; she seemed to be in a dusky haze. He opened his eyes again, staring through this shadowy, almost spectral twilight—for such it seemed to him.

Her face was rounded, her eyes a lustrous brown, and her brown hair was parted in the middle and drawn back into a thick braid. She wore a white cotton blouse with a drawstring neckline, a black cotton skirt, and huaraches. He stared at her, and a vague remembrance stirred within him. The name of Magdalena crept into his mind, the Magdalena who had saved his life after he had been shot in the back and left for dead so many years ago, when he was riding with Diego Macaras. Magdalena—the name of his mare as well, who so valiantly, so unprotestingly, had carried him for more miles than he could count, through heat and rain and thunder and lightning, unfalteringly taking him on this will-o'-the-wisp search that had no beginning and no end—and even now was no nearer ending than it had been at the very start. *Magdalena* . . . Suddenly, he began to weep, great wracking sobs that shook his body, and he turned his face to one side and covered it in the crook of his right arm.

Her soft hand touched his hair, stroking his forehead, stroking the side of his head and his neck. "It is good for a man to weep at times. I have been worried about you, *hombre*. What do you call yourself?"

"It is—my name is—Ramón. Ramón Hernandez. And you? Did you tell me your name?"

"I am Señora Juana Perez, Ramón. Call me Juana. We are

two people who have known grief. This is why I did not let them throw you out of my cantina." She laughed gently. "You were very drunk, and you were abusive, and you wanted to fight with everyone because they would not tell you where your child and that woman who stole her were. Believe me, Ramón, they could not know . . . they did not know."

"I begin to understand now. It has been so long since anyone has spoken kindly to me—I cannot help this—I am no less a man because I weep, but I had forgotten what kindness is. And now you have given this to me—you have taken me in, and I think I understand how badly I must have behaved in your cantina. Forgive me, Juana."

"There is nothing to forgive. A man who sorrows, a man who loves, a man who has lost his child, is not a criminal or an evil man. I knew this from the first. When you came into my cantina and I saw how tired you were, the sweat dripping from you, plastering your *camisa* to your body, I told myself that here was a man who had traveled a terribly long way and who was sorrowing and could not help himself."

He tried to sit up again, and this time she helped him, an arm around his shoulders. "All of you men," she uttered that soft vibrant laugh, so throaty and sensual, "you try to show yourselves to be *macho*, when you are really little children at heart. It is we women who know what is in you, when you do not know yourselves. Now, will you take some broth and perhaps one of my fine tortillas?"

"If—if you want . . . Yes, I feel I could eat. I do not know why you do this for me, but I have a few *pesos* in my saddlebag—my saddlebag!" He looked around in alarm.

"Hush, Ramón. Your saddlebag is over there in the corner. I live here at the back of my cantina. My husband died four months ago, and he left me this place. He was a good man. He longed for children, but I could not give them to him, yet he was so good and kind he did not hate me for it. Nor did he go after other women. Many men would have done that. I am grateful to *El Señor Dios* for the happiness we had together—it was eight years, Ramón."

"I do not know what has brought me here, but I think that I have been very fortunate. If it had been anywhere else, or anyone but you, Juana, perhaps I might have died. I am very grateful to you."

"I do not want your gratitude. I want you to be well and

strong again, and then we will talk about your Gatita. There is so much hate in you, and this I understand, also, because a man's child, the flesh of his flesh and blood of his blood, is sacred to him.''

Her unexpected gentleness, her deeply sensitive compassion, had unleashed the torrent of pain and desperation in his heart. He wept again, wept like a child, and she held him close to her.

"He was a lucky man, this *esposo* of yours, Juana," he said at last in a trembling voice. "I had forgotten there are women like you. I thought only of the one who took my child from me—a liar, a vicious woman. There is so much I can tell you—''

"It will keep. If it has been locked in your heart and in your mind all these months, it will keep. Lie back now, and I will prepare for you the soup and the tortilla. Then, when you are rested and nourished, you will say what is in your heart, and perhaps I can help you.''

"You have helped me already. You have given me back my life—as once another woman did. She, too, was a widow. Oh, I have been a fool, a monster! I have blasphemed. I have been—''

Her hand pressed against his lips. "That you can say these words now shows that you have no evil in you. And God knows this. When I heard what you said in my cantina, I was horrified—until I looked at you and understood, until I heard you talk about your child and the loss of her. I can understand how a man would abuse Him who gave us life, for none of us can truly understand His ways. There is a reason for everything, Ramón Hernandez. There is a reason that my husband was taken from me. I do not know what it is, but I have learned to accept it. And somehow I feel that his spirit is with me now, and perhaps it was his gentle spirit that told me I must help you when you needed help—when you came, a stranger, to my cantina here in Mazatlán.''

He lay back again, closing his eyes, exhaling a long, deep breath. Once again, he felt his clean face. His skin was cool now; the fever had abated, and he began to feel an emptiness in his belly—the first good sign, the true sign of hunger. The sweat, the heat, the exhaustion, and the agony had purged him of not only the fever in his blood but that in his mind as well. He did not understand much as yet, but he felt more rested and at peace than for what seemed a lifetime. He was content to lie there and to breathe in deeply, and to wait.

It was cool at the back of the cantina, where Juana had made a comfortable private room. Ramón lay covered by a light blanket upon a straw pallet that served as a bed. Though the floor was only of dried earth, there were small, colorful rugs here and there. A crucifix hung on the wall at the opposite end. There was a single window in the middle of one wall, and a shutter had been drawn over it. He did not as yet know what time it was, but he vaguely remembered that she had said he had been here two days. *Gatita.* She and that woman were farther away from him than ever now. In those two days and nights they had outdistanced him, no matter where they had been. Would he ever find them? He was so very weary of such thinking.

"Here you are. Eat as much as you can, but very slowly. There is no need to hurry."

"But the cantina—what time is it?" he hoarsely asked.

"It is late evening. I have closed the cantina. After all, a woman needs a rest at times from her labors. We are not so strong as you *hombres machos.*" There was a gentle, mocking laughter in her vibrant voice, and it pleased him.

"I will pay you. What you have lost in taking care of me, I will make it up to you. I told you I have a little *dinero* in my saddlebag—"

"Have I asked you for money, *hombre*? Do not insult me. It is true that I have no man now, that I am a widow, but I have my pride. If I choose to do this for you, it is of my own free will. No one has forced me, and you yourself did not ask for anything. You could not—you were beyond asking. Perhaps you were very near death, more than you knew."

In a way, the husky, soft gentleness of her voice and the words she used, singularly logical and simple and yet not those at all of an educated woman, made him feel, very strangely, as if he were a boy and this a wise woman who was being benevolent to him, compassionate and forgiving. It touched him, and he felt tears come to his eyes again. "I am hungry," he humbly confessed.

"That is very good. It is a very good sign. You are not to have any more tequila. *Hombre*, you drank more than most men could in a short time. And I do not think that it was the first time you had drunk so much—I do not think, also, that

352

you had not had any till you came to my cantina." Once again her words had that soft, pleasant mockery that did not deride him, but seemed to share a joke between the two of them. He felt very reassured and restful. Then suddenly he realized that he no longer stank, that the clothes he was wearing were clean, not dirty and tattered. "You—you cleaned me," he muttered.

"Yes, I bathed you. Now you are wearing a shirt and trousers that belonged to my husband. Ramón . . . you and your clothes were filthy, so I tended you."

"What must you think of me?"

"I told you that I am a widow. Do you not think that I saw my husband without his clothes? Why, then, should you feel ashamed because I saw you, when you were disabled? I saw you only as someone who needed help."

"Once before—once, a long, long time ago," he said in a voice that was faint with reminiscence, projecting far into the past, "someone like you saved my life. Perhaps it is a sign, and yet I do not deserve it. I know I have sinned. I know I have said things that He must judge me for and punish me for—"

"But now you repent them, and so He will know and understand why you said them, and He will know also that you did not mean them because you were stricken with grief. He will know that it was because you loved your child so much that you said what you did. If He made this world, as we are taught, Ramón, He knows more than you or I what is in the heart and the mind of a man or a woman. Be sure of that, as I am.

"I cling to my faith because, when my husband was taken from me—a man who had been healthy all of his life—without any reason or explanation, I too felt that it was unjust. Yet I prayed, and I asked for strength to keep me here and to continue the work my husband had done, for he had made many friends in Mazatlán. So I serve tequila and *cerveza* and a little food. I do not charge very much, just enough for my living, because I want his friends to be my friends, also. Thus I can live, and I can live with myself in my grief. I think my husband's spirit looks down upon me and is glad that I have done what I have done in his name and in his memory."

He had not heard such words since Magdalena had comforted him, when he had been a young man seeking a freedom that would avenge martyrs like his own murdered father. He was awestruck because now it seemed to him that there was a pattern to all this—a pattern that had begun in that other small village and brought him all across Mexico to where he had found another such woman to save his life and to help him see things as they must be.

He felt stronger now and sat up by himself. She placed a hardened clay tray on his lap, holding a bowl of soup and two baked tortillas. It smelled heavenly. He could not remember when last he had eaten. He began to drink the soup, gulping it down, till she gently chided him. "There is no hurry. Eat, enjoy it, but slowly. It will be better for you this way."

He forced himself to obey her, as a child might, understanding that an elder had greater wisdom. How good the soup was; he had not had food like this in so long! He finished it all and then belched, coloring as he did so.

"*Gracias,* señor. You like what I prepared for you, then, Ramón?"

"I—it was a feast, Juana. But my stomach—"

"Do not make excuses. Naturally a hungry man's belly responds when it has food put into it after a long while. I'm sure that you have not eaten as you should have all this time you have been searching."

"Not, that is very true. I do not know how to thank you—"

"Then do not try. I am happy that you are going to live, that you already feel better, and that you are speaking sensibly. As I said before, when you came into my cantina I was a little afraid of you."

He uttered a hollow little laugh. "The fact is, Juana, I've been afraid of myself, as well."

She smiled at him, then stood up. "I will make coffee. I think a little of it would do you good."

"I should like it very much."

"Then lie back now, take a little siesta, and I will prepare it. I will have some too, to keep you company."

"*Gracias, gracias por todo, Juana.*" Once he lay back, a blessed torpor came over him, and before he knew it, he was snoring, deep in slumber. The handsome widow stared at him, smiled, and quietly moved to the table. She lifted a blanket that was draped over a chair, then spread it out on the floor beneath the crucifix. This done, she looked back at

Ramón and, assured that he was fast asleep, turned off the oil lamp. Then, kneeling down on the blanket, clasping her hands in prayer, she bowed her head and prayed silently to the crucifix. When she had finished her prayers, she stretched herself out on the blanket, closed her eyes, and let the silence and the peacefulness of the room absorb her and carry her off into a deep sleep.

Ramón did not know how long he had slept, but when he wakened, the pleasant-featured widow was kneeling beside him, watching him carefully. He smiled at her, a wan smile, and asked, "What time is it now?"

"You have slept until morning, Ramón. Your body needed it, and I saw no reason to wake you. Now, I shall bring a basin of water and a towel for you. Then, we shall have some breakfast together."

"You are very kind. I do not deserve all this."

"There you go again, punishing yourself for something that was not your fault."

"Woman," he angrily declared as he propped himself on an elbow, "you know nothing about it. You are not to judge, *comprendes?*"

"*Sí*, Ramón, as you wish. But you will tell me the story, and then I will tell you that *El Señor Dios* did not intend for us to punish ourselves constantly."

"Woman," he shouted, clenching his fist, "stop saying that to me! You know nothing of my life! I am a total stranger to you."

"But we are all made by the same God, Ramón, and so I feel what you feel. When my Alonso was taken from me, I argued with *El Señor Dios*, and I asked Him why He had done this to me. And that was selfishness."

"I see," he almost mocked her, "and you fancy yourself an ecclesiastic because of your experience, do you?"

She shook her head and looked at him, with a sad, wistful expression. "I am a humble woman, a peasant. I married a fisherman. He was very lucky and that is why he could put away money and finally buy the cantina. Without it, I should be starving now. It is true that some of the villagers would have pity on me, but it is much better this way. But my husband, my Alonso, got down on his knees and thanked *El Señor Dios* each night for His bounty. How, then, could I rebuke *El Señor Dios* because He chose to take my husband to Him? I had a husband who was better than most men. He did not lie or cheat or steal—he did not go to other women, even if I did not always please him. And he never told me, either—though I knew even in our first year of marriage—that I was not the real *novia* he might have wanted." She shrugged. "But the two of us came together; each of us had needs, and we each filled them for the other. We believed in each other, and we had our faith in *El Señor Dios* to strengthen us when things were bad."

"That is all very well. You have lost a husband, but you have your freedom and this cantina, and you have friends in Mazatlán. I have no friends left now. Even my vaqueros do not want to ride with me any longer. They say of me, 'There goes Ramón Hernandez, and you cannot say even a single word to him before he flares up and looks daggers at you. And when he looks at you, you see hate in his eyes, not the look that one *compañero* should give to another.' Yes, Juana, for almost two years now, because of what has happened to my little girl, I have been driven by a fever, driven by the need to bring my daughter back and to punish the woman who took her from me. That woman was responsible for still another crime: The loss of my child turned me from every occupation I had on the ranch. Even from my wife and brother-in-law, whose father had given me a chance, who had agreed to my marrying his daughter—I, a lowly Mexican whose father had been a *peón* whipped to death by a *rico*. I have even broken up my marriage hunting for my child."

"It will do you good to get it out of your mind and heart, Ramón. Tell me all that has happened to make you this way," Juana Perez murmured as she put a hand on his shoulder.

He glared at her, but the gentleness of her face and the concern in her eyes made him wince inwardly. He gave a bitter little laugh. "You have asked, and I will tell you. I said to you that I had been a *peon* once, the son of a *peon*. I was fighting with a man I believed to be a leader for Juarez but who was actually a bandit and a liar and a murderer. He shot me in the back and left me for dead. A woman nursed me back to life, and when I could, I rode to a Texas ranch because I knew that it was in the *bandido*'s plan to attack them. I stayed on there. I became a vaquero, the head of the *remuda*, because I am good with horses. And then I met Mara Bouchard, the sister of Lucien Edmond. She looked down upon me at first because I was a Mexican. Yet we overcame that, and we married and had children.''

"I understand you. Tell me in your own words and leave nothing out," Juana encouraged him.

Ramón rolled over onto his side, away from the widow. In the dusky haze of this room, where it was cool and pleasant, he was remembering. All the hatred had been poured out, had been sweated out in his exertion and his exhaustion and his fruitless quest all these months throughout Mexico. He felt a compulsion to tell this gentle, hospitable woman what had made him abandon his family and come searching for Gatita.

He told her how, after the silver mine was discovered, he and some other ranch hands had gone up to work the load. A lovely young woman had presented herself one day, looking for work, and needing a cook, they had hired her. When his brother-in-law, Lucien Edmond Bouchard, returned to Texas from Colorado, he had taken the woman back with him to work on the ranch. "She told us," Ramón said bitterly, "that she preferred the warmer climate."

"Yes, I follow you. Go on."

"Our last child, who was three, was named Mara after her mother. But we called her Gatita, first because her hair was as soft and silky as a kitten's fur, and later it was even more fitting because she was so sweet and innocent and playful, exactly like a kitten—" He broke down and started crying, unable to complete his story.

"Please continue, Ramón. It is good for you to talk this way," Juana said gently.

"I—I begin to feel this, too. Yes, you are an angel of mercy, and you have helped me. Finally some of the hatred is beginning to spew out of me. Well then, this woman, she was pleasant, attractive—everyone liked her. And she looked after the children. Oh, my God!" he suddenly broke out, his face darkening with pain.

"I don't understand. Tell me what happened then."

"One day, while I was still up in Colorado, Maxine—that is, Lucien Edmond's wife—and my Mara went to San Antonio to do some shopping. They left this woman, who called herself Rita Galloway, in charge of the children. Instead, the devil-woman rode off with Gatita! She left a note saying that she was taking the child to Mexico.''

"But why would she do a thing like that?''

"To this day, I do not know; I cannot tell you this. We trusted her. She was kind—the children loved her. So did my vaqueros. And out of the clear sky, I received a wire that Gatita was missing and that this woman had made off with her.''

"But why should you feel such deep guilt?''

"Because Lucien Edmond and I did not check her story. We knew nothing about her, yet we accepted her on trust. We saw by her actions that she was a good cook, and that she was friendly and gave us respect, but we had no way of knowing who or what she really was. If either he or I had been more careful, perhaps this would never have happened.''

"You mustn't blame yourself!''

"It's easy for you to say this, for you're not involved, Juana.'' He gave her a fierce glare. "Let me finish now. You may as well know all of it. Lucien Edmond wired me, and I came home at once. We knew nothing, except that she had said she was taking Gatita to Mexico, and so we went off looking for them. But we found nothing, learned nothing. I went out searching a few more times . . . short journeys . . . then this past February I left home, vowing not to return until I had found them. I have ridden through many provinces. I have made inquiries at every cantina and *posada* in every village, no matter how small it is, to see if anyone ever saw a *gringa* with a little child. And so far, no one has.''

"So in all these months you have been riding through Mexico to try to find her?'' Juana sympathetically asked.

He nodded grimly. "Yes, Juana. And now I am very much feeling that I never will find her.''

"Then, first of all, you must get well and get your strength back. Then you will go back home, and you will make it up to your wife and your other children. They love you dearly—I am sure they do—and it is not right to deny them. All you can do now—all you should ever have done—is trust in God.''

"If what you say is true, Juana, I have wasted months of agony and torment, and I may have lost my Mara and broken away from my other children.''

"No,'' she shook her head. "They love you and are concerned for you. And you will go back home when you are strong again. Someday you will know exactly where to look for Gatita, for *El Señor Dios* will give you a sign. I know this, as surely as my name is Juana Perez.''

He stared at her, incredulous. The warmth and the conviction in her voice had penetrated his innermost core. "What you say makes sense, Juana. I have been going off irrationally. I have been oppressed by the burden of my guilt, and all that I have done has been the result of it. Now I begin to see things in another light. Yes, I will rest and get my strength back, and then I will go back to my home. If it is not too late, I will make up with Mara and with Lucien Edmond Bouchard—and I will try to overcome the vaqueros' resentment of me. I cannot go on living this way. It is a life of torture, and it seems to have no end to it.''

"It can never have an end, so long as you deny God. He alone can help you, Ramón,'' she said firmly.

Again he stared at her without speaking. It was incredible how this gentle widow gave him peace and sparked the glimmerings of the restoration of a belief that he had so long put aside with such a vindictive and hostile spirit.

"Woman,'' he said hoarsely, "I do not know who you are or what brought me here, but your words waken in me feelings I have not had since I cannot remember when. Why should this be?''

"Perhaps it is because God wills it, Ramón,'' was her simple answer as she put a hand on his shoulder and stared deeply into his eyes. "A week after Alonso died, I went to Padre Cuernaba, who officiates in the church I attend. I was crying—I was very bitter—and I told him that I had lost some of my faith because I did not know why my good man should be taken from me. He had done no wrong. . . . He was still young, we pleased each other, and even if there were no children, we thought that one day we might adopt some— perhaps some of the *niños* who were in the orphanage just outside Mazatlán. Then he died, and all I had was this cantina. There was nothing left of him once the priest buried him and said the words over his grave. I asked myself, and I asked Padre Cuernaba, 'Why did this have to happen? What did I do to be punished so?' ''

"But that, *mujer*, is exactly what I said when I looked up

to *Dios* in the sky and demanded a reason for the loss of my little Gatita!'' Ramón fiercely answered.

Her fingers tightened on his shoulder as she responded, "But you cannot demand that *El Señor Dios* do what you want. That is not His way. Do you think He is a dog, and that you can summon Him just by calling Him?'' She shook her head. "No, Ramón. You must trust Him. You must understand that He has a reason for whatever is done upon this earth. To question it, to question His judgment, is to be left with nothing. And that is what Padre Cuernaba told me. He said to me, 'Juana, now you are hurt, and you strike out, and you say words you do not mean. But He, the All-Knowing, understands your hurt and feels your pain. And in good time, He will reveal to you why Alonso Perez was taken from this earth. You must go on living. It is what He demands of all of us. Life is the adventure that leads to paradise—if we are devout and believe and are good to those whom we meet on our way along the road. Be assured of this, Juana Perez.'

"Yes, Ramón, and those words comforted me. So why do you condemn yourself and renounce Him who brought you here? Do you think it strange that you did not die when you wished for death? Do not shake your head, *hombre*, I know that is what you wished. And it would be easy—to die, to belong to nothing, and to have all these torments healed once you are in the eternal sleep. No, that is not what He intended. Think of it rather as a test, Ramón. And when you pass it, just like a schoolboy who is promoted to another grade in the classroom, you will know why this happened to you, and you will no longer curse Him who made you and who made your Gatita and your wife, Mara. Think of this and ease your mind and let yourself be at peace, as I have learned to be.''

Ramón lay back, closing his eyes. He could not believe that this simple peasant woman could be so wise, so gently comforting. The words she had used, doubtless, had been told her by the priest of the town, but as she phrased them, he felt that they particularly applied to him, and they were balm to his agonized spirit.

And yet he was still troubled. He had lived with his guilt so long that it was not so easily washed away. He opened his eyes and considered her. Then he said, "Juana, what if I never find Gatita? What am I to do then? How am I to think, how am I to speak? Am I to accept Him whom I renounced in

360

the hope that He will pardon my transgressions and bring back my child to me?"

"No, Ramón. You do not bargain with *El Señor Dios*. But you must live. You have other children, and you have a wife who loves you and is distressed because you despair and leave her for long months. It is not right to leave this good woman, who has meant so much to you all these years, Ramón. If it is His will that Gatita be returned to you, she will be—be sure of it. Have faith, and have faith in yourself. You must go back, and you must be patient, and you must tell your wife that you have always loved her and will always love her, and you will be kind to your children because they should not suffer because you have not found the little one. God will know this, and then you will not have to bargain or call in *El Diablo*, as I heard you do in my cantina."

"I—I am sorry I was such a fool, Juana. When you see those other men, tell them that I apologize."

"But they have already forgotten it. And they do not hold it against you. You see, Ramón, while you slept your exhausted sleep, they came and asked me about you because they were worried. They thought that you might do me harm. I told them that you would not and could not because you were not that sort of man. No, they have forgiven you. They know what grief can be. Many of these fishermen have had hardships. Either their children or their wives have died, or they have been very poor, or they cannot pay the tax on their little boats so they can catch the fish and bring food to their families. They understand you, and they pray for you, as I have and will."

He could not speak. The sound of her voice in this darkened, cool room, the thought of her kindness toward him, made him reflect upon his aimless, agonized wanderings all these long months. Perhaps it was true. Perhaps this was a test, after all, of his strength and his endurance and his faith.

"I will see this Padre Cuernaba of yours, Juana. I will confess to him my great sins of envy and pride and of blasphemy. I will pay penances, but I will not bind myself in absolution."

"You cannot. When you confess to Padre Cuernaba, the Almighty One, will read your heart, and He will judge you."

"I could ask for no more. Now I must sleep a little. I am still weak from the long months in the saddle on poor

Magdalena—my beloved mare. I wish she were still alive, so I might ask her pardon for having driven her without stint or pause. Her heart gave out because I demanded more of it than she could give. For her, too, I have guilt in my heart that I did not deal with her as she deserved."

"But she loved you; she served you. She did not hold it against you because it was her very nature to serve your needs, Ramón."

"You are right." He slowly sat up, rubbed his hand over his cheeks. "And what you have said to me has given me greater strength than I ever had before this sickness of mine."

"I am glad of that. Now lie back and rest."

"*Gracias*, Juana. I am very lucky to have found you. And perhaps it is part of a plan, which I do not yet comprehend but am eager to."

She nodded vigorously, her smile radiant as she leaned toward him. "Yes, it is a plan, and you will one day learn the reason for it and what the plan itself was. I feel this here." She touched her heart. "You are still young. . . . You have all of your life ahead of you, Ramón. Your Gatita will come back. I feel it. . . . I know it."

He began to dream. He had just left Windhaven Range after bidding Mara farewell, riding off on Magdalena, crossing the Rio Grande and heading to provinces he had not yet visited. Out of a thicket came a huge puma, snarling and charging at him, and his courageous mare reared up. He reached for his hunting knife and flung it—and missed the cat. And as its fangs neared the front legs of Magdalena, he awakened with a shout of fear and horror. "*¡No, pero no!*"

"Hush, hush, *Ramón*. You had a bad dream. Keep your eyes closed. Do not move." She murmured this vibrantly, and he obeyed. His heart was pounding swiftly. He heard the rustle of garments, and then Juana Perez lifted the blanket and moved beside him on the straw pallet. He felt the warmth of her naked flesh, he felt her hand stroke his shoulder, and he felt her lips fuse with his. He uttered a stifled groan, for this was maddening, totally unforeseen.

"Hush," she repeated in a sibilant whisper. "You need me, and I need you. Together, let us give each other some comfort and some peace. Certainly it is time that you enjoyed these. You have whipped yourself far too long and to no avail."

He was about to speak, but her soft palm silenced him, and then her lips touched his forehead and cheek and ears, and her other hand glided down his shuddering naked body.

He uttered a gasp, then his arms embraced her, seeking the solace that she could give him.

"How kind you are—oh, *mujer,* you have made me a man again—may the good God bless you. . . ." He groaned as her body merged with his.

There was no need for words. Between them, in the darkness, their bodies spoke and answered, and they were renewed and fulfilled with a joy each gave the other.

Much later, he wakened to find her beside him, and his arm caressed her. He turned to her, burying his face against her breasts, and then again he fell asleep.

Chapter Thirty-Six

Ramón Hernandez woke with a start the next morning and turned his head to see Juana Perez still lying beside him, still fast asleep. He rose carefully, not wanting to waken her, and went to a corner of the room where there was a basin of water. As quickly and quietly as he could, he washed his face and hands, then dried himself with a piece of clean toweling. Lying on the table was a hand mirror, and picking it up, he stared curiously at himself. There were new lines drawn in his face, and he saw that his hair had turned almost completely gray. But at least he now had only a tiny stubble of beard; he was, in fact, better groomed than he had been for months.

He turned back to look at the sleeping woman, and his eyes softened and grew tender. How natural, how uncomplicated, it had been between them last night. She had sensed his needs and had given him warmth, compassion, and an understanding that transcended their physical coming together. She had, he reflected, helped him regain his sanity. The craving for drink that had consumed him—and which, he now could perceive, had been part of his frenzied obsession, a means of escape from the torment of his loss—had left him. The thought of tequila now made him grimace with revulsion.

He sat down on a stool and began to think. Mazatlán. It was at the westerly edge of Mexico, a fishing town to which, in ordinary circumstances, he would never have thought of coming. Recalling the past months more calmly now, he could see that he had made innumerable comings and goings, aimlessly wandering through the provinces, and yet was no closer to finding his daughter than when he had left Windhaven Range. His mind now clear for the first time in weeks, he began systematically to weigh all the possibilities of where she could be. Suddenly a thought struck him with all the force of a rifle shot: Perhaps Gatita had never really been taken to Mexico; perhaps Rita Galloway's note had been a ruse to throw all of them off the track. That might explain why there had been no sign of her, not even at the very outset, when he and Lucien Edmond had crossed the border leading two separate search parties, visiting towns and villages to see if anyone had sought refuge there.

He ground his teeth in a sudden surge of frustrated fury. Why had he never thought of this before? How could he have overlooked the obvious? He reproached himself bitterly, but then he realized, with the awakening clarity of the healing mind, why it was that he had not seen the possibility of this before: So obsessed had he been, so clouded and confused had his mind been with hatred and strong drink, that the simplest truth had eluded him. It was ever thus, with men: Their obsessions and cares deluded them and led them astray.

Now, at last, he could calmly and rationally give thought to the various possibilities. What if Rita Galloway had gone northward, all the time knowing that he and Lucien Edmond would search for her and Gatita in Mexico? Perhaps even back to Leadville—no, that would not be too logical, for although by now surely everyone had left the worked-out mine, there might be those, like the good sisters who lived with the Widow Boyd, who would have recognized her.

His mind was working feverishly now, but at least it was proceeding with clarity, a step-by-step piecing together of what facts he had gleaned in his nearly two years of futile searching.

He glanced at the mirror again, then laid it back down on the table, shaking his head. What a price he had paid for all of this traveling, distressing his family and Lucien Edmond and all the others—*what a terrible price*. Even the joy and the beauty of sweet Mara's face, that face he had always cherished and loved beyond any other on this earth, even that had changed because of his obstinate—yes, even crazed—determination to find Gatita and reunite her with her family on Windhaven Range.

He would have to make amends, and not only in the confessional with a priest in the sanctity of a church where he could purge himself of his guilt. This was a new guilt, added to that he had already inflicted upon himself, bearing it like a weighty cross that bowed him to the earth and humbled him; for he knew that all his skill and cunning, all his horsemanship and daring, had been useless in finding his abducted child.

Once again he turned to look at the sleeping woman. Juana was comely, and she was good and kind. There were few comforts in this cantina, but at least it gave her a livelihood. And as she had said, she helped the fishermen of the town by not charging too much, by giving them a place where they could enjoy their camaraderie and their drink at prices that did not deplete the money they should be spending on their wives and children. She was doing a service, and in her way she was as valuable to Mazatlán as its most influential *rico*. At least, that was how he felt about it.

He must repay her. She was too proud to take money, but there were things he could do around the cantina to make it more livable. Instead of this straw pallet, heaven knew a bed would be more comfortable. Surely somewhere in Mazatlán he could buy a bed where she could sleep after a hard day of working behind the bar, waiting on all sorts of men who did not mind their language and who cursed—he grimaced to himself, sheepish all of a sudden. He began to remember how vilely he had behaved when he had come here that hot, withering afternoon, saddened by the death of his faithful mare. Surely he must have frightened Juana with his bushy, unkempt beard, his dirty, sweaty clothes, and his oaths renouncing *El Señor Dios*. . . .

He would make it all up to her. She deserved more from him after what she had done for him. She had given him back his life, and now he must use it wisely, because that was the only payment she really had sought. His face relaxed into a grateful smile as he stared at her again.

Abruptly, he rose and began to make breakfast. There were some eggs, some sweet peppers, a few tomatoes, and tortillas. He would make *huevos revueltos*. Rummaging in the cupboard, he found the strong chicory that she used for coffee. He made a mental note to find the telegraph office and wire his bank for a draft. He chuckled to himself, realizing that he had been so crazed all these months that he had forgotten this resource: He could have wired San Antonio for funds at any time instead of laboring for a few measly *pesos* at those terrible jobs. He wanted very much to give Juana the things she deserved, like some good coffee—mellow to the taste and as strong as chicory, but without its harsh bite—and the bed, of course. He smiled to himself as he began to prepare the omelet, then he put the coffeepot on. Soon the smell of food made his nostrils crinkle with anticipation. *Dios,* but it was good to be alive! He had much to be thankful for—his health, his strength, and the smell of a breakfast in a room where a kind, handsome woman slept, a woman who had brought him back to reality, to appreciate what he had very nearly cast away in his frenzy. . . .

Five minutes later, as Ramón was completing the meal and was about to wake Juana, she stirred gently. Ramón heard her utter a little moan, and then her eyes opened. They widened, and then there was a soft, sweet smile on her face as, lifting herself on one elbow, the coverlet fell away and revealed one full, firm breast. She murmured, "Ramón, what a nice surprise—you've made breakfast for us. It smells wonderful, *hombre!*"

"It is nothing," he declared. "After all, I have been on many a cattle drive in my time, and I learned to prepare food in a hurry. This is easy."

"*Gracias,* Ramón. But that is a woman's work."

"No, *querida.* You have done a man's work—more than a man's work—in restoring me so that I do not look like a bearded scarecrow, or a *borrachón.* This is only one of the many things I wish to do to show you my gratitude."

"There is no need for gratitude. I am happy that you are easier now in your mind than when you first came to my cantina," she said, starting to rise.

"No, do not get up. Let me serve you. Here we are—a breakfast fit for a queen. It lacks only flowers in a silver vase. Alas, I do not have these, but when I explore Mazatlán this afternoon, I will try to find something appropriate."

"Please, I do not ask this of you—"

"But I wish to do it. It is my pleasure. And I will stay here for a time, if you will keep me, and I will work about the cantina. I see a few things that I can do that will make it easier for you, Juana."

"That's very good of you, Ramón." He had knelt down, putting the clay tray on her lap, carefully arranging the plate and the cup and saucer. She began to eat, quite unashamedly and without concern that the coverlet had fallen to her waist and bared her magnificent torso. He smiled at her, and there was no lust in his gaze, only a warm, glowing appreciation of this earthy, natural, candid woman.

He made a vow to himself that he would pray in church that one day, if He so willed, she would find a true *hombre* to replace the Alonso she mourned and with him have many happy years. Juana was one in a thousand; she would make a man a wonderful wife. If he, Ramón, were free, he would assuredly believe that his future lay here with this woman.

The least he could do to show his appreciation was to help her and make her lot easier before he left. He knew his stay with Juana would hold no future obligations and that he would probably never see her again, but a warm and lasting friendship had evolved, one that he would remember to the very end of his days. It was a good feeling, and it salved the bitter hurt that had lurked so long within his spirit. He watched her eat as he filled his own plate, then came back to sit beside her.

"Oh, it is so good, Ramón! You could have earned a living as a cook for your vaqueros, I think." She made a face at him and uttered her soft, throaty laugh, which so enchanted him. Then she stared at him, and there was such invitation in her eyes, such eagerness and joy, that he could not resist it. In thanksgiving and humble gratitude for her gentleness and perception, he took Juana in his arms, and they kissed, expressing their rapture slowly and tenderly, like two friends who have just discovered each other after a long time and rejoice in their reunion.

Her hands stroked his cheeks, and she murmured, "You are *muy macho*, and yet so gentle a lover. In a way, you are like my Alonso."

"I would to God—" he began, then halted as her finger touched his lips.

"Hush. I see at least now you do not fear to speak His name, and you do not take it in vain."

"Yes, Juana, but because of you. Because I see how He has touched you and made you a miracle of sweetness and goodness—"

"Oh, please, I am only a humble peasant woman! You flatter me too much. I am not worthy of such—"

"Juana," he interrupted. "Hear me out! I was like a drowning man, and I did not even know that I was drowning— nor did I care. Out of nowhere you took me in, and you drew me out of that vortex of madness—and now, because of you, I have renewed hope in my life. I know what I have done to those who love me, and I am ashamed, and I will make restitution. All this because of you, Juana. Through you, I have seen His goodness again upon this earth.''

There were tears in her eyes as she kissed him, and then she murmured gently, ''God has been good to me, too, Ramón, because I was very lonely. Then you came and eased my hurts, just as I have eased yours. It was God who brought you here to me, and it was God who saw to it that I was here to help you. Each of us will now be stronger and happier, no matter what awaits us, to the end of our days, Ramón Hernandez.''

''How beautiful you are, and how I pray that you will very soon find someone who will cherish you and be grateful for your love and repay it with greater love still,'' he whispered.

A week later, having received the draft from his San Antonio bank, Ramón went to make some purchases. Mazatlán was two miles long from one end to the other. It was still hot and oppressive, with little relief given by the breeze carried in from the Pacific Ocean, but this time—purged as he was of alcohol's effects and having rested and eaten nourishing food— Ramón was able to ignore the heat.

Walking through town, he saw a general store, and went directly to it. The proprietor, a thin man in his early fifties sporting a gigantic handlebar moustache, greeted Ramón effusively. Yet the shopkeeper was speculatively curious about this distinguished, gray-haired stranger, and he commented, ''Señor, you are new to Mazatlán, I think.''

''*Es verdad. Hombre*, I wish to spend some *dinero* with you. First of all, I need a horse, a spirited, reliable horse— preferably a mare. Do you know where I can find such an animal?''

''I have such a one at the back of my shop, señor, in the stable. For you, a hundred *pesos*.''

''Do you take me for a country simpleton?'' Ramón countered. ''I will give you sixty *pesos*. You see, I intend to make many other purchases if your prices are good. If I find you honorable, I will pay you three *pesos* for every dollar's worth of goods—a very good rate of exchange, as you know.''

Good sense overcame the shopkeeper's desire to haggle,

and his eyes brightened. "I'm a poor man, señor, and what you offer me is more profit than I could make in four days. I will not stand here and argue with you. How else may I serve you?"

"I am staying for the time being at the cantina of the Señora Juana Perez—"

"I see." Lubricity entered the man's eyes. Ramón glowered, then reached across the counter and took him by the collar of his shirt and tightened it. "Do not say what you are thinking, or I will cut off that moustache of yours and then what will the women do when they see you coming, *hombre*? I have lost my horse. It died as I reached Mazatlán, and Señora Perez was kind enough to take me in. That is all there is to it, and you are to say nothing, *comprendes?*"

"*¡Pero sí, señor!*" the store owner gasped.

"That is much better." He released his grip and continued, "Now, I am sleeping on a straw pallet, and I live on a ranch in Texas where I'm used to a bed. Can you sell me a bed, a sturdy one, and as wide as you have it?"

"I have just what you want, señor. I ordered it for an old man who died before he could marry his third wife, a pretty *muchacha*." The storekeeper rolled his eyes and licked his lips. "I think that if he had married her, he would have died anyway. Of course, it would have been a more delightful way to go. . . . But, at any rate, I have the bed, and it will cost you ninety *pesos*."

"I will not argue with you on the price; however, I insist that you deliver it to the cantina of the estimable Señora Perez," Ramón countered.

The shopkeeper shrugged his shoulders. "Because I can see that you are a man of purpose and character, I will allow it. And what else do you wish to buy from me today, señor?"

"I come from Texas, as I told you, and I have a hankering for good beef. Is there any in Mazatlán?"

"This is a fishing town, as you must know. Mostly, the people here eat seafood. They make stews, soups, and they serve it in many ways. It costs them nothing except their labor in bringing the catch in from the ocean."

"I understand that, but you have still not answered my question—have you any good meat to sell?"

"I think so. Yes, I am sure of it. There is a large cut of

beef that is only a week old in my cold cellar below the store here. I will let you have that for fifteen *pesos*."

"You will take ten. I suggest you write all this down."

"I will, señor. I will at once," the proprietor exclaimed as he looked around, finding a piece of paper and a pencil. "Now, I am yours to command."

"Write down the meat and the bed and the horse and the prices we have agreed upon."

"Of a certainty, señor." The storekeeper showed alacrity and enthusiasm. It was very likely the best sale he had made all year long.

Ramón thought a moment, and then his face brightened. "Oh, yes, I was very nearly forgetting. You have dress materials?"

"Of abundance, and with great variety. They come all the way from Mexico City, señor."

"You say you know Señora Perez—"

"Assuredly, and I knew her husband, peace to his soul." The storekeeper reverently crossed himself and looked solemn.

"Well, then, you will help me choose dress materials that will suit her. You know her coloring. . . . You must know what fabrics will become her most."

"Yes, señor, I think I can satisfy her."

"Very good. Choose appropriate material then for two or three dresses. Is that clear?"

"Decidedly, señor. Now, can you think of anything else you may need?"

"Yes, but let it be understood that I wish all the things I am buying to be delivered by evening to the cantina of Señora Perez," Ramón ordered.

"I have a helper, who is off now on an errand. When he gets back—"

"He will deliver it," Ramón quietly stated. "Now then, I should like a brush and comb, of the very finest quality, for the señora. And some good coffee, the choicest coffee beans you have. Do you have some chairs? I did not see very many in her cantina—"

"She has mostly stools, señor. The fishermen here do not expect chairs—"

"All the same," Ramón interrupted, "I wish to buy some chairs."

"I can sell you six for about seventy *pesos*, señor."

371

"Very well, I will take them without any more haggling. I will look at the horse now and take her if she is satisfactory," Ramón said to the proprietor. He eyed the man, then laid down a gold coin. "This will enable you to pay two men to deliver the rest, a few *pesos* for each of them. What is left can go into your own pocket."

"It is a pleasure to deal with a man who is as wise and generous as you are, señor," the storekeeper ingratiatingly purred. "Rest assured, everything will be in order, as you wish."

"*Bueno*. Now let me see this famous horse of yours. Tell me about her."

"She is three years old and roan in color. Strong withers and flanks, and she is very docile, but intelligent."

"That is exactly what I seek. Take me to her."

Ramón accompanied the storekeeper out to the tiny stable behind the store, put out his hand, and stroked the muzzle of the roan mare, who whinnied and nuzzled him. He smiled and his face was transformed. "I like her. She seems very sound. You can figure the total, and when your men bring the things I have ordered to the cantina of Señora Perez, I will pay you what I owe," he curtly remarked.

The mare, whom he had decided to name Querida, reminded him in some ways of Magdalena. Like Magdalena, she was docile and gentle, yet with a mind of her own and tenacity that spoke well of her stamina. He had carefully inspected her from head to tail, and the ride back to Juana's cantina confirmed his judgment.

Tethering Querida to a hitching post outside the cantina, he went in and saw Juana sweeping the floor near the bar counter.

"Let me do that for you, Juana," he offered.

"*Pero no*, Ramón," she turned to him, her eyes very wide. "It is a woman's work, not for one like you. You came back much more swiftly than I thought."

"That is because I bought myself a mare to replace the one that died when I arrived here. I have called her Querida, to remind me of you. By the way—by the time the sun sets, there will be some deliveries made here by that man with the huge moustache who runs the general store in the town."

"I don't understand—"

"It is a surprise for you. Let us say that, if I am to stay here for a bit more, I should like a few comforts, too. And, since I have *dinero* enough, it is fitting that I pay for them."

"I hope you have done nothing that you should not have done, Ramón. I am happy that you are happy, and I never asked—"

"I know you didn't," he interrupted. "But it pleases me to give, exactly because you ask for nothing. This is my nature, my dear one. Be satisfied with it."

"As you say. I am glad that you have a horse now. You will be able to ride back to your ranch in Texas and take up your life again."

"A life I could never have had, had it not been for you and the kindness you showed me, Juana." He looked at her with a faint smile on his face.

"What are you thinking of now?" she suspiciously demanded.

"How well you will look in a nice new dress. I asked the man at the store to send some material. I suppose you can sew?"

"But of course I can! Do you think I travel into Mexico City and buy beautiful dresses from elegant shops?"

"Heaven defend me!" he chuckled as he raised both hands above his head, as if capitulating to her tartness.

"Is it too much for me to ask more of what you have done in Mazatlán, while I have been working here to clean things up?" she warily asked.

Again he grinned and laughed. "No, it is not. You may ask all you like, and I will say only that there will be some surprises." Then, because he could not keep it inside, he hinted, "For one thing, you need more chairs."

"That's true," she admitted, with a rueful sigh. "But there are times that the cantina is nearly empty, and then, if there were more chairs, I should be sorry that my business is not doing well."

"Not only for the cantina, but also for the back room of yours," he went on. "And there is something else that I bought for the back room. . . ."

"And what is that?" She eyed him almost with irritation.

"I can't believe that you and your husband slept on this pallet all these years."

"But we did! And there was nothing wrong with it. What have you done now? Tell me!"

"Well, since you insist, I asked the storekeeper to deliver a decent bed. It will be more comfortable for you."

Then she giggled, sending him an arch look as she whispered, with a teasing, provocative note to her voice, "And probably for you, as well."

"I protest that! It is not true," he indignantly responded. "Long after I have left you, you will sleep well on the bed, and if you think of me, so much the better. But I swear to you, I did not think of our making love—"

"Be truthful, Ramón. You know that you desire me now, and I desire you too, *hombre*. But I think we shall wait for this famous bed, *no es verdad?*"

Now it was his turn to laugh. "*Seguramente*, Juana" was his laconic answer.

She tilted back her head and laughed softly, then came to him, dropping the broom, and embraced him. He felt the thrust of her bosom against his chest, and their lips met as his hands gently caressed her hips and thighs and her smooth, firm back. There was a sweet fragrance to her hair and her skin that delighted him; he felt himself young again, as if he had never known a woman before. "You are *muy bonita*," he murmured, his voice hoarsening with desire.

"Do you think," she whispered, as her fingers played with his shoulder blades and ran down his back, "do you think that we might have time before the goods are delivered to us from Mazatlán?"

"I think it is possible," he slyly conceded, his blood hot in his veins at the thought of her implication. "I think it is more than possible. Unless, of course, you wish me to prepare some food for you—"

"There are times, *hombre*, when I feel like taking the broom to you." She drew back, put her hands on her hips, and stared him down. "When a woman hungers, it is not always for food. Because you men rule the world you do not allow us women to say what is really in our minds and souls. I want much more—*comprendes?*"

"Yes, I comprehend you perfectly. Come here, *mujer*," he said with a rough tenderness.

With a gay little laugh, she moved to him, her arms around his shoulders, and their lips met. He felt the throbbing of his virility, and he rejoiced that he was whole once again.

Chapter Thirty-Seven

The storekeeper had kept his word, and late that afternoon two young men drove a wagon to the cantina to deliver the bed, the chairs, the side of beef, the dress materials, and the other items that Ramón Hernandez had ordered. Juana could not believe her eyes and stood almost spellbound, an incredulous smile on her attractive face, as Ramón dictatorially ordered where the chairs should be put and where the bed should be placed. Then gesturing to the straw pallet, he declared, "Take this and dump it. Or, better still, give it to someone poor, who may have no bed at all."

After they had left, Juana turned to Ramón. "I can't believe you've done this for me, Ramón. And think of all the *dinero* you spent—"

"That is my affair. I have it, and it gives me pleasure to spend it as I wish. Please do not spoil my delight in making your cantina more attractive and giving you more comforts," he responded.

"And the beef—it is the very best, I can tell. Fortunately, my poor Alonso dug a cellar when he first built the cantina, to keep cheeses and things that need chilling. There are no ice houses around here, except for the larger fish sellers, so it is the best I can do."

"Where I come from in Texas, the ice is shipped by steamboat from Chicago and St. Louis in the winter, down to New Orleans, and on to Galveston and Corpus Christi, then taken by wagons to nearby places. Strangely enough, it seems to last a long time. But this meat will do very well, since it has been salted to cure it. Tomorrow, if you like, we can make meat-filled enchiladas for your customers. And perhaps we will put a sign in the window and announce that there will be an evening of entertainment.''

"Entertainment?" she blankly echoed.

"Of a certainty! Are there not, in Mazatlán, men who play the fiddle and the accordion and the guitar?"

"Yes, there are," she said somewhat doubtfully, "but my husband was never really able to afford entertainment. This is an out-of-the-way place at the end of the town, Ramón. We have an established trade, it is true, but we do not have those from the other end of Mazatlán coming out here for their tequila and *cerveza*."

"Then it is high time we did! Leave it to me. Tomorrow morning, I will go back and tell that obliging storekeeper that I will give him a commission on any new customers he sends to you tomorrow night. You will recognize those who are new to your cantina, won't you, Juana?"

"*Seguramente, Ramón, pero—*"

"Then it is settled," he interrupted with a smile and came to stand with his arm around her shoulders. "Trust me, *mi linda*. It pleases me to put my mind to work on such pleasant affairs. Leave the mariachi to me. I will pack this cantina tomorrow night. There will be joy and music and laughter and good food and plenty to drink. And then they will say in town that Juana Perez's cantina is the best in all Mazatlán."

She lowered her eyes, and her hand pressed his wrist. "You are a good man, and now it is I who am grateful to you. You do not know what it means to a widow to have someone who looks after things, who is attentive to her, and who, though I know he will not stay too long—but you will not go too quickly, will you, Ramón?" She interrupted her thought to ask him this with a plaintive note in her voice, looking imploringly at him.

"Juana, I shall surely stay until I know I have the strength to journey back to Texas and my family. I have been thinking a good deal about how Rita Galloway may have tricked us all by saying that she took Gatita to Mexico, when she had no intention of doing so. If that's true—if in my insanity I failed to take this possibility into account—then I've wasted all these terribly long, cruel months away from my family and away from where Gatita is really hidden. I was stupid, and I was selfish. I have cursed God, and for that sin I heartily repent.''

"I know that by now He has forgiven you, Ramón," she said gently.

"I do not think so. I have not yet earned it. Now that I can think clearly again, thanks to you, Juana, I remember the many times I cursed Him, I defied Him, and I challenged Him. I was wrong. Without faith, a man is nothing—just as without the faith of a woman like you—like my Mara, who in some ways reminds me of you—a man cannot hope to reach that goal that he sets for himself from the very beginning. I know this now. When I go back to Texas, I shall try to make amends. I shall try to have Mara forgive me, and I shall try to make up to her for the misery that I have caused her and my other children. Yes, Juana, I was absorbed by my selfish, personal vendetta, a vendetta that let me forget that I was really seeking only the return of my little girl. That is why I have much to make up for. And that is why, also, I wish to show my gratitude to you. After I have gone, these chairs, this bed, and the other things I have brought you may remind you of me, and one day you will remember that you were kind to a stranger and you showed him the way back to the road of life. This I have learned from you, Juana. In a way, it is as if I had been to a church and there atoned for some of my sins."

"Please, Ramón, I am not worthy of such praise. I am the humblest of His servants. I know this and have always known it. If I was blessed, it was because He gave me Alonso, a good, honest man, who worked hard and did not try to take advantage of his neighbors. It is the way we lived, *hombre*. I cannot take credit for it entirely. But I am happy that you have regained your strength and the peace that your mind must have to go back home again."

That night, when he had taken his sleeping blanket out of the saddlebag and curled up on it in a corner, wanting to show her that he had not bought the bed simply to have his way with her, it was Juana who tiptoed toward him when he was asleep, knelt down, began to stroke his face, and wakened him with kisses. And then, laughing like a child who is amused by her own sly behavior, she took him by the hand and whispered, "It will be much more comfortable in the large bed that you so thoughtfully bought for me, Ramón.

Besides, I do not like to see you sleep on a blanket on the floor.''

He turned to her, and her warm embrace and her soft kisses enchanted him—but he thought at the same time of Mara and how he had neglected her. He swore to himself that because this kind widow had shown him what love could be by way of redemption, he would make Mara's life happier than ever when he returned home.

The next day, after asking questions here and there in town, he hired a group of mariachi to play at the cantina that evening. He talked to the storekeeper who had sold him all of the new goods and the storekeeper agreed to tell all his customers that there would be a special fiesta at the cantina of Señora Juana Perez this night.

That afternoon, Ramón insisted on helping Juana prepare enchiladas, burritos, and *chile relleño*, and helped her also bake fresh corn tortillas. There were frijoles, cooked with jalapeño peppers, and there was even a guacamole. Then, making her laugh until she nearly cried, he donned an apron and went behind the counter as the first of the evening's customers entered. It was he who served them, making jokes and welcoming them, telling them that this was a special celebration. To those who bought a whole bottle of *cerveza* or tequila, he saw to it that they had food with the compliments of the señora.

The mariachi played, and three of the fishermen, overjoyed at the festivities, actually went home to their houses and brought back their wives so that there was dancing.

It was well after midnight when the last customer left, after effusively thanking Juana and Ramón for the entertainment and the food and the music.

He turned to her. ''Well, *mujer*, do you think I am capable of running a cantina, if I put my hand to it?''

''I think you could do anything you wished, Ramón. *Mi ayudante*, I have not had so much fun since my wedding day—''

Suddenly, she fell silent and turned her face away, stealthily dabbing her eyes, into which tears had sprung. He put his hands on her shoulders and slowly turned her to him. ''Juana, I did not mean to make you cry. Forgive me.''

''No, no, there is nothing to forgive! What a lovely, happy

night it was! I think Alonso must have looked down from heaven and smiled and been content. He knows what you have done for me, Ramón. I think that he would be pleased, and I pray that *El Señor Dios* will grant you pardon for those sins you think you have committed."

"*Gracias, mujer*," he murmured. "And the money—we took in a good deal tonight, didn't we, Juana?"

"Yes, over two hundred *pesos*! That is the best day we have ever had, better even than the day Alonso first opened the cantina. It is all due to you, Ramón. The things you bought—the chairs came in very handy, and the special pan for washing dishes and glasses—they will help me a good deal in the times to come."

"Yes, it was a wonderful evening. And it was very good for us."

"Very good for us," she repeated. Her arms slipped around his waist as she whispered, "And I am very tired. But not too tired that I cannot hope that you will come to me when I am ready, *querido*."

Now at the end of the fifth week, Ramón Hernandez wakened at dawn, dressed quickly, and went to the stone church two miles southwest of the cantina. There he made his confession and then attended mass. He lit candles, one for the soul of Alonso Perez, and two for the long and happy life of Juana. Then he lit one for his Gatita, and he prayed silently that *El Señor Dios* would now hear him, a sinner who had repented, and spare Gatita and—if it be His will—return the girl to Windhaven Range.

He left the church, stopping to chat with the priest who had come outside to talk with the parishioners. "*Padre,*" he said, "look after Señora Perez. She is a wonderful, generous woman. See what you can do to find her a man as worthy as her husband."

"I will do what I can, my son. All Mazatlán speaks of how you came to us, drunken and blasphemous, and how she gave you shelter. They speak also with admiration for what you have done for her, for the cantina, to bring more trade to her, so that she will have money enough to live comfortably. I do not ask what happened between you, for it is not my business. But I know that you have treated her with kindness. And I see from your face that you have made a decision—"

"Yes, *Padre*. I shall go back home to my wife and my children. I have prayed this morning that my Gatita will be returned to me, if it be God's will."

"Do not fear, my son. He will hearken to your prayer."

"I know, *Padre*. Though my heart is still bitter, my faith is restored. I regret only the long months I spent, months I should have been at home caring for my wife and the others. But I will make it up to them—this I have sworn."

"I know you will, just as I know that God will heal you, cure you of the anger that even now burns within you. *Vaya con Dios*, my son." The priest made the sign of the cross over Ramón's bowed head.

"I shall leave now, Juana."

"So the time has come. . . ."

"*Querida* . . ." He shook his head and gave her a rueful smile. "It would be too easy to stay here, to fall in love with you, to forget where I came from and what duties and obligations I have. It would not be fair to you. No, Juana, I shall mount my horse and ride back to Texas."

"I wish—" She straightened, bravely composing herself. She took his hand in both of hers and pressed it against her bosom. "There is no need for words of farewell between us, Ramón. You will go back to your life, and I will continue with that which is meant for me. But it will be a happier life, thanks to you."

"I feel the same, Juana. You have brought me back to life, when I wished for death. You have taught me how there is goodness and kindness if one only has the vision to see it. Best of all, you have given me back my faith in *El Señor Dios*." He took her hand and put it to his lips, bowing his head over it, as if she were a princess. "I will think of you for the rest of my life, and I will pray that you will be as happy as you have made me all this while, Juana."

"Promise me you will be careful. It is a long way back, and there are *bandidos*—"

"I do not fear anything now. I know my way, Juana, and I shall find it safely. My God bless you, and may He keep you and protect you and give you an *esposo* who will look after you and love you, as you deserve."

He shouldered his saddlebag, turned for a last look at Juana, and then strode out of the cantina. He went to the roan mare, saddled her, mounted, and with a long sigh headed her toward the northeast. The sun was hot, the sky was cloudless, and the blue water was serene and glistening with facets of light from the midday sun. It was a day very much like that day when he had come to Mazatlán. Only now, Ramón Hernandez knew, he had been delivered from hell through a purgatory back into life. He would welcome this second chance, and not waste it. Yes, he told himself, as he turned in the saddle for a last look at the little cantina, he could now even bring himself to think of Rita Galloway with a kind of bitter resignation, his anger tempered by patience. Putting a hand over his eyes and glancing up at the sun, he murmured, "I thank You, *mi Padre*, for leading me to Juana—that kind woman who was Your own angel of mercy and who has restored me to my family." He made the sign of the cross, and then he rode on, his eyes fixed on the road ahead.

Chapter Thirty-Eight

It was a hot afternoon in late September, and as Rhea Penrock walked to her vegetable garden, preparing to pick the last tomatoes for canning, she thought that she had never been happier, or at least, had known no such contentment since her marriage to the young outlaw, Gabe Penrock—brief and marred though it had been. Now, nearly two years after she had abducted young Gatita Hernandez from Windhaven Range, she lived the most placid and predictable of lives. Her only devotion and obligation—her only purpose for being, indeed— was to care for the five-year-old girl to whom she had become so intensely attached.

She had by now come to feel thoroughly at home in the old farmhouse near Preston, Kansas, that she had taken over almost two years earlier, adding comfortable furniture and planting a garden. The dwelling might well have been a palace, such was the comfort Rhea had found there. Gatita was a partner in the bucolic enterprise: When Rhea worked the garden, plowing the rows for the vegetables, the playful girl pranced along, laughing, finding pleasure in the sudden sight of a grasshopper leaping high over a furrow or a butterfly taking to wing, and her comments and observations brightened each new day.

The monotony of these chores would, some years back, have chafed Rhea to boredom and even anger; strangely, with Gatita as her constant companion, she actually looked forward to the work. The citizens of Preston had quite readily accepted her. They did not question her story that her dead brother's wife had run off and abandoned the little girl, and that Rhea had undertaken to bring her up because there was no one else who would look after her.

The winter of 1881–82 had been not nearly as severe as the preceding years, and thanks to her frugality and her ability to get along on very little for herself, Rhea had stretched the money she had taken from Jeb Cornish's body far beyond what she had originally estimated it would last.

Still, the horizon had not been without its occasional cloud. Last mid-March in this year of 1882, it was Gatita's birthday, and Rhea had baked a cake and put five tiny candles on it. She lit them and then urged Gatita to blow them out and make a wish without saying it aloud.

The black-haired, dark-eyed, pretty little girl had taken a deep breath and then, leaning toward the cake, blown them all out with a single puff. "Sweetheart, you did it!" Rhea exulted. "Now what did you wish for? It's all right, you can tell me now."

"Well, Auntie Rhea, I wished you could be my mommy— you're so nice, and I love you so much," Gatita had said. Her charming heart-shaped face was radiant, and she turned to Rhea with adoring eyes.

The striking young widow had inwardly winced. The child's innocent remark had reminded her that she was, assuredly, not Gatita's mother, nor ever would be. Not only that, if she ever did return the child to her rightful mother, what could she expect in return? A trial and probably being led to the scaffold at dawn some morning, the black hood over her face, the noose around her neck, shuddering and praying as she waited for the sheriff to give the signal that would spring the trap. No, she could not yet part with Gatita; in a sense, the child was her hostage against ill fortune.

After a moment's reflection, she had answered, forcing an endearing smile to her lips, "That's very sweet of you, darling. I'd love to be your real mother, I truly would, but I don't think it's going to be possible. I'll tell you what—you can have another wish. Think about it and then tell me what it is you want."

Gatita had closed her eyes, screwing up her pretty face in absorption, and Rhea had laughed softly, for it was an enchanting sight. Finally, the little girl said, "All right, Auntie Rhea, I thought of something else. I'd awfully much like a brand new doll, a friend for the one you made before."

"Why, honey, that's easy. I'll start making you a new doll

tonight. Right now it's time to cut the cake, and you can have an extra large piece because it's your birthday.''

"Oh, goody! You're so good to me! I love you so much!'' the child gleefully exclaimed. Rhea moved near her, and Gatita sprang up from her seat, flung her arms around the slim young woman, and gave her a big hug.

Rhea trembled, and her eyes moistened. No one—perhaps not even her husband, who had been direct and forthright—had shown her so much tenderness, so much devotion and respect. It was a new experience for this woman who had been hardened by the adversities of a life not of her own choosing or making. Gatita's unwavering acceptance of her had, with each new day, begun to lessen the fiercely hostile and vindictive outlook that had driven Rhea Penrock almost from the day she was born.

That evening, true to her word, after she had put the little girl to bed and told her a bedtime story—"Little Red Riding Hood" and "Jack and the Beanstalk" were Gatita's favorites, of which she never tired—Rhea began to make a doll out of some red cotton dress material, black buttons, and cornstalks, which she ingeniously sewed together and then painted with bits of charcoal and crayons she had bought at the general store in Preston.

In the morning, when Gatita came down for breakfast in her dainty cotton flannel nightgown, she saw the doll at her place and stood wide-eyed and speechless with wonder and delight. Then she seized the doll with one hand and ran to Rhea. "Oh, thank you, Auntie Rhea, thank you so much! It's just beautiful! It's the best doll I ever had in all my life, honest it is!''

On this very day, Mara Hernandez—now forty-five, her hair almost all gray from the anguish and grief caused by the loss of her child—went into the chapel on Windhaven Range. There, alone, she knelt before the altar, clasped her hands, bowed her head, and prayed aloud. "Oh, Blessed Virgin Mother, oh, Mary full of grace, Thou who gave Thine only Son to the world to die upon the cross for the redemption of man's sins, hear my prayer. Ramón and my youngest child, the last child I shall ever bear, are gone from me. I pray You to intercede for me. If Ramón has offended our dear God, do forgive him, for he did so out of sorrow, and my sorrow, as

384

well. He is only mortal, as all of us are, dust and ashes in Thy holy sight. I will make no promises or pledges, but You, Holy Mother, know full well that I believe unswervingly in You and Your divine Son and Him who is Lord of all of us. I ask only pardon for Ramón, and I ask that Gatita not be punished for either my sins or Ramón's. Grant that I may see them both again before I die.''

Tears streaked her cheeks as she crossed herself, and then she wept silently. She thought to herself, *Oh, God, where is she? Does that horrible woman still have her? Or is she dead, perhaps from some sickness, or from maltreatment? God, hear me! Let Gatita not be harmed or scarred or maimed, or in any way blemished by what has been done to her, for she surely is innocent in Your divine sight.*

She rose slowly, her shoulders shaking with her weeping, and she moved out of the church and headed back to the house. Her heart was heavy, filled with sorrow at the loss of her child—and her husband. She did not know if she would ever see either one of them again. . . .

A furious howling suddenly reached her ears, coming from over by the bunkhouse. She heard Robert Markey calling to his dog. "Tramp! Stop it! What are you barking at anyway, you silly creature? There's nothing there, can't you see? No one's—"

The cowboy stopped in midsentence as his eyes lit on what the dog's keener senses had already perceived. "Oh, my God! Mrs. Hernandez! Come here, quick! Look, over by the south gate. . . .''

"*Ramón!*" The one word feebly escaped her throat, and she clapped her hand over her mouth, as if fearing that were she to say anything more, the image of her husband would vanish, that what she was seeing was no more than a cruel illusion. But the figure came steadily onward, growing larger by the seconds. Mara gathered up her skirt and ran toward her husband, stumbling every now and again in her haste to reach him.

Ramón spotted his wife and steered his mare toward her, urging the tired animal to one last gallop. A few yards remained between husband and wife when Ramón pulled on the reins and leaped down from his horse, running to swoop Mara up in his arms.

"*Querida!* Oh, my beloved one!" he hoarsely whispered.

Mara silenced him with kisses, her hands tenderly holding his head, stroking his hair. They clung tightly to each other, saying nothing, for a long time.

At last Ramón held his wife back at arm's length, studying her face. That she had forgiven him, was overjoyed to have him home, was evident. Evident, also, was her now dashed hope that when he returned, he would have their daughter with him.

"I am sorry, *querida*. I have caused you great grief, and it was all for nothing."

"Hush, my darling. Don't say that. I know that you had to do what you did. I am grateful that no harm befell you and that you are now home safe and sound. One day, if God so wills . . ."

"He must!" Ramón replied, almost fiercely. "And He will. We must believe in His goodness and His compassion. That is something that I for too long forgot."

That evening at dinner, their other children—Luke, Jaime, Dolores, and Edward—plied their father with dozens of questions. Ramón patiently answered them all, telling them about his adventures, his travels.

"One of these days," he promised, "we will all go down to Mazatlán and I will show you the Pacific Ocean, the likes of which you cannot imagine."

Unspoken by the children was the question of whether Gatita, too, would take this trip with them. They all carefully held their tongues, reveling only in the joy they felt at their father's return. And just as the children intuitively knew that to speak of their missing sister would cast a pall on this homecoming, so Ramón knew that he would never say anything about Juana Perez. She would be nothing more than a wonderful memory for him and him alone until the day he died.

After they had all eaten, the entire family went over to the hacienda to visit with Lucien Edmond and Maxine Bouchard. Earlier that afternoon, Ramón and Lucien Edmond had met briefly, but Lucien Edmond realized that Ramón was anxious to be reunited with his children, and did not keep his brother-in-law long.

Maxine now threw her arms around Ramón the moment he walked in the door, and then, with her arms around Ramón and Mara's waists, she led them into the parlor while the children tagged behind.

The Bouchards asked nearly the same questions that Ramón's children had, and he again patiently answered them all. Later, when it was time for the children to be put to bed, Mara escorted them back home, leaving Ramón to linger with Lucien Edmond.

Lucien Edmond poured his brother-in-law a glass of port wine, but—as he had done earlier—Ramón refused. "I am ashamed to say that I became a lowly drunk," Ramón explained. "When I had recovered my senses, I made a promise to myself that I will drink no spirits until Gatita is returned to us. You see, I am afraid that I will be moved by my grief to drink more than is good for me."

"I understand. But tell me, is your grief as strong as ever, my friend?" Lucien Edmond asked, a concerned look on his face.

Ramón thought a long moment before he replied. "It is a curious thing, Lucien Edmond. . . . I now grieve only for the time that we have lost together, my daughter and I, for in my heart I know that God will return her to us."

"What about your search for Rita Galloway?" Lucien Edmond cautiously asked.

For just a brief moment, Ramón's eyes flared with anger, but then he replied, "A good friend of mine—a friend I made down in Mazatlán—made me see that living in the grip of an obsession was doing *me* more harm than anyone. It has kept me from all those I hold dearest to me. It has been a spell that I have cast over myself. Yes, I suppose I do still hate that woman for what she has done, but I know I must be patient and let events take their course. For the moment, what is done is done, and in the end I want only to have my child returned."

Chapter Thirty-Nine

"Good morning, Mr. Ellerton," Rhea Penrock greeted the slim, aging head of the Preston National Bank who, seeing her enter the door, had held it open for her.

"And to you, Miss Penrock," the man replied cordially.

"I'm afraid I have to make another withdrawal from my account—but I need to know what my balance is." Rhea gave him a winning smile. "You see, there's been a lot of trouble over my poor brother's estate with the probate court, and with some lawyer who's trying to defend my brother's faithless wife—"

"Tsk, tsk." The banker shook his head and clucked sympathetically. "I know exactly how it can be with those slick Eastern shysters. Well, Miss Penrock," the banker said, chuckling at his own wit, "you're not the only one interested in withdrawing money. We had a holdup here last week."

"You did?" Rhea was dumbfounded.

"That's right," Silas Ellerton declared, a note of disbelief in his voice. "I wouldn't have thought that our little town would be of interest to bank robbers, but sure enough, there were two fellows in here last Thursday, just around closing time. One of them held a big Colt on us, and the other told my teller to put all the money he could in a sack, or else. Well now," the banker shrugged, "I learned a long time ago not to argue with a man when I was on the short end of a gun." He paused, then said, "I hope you don't find this too upsetting, a woman of your fine character. Perhaps I should say no more—"

"Oh, no, please—I want to hear," Rhea replied.

"Well," the banker went on, "as luck would have it . . . you know Mr. Dansworth, the owner of the general store here?

388

"Yes, I—I know him, Mr. Ellerton."

"Anyway, his daughter, Penelope—just seventeen—poor gal, she came in to make a deposit right after the robbers did, and the man with the Colt, he got nervous, turned halfway around, and fired. She got it in the shoulder. Could have been a lot worse."

"My God!" Rhea ejaculated. "What happened then?"

"Well, not much we didn't expect. The man who had the sack full of cash cussed out the man with the gun for shooting, then the two of them skedaddled. They had horses tethered outside, and they got away before the sheriff could do a darn thing. They got about three thousand dollars—but we made enough profit this year when the farmers paid us back from last year's loans, so we didn't suffer too much."

"That was lucky."

"But here I am, talking a blue streak and forgetting why you've come here, Miss Penrock. Oh, Mr. Kinderson!" He said this to a bespectacled middle-aged clerk who was behind the window nearest the door.

The teller looked up. "Yes, Mr. Ellerton?"

"Please tell Miss Penrock what her balance is." Then, with a beaming smile, he turned to Rhea. "If there's anything else we can do to help you here, please let me know."

"That's very kind of you, Mr. Ellerton. Thank you very much." Rhea was badly shaken by the news of the holdup, but she took pains not to show it.

She stood at the window while the teller went through his files. After a moment or two of computation, he said, "The balance now is two hundred eighteen dollars and ninety-three cents, Miss Penrock, interest compounded and all. That's it right now, as of this minute."

"I'm much obliged to you. Thank you so much. Now, I'd like to withdraw fifty dollars, please."

"My pleasure, ma'am."

When Rhea left the bank, her face was taut with her inner reflection. She was thinking to herself, *My God, I know Penelope! She was just plain lucky she didn't get killed. If she'd been a few inches one way or another, she might have been. And those two men, they didn't care a hoot what happened to anybody so long as they got what they wanted— hard cash. My God! Gabe was an outlaw just like those two men—and he wouldn't have cared at all if some innocent*

389

person had suffered so long as he would gain by it. And here I thought he was the best man that ever crossed my path. . . . Well, I guess maybe he was, at the time. Oh, what have I done? What have I made of my life, and what have I done to poor Gatita?

She had left the little girl in the general store after giving Gatita two pennies for candy. Rhea walked across the street and entered the store, grinning to see the child perched on the counter, watching intently as Mr. Darnsworth counted his change. The sight of the money abruptly brought Rhea back to reality. Two hundred-some dollars! That would never get them through the rest of this year. She needed to buy more sides of beef, and there were still so many things that needed repair or replacement at the old house. She'd put them off hoping that somehow there'd be more money.

Well, there wasn't. And she realized that she had to make a decision and make it rather quickly.

She made some small purchases, then gathered up the child. As soon as Rhea got into the buggy and began to drive it back to the farmhouse, Gatita piped up, "Mr. Dansworth's real nice. He gave me extra candy—look!"

Rhea turned to send the little girl a warm smile, but her thoughts continued, unabated, and she could not suppress them. They crowded into her mind as if they were a voice of conscience talking to her, demanding answers. *I know what Ramón and Mara Hernandez and the Bouchards must think of me. They must think I'm worse than a murderess. God, what have I done? I hate myself for putting this sweet little kid through such a hard life, taking her away from her folks.*

"You're so quiet, Auntie Rhea," the child spoke up, tugging at Rhea's free arm.

"I know, honey. You'll have to excuse me. I'm doing a lot of thinking because I have to decide what we're going to do this winter."

"I wish I had someone else to play with," Gatita continued. "You're lots of fun, but you don't want to play all the time."

"Not when there's work to be done and nobody else to do it, darling. That's why a girl's mother—" She bit her lip.

She went on thinking inwardly, while mechanically smiling at Gatita as the child pointed out this or that landmark along the road back. *The really worst thing about all of this and something I didn't consider when I went through with my plan, is that I love her—I mean, I really love her, just as if she were my own flesh and blood.*

They reached the farmhouse; Rhea got out of the buggy and lifted the little girl down, hugging and kissing her. The gloomy thoughts persisted, and she could not shake them. *Back to this run-down old house. Sure, I've spent a lot of money fixing it up, and it got us through all these months without any major disasters. But it's out in the middle of nowhere, and I hardly know a soul out here. We've had maybe three or four neighborly calls since we came in here, and that's not fair to Gatita. If I hadn't taken her away from her folks, she'd have her brothers and sisters around and all the other kids down on that ranch, and all the advantages and easy life—instead of having to work and help me out here doing these chores. Oh, sure, we've made a game of it, but it's not right for a kid her age.*

That evening, having put the child to sleep following a dinner of eggs and a bit of bacon, an ear of sweet corn, and a fruit tart, Rhea Penrock sat watching the little girl as she slept to one side of the bed, hugging her doll to her, a beatific smile on her innocent, piquant face. She stared at Gatita with a longing that brought her close to tears, and there were lines in her forehead as she contemplated her surroundings.

The prospect of another winter in this desolate farmhouse was hardly encouraging. There was no future here; it would lead to nothing; it would only be further hardship for the little girl who had done nothing to warrant such harsh living conditions.

She rose, rolled a cigarette, and lit it. As she struck the match, the light illuminated her tense, brooding features, making her, in some ways, look lovelier than she ever had before. For in her deep gray eyes there was no longer hatred or the glow of vengeance or a sneering look of derision; rather, conversely, there was deep concern and love as she watched Gatita asleep with her doll.

She puffed nervously at the cigarette and paced the floor. Her thoughts crowded in upon her, and outside, except for the chirping of the crickets and the soft calls of the night birds, there was a stillness that augmented these thoughts and made them come more vividly into her mind: *If I take her back, the first thing that Ramón Hernandez and his wife will do, and I'm pretty sure that Lucien Edmond Bouchard and his wife will be on their side to do it, will be to have me arrested and sent to trial. They'll probably hang me for keeping this poor little kid away from her folks—not to mention Cornish's murder.*

Again, she began to pace the floor, like a cat, softly and subtly, her hackles rising at the thought of danger. She paused to look for a long moment at the sleeping child, then uttered a deep, heartfelt sigh.

She turned, put the cigarette out in a small clay bowl, and walked over to the bed. She knelt down and very gently stroked Gatita's cheek. The child murmured in her sleep, automatically hugging the doll even closer to her. Rhea tightened her lips, but there were tears in her eyes. She thought to herself, *You're becoming as straight as a schoolmarm, Rhea Penrock!* She leaned over and kissed Gatita's little ear, then stroked her hair and abruptly turned and strode out of the old farmhouse into the night.

There was a full moon, and it shone down on the rows of cornstalks and the small garden. But beyond, there was nothing but the bleak loneliness of the level Kansas plain, ground that had frustrated many a would-be farmer from the East, unprepared for the desolate isolation of his farm and his lack of proximity to any neighbors.

She looked up at the sky and at the moon. It sent down a warm glow, and it touched her face with silver. There was a softness and tenderness and a vulnerability to her features, which had never been before. Even Gabe Penrock, if he had been alive, would not have recognized her at this moment. It seemed as if she were transfigured, caught in the web of her own devising, for she had fallen in love with Gatita, and she could do nothing about it. Because of that, the voice of her conscience, wakened now after this long while when she had had time enough to retrospect to see the folly of her act, began to gnaw at her with an insistence that would no longer be denied.

She called out loud in her torment, "I know, dammit, I know! What am I going to do?" She started crying, tears running unchecked down her face, and looking up at the moon again, she whispered, "What are we going to do? What in the world are we going to do about this?"

She lit still another cigarette, impatient with herself for yielding to such a show of nervousness. Hitherto, she had always been cool and secure, poised; as Jeb Cornish had once said, "a little bitch who knows exactly what she's going to do and where she's going all the time." That remark had been carried back to her by Gabe himself, who had been told it by one of his cronies. And she had laughed, sidling up to her young husband, winding her arms around him, and huskily whispering, "That's right, especially when I'm with you."

She remembered that now, and she laughed softly and bitterly to herself. Far off, a coyote bayed, and she burst into a nervous flurry of sobs as she said aloud to herself, talking as one might to give oneself false courage while walking from a cemetery, "I was as lonely as that damn coyote out there. I've had nothing but bad luck all my life—starting with that damn river pirate who killed my mother, forcing me into prostitution. I settled his hash, just the way I did Cornish's. But suppose all that hadn't happened to me . . . suppose my mama had been born in a nice decent house, and I'd had a father and brothers and sisters and grown up the way Gatita did? I wouldn't have been like this; I never would have come out here and married Gabe Penrock. I would have steered clear of conniving louses like Cornish. But that's the only life I know—and I don't want it any more! Oh, my God, won't You show me the way to go, tell me what to do, if You're really up there the way the Good Book says?"

She sank down on her knees, covering her face with her hands, and sobbed. She did not recognize herself; she'd never done anything like this before. She did not know that she was weeping for her lost youth, for the innocence, for the childhood she had never had, for all the happiness that had been denied her, for the brutal way she had been forced to live, which had turned her natural feminine inclinations and instincts toward vengeance, even at the cost of a little child's life and happiness.

It purged her; it was cathartic, that hysterical fit of weeping, so unlike the cool and undaunted young woman who had stared down all the lustful desperados of Cornish's band and dared them to try something with her. Now she was vulnerable, now she was human and frail, and she knew her weaknesses.

But there was no sign, no flash of lightening or rumble of thunder, no sudden wind, no burning bush, and no miracle to tell her that He to whom she had addressed her first real prayer of her entire life had heard and recognized her need. Nor did she or could she expect such a reply. Wearily, she got to her feet and trudged back to the farmhouse. Before she opened the door, she said aloud, "I guess that's what life is. You get a lot of hard knocks, you try to give a few back, and then you're stuck. Maybe that's the way it's planned up there. . . ." She glanced up at the serene sky. "Well, whatever, we'll just have to play things by ear and see what happens. I don't know where we're going yet, but I know only one thing: We can't stay on here in Preston much longer. I'll think of something. I'll *have* to."

Chapter Forty

By the beginning of October of this year of 1882, Rhea
Penrock's bank balance had fallen to eighty-six dollars and
forty-one cents for two reasons. One of the horses she had
been riding and harnessing to the buckboard had died
unexpectedly, and part of the roof had begun to collapse. She
had purchased a sturdy black gelding, three years old, which
had cost her nearly fifty dollars, and it had been necessary to
employ two itinerant workers to replace the sagging roof of
the farmhouse, at a cost of another fifty dollars. This made
her come to grips with the impossibility of her situation: She
and Gatita would never be able to exist through the winter
with a stake of under a hundred dollars.

And so, dressing Gatita in her prettiest blue cotton dress,
dainty shoes, and stockings, Rhea drove into Preston to confer with Silas Ellerton.

"Good to see you again, Miss Penrock. Mighty warm
autumn, this one, isn't it?" The banker mopped his brow
with a crisp white handkerchief.

"It certainly is, Mr. Ellerton." She paused a moment to
gather her thoughts, then declared, "I'm thinking about leaving Preston, Mr. Ellerton. I thought maybe you could give me
some advice."

"Oh, I'm sorry to hear that, Miss Penrock. Why don't you
step into my office, and we'll talk a bit?" he suggested.
During the past months, Rhea had made two trips into Preston
to purchase supplies and had stopped at the bank to withdraw
funds. On each occasion, Silas Ellerton had made a fuss over
her, making her curious about his unexpected attention.

Once inside his office, Rhea learned the reason. After
offering Rhea a seat, the banker proceeded immediately to

speak in a serious tone. "Miss Penrock, I don't know if I've got any right to say anything to you, but now that you said you need advice and you're thinking of leaving our fair town, would you mind if I said something quite personal?"

"Not at all. Say what's on your mind, Mr. Ellerton."

Silas Ellerton grinned mechanically, then cleared his throat portentiously. "Erhummph. Miss Penrock, as I understand it, this little girl you've been looking after is your deceased brother's child?"

"That's right, Mr. Ellerton."

"Well now, and if I remember rightly, you said that his wife took off and left him and can't be found anywhere?"

"That's also true. That's why I brought my niece up, because I loved my brother."

"And it does you great credit, Miss Penrock—indeed it does. Great credit. Er—ahhumph!" Again, Ellerton cleared his throat, and then, lowering his voice and leaning forward, he said, "I wonder now, ma'am . . . I'm a widower, myself, you see. I've been alone out here in this town about twenty years. It's a hard life to be alone. It's true I'm fifty-six, and you're probably half my age or thereabouts, but . . . well, I'd be mighty proud if you'd consent to marrying me. Now I probably know what you're going to say, but think it over a mite. I'd be devoted to you, and you wouldn't have to worry about money, and I'd like to take care of your niece. As you can tell, I'm much too old to want to start a family now, but if I marry you, I'd already have a family ready-made, so to speak. Well now, you'll forgive me for getting right to the point, but I think a man should always do that, don't you?"

Rhea did not know whether to laugh or cry. She certainly had no desire to insult the earnest and kindly banker, and so, with a sincere smile on her lips, she murmured, "It's very kind and most flattering of you to say you want to marry me. But you don't know anything about me, Mr. Ellerton—and more importantly, I don't want to live in Preston any more." She began to improvise quickly. "You see, I had a friend, and I thought he was going to marry me. But he went off with another woman, just the way my brother's wife went off with another man. Well, since then I've learned to enjoy my independence, and I want to make my own way in the world."

"That's quite understandable, I have to admit."

"So it wouldn't be fair of me to wish myself on you just because I don't have a means of support. Besides, I'd like to get back to a bigger town. I have to find some way of earning a living. You know yourself there's no work here in Preston."

"That's true, Miss Penrock. I'm sorry to say, but the town is just about dead, right now. No cattle are coming to market, no cowhands on a drive—it's mighty tough, and a lot of the farmers are going to have trouble this year making their payments to this bank—I can tell you that in all confidence."

"So now you understand my position, Mr. Ellerton."

"You're a smart woman, my dear. I knew that from the first moment you walked in here and deposited your money. I said to myself, 'Silas Ellerton, this is a fine woman, an upstanding woman, and she's chosen you to handle her money, all her capital in life. And I, Silas Ellerton, am going to see to it that her savings are handled properly.' Yes, ma'am, that's exactly what I said to myself."

"Again, that's very kind of you. But I was wondering—" Rhea thought quickly, and then went on. "Is there some sort of home for women and children who don't have any money or any relatives or anything? A place to stay temporarily until a job is found?"

"Now that you mention it, I seem to recollect that there is one. A fellow riding into Preston last week brought me a copy of the *Wichita Blade*. There's a story there—yes, I remember it now because what you just said reminded me of it. The Quakers in Wichita have started a sort of settlement house, you might call it, where they'll take a woman and her children in and give them food and shelter and they don't charge a penny."

"That's wonderful! You understand, Mr. Ellerton, I'm not seeking charity. But I want to find the right sort of job for myself so I can make a good home for Gatita. I'll call on this place you just mentioned."

"You do that, and I'm sure they'll take good care of you. Quakers are good people, Miss Penrock."

"I wonder if you still have the newspaper, Mr. Ellerton," Rhea pursued.

"I believe I do, ma'am." The banker scratched his head, screwing up his face in an attempt to remember. "We don't often see Wichita papers here, and I wanted to read it all and see what was happening around that part of Kansas. Now, where did I put it?'' He rose and walked over to his file cabinet. "Sure enough, here it is, Miss Penrock! Take it along, if you like.''

"Oh, no, I know you want to read it. I'll just look at the article and find out the name of the place. Then I'll go to Wichita and make inquiries.''

"You wouldn't go wrong if you're dealing with Quakers, as I said, Miss Penrock.'' He gave her a wistful look. "Are you sure I can't change your mind about staying here? I mean, I know I'm no great shakes for looks, but I've got a nice house and money in this bank, and I'm solid here. And I'd be good to you and your niece.''

"That's really very kind of you, Mr. Ellerton. I certainly don't want to hurt your feelings. And your looks have nothing to do with it. You're a kind, decent man, and I know that you would treat me nicely. Only, as I said, I just can't stay any longer in this little town.''

"Yes, I understand. Well, no harm asking and no offense taken, I hope?''

"None in the world, Mr. Ellerton.'' She gave him a warm smile. Quickly looking at the newspaper article about the Quaker settlement, she saw that it mentioned Dr. Ben and Elone Wilson as the founders and went on to say that Dr. Wilson's wife had drawn contributions from the citizens of Wichita to offer a shelter for homeless women and children, regardless of race or religion. Rhea thought to herself that here was certainly a safe, if temporary, haven for her and Gatita until she could decide what was best for them. And if she finally decided to return the child to Ramón Hernandez and his wife, it would be very easy to send a wire or even a letter saying that the child could be found in this shelter, while she herself took off and put distance between her and the most likely vengeful father and mother.

She drew a deep breath and gave Ellerton another smile. "I think this is exactly what I've been looking for, Mr. Ellerton. So, I suppose I'll draw out the rest of my money now, and I'll go on to Wichita.'' Rhea stood up and offered her hand. "Thank you again for all your kindness. You've helped me a lot since I came to Preston, and I'll always value your friendship.''

Silas Ellerton warmly shook her hand, then rose from his desk. "I'll take you to the teller, Miss Penrock.'' He escorted her to the teller's cage, then said, "It's been good doing business with you, but . . . er . . . are you sure you won't change your mind? You know, about what I just said?"

She gave him a quick, warm smile and shook her head. "I'm afraid not. But you'll find someone who'll appreciate all you have to offer, Mr. Ellerton. I'm certain of it. You're a good-hearted man, and that's rare, believe me."

"It's kind of you to say that." He grinned at her, and the smile lit up his plain face. "Good luck to you, Miss Penrock. And stop in to say hello, if you're ever passing through."

Rhea Penrock walked out of the bank with the money in her reticule. Gatita had obediently remained in the buckboard all this time, but she was anxious, and the sight of Rhea made her cry out, "Auntie Rhea, are we all done now?"

"Not quite, honey. I've got to stop at the store and get a few things. Then we're going."

"We're going to leave here?"

"I told you that this morning, sweetheart. Yes. We're going to Wichita. I—I know someone there who'll take good care of us. And it's a lot nicer place than Preston."

"I'll miss the house . . . what about my dolls, Auntie Rhea?" the child anxiously demanded.

Rhea smiled, stroked the child's head, and then leaned over to kiss her on the cheek. "I wouldn't think of leaving the dolls here, honey. We'll go home first and pack up our things. But you know what? When we get to Wichita, I'm going to buy you the best doll I can find there. It'll be just like a real baby—much nicer than the ones I had to make from scratch."

"But I like the ones you made for me, Auntie Rhea! I want to keep them."

"And you will, sweetheart. But you'll have another one, a real special one."

"Oh, golly, Auntie Rhea! I can't wait!" Gatita looked up at the slim young woman with expectation shining in her eyes.

Chapter Forty-One

Eight years earlier, Wichita had been the leading beef shipping center in Kansas, and as many as two hundred thousand cattle and two thousand cowboys entered its boundaries during the summer months. But as more and more farmers settled in Wichita and decided that they wanted law and order, cattle had given way to other markets. It was an ideal trading center. Government contracts were negotiated, and farm tools were sold in abundance. Families came to live in Wichita knowing of its safety, as compared with the border towns and the frontier vistas where lawlessness reigned.

It was a full two days' journey from Preston to Wichita, but the weather was fairly mild and dry, as Kansas generally was this time of year. For Gatita's sake, Rhea Penrock was making a game of their move, just as she had previously done. Of the money she had drawn out of the bank, she carefully set aside fifty dollars for absolute survival, and with the balance bought a few foodstuffs for the journey, for they would camp out until they reached Wichita. Rhea also bought some presents for the child: a pretty dress in a blue-and-white checkered pattern and some new shoes and stockings, as well. Nor did she forget Gatita's sweet tooth—she purchased a large bag of penny candy, ranging in variety from licorice whips to jawbreakers.

The storekeeper made Gatita a present of a bag of marbles and some crayons, as well as a tablet on which the child could draw to her heart's content. He and his daughter wished Rhea and Gatita well, and—as had the banker—told her to stop in and visit again.

Rhea was touched by this show of affection and told the storekeeper and his daughter that she was sorry to be leaving

Preston; however, it was important that she be able to find a job so she could give her brother's little girl a home where she could have every advantage in comfort and education. After a final goodbye, she helped Gatita into the buckboard, took up the reins, and drove down the main street of Preston for the last time.

Silas Ellerton came out of his bank to bid her farewell and looked wistfully after her. His secret wish was that, at the last moment, she might succumb to the security he could offer her and remain in Preston as his wife. A few years ago, Rhea would have laughed in his face after hearing his awkward, ingenuous but sincere proposal; yet when she smiled back at him this afternoon, she felt a curious wave of sentimentality come over her, along with a rueful remembrance of her past.

Of late, she had had dreams and recollections of the lurid events that had channeled her into the life she had led and whose final effect was to motivate her in a vindictive, hateful desire for vengeance against Ramón Hernandez. Now, she was filled with contrition and with a gloomy presentiment that not only would she have to give the child up forever—which she had already resolved to do when the time was propitious— but also, when that moment came, forfeit her own life to the law.

As she turned the horses down the road toward Wichita, she looked back in the direction of the old farmhouse. There it stood—its beams sturdy, the roof shingled, ready for another winter. It was comfortable, and the second-hand furniture she had bought and taken such excellent care of would serve some other refugee in time of need. Indeed, she had mentioned this to both Silas Ellerton and the storekeeper, suggesting that if any new settlers came to Preston and did not have enough money for materials to build a house, those men recommend the use of the farmhouse that had served her and Gatita so well all these happy, idyllic months.

All that time, Rhea had fulfilled the roles of mother, of solicitous companion, of nurse, and of protector. Since her previous life had inured her to hardships, to violence, and to the worst forms of debauchery—having grown up in a bordello would compel any woman to adopt a callous outlook, if she hoped to survive—Rhea had barely known what it was to give and receive affection, save for her brief marriage to Gabe Penrock. But this existence with Gatita had softened her, ameliorated the harshness of her nature, her cunning suspicions, and her easy hatreds. When Gatita turned to her and anxiously asked, "Is it a long way to where we're going, Auntie Rhea?" Rhea uttered a soft, almost silent sigh and then, smiling at the charming little girl beside her, declared, "Not really, darling. We'll camp out—we'll have picnics under the stars—and we'll be there in about two days. It'll be a fine place, and there'll be lots of other children for you to play with. I know it's been lonesome for you."

"What is Wichita like, do you know?"

"It's a big city compared with Preston. There're lots of nice people there. And there are Quakers."

"What's a Quaker, Auntie Rhea?" Gatita asked, wide-eyed, with curiosity.

Rhea frowned, trying to find an explanation that would not be too difficult for the child to understand. Finally, she said, "Well, honey, a Quaker is somebody who doesn't believe in fighting, who doesn't ever carry a weapon. You know, cowboys go around with guns in their holsters, so they can fight if they have to."

"I know. In case they have to fight Injuns and outlaws, right?"

"Yes, that's right, dear. But the Quakers would never use guns because they don't believe in hurting people. And if someone hurts *them*, they just pray for them. They're very kind, good people. And they love children."

"As much as you love me, Auntie Rhea?"

That naive question tore at Rhea's heart. She looked at her and was irked at herself because tears had sprung to her eyes.

She replied softly, "Yes, honey, they'll love you just as much as I do, you wait and see. My, you're a little chatterbox this afternoon. Oh, look—the sun is starting to set. Why don't you watch for a good spot where we can camp and have our picnic. Then you can play with your dolly, and I'll tell you a story before you go to sleep."

"That'll be fun! I love your stories!"

"I'm glad. It's a good feeling to make the ones you love happy—" She hadn't meant to let that slip out, but she wasn't sorry. She looked almost defiantly up at the sky, as if to say, *I hope I haven't hurt her. I know it won't count for much in the final score—and I've done a lot of things I'm ashamed of now—but I love this little girl. Please, God, if I have to be punished, don't let Gatita know. That's all I ask of you.*

As the sun began to sink lower, Rhea looked around to find a safe place for camping. Suddenly she was conscious, as she had never been before, of the dependency of this little girl upon her—that someone else's life was inescapably linked with hers, and that her own conduct might well jeopardize that other, precious life. Gatita might get severely chilled, or—who knows—maybe there were wolves around here. . . .

As it began to grow dark, Rhea saw the light of a nearby farmhouse and decided that rather than camp outdoors, it would be much wiser, considering the ever-present danger of a sudden change in temperature or even a sandstorm—a phenomenon that had plagued many a cattle drive in this part of the country—to seek shelter for the night. She had money to pay for it, she was surely presentable, and the child would reassure these strangers that she was not a decoy for some bandit gang. She still had the derringer she had taken from Cornish's body, and this she had tucked into the wide pocket of her brown cotton jacket and covered with a kerchief, so that it would be handy in the event of some unforeseen danger. What she feared on this ride with Gatita some sixty miles between Preston and Wichita was the sudden appearance on the lonely road of some cowhands or desperados who, seeing an attractive young woman traveling alone with a five-year-old girl, would conclude that she was prey for the taking.

She drove the buckboard up to the farmhouse, got down and tethered the reins of the geldings to a hitching post, and then lifted down Gatita. "Maybe we'll stop here for the night," she murmured to the child.

"Aren't we going to have a picnic, like you promised, Auntie Rhea?"

"Well, honey, I really wanted to, but . . . I'll tell you what—we'll have an extra-big one tomorrow noon. You see, I don't know of any place to camp around here, and there might be coyotes and wolves and all sorts of things. So it would be better to have a nice warm bed to sleep in tonight. You'll see."

"All right," Gatita drowsily murmured. The long ride in the fresh air had tired her out early. Also, her young mind had much to digest: She was suddenly moving away from one place, a place she had come to love, to go to a mysterious place called Wichita, about which she knew absolutely nothing—except that there were something called Quakers there.

Taking Gatita's hand, Rhea walked to the door of the farmhouse and knocked. After a few moments, it was opened by a stocky, gray-bearded farmer who at first glared at her, then, seeing the child, relaxed his homely features into what passed for a smile. "Can I help you, ma'am?"

"My name is Rhea Penrock, sir, and this is my niece. I'm on my way to Wichita with her, to find refuge with the Quakers. I was wondering—I've money, so could we pay for dinner and a place to sleep, if we wouldn't put you out too much?"

"Of course we'll help you out, dear," came a woman's pleasant voice. Emerging from the kitchen, the farmer's stout wife came forward. A smile was on her face, and seeing Gatita, she at once squatted down and held out her arms, saying, "Come here, child. What's your name?"

"It's Gatita," the child proudly replied, somewhat shyly stepping back a little and reaching out for Rhea's hand.

"Gatita—that sounds sort of Spanish," the farmer declared.

"It's my name, mister."

"I see. All right. Well then, come in. You've tied your horses and your buckboard to the hitching post, I see. I'll take them around to my stable. You go in and freshen up a bit and chat with my wife, Della. Fact is, we were just about to sit down to dinner, and you're welcome to share it with us."

"That's very kind of you, sir."

"Name's McFarland, Miz Penrock," the farmer called over his shoulder as he went outside, untethered the reins of the geldings, and led them toward the stable at the back of the small frame house.

Della McFarland beckoned the two into the house and showed Rhea to a room off the kitchen, where she might wash her hands in a bowl of water and dry them on a fresh towel. Rhea took Gatita and gently sponged the child's face, which helped waken the little girl.

After they were all seated at the kitchen table, the farmer said grace, and his wife served them stewed chicken, mashed potatoes, corn on the cob, and hot biscuits. For dessert, there was coffee and blueberry pie with whipped cream. Gatita was

404

given milk, and Rhea, an arm around the child's shoulders, made a game of urging her to drink it all down.

"You're going to Wichita, you say, Miz Penrock?" the farmer asked Rhea.

"That's right. I've heard the Quakers there take in women and children who don't have homes. I've taken care of my niece for almost two years—she was appointed my ward because my brother's wife abandoned him, and then he died—but what money I have won't last too much longer." Gatita, who had heard this tale several times before, never understood what Rhea meant by those strange words and so didn't contradict the story. Further, after all this time, she had only a dim memory of her real family and never asked after her mother and father anymore.

"That's just dreadful!" the pleasant-faced wife sympathetically put in, shaking her head and uttering a sigh of lamentation. "Now my husband—" here she gave the farmer an endearing look—"has abided by the Ten Commandments all of his life—even from the time we went to school together. Although he did dip my braids in the inkwell."

"That's right, Miz Penrock," the farmer chortled. "That was the start of our sparking."

"My! You've spent a good many years together," Rhea exclaimed. "Do you have children of your own?"

The woman's face fell. "We had a daughter—many, many years ago—but she died of smallpox when she was barely old enough to walk. I could never have another, though Lord knows we tried—"

"Woman, hush! Such talk's not fit for strangers—begging your pardon, Miz Penrock," the farmer scowled at his wife.

"I'm sorry. I didn't mean to pry," Rhea apologized.

"No harm done, I'm sure," Della McFarland assured her, ignoring the look on her husband's face. "I must say, when I saw your niece standing there in the doorway, I immediately took to her. She seems so sweet, and she has such a lovely smile."

The farmer looked at his wife, who was now staring at Gatita.

Rhea felt tears sting her eyes. Here was a couple who loved children, yet who could not have them. By the odds of chance, by her own selfish and hateful will, she had stumbled upon what these good, decent people would never have: the love of a child for her, who was least worthy of such love.

She took a swallow of her coffee, and its bitter strength made her wince. Gatita, she noticed, had bowed her head in her arms and was almost fast asleep. Rhea's smile was that of a happy and fulfilled woman, though she did not see herself. But the farmer and his wife did and exchanged a knowing look, a look full of remorse and envy and yet of tender admiration.

Rhea felt compelled to say something to ease the tension that had suddenly sprung up around the kitchen table. "You know, folks, I've met a lot of people—good ones as well as riffraff. Now, you folks . . . well, obviously I've never met you till tonight, and yet I can see immediately that you love each other, and you've been true to each other all these years. So maybe even if you don't have children you're blessed, because you have each other. Lots of folks with children can't say that. They wind up hating each other, and they stay together only because of the kids."

The farmer stared at her. Then he turned to his wife and said, "Della, you know, Miz Penrock's right. And that's what it says in the Good Book, too. So maybe we weren't such failures after all."

"Of course you're not failures! You've each other, and you've this fine farm—and lots of folks around here respect you, I'm sure. You were kind to us—you let us in, and you didn't care about who we are. By the way, I want to pay for the meal and our shelter—"

"No, Miz Penrock, I wouldn't think of it; I wouldn't charge you a penny. Please don't say any more about it," the farmer insisted.

"All right, if that's the way you feel. God bless you." The phrase was strange on Rhea's lips, and yet it came swiftly. She looked down at the sleeping child. "I'd best take her off to bed now, before she wakes up. She might not be able to get back to sleep if she does."

"There's a spare room at the back, just to the right of the kitchen, Miz Penrock," the farmer offered. "You take her right in—and you go to sleep, too. Breakfast'll be ready when you get up. Come on, Della."

"I'd like to do the dishes, Mrs. McFarland," Rhea offered.
"Oh, land sakes no! That would be awfully rude of me to

let you do them. It was my pleasure having you and that sweet little girl here. Just you forget about the dishes. You get your niece and yourself off to bed now," Della McFarland urged with a smile.

The next morning, the McFarlands insisted on preparing a large breakfast of flapjacks, scrambled eggs, sausages, and fruit. With a pang of remorse, Rhea remembered that one of the few other times in her life she had received kindness from strangers was when Ramón Hernandez had hired her on as cook in Leadville, simply on her own word.

After breakfast, the farmer rose and patted Rhea on the shoulder. "Now I'll just get your horses and buckboard out, so you can leave when you've a mind to. Simply follow the road west and you'll make it fine."

Mrs. McFarland hurried out, just as Rhea was about to drive off, with a parting gift of half a slab of bacon, which she had carefully wrapped. "You can cut it thick or thin, as you like. Zeke smoked it himself, and you'll find it mighty tasty. God bless you both, and I hope the Quakers are real good to you."

"God bless you both, too," Rhea found herself saying and meaning it. Flicking the reins, Rhea drove off, following the road that led to Wichita.

By about noon, Rhea and Gatita reached the outskirts of Wichita. The young widow knew the settlement house was on Paine Avenue and headed for it.

As Rhea drove down the main thoroughfare of Wichita, she was surprised at the almost cosmopolitan nature of the growing city. Turning onto a side street, she caught sight of the settlement house, a two-story building built of wood and brick, and drove up to it. Descending from the buckboard, she tethered the geldings to the post, took Gatita down in her arms, and carried her toward the door of what seemed to be an office.

As they entered, Elone Wilson was in the process of writing a letter. Rhea left Gatita seated in a chair by the door and approached the attractive Indian woman. Elone looked up. Her jet-black hair was braided into a single thick plait at the back of the neck, descending almost to her waist. She wore a blue cotton dress, and there was a warm smile on her delicately featured face.

Elone put her pen down and rose, extending her hand. "Welcome, friend. How may I help you?"

"Are you in charge of this settlement?"

"Yes, I am. My name is Mrs. Ben Wilson, but you may call me Elone."

"My name is Rhea Penrock. I read about your settlement, and when my money started running out, I thought it best to seek shelter with you." She then told her usual tale about taking charge of her dead brother's daughter, concluding, "So you see, I couldn't stay in Preston, because I have to earn a living. Unfortunately, it might be necessary for me to leave my niece for a time until I find employment. She ought to be in school, for she's a very bright little thing. Her name is Gatita."

"I am glad you read about our settlement house. It is true, Miss Penrock, we do help the homeless, with special care for the children. But you should not make a hasty decision about leaving her."

"What do you mean?" Rhea asked, somewhat startled.

"Why, there are positions here in Wichita. Perhaps I might be helpful in getting you one, so you wouldn't have to leave your niece at all."

"Why, that—that would be wonderful!" Rhea stammered.

"You see, Miss Penrock," Elone explained, "Wichita has outgrown its beginnings as a cattle town, and it's now attracting all sorts of people and businesses. You seem bright and personable—I'm sure there would be opportunities for you. Have you ever done any sort of work outside the home?"

"Oh, yes, I—well, I was a cook for a while, but I can read and write, and I'm also pretty good at figures." Rhea remembered how Gabe talked to her about the robberies in which he was involved and the money he had taken, and how she would write down the figures, determining his fair share.

"You haven't done any bookkeeping or anything like that, have you, Miss Penrock?" Elone persisted.

"No, not really. But I can add sums, and I'm quick."

"I see. Well, it's just possible that I might be able to get you a job at the bank. In a way, they owe me a favor."

"They'd hire me? Really?" Rhea was incredulous.

"I think so. We'll go and talk to Mr. Mellers. He's the president."

"That would be wonderful. I'd really like to stay with Gatita, if I could."

"Of course you would. It's natural for you to want to be with your niece and watch her grow and learn and be happy in life," Elone responded.

"Well, then, would we be able to room here? I don't have any place else to stay, but I do have some money. I could pay for it. . . ." Rhea declared.

"We will be glad to have you, Miss Penrock. We have fifteen rooms in this building—each furnished with beds, bureaus, tables, and chairs—and we'd be happy to put you and your niece up for as long as is necessary. After we've seen Mr. Mellers, perhaps I can arrange to find you a more spacious place that you can rent at a reasonable figure."

"That's very kind of you."

"Not at all. You see, I am of the Quaker faith, as is my husband, and we deem it a blessing to help those who are in need. Our goal here is to make women and their children comfortable and get them settled so that being alone in a strange town does not terrify them. It is particularly harmful for a young, impressionable child not to know where he or she is going to stay."

"As I said, I'd like to pay something—"

"We don't ask for money, Miss Penrock. If some day you get on your feet—when you're settled and working and you have a few extra dollars to spare—we'd be grateful for a contribution to the settlement house. But even if you didn't have a penny, we'd still be happy to take you in."

Rhea found herself nonplussed by the evident sincerity and kindness of the attractive Indian woman. "It's really wonderful what you're doing for people, Mrs. Wilson. I'm very grateful. Oh, incidentally, I drove here in a buckboard. I'll have to find a stable—"

"That is no problem at all, Miss Penrock. There's a stable around the corner from here, and Mr. Finney's rates are extremely low." Elone Wilson looked over to where Gatita patiently sat, and she held out her arms. The child came running to her.

"May I hold your niece?" Elone asked.

"If you like, of course, Mrs. Wilson."

"How very sweet you are, little one. And I heard your aunt

say your name is Gatita—I know some Spanish, and it means kitten," Elone said to the child.

"Yes, lady, it does," Gatita agreed. She reached out a hand to touch Elone's braid. "Oooh, what pretty hair! I remember somebody I once knew wore it tied up in a long tail like that!" Her face screwed up in concentration at the elusive memory of her mother's own braided hair.

"It is called a braid, Gatita." Elone turned to Rhea Penrock. "She's really an adorable child. She seems very quick, bright, and happy. I do hope it will be possible for me to find you a position, Miss Penrock, so that you will not have to be parted from her. I know what a hardship that would be, since I am a mother myself." Elone drew out a printed form from her desk. "If you will fill out this paper for me telling me about yourself, then I will take you to see Mr. Mellers at the bank. Mrs. Hartmann, the widow of our former pastor, is upstairs at the moment. She can look after Gatita while you and I go over to see Mr. Mellers."

"You're going to a great deal of trouble for me. I really appreciate it," Rhea responded. "Would you mind waiting here a little bit for me, Gatita dear?"

"Oh, no, Auntie Rhea," the girl piped up. Elone put Gatita down, stroked her head, and said gently, "Do you see the blackboard at the end of the room? There are pieces of chalk there, and you may draw something, if you like."

As Gatita gleefully hurried off to the blackboard, Rhea smiled at the attractive Indian woman and said, "You are a real godsend. When my brother died—that was about two years ago—well, it's been touch and go . . . I mean, the money—supporting the little girl and myself at the same time."

"I understand," Elone said sympathetically. "Well now, let me go upstairs to get Mrs. Hartmann, and then I'll take you over to the bank."

Chapter Forty-Two

Abel Mellers, president of the Drovers Commercial Bank, was predisposed in advance to Elone Wilson's appeal for help. More than three years earlier, Elone had been in his bank when three outlaws had entered it, taken a sack of money at the point of a shotgun, and then seized Elone as a hostage. But, riding on horseback with the leader, Elone had ingeniously torn off bits of her yellow petticoat and dropped them at various stages of the journey, enabling the posse that had formed to follow the trail and ride after her. Abel Mellers had paid her a reward of two hundred and fifty dollars for the recovery of the stolen money, and he had publicly expressed his gratitude and admiration for Elone Wilson's courage.

Years before, when Dr. Ben Wilson had first brought her to Wichita, there had been resentment among the less enlightened citizens that a doctor should be married to an Indian woman, and a few had even gone so far as to call him "squaw man." But by now, Ben Wilson's reputation as a doctor intensely devoted to all his patients and his obvious love of his wife and children had eliminated all of that ugliness. The story in the Wichita paper about Elone's resourcefulness had further given her a special status as a heroine, much to her embarrassment.

"I think we can work something out, Miss Penrock." Abel Mellers clasped his hands over his plump belly and leaned back in his chair with a benevolent smile. "One of our tellers is leaving us for San Francisco in a few weeks. What I'm thinking is, you could train for his job. The salary wouldn't be too much at first, you understand, till you make yourself valuable. But I think we could start you off at about sixty-five dollars a month."

"I'm most grateful, Mr. Mellers. I'll work very hard, and you can trust me," Rhea Penrock radiantly declared.

"I'm sure I can. You come highly recommended by Mrs. Wilson here." Abel Mellers favored Dr. Ben Wilson's wife with a smile, then told Rhea, "Why don't you plan to come in Monday morning about eight-thirty, and I'll get you started. Jack Menifee, the teller I mentioned who's leaving, will be staying until the end of next week, and he can work with you and train you for your duties."

"I'd like that very much. I'm sure I can learn quickly."

"I'm sure you can, too. Well then, it's settled."

Mr. Mellers rose, held out his hand, and Rhea shook it. Then she turned to Elone. "I can't begin to thank you enough for all you've done."

"Not at all. That's what our aim is, Miss Penrock. So, then, we'll put you and Gatita up for now, and over this weekend we can look at a few boardinghouses where you could live very cheaply. With the salary you'll be getting from the bank, I'm sure you'll be able to make ends meet. Did you mention that you had some money of your own?"

"Yes, that's right, not quite a hundred dollars."

"Well, you'll be surprised to see how far it can go, if you watch your expenses. And if you settle here in Wichita, you could always sell the horses and buckboard to have little extra money in reserve."

"Yes, that—that might be a good idea," Rhea nodded. She was swiftly thinking that she could do much worse with her life than have a steady job, even if it meant a lot of application and study. The thought of herself as a bank teller handling all that money brought an ironic smile to her lips. Her late husband had been a bank robber, although she'd never stolen a penny herself—well, not technically. What she'd taken from fat old Jeb Cornish's wallet was more than due her. And if she and Gatita could stay here untroubled for some months, maybe she could figure out how to get the girl back to her parents in a way that would not jeopardize her own welfare.

An hour after they had returned from the bank, Dr. Ben Wilson came to the settlement house to call for his wife and to take her home. Elone introduced him to Rhea, who liked him at once for his directness and humility. Indeed, if he had been present during that past hour, he would have blushed with embarrassment, for lovely Elone had praised him to the skies and told Rhea how they had met, how his medical skill had saved her life and that of her daughter, Tisinqua. Now thirteen years old, Tisinqua was already a young woman, grave and keenly intelligent, but slow to speak her mind—unless she was prompted by her ten-year-old half brother, Bartholomew, or their brother, Jacob, who had turned nine in June. Her principal chore was looking after her half sisters, six-year-old Amy, and Dorothy, a year younger.

Rhea had been greatly impressed by the Wilsons' modest, self-effacing manner and still more so by their sympathy and kindness. What had really caught her attention, however, was a passing reference Elone had made to her belief in the equality for women. This was an idea entirely compatible with what Rhea herself had always believed: that a woman is not necessarily inferior to a man simply because she is a woman. She, who had had to fend for herself all of her life and had grown up within the walls of a bordello, knew only too well the inferior role to which the majority of men assigned those of the opposite sex.

By early November, Rhea Penrock began to believe that perhaps fate was finally on her side. She had taken the job at the bank with a certain amount of trepidation, not sure that she could meet the requirements of handling money, making change, entering transactions, and keeping up a pleasant rapport with the bank's customers. However, she had been pleasantly surprised to find out how quickly she could assimilate the intricacies of the work. The teller who had left to accept an offer in San Francisco had been an enthusiastic teacher—doubtless because he was eager to leave Kansas behind him for the greener pastures of California and, to be sure, because the apprentice was a lovely, slim, black-haired woman about whom he had erotic inclinations from the very first moment he was introduced to her. Rhea, however, had tactfully but firmly given him to understand that she was not at all interested in him, and the most overt display of his feelings was an occasional sigh. At any rate, Rhea learned quickly, and at the end of the week, the teller had been able to report to the bank president, "Miss Penrock seems to do pretty well, Mr. Mellers. I think it's safe to trust her behind the window. And

413

since she's certainly a looker, she's bound to bring more business into the bank.''

There had, indeed, been a noticeable influx of new customers, all of them male, since it had been bruited around Wichita that the Drovers Commercial Bank now had a new teller who was very definitely "a real eyeful." She found the work pleasant enough, albeit occasionally repetitive and routine, but certainly in no way overtaxing. She had not expected the friendliness with which regular bank customers greeted her and their solicitous inquiries as to how she and her child were enjoying life in Wichita. Having always been a loner, she now found herself the center of more attention than she might have normally wished, and yet she found it strangely gratifying.

In addition to finding Rhea a job, Elone Wilson had found her a boardinghouse about three blocks from the bank where she and Gatita could lodge for the low cost of fifteen dollars a month, including breakfasts. Mary Jamison, the widow who operated it, was also a devout Quaker like Elone. She felt that she was showing her charitable side by providing a comfortable, clean, and spacious suite of rooms for this woman who had so readily assumed responsibility for her adorable young niece. Mrs. Jamison's breakfasts were lavish, and indeed, Rhea needed very little food for the rest of the day, though she saw to it that Gatita received three square meals.

Although, much of Rhea's time was spent at the bank, including part of Saturday, Sundays and evenings she had all to herself and the child who had made such a profound change in her outlook. There were times when she began to wonder if it would not be possible—after staying perhaps a year here in Wichita and putting away savings—to take Gatita to the East, and there begin life all over again, bringing up the girl as her own daughter with every possible advantage. Thus far, there had been no sign or word of any pursuit, and that was why Rhea at times hoped that what she had done might yet turn out happily for her. She liked to pretend, at these times, that she and Gatita would be together always. As false as her reason told her this notion was, it nevertheless brought stability to her life, and it enabled her to surround Gatita with an atmosphere of calm and tranquility.

On this Saturday in November, Elone Wilson had invited her to go shopping, knowing that Rhea had been given half the day off at the bank, which had closed down for an audit.

The young widow thought to herself what Gabe might think or say, if he could see her working in a bank, greeting customers by name, exchanging pleasantries with them, and handling their money with swiftness and efficiency.

She looked forward to shopping with Elone, and, of course, Gatita was to accompany them. When Rhea and Gatita came down for breakfast, they were all smiles, excited over their outing together. Rhea cheerfully said "Good morning" to her landlady and the three other guests who occupied the house. One was an aging, retired cowboy who late in life, having received an unexpected legacy of twelve thousand dollars from an uncle he had completely forgotten, had decided to settle down in Wichita. The other two boarders were man and wife, stolid, dour Scotch Presbyterians who had left Dundee eight years before to visit a first cousin here in Wichita, then stayed on to open a tailor shop. The wife was an expert seamstress, while the husband could fit men's clothes with almost miraculous ease. They rarely spoke at the table, though both of them did rather glumly acknowledge Rhea and Gatita, and at least they did not concern themselves with speculative gossip on why an extremely attractive young woman would isolate herself in a rather dowdy Kansas boardinghouse. If anything, they admired the fact that she had gone to work in a reputable institution—for the Drovers Commerical Bank was where they had their own lifetime savings.

Rhea was in an exceptionally jubilant mood today. Only late yesterday afternoon, Abel Mellers had called her into his office, told her how satisfied he was with her work, and informed her that, effective the next week, her salary would be raised to seventy dollars a month. It was a triumphant milestone for her: Other than the brief period she worked as cook for Ramón Hernandez, this was actually the first time she had worked for wages in any sort of job outside the warped confinement of a bordello. Moreover, it made her feel that she had thoroughly adapted herself to her new life, though she knew that she was playing a dangerous game that might boomerang at any moment.

Nonetheless, she was pleased with the growth of her own self-esteem caused by this raise in salary. The night before, after Gatita had fallen asleep, she had smoked one of her hand-rolled cigarettes and, studying her reflection in the mirror, said softly to herself, "If only you could have started life this

415

way, Rhea girl, you might have amounted to something. I don't know what use it is now even saying a prayer that things will work out, but right now, I'm very happy and very proud of myself—and it's a very good feeling."

This morning, Elone, Rhea, and Gatita went first to the general store, where Rhea wanted to buy some hard candy for the child as well as some dresses that would be warm enough for Gatita during the winter and a new dress for herself. As they entered the store, Elone mentioned that she needed to buy some additional foodstuffs. "Relatives of my husband's first wife are coming to visit us for a few days."

"His first wife?" Rhea looked blank.

"Yes. My husband was married to a dear woman who served as a nurse during the Civil War. Ben himself was a member of the medical corps."

"I understand," Rhea nodded, as she riffled through a number of children's dresses, studying them with absorption.

"They fell in love, and when the war was over, my husband went back home to Pittsburgh with this young woman. However, she died from diphtheria, and Ben took their two children, Thomas and Sybella—oh! I don't believe you've met my stepchildren yet, have you? They've both been out with friends the few times you've come to visit. Anyway, Ben took them to Texas to her mother, and then in his sorrow, he went to Indian Territory."

Rhea stared curiously at Elone, but said nothing, except to favor the beautiful Indian woman with an encouraging nod.

"There he met me and my daughter Tisinqua. We fell in love and were married. But you see, my husband continues his friendship with the family of that woman who first loved him."

"How nice for you to have such a large family," Rhea said somewhat wistfully. "You say they're coming here to visit?"

Elone was intent upon selecting some material from which she intended to make Bartholomew a pair of trousers, but she finally nodded. "Yes, I expect them tomorrow, or Monday for certain. And I do want you to meet them. You and Lucien Edmond Bouchard certainly should talk with each other. He is a highly respected rancher, so perhaps he can exert some pressure on the authorities to find your missing sister-in-law."

"Lu-Lucien Edmond B-Bouchard . . . My—my missing sister-in-law—" Rhea echoed, instantly thrust into frantic self-

416

searching, unconsciously moving back into the shadows near the entrance of the store as if to hide herself.

"It's true, dear, you may not want to give Gatita back, but at least her mother should be made to meet her financial responsibilities to you and your niece," Elone continued.

"Yes—yes—I—I see what you mean," Rhea stammered. Her heart had begun to pound violently, and she was very pale.

"Is anything the matter, dear?" Elone innocently inquired.

"Er—n-no. Oh, no, Mrs. Wilson. I was just thinking of something. I suppose you're right; this Mr. Bouchard might help me find my sister-in-law."

"Of course he could. You see, he has a great deal of influence not only in Texas and Colorado but also in Alabama, Chicago, Galveston, and New York, all places where he has relatives. He could very easily arrange for a private detective to track down this irresponsible woman."

"I—I guess he could, w-with connections like that. Well, thank you very much, Mrs. Wilson. I—I'll look forward to meeting him. Well, I guess we'd best get on with our shopping."

Rhea tried to keep her voice casual and level, but there was a trembling to it, for her mind was overwhelmed by the sudden, awful news that Ramón's brother-in-law was soon to be in Wichita. And once that happened, she knew that she would be found out—and then only the worst would happen.

Chapter Forty-Three

Rhea slept only fitfully through part of the night and well before dawn had already packed the single valise she had carried with her since leaving Dodge City. She quickly scribbled a note for the pious Quaker landlady, expressing her regrets that business affairs in the East had forced her to leave so abruptly, and enclosed a five-dollar bill. Then, walking Gatita and putting a finger to her lips to indicate the need for silence, she quickly dressed the child. Carrying the valise in one hand and holding on to Gatita with her other hand, Rhea hurried to the stable for the horses and buckboard.

Fortunately, a young hand had already started work and was present when she knocked at the door of the stable. She gave him a dollar, and he harnessed the geldings and attached the buckboard shafts, then courteously helped her climb into the driver's seat, lifting Gatita up beside her.

"Where do we go now, Auntie Rhea?" the child drowsily asked as she yawned and stretched.

"We have to go see someone very important, darling. Don't you worry now. If you like, lean your head against my shoulder and try to go back to sleep."

She smiled at the stable hand. "Thanks, Tom, and tell Mr. Perkins I probably shan't be back."

"Sure will, ma'am. Want me to tell anyone where you're going?" the young man asked.

"No, I—well, you see, I got word that someone has spotted my niece's mother, so I want to see if I can catch up with her."

"I understand, ma'am. Well, good luck. I hope everything works out all right for you."

She nodded her thanks, shook her reins, and started the

geldings off. They moved eastward, along the main street of Wichita and out beyond the town's limits. Dawn was breaking, a magnificent sunrise tinged with purple and red, a burnished light announcing the sun's imminent appearance on the Kansas sky.

The day after Rhea Penrock fled from Wichita, Lucien Edmond Bouchard and his wife, Maxine, disembarked from the train at the Wichita railroad station. Dr. Ben Wilson was waiting there for the Bouchards, as was his wife, Elone.

"How good it is to see you again, Ben." Lucien Edmond held out his hand, which the Quaker doctor warmly gripped. "And you, Elone—you're as beautiful as the day Ben married you."

"Now that is flattery I cannot entirely accept, but you are very kind to offer it to me." Elone smiled. "If I am still attractive, it is most likely because I am happy and fulfilled."

"There, you see, Maxine?" Lucien Edmond turned to his handsome wife. "Despite what Carla may think, it is entirely possible for a woman to find happiness through marriage and children." His handsome face momentarily flushed with anger; then he realized he had committed a social gaffe. "Oh, forgive me. We're having a slight family dispute, but this is hardly the time to bring it up."

"Indeed, it isn't," Maxine agreed with a smile. At forty-two, she was still as stunning as the day she had come from Baltimore and captured Lucien Edmond's heart on Windhaven Plantation. There was only a little gray to her chestnut hair, and her face was sweet and full, though the lines of worry occasioned by her concern over Ramón and Gatita Hernandez and, most recently, by her daughter's decision to adopt a bohemian way of life were visible. Speaking to Ben and Elone, Maxine explained, "There's so much that we can be thankful for. You see, we thought we'd take a little vacation because Ramón has returned from his search for his daughter. She's still missing, and we're all heartsick about it, but at least he came back to us in a better frame of mind than when he left. I think somehow he's found himself again, and he's found the faith he had renounced."

"God saw to that," Ben Wilson replied simply. "But come along now. I'll take your baggage, and we'll get you settled in your room so you can freshen up."

419

Ben drove the buggy, while his wife sat in the back seat with Maxine and Lucien Edmond. "You know, Lucien Edmond," Elone said, "you've come at a very good time. You might be of great aid to a very needful young woman."

"Oh? Tell me how," Lucien Edmond asked.

"Well, her name is Rhea Penrock, and she has a niece, a very sweet young thing, named Gatita," Elone began.

"What? Wait a minute—did you say Gatita?" Lucien Edmond stared at her, his face taut.

Elone nodded. "Why, yes, that is her niece's name. She said that her brother died and her sister-in-law took all the girl's inheritance and then abandoned her. Rhea was appointed her ward, but she ran out of funds and came to our settlement. I helped get her a job as teller at the Drovers Commercial Bank."

Lucien Edmond turned to his wife, whose face was pale. "Maxine, this can't just be a coincidence can it? I know the odds are at least a million to one, but is it possible that the child is Ramón's?"

"I don't understand," Ben declared, turning to look back at the Bouchards.

Lucien Edmond tried to compose himself a bit before he answered Ben's question. Finally, he said, "You know, of course, about Ramón's kidnapped daughter, Ben. But do you know the details?"

"Why, yes, I think I do. You wrote to us when she was first kidnapped that she was taken away by some woman whose cruelty is—I must confess—completely bewildering to me. I cannot understand, for the life of me, how anyone could be so reprehensible as to take an innocent child from her parents. But what has that to do with Rhea Penrock and her niece?"

Maxine burst out, unable to contain herself, "Ramón's daughter's name is Gatita—at least, that has always been her nickname in the family. I'm astonished that we never told you this. No matter, it can't be helped now. The main thing is, it's an unusual name, so it's unlikely that it's mere coincidence that this child is also named Gatita. Besides, 'Penrock' doesn't sound the least bit Spanish to me, so why would this so-called niece have a Spanish nickname? Unless—"

"Elone," Lucien Edmond cut in, "how old would you say the child is?"

"Why, I believe Miss Penrock said she is five years old."

"Oh, my God! She *must* be Ramón's daughter!" Lucien Edmond exclaimed. "What does the woman look like, Elone?"

"She is in her middle twenties, I would say, and she has long black hair and the most beautiful deep gray eyes."

"That's her! That's Rita Galloway!" Lucien Edmond seized his wife's hand, practically crushing it in his excitement until he noticed Maxine wince.

Ben had halted the wagon and was staring wide-eyed in amazement at his passengers. "I can't believe it!" he managed to say. "She seemed like such a lovely, sweet young woman the few times I met her. And she is so obviously devoted to the child."

"Ben, Elone, I'm sure you'll understand that we must go and speak to this woman immediately. Where can we find her?"

"I presume she is at the bank at this hour," Elone said in a distracted tone of voice. She mumbled under her breath, "I can't believe it of her. I simply cannot believe it."

"I'll take you there immediately," Ben offered.

Five minutes later the buggy drew up to the Drovers Commercial Bank, and Lucien Edmond jumped down, then helped Elone alight. They strode into the bank and up to the tellers' windows. Elone then shook her head, declaring, "She's not here. Perhaps she's in Mr. Mellers's office. Let me go back and see."

She emerged from the bank president's office only a moment later, a frown on her lovely face. "Mr. Mellers said she didn't come in for work. He sent someone around to Mrs. Jamison's—that's the boardinghouse where she has a room—and the landlady said she left town sometime early Sunday morning. Apparently Miss Penrock notified Mrs. Jamison that she had to go East—something about business affairs that required her presence." She saw the crestfallen look on the Texan's face and murmured, "Oh, Lucien Edmond, I'm so sorry."

"Damnation! So close, after all this time! And now she's gotten away again!" Lucien Edmond groaned. Then he asked, "Elone, is there anybody who might be able to help us?"

"I don't know. Wait! Perhaps when she got her buckboard

from the stable someone was there and might have spoken with her. I can take you there if—"

"Yes, immediately!" Lucien Edmond cut in.

They leaped back into the buggy and Ben drove over to the stable, where as luck would have it the same hand was working as had been there the morning before. However, after questioning the boy, all they could learn was the direction that the woman and child had taken when leaving town.

"Well," Lucien Edmond sighed, "I guess that information is better than nothing. Elone, Ben, I'm going to hire a horse right now and seé if I can track them down. You can take Maxine to your house and—"

Ben Wilson interrupted, "Hold on a moment, Lucien Edmond. I know Kansas a good deal better than you do, and I've many friends and patients here. Perhaps I can be of help in locating this woman and Ramón's child. First off, I can more easily talk to the farmers around here, get information from them, than a stranger could. That might give us a clue as to where we might find her. With a child, she would take more time and obviously stop for the night. Even though it's been almost two days, it's not hopeless. I'm sure we can find her."

"That makes sense. Tell you what, Ben, I'll have Maxine send a telegram to Ramón to come at once to Wichita. And just as soon as we've left our baggage at your place, I can make some inquiries."

"That would be fine. I have a friend who might go with us. He often rides on horseback by himself for quite considerable distances, for he enjoys being active and loves the outdoors. His name is Dave Haggerson," the Quaker doctor suggested.

"That's great. We can certainly use all the help we can get. Well then, Ben, is there a telegraph office nearby?"

"Sure is. It's back at the railroad. I'll get you over there in a jiffy."

A few minutes later, Maxine Bouchard got out of the buggy and hurried to the window of the telegrapher, where she composed a message to Ramón:

Have traced Rita Galloway and Gatita. Come at once. Lucien Edmond and Ben Wilson are starting out now on their trail. Come to Dr. Wilson's house as soon as you arrive. All love and best wishes to you and Mara.

Maxine Bouchard

They quickly headed back to the Wilsons' house, and when they arrived, Elone showed Maxine to a spare room.

Lucien Edmond and Dr. Ben Wilson followed with the luggage, and after Lucien Edmond had freshened up, the Quaker doctor proposed, "Let's go have a chat with Dave Haggerson."

The bell ending the last class at the rural school where Dave Haggerson taught had just rung as Lucien Edmond Bouchard and Dr. Ben Wilson got out of the buggy and headed toward the one-story brick building. Dave emerged with two eleven-year-old boys following him, one on each side, asking him questions about the next day's lessons. He was in his middle fifties, tall, with dark-gray hair and neatly trimmed sideburns, frank brown eyes, and a firm, incisive mouth. He had been a schoolteacher when he married a gentle, intelligent, mature pupil of eighteen. Then he had served during the Civil War in an Iowa regiment for two years and, after being severely wounded, was mustered out three months before Appomattox.

A few months after the war was over, one of his cousins, who had moved to Wichita, died and willed him a small farm on the northern outskirts of the city. He and his wife, Elaine, eagerly moved there. But a year before Dr. Ben Wilson made his first visit to Wichita to buy supplies for the Creeks, Elaine died in childbirth, and her sickly baby boy followed her to the grave scarcely a week later. To lessen his grief, Dave Haggerson had gone back to teaching in the small Wichita rural school.

He had, all this while, evinced no interest in any other woman. His good friend, Dallas Masterson, who ran the faro table in the gambling hall, had once told the Quaker doctor, "Dave doesn't want sympathy, and he really loved Laney. It shocked him when she and the kid died so sudden-like, and it hurt him a lot. He'd never let on, but he's not especially happy being lonely like this. So that's why he works like a dog in that school, where they don't pay him enough or appreciate him enough, though there are some kids with brains who really know what a great teacher he is. One day he's going to find the right woman—at least I sure hope he does. He's got a lucky break coming because he's the most decent guy I know."

Now, as he saw the homely, lanky Quaker doctor come

quickly toward him, followed by Lucien Edmond Bouchard, Dave Haggerson quipped, "Well now, Ben, don't tell me you want some extracurricular training—say, perhaps in history."

"I'd mighty like to take a class of yours, Dave, and one day I will. This is Lucien Edmond Bouchard. You've heard me talk about him a good deal. He's my late wife's half brother, if you'll recall."

"Pleased to know you, Mr. Bouchard," Dave said as they shook hands.

"Ben mentioned you in his letters—I'm delighted finally to meet you. That's the reason I feel I can ask for your help," Lucien Edmond declared.

"Ask away. Anything I can do for Ben and for you—being in the family, so to speak—I'd be more than happy to do," Dave replied.

Quickly, Lucien Edmond explained the situation to the schoolteacher. Dave nodded, frowning. "I guess when Rhea heard that you were coming to Wichita, Mr. Bouchard, she knew the jig was up. So she took off with the child. Well, I think we can find her, just the three of us. She's by herself, obviously, so we don't need a big posse. First off, I'd suggest we go back to the stable and talk to that young fellow who saw her ride away from Wichita. Maybe he'll remember something he hasn't already told you."

"Good idea. Can we go right now?" Ben asked.

"Of course, Ben. Your bringing the buggy saves a lot of time," Dave smiled as he clambered aboard.

A few minutes later, the three men talked to the stableboy. However, the boy only reiterated what he had said earlier: She left at dawn the previous day, and as he had walked out of the stable to wave goodbye to her, she was heading east.

"We'll rent some horses from you," Lucien Edmond said, pulling out his wallet and handing the stable hand two ten-dollar bills.

"Shucks, they don't cost that much—"

"Take it. It's more than worth it to us. The chances are," Lucien Edmund turned to Ben and Dave, "she can't have gone more than thirty miles a day. She'd be bound to stop at night, maybe at some farmhouse, because it is too cold for camping out. She had some money, Elone told us, but unless she kept it in her room, she couldn't have withdrawn it from the bank. She's abandoned everything. Her one concern is being caught. That means she's bound to make mistakes."

The stableboy brought out three sprightly geldings, and Lucien Edmond, Dave, and Ben mounted them and rode off in an easterly direction.

"I'm going to telegraph Maxine at your house, Ben, whenever we stop off. That way, when Ramón gets up to Wichita, he can head out to find us. I want him to be there when we find that woman and Gatita," Lucien Edmond sternly declared.

"I understand that," the Quaker doctor said. "Lucien Edmond, what are you going to do to her?"

"She committed a criminal act, and it was exacerbated by the length of time she kept us all in agony. All this time we believed that she had taken Gatita to Mexico. However, according to what she told Elone, it seems she's been in Kansas all this time. I think the law would take a dim view of her act, and if the child is hurt in any way, she might very well be sentenced to the gallows. But, since the child is Ramón's, it's for him to decide what punishment Rita Galloway ought to have."

"Well, she must have had a reason. Unless she's entirely deranged, a woman wouldn't take a child for whom she obviously showed a good deal of devotion without some reason," the Quaker doctor remarked.

"I don't hold with criminals or lunatics, I'm afraid—and certainly not with women who steal other people's children. You don't know what Ramón's been through, and it just about destroyed his marriage," Lucien Edmond stubbornly declared.

Chapter Forty-Four

Rhea Penrock and Gatita Hernandez had stopped at farm-houses on the two previous nights, paid for their keep and the meals that the farmers' wives had provided, and then set out eastward. The farmers themselves had been curious about her apparent anxiety and her interest in leaving quickly the next morning, almost before breakfast could be served. When they had questioned her, she had given them the evasive answer that her estranged husband, who had abandoned her, had threatened her life and that of the child, and she was riding away from Wichita. This won their sympathy, and the two women who had cooked dinner for Rhea and Gatita saw to it that they were provided with a bundle of food to enjoy during their travels.

They had reached Eureka, some sixty miles from Wichita, in the early afternoon of the third day following the flight from Wichita. By the time Lucien Edmond had enlisted the aid of Ben Wilson and Dave Haggerson, and started tracking their quarry, Rhea and Gatita had come as far as Batesville, some twenty-four miles further east. Gatita was running a slight temperature, which greatly concerned the slim young woman. Accordingly, she had gone to the little town's only hotel and rented a room. She had asked that the town doctor be sent to her, and he diagnosed Gatita's ailment as a simple cold, recommending that the child stay in bed for a day and drink plenty of liquids and fruit juices. By now, the November cold was touching all of Kansas, and Rhea herself was exhausted, not only from the physical exertion of this un-planned flight, but also from the tension and the fear that had redoubled when she had been told by Elone that Lucien Edmond Bouchard was on his way to Wichita.

Gatita's cold improved the next day, but Rhea, concerned about the rigors of travel on the child, called in the doctor. He recommended that Gatita rest another day before they continued their journey. Rhea had, as she had with the farmers, informed the doctor that she was fleeing from an estranged husband who had threatened her life and that of the child. The physician had been most sympathetic and suggested that when they were both rested, they go northward to Topeka where, he informed Rhea, there was a Quaker settlement that would give them both shelter and a lawyer who would see to it that her malevolent husband was prevented from any violent action.

The three men rode swiftly in pursuit, making inquiries wherever they stopped. Lucien Edmond, true to his promise, sent daily telegrams back to Maxine in Wichita to advise her where they were and where they were heading. By now, Ramón Hernandez had arrived and, renting a spirited mare from the stable owner, set out to meet them.

On the day when the Batesville doctor told Rhea that Gatita could travel, Lucien Edmond Bouchard, Dr. Ben Wilson, and Dave Haggerson reached Eureka. There they found the farmer who had given shelter to the fleeing couple, and the farmer's wife volunteered, "She was in a great hurry, mister, afeared her hubby was going to do her and the little girl some terrible harm. I do hope you mean to help her. She looked so worried, and the little girl herself looked plumb tuckered out."

"Where do you think they would go from here, Mrs. Grorty?" Ben Wilson anxiously asked.

" 'Peared to me they'd headed on toward Batesville. It's not far from here, and they could rest up there for a spell."

"You've been most helpful, Mrs. Grorty. God bless you," Ben had said.

A few hours later, Ramón Hernandez caught up with the three riders on the road from Eureka to Batesville. They halted their horses, waiting for him. Exhausted, dripping sweat even though the day was cold, Ramón was trembling with anticipation as he reined in his mount, and his energy seemed almost demonic, thanks to the news he had received. "I've found you at last! I haven't ridden a horse this hard in a long while—except perhaps poor Magdalena," he panted.

Lucien Edmond looked at his brother-in-law, then exchanged uneasy glances with Ben Wilson and Dave Haggerson. The three men could see Ramón's eyes glowing with a fierce anger, as if the proximity of Rita Galloway and Gatita, after so many months of waiting, had served to rekindle his old desires for retribution. It was almost as if the long ride across the Kansas plains had reminded Ramón again of the bitter, wearying days of travel he had endured on the lonely trails of Mexico, on his vain quest for his daughter and her abductor.

"Take it easy, Ramón." Lucien Edmond sought to calm him, clapping him gently on the shoulder. "I think we're nearing the end of the trail. How long it's been! At last you'll have the joy of finding Gatita. By now, I'm sure that woman has figured that either no one is after her, or she's got a wonderful head start. So she'll probably slow down because she'll be thinking of the child—for the fact that Gatita's still alive and well means that she's learned to care for your daughter. That's all in our favor."

"I think that's very sound reasoning," Dave Haggerson nodded. "You know, speaking as a schoolteacher with a little experience on the matter, I can tell you that children who are taken away from their parents at an early age and have foster parents or some other relative taking charge of them can quite possibly and understandably fall very much in love with that substitute. Even going so far as to consider a governess or a nurse or even an aunt the same as a mother."

Ramón's face darkened. "I have no desire to argue with you, Mr. Haggerson, but to suggest that this evil, vindictive woman could in any way resemble my wife is, in my mind, little short of blasphemy!"

"Come now, Señor Hernandez," Dave soothed him, "I didn't say this pertained to you personally. I only say that it's understandable, and it's probably why your little girl has been able to survive under the supervision of the woman who has kept her, as you've told me, two years away from all of you. But we'll find her. Let's ride, gentlemen!"

On Friday morning, Gatita sprang out of bed and ran to hug Rhea, her eyes sparkling with vivacity and affection, and the young woman was certain that it was safe to continue their journey.

There was a restaurant on the same block as the hotel, and

telling Gatita that they were going to have breakfast before they started off again, Rhea dressed the child and then took her down to the restaurant. She ordered a large batch of flapjacks, suggesting to the waitress that she ask the cook to make them as thin and fluffy as possible. Remembering all too well how Gabe had grumbled that the flapjacks he had been served on long forays with the Cornish band had been leather tough, she emphasized this to the bony, efficient waitress, who was quite taken with Gatita.

Rhea enjoyed some bacon with the flapjacks and two cups of coffee. Then, rolling a cigarette, she leaned back and sighed with repletion.

"That was just wunnerful, Auntie Rhea," Gatita said, reaching over to squeeze the young woman's hand.

"I'm glad you liked it. I love you, Gatita darling."

"And I love you too, Auntie Rhea."

The homely waitress, overhearing this, sighed rapturously and, approaching the table, solicitiously murmured to Rhea, "Maybe you'd like another order of flapjacks? They're on the house this time—the chef says he likes folks who 'preciate his cookin' something special."

"Tell me, Gatita, could you eat a few more flapjacks?" Rhea asked.

"Oh, yes!"

"Okay. Thank the chef for us. Tell him how much we enjoyed them," Rhea told the waitress.

The pancakes came in about ten minutes, with more coffee for Rhea and another glass of milk for Gatita.

It was a pleasant little town, Rhea told herself. She rolled another cigarette and finished the last of her coffee, then reached into her reticule and drew out the worn wallet in which she had kept the last of Jeb Cornish's money. She left a generous tip for the waitress, who effusively thanked her.

"It was a pleasure waiting on you, ma'am, you and the lovely little girl. It's nice to see a woman who loves her kid. Me, you can see from my face that would stop a clock no feller'd ever want anyone like me, but all my life I wished I could have a kid," the waitress told her with a nostalgic sigh.

"Don't give up hope. One of these days some man will come along who'll appreciate your kind heart," Rhea reassured her with a smile. "It was really a marvelous breakfast.

Thank you so much, and don't forget to tell the cook how much we both enjoyed what he did for us.''

''I won't, and thanks a lot for the tip. Are you going on from here?''

''Yes, I'm afraid we have to. We're on our way east, to Baltimore.''

''My goodness, so far!'' The waitress shook her head. ''Well, a good morning to you—and to you, sweetheart.'' She leaned forward and patted Gatita on the cheek.

When the waitress had gone back to the kitchen, Gatita turned to Rhea and asked, ''Where do we go now, Auntie Rhea?''

Rhea took a moment before answering. Then she stubbed out her cigarette in the saucer of the coffee cup. ''We might just go on into Missouri, honey. I know some folks in St. Looey. You'd like that town—it's really big, and there are lots of things to do and to see.''

''Can we stay there forever, Auntie Rhea?''

''Of course we can, honey. Come,'' she said as she rose. ''Take my hand, and we'll go back upstairs to our room and get our suitcase.''

''Look, there—up ahead! There's a woman and child in that buckboard! Perhaps it's them!'' Lucien Edmond shouted as he pointed straight ahead on the narrow road from Batesville.

''I can hardly wait for this moment! It has been an eternity of hell for me,'' Ramón Hernandez cried aloud, his eyes blazing with eagerness.

''We must show no violence to the woman,'' Ben Wilson admonished. ''She must tell us why she did what she did.''

''By all means,'' Ramón said between his teeth, as he spurred his horse after the fleeing buckboard. ''Look at her! She drives her horses hard because she knows that her time of treachery is at last over—God, how I have prayed for this moment!''

''You'll not harm her, Ramón,'' the Quaker doctor called to him. ''Look—the child has spotted us and is waving! She seems well, praise God for that. Ramón, hold your hatred within yourself, I beg you!''

''Very well,'' Lucien Edmond's brother-in-law replied, his face a stony mask. ''But when she's had her say, there'll be a trial. The gallows for a vicious, treacherous *puta* like that one!''

''No, Ramón, no! We must not judge her in advance!'' Ben earnestly shook his head.

Rhea Penrock had glanced back and, with a cry of terror, saw the four horsemen approaching, forging closer and closer to the buckboard. She used the whip, but the valiant geldings could go no faster, and the wagon began to rock perilously. Gatita began to cry, and Rhea, with a groan of defeat, drew in the reins. ''Whoa, whoa, boy! All right, that's enough. We can't outrace them. Don't cry, honey, don't cry. We're stopping now!''

The geldings at last slackened their gait and came to a panting halt, their sides heaving. Ramón rode up first and uttered a cry of indescribable joy. ''Gatita, my little Gatita! Oh, my sweet darling—my Gatita—I've found you at last!''

The girl stared at her father, at first not recognizing him from his gray hair and the taut, weatherbeaten set of his features. And then, slowly, remembrance and comprehension came, and she cried out, ''Papa! Papa!''

He curbed his horse and came beside the buckboard, then reached out and seized his daughter in his arms, covering her with kisses. Rhea, very pale, sat stiffly in the driver's seat, the whip drooping in her hand, waiting. Lucien Edmond and Ben rode up on the other side, while Dave Haggerson grabbed the horses' reins, forestalling any attempt at escape.

''Rita Galloway, or Rhea Penrock—whatever your name is, you damned, cursed *puta*!'' Ramón cried out. ''Why did you do this? What did I ever do to you that you would steal my child and leave a note and say that we would never find her again? You never were in Mexico, were you?''

Rhea shook her head, mute, stunned.

Ramón moved his horse a little and handed Gatita to Ben Wilson. ''Hold her for me, so I may have my hands free to deal with this woman—''

''No, Ramón, not that way. Let her talk! We must know why she did what she did,'' Ben calmly responded as he shifted the child in his arms.

Gatita clung to him, looking back at her father, and cried out, ''But I love Auntie Rhea. I love her, Papa! Why are you so angry with her?''

''She does not know what she is saying—this *puta* has

431

bewitched her! She is a *bruja*, too!'' Ramón gasped, making the sign of the cross.

"Tell us,'' Lucien Edmond urged. "Weren't we good to you? Didn't we give you work when you said you needed it? And in Texas, we were kind to you. Is that how you rewarded us? What made you take the child?''

"I—I thought I had to—'' Rhea began.

"Thought you had to! What sort of answer is that, woman? Tell us the truth, or by the Eternal, I'll strangle the breath out of you!'' Ramón swore, clenching his fists and glaring at her.

"No, Ramón!'' Ben shouted. "Threatening won't get the truth out of her. Miss Galloway, or Miss Penrock, or whatever your real name is, you know me. You know I'm a Quaker who speaks the truth when I promise that we shan't harm you. We ask only that you tell us why you stole Ramón's child.''

Rhea stared at the Quaker doctor and then burst into tears.

"Crocodile tears because she knows she's guilty, because she's going to jail or hang, and as swiftly as we can manage it,'' Ramón growled.

"Stop it, Ramón. The child is safe now, and you've had your prayers answered. There must be a reason—she has seemed to me like a sensible young woman. Tell us, Rhea,'' Ben Wilson pleaded.

Rhea slowly raised her tear-stained face to meet his gaze and saw the sympathetic look on his face. "All right, I'll tell you. My name's Rhea Penrock—it used to be Rhea Galloway, till I married Gabe Penrock. He was one of Jeb Cornish's men.''

"I knew it, I knew it!'' Ramón shouted, "I had a feeling that you were tied up with that crooked Indian agent who tried to have me killed! Oh, yes, now it's all very clear—''

"Wait! You—you don't understand, Mr. H-Hernandez. I—I know you've got me, I know I've done a wrong thing—but I want to tell all of why I did it. . . .''

"Go ahead and tell us, then, Mrs. Penrock,'' Ben urged, as he shifted Gatita in his arms and kissed her cheek and smiled at her. The little girl clung to him, but looked anxiously back at Rhea, then at her father, her eyes filled with tears.

"You see, my mother—my mother was Lucille Galloway, and she worked for a cotton planter near Chattanooga. His son got her with child—me—and they kicked her out. So she had to go to work in a bordello on the outskirts of that town—and there I was born.''

"How terrible!" Ben sympathetically murmured. "Go ahead, Mrs. Penrock."

"Well, my mother kept me with her in the house there—but she took good care of me, I'll have you know!" She looked up at them with almost glaring defiance, then again burst into stifled sobs. After she had recovered, she went on, "When I was fourteen, Mother went to a house in Natchez. And a year later, a riverboat pirate who was one of her regulars knifed her. Then he—he went into my room where I was asleep and he—he raped me—"

"You poor woman! I begin to understand a little," Ben murmured. "Ramón, listen carefully. She has had a life that would have made even a saint have doubts of salvation."

"I will listen," Ramón growled, "but I haven't heard enough yet to pardon her for what she did to Mara and me—or to my daughter! Finish it, woman!"

"Mrs. Penrock, take your time. Say what you will," Ben interposed.

Rhea, who looked older than her twenty-four years with tears on her face and the anguish in her eyes, looked up at the Quaker. She drew a long, shuddering breath and then went on. "The madam there—after what happened—told me to take Mother's place. I had nothing else left to do—nobody would hire me—the daughter of a wh-whore—and so I did. But, one day, that man came back and—and he had me, and I stabbed him and killed him."

"My God!" Lucien Edmond ejaculated.

Dave Haggerson shook his head and gave Ramón a meaningful look, muttering softly, "This poor woman has been through hell, a hell of her own, long before she made one for you, Mr. Hernandez."

Ramón sat on his horse, stonily silent, still glaring at Rhea. Then at last he said, "Let's have the rest of it. A woman's tears won't wash out a crime, Mrs. Penrock, if that's really your name—"

"It is—Gabe was my husband, and one of your men killed him. But I'll tell you the rest—you may as well know everything. I went to St. Louis, where I worked honest jobs, but men there wanted me—they probably learned that I'd been a whore and the daughter of one. Then, about seven years ago, I got to Dodge City. I was a dance-hall girl in a saloon until I met Gabe—Gabe Penrock. He had Jeb Cornish hire me. And I liked Gabe—he treated me right—and then he married me. And when he died, it was one of your men, Mr. Hernandez, who shot him—there in Leadville—and when I found it out, I told Cornish I'd pay you back on my own way, without anybody's help—"

"But it wasn't I who killed him. I don't even know who you mean!" Ramón burst out.

"He was one of the men who robbed the train for the payroll, and then—and then he tried to get the miners to strike against your mine, yours and Mr. Bouchard's. He was going to dynamite it—"

"It was Robert Markey who shot that man just as he was going to press down the plunger! You mean to say for that reason—for that reason, woman—you played your sick game? You deceived us all? You stole my Gatita?" Ramón incredulously demanded.

Rhea covered her face with her hands, bowed her head, and nodded. After a few moments, in a muffled, tear-choked voice, she went on. "So, when Jeb Cornish told me that my man was killed, I blamed you for it, Mr. Hernandez. I knew that it wasn't you personally, but I thought that because Gabe had gone up there and got in the way, you'd had him done in—and so I swore I'd pay you back. Well, anyhow, you know what I did in Leadville and how I came down to Texas with you—"

"Get on with it! Get on with it, woman! I want to know why you kept her so long. I spent months searching all through Mexico, going mad with grief and drink, ruining my marriage, being hated by my men—all because of you!" Ramón hoarsely interrupted.

"I—I thought at first I'd bring her up the same way I'd grown up. It would be a way of paying you back—a just way, I thought. But I couldn't—no, I couldn't. Even when I first went back to Dodge with her after I'd taken her away from the ranch, Cornish wanted to hold her for ransom. He said he'd cut off an ear or a finger and send it to you—"

"I should have killed him with my bare hands years ago!" Ramón growled, clenching his fists again.

"I did that for you, Mr. Hernandez." Rhea raised her face

to his. "I told him I wouldn't stand for that. He said he was going to teach me a lesson for defying him, and I had to defend myself—I killed him—and his men there didn't turn me in because they wanted to take over all his dirty business and make money for themselves. Then I helped myself to what I could find in his wallet—that was to take care of me and Gatita. What I didn't count on, what I couldn't help, was falling in love with her. That's why I didn't return her to you and your wife, Mr. Hernandez! It's the truth! Even when I was down in Texas hating you and planning all this, I couldn't help loving her, and yes, I wanted to keep her. Sure I was afraid to bring her back because I didn't know what you'd do to me, but most of all—and I'm not afraid now, and you can do whatever you want—I loved her as if she were my own flesh and blood. It's the truth before God, I swear it is!"

Once again, she was overcome with weeping and covered her face with her hands. Gatita began to cry too, and Ben Wilson soothed her.

"Well, Mr. Bouchard, Mr. Hernandez," Dave Haggerson finally spoke up, "I'm just a small-town schoolteacher, so maybe I'm no expert, but I'd say this isn't a bad woman. This is a woman you can read about in the Bible where it says more sinned against than sinning. That's my humble opinion."

Lucien Edmond had been deeply moved as he had listened to Rhea Penrock's confession. He eyed his brother-in-law, and then said softly, "I realize that you've gone through hell, Ramón, and I know exactly what you thought. But somehow, now that you have Gatita back, and now that I've heard all this, I for one wouldn't want to send her to jail and certainly not to the gallows—"

"*Damn it!* Do you take me for a man without conscience?" Ramón suddenly burst out. He took out a bandanna and violently blew his nose. "Devil take it all, woman! If only you'd told us the truth, if only you'd leveled with us and told us what had happened to your husband—"

"I know! I know how wrong it was. But I took good care of her, she'll tell you that. I'd do anything for her, and if—and if you want to send me to jail, or—or—even ha-hang me, Mr. Hernandez, you've every right! I know I have to pay for my sins, and maybe I have it coming for killing the man who killed my mother and had me—and maybe even for Jeb Cornish—"

"You know," Lucien Edmond dryly interposed, "I rather think there might be a reward out for ridding the world of that conniving Indian agent, that head of bushwhacking and rustling gangs! I'm going to do some investigation on my own in Dodge City. I've a friend there who will find out from the sheriff exactly what the situation is. Were there any witnesses?"

"Oh, yes! There were some men in his gang playing cards with him. He always did that when he thought up his schemes. . . ." Rhea answered unsteadily.

"I'm just guessing, Mrs. Penrock," Lucien Edmond gently remarked, "chances are they thought up a good tall yarn to tell the sheriff by way of explaining why Cornish was found dead in his own dance hall. You leave that part of it to me."

"I—I don't deserve your being kind or nice to me at all, Mr. Bouchard, not after what I did. . . ."

Rhea had begun to cry again, and Gatita, restless in Ben Wilson's arms, called out, "Please don't make her cry, Papa! Please don't! She was so good to me—she made me dollies. She told me stories before I went to sleep, and we had lots of picnics. . . ."

Again Ramón blew his nose. His face was fiercely taut, but his voice was unsteady as he said, "You must have loved that man of yours very much to have thought all this up by yourself. That I can't blame you for. I guess if someone had killed me, my Mara would have wanted to pay him back." Ramón paused, for unexpectedly, Juana Perez's words came back to him: *You must understand that God has a reason for whatever is done upon this earth. To question it . . . is to be left with nothing.* The handsome Mexican looked at his beloved daughter, whose face was streaked with tears. Evidently, Gatita loved this woman very much—and Rhea Penrock must have been very good to the child to receive such affection.

For another long moment Ramón remained silent, as did his companions. Only the faint wind could be heard, stirring the dried prairie grass. Finally Ramón reached over to Gatita and gently brushed away her tears with his finger. Then he took a step closer to the buckboard, facing Rhea directly. "A good friend of mine gave me excellent advice not long ago—about faith in God and in His purposes. It is advice that I will take now." Ramón paused and, swallowing hard, looked at his feet. "You have obviously taken good care of Gatita. I

436

will think only of this now, and I won't hurt you. I won't bring any charges against you.''

"God will bless you for that, Ramón," Ben murmured. Then he said to Rhea, "I've an idea for you, Mrs. Penrock. I want you to come back to Wichita and go to work in my wife's shelter. With your background and your experience, with the hardship you've known and the courage you've shown and your showing us how you truly redeemed yourself, I know that you can help other unfortunate women to regain their footing toward a decent life.''

"Oh, I can! I want to do something good! I was a teller there for a time at the Drovers Commercial Bank—you know that, Dr. Wilson—and I liked the people, and I was happy. But when I heard that Mr. Bouchard was coming to visit you, I got scared—and I was afraid that I'd lose Gatita forever—''

"You can see her again, I promise you that," Ramón broke in. "We'll come visit once in a while, my wife and I. And about that man Cornish—I feel the way Lucien Edmond does. Even if they brought you to trial, they'd let you off because it was a case of self-defense. I don't think any court would convict a young woman who tried to protect a little child, not when you tell them what Cornish wanted to do to my Gatita.''

"I quite agree," Lucien Edmond nodded, "and in the event of a trial, if worse came to worst, I could wire my adoptive brother, Lopasuta Bouchard, in New Orleans. He's an excellent lawyer, and he's always helped those who are really in need. He'd be able to recommend someone to defend you.''

They took their time getting back to Wichita, and during that week, Rhea Penrock and Gatita rode together. The four men observed how devoted she was to the girl and with what loving care she prepared the "picnics" by which term Gatita had always characterized their simple meals.

Lucien Edmond Bouchard had stopped at Batesville to send a telegram to his friend in Dodge City, asking him to investigate the death of Jeb Cornish and to wire him what he had learned in care of Dr. Ben Wilson in Wichita. He sent a second telegram to Maxine, briefly telling her all that had occurred, and Ramón sent a wire to his wife and children, telling them the joyous news that Gatita was found.

When they reached Wichita, Elone, her face radiant, came hurrying out of her house, waving a folded telegram in her hand. "She isn't wanted at all, Ben! Not at all! The sheriff told Lucien Edmond's friend that the outlaws explained that some renegade did Cornish in and got away before they could do anything. And the sheriff says it was good riddance, and Dodge City is a lot better without him."

"There, you see, Mrs. Penrock?" Dr. Ben Wilson turned to the young woman, his eyes shining. "This is truly a case of redemption, and restoration as well. Elone, my dear, Miss Penrock is going to work in your settlement, and she'll help the unfortunate women who come there for spiritual comfort and material aid."

"I'll work very hard. I'll make you both proud of me," Rhea tearfully promised.

The next morning, Lucien Edmond and Maxine accompanied by Ramón, who carried Gatita in his arms, were driven to the railroad station, to begin their return to Windhaven Range. Rhea stood on the platform embracing Gatita for what, as Ramón had promised, would certainly not be the last time.

As the train pulled away, Rhea turned to the Wilsons. "It's like a dream! It's like a dream, and this nightmare is all over! I look back now and I wonder how I could have been such a fool, how there could have been so much hate in me—"

"Hush, my dear," Elone said as she put her arm around the young woman's shoulders. "All that will be forgotten."

"In my book, it already is," Dave Haggerson spoke up. He had accompanied the Wilsons and Rhea to the railroad station, and he now gently smiled at Rhea.

"Th-thank you, Mr. Haggerson, I—I just don't have words to thank all of you for what you've done. It's like a miracle—"

"A miracle accomplished through love, Mrs. Penrock," Ben interposed. "And according to our Quaker faith, God is happiest when hate can be turned into love because that is how all men become brothers in His just eyes."

Chapter Forty-Five

It was December 18th, 1882, the one hundred twentieth anniversary of the birth of Lucien Bouchard, founder of the Bouchard dynasty. Laure and Leland Kenniston and their children—including young Lucien, on a long vacation from St. Timothy's Academy in Dublin—had returned to Windhaven Plantation for the Christmas holidays. Laure had made a special point of arriving in time for the commemorative that always marked the birth of the founder of the Bouchard clan.

High on the bluff overlooking the river, at the gravesites of that valiant pioneer and his beloved woman, Dimarte, Laure and Leland stood together, and their children beside them, along with Marius Thornton and Benjamin Brown, stewards of the estate that old Lucien Bouchard had built out of the generosity of the Creeks with whom he had come to live after his departure from Normandy.

They had knelt, the children imitating their elders, awed and hushed by the reverent aura of this memorable place. Laure had praised old Lucien Bouchard, and then she had said, "Almighty God, we thank You in watching over the destiny of Windhaven, in each part of the land where Windhaven is found. We thank You humbly and gratefully for returning Gatita to Ramón and Mara Hernandez, and also for the safe return of my son, Lucien. May the families thus reunited find joy in one another, and may they continue to do Thy bidding, enjoying as a privileged legacy the fruits of our growing nation."

Those about her murmured a soft, "Amen."

After a pause, she raised her face to the gray, gloomy sky. "As St. Paul said, we should 'Follow righteousness, faith, charity, peace, with them that call on the Lord out of a pure

439

heart.' Almighty God, I pray for all of us that we may lead lives which are goodly in Thy sight. We are bound, all of us, by faith and belief in the unity of our fellow men under Thy will. Grant us the wisdom and the courage never to swerve from Your Truth that makes us finally worthy in Thine eyes.''

The faint chorus of ''Amen'' was a murmur in the wind, which stirred the trees around the gravesites of those who had so heroically inaugurated and perpetuated the destiny of Windhaven.

THE END